Imagine the worst thing
that could happen
to an innocent little girl...

THE SHARING

D0851053

THE SHARING

M. M. Faraday

BANTAM BOOKS
TORONTO · NEW YORK · LONDON · SYDNEY

THE SHARING

A Bantam Book / November 1982

ISBN 0-553-22579-0

Bantam Books are published by Bantam Books, Inc. Its trade-
mark, consisting of the words "Bantam Books" and the por-
trayal of a rooster, is Registered in U. S. Patent and Trademark
Office and in other countries. Marca Registrada. Bantam
Books, Inc., 666 Fifth Avenue, New York, New York 10103.

PRINTED IN THE UNITED STATES OF AMERICA

O   0 9 8 7 6 5 4 3 2 1

For Dennis, Pickwick and Boo.

PROLOGUE

She was old, of an age beyond years or pity. She freely admitted the sum total of her remaining substance was invested in this last, unlawful promise.

Bryna stirred in her sleep, her fat little arm closing tighter around the dead girl's doll. The old woman who spoke to her was ugly and smelled bitter as brass. She hovered, weightlessly it seemed, over Bryna's bed, suspended in midair, flabby arms spread wide like a giant bat. But she seemed to be merely an outline, little more than pale blue air. Only her face, as wrinkled and withered as an apple that has rotted and dried in the sun, had any real color, a corrupt brown, interlaced with spidery purple veins. Her eyes were black holes. And her mouth, out of which partially protruded a thick, black tongue, was a black hole, too.

At first Bryna thought she was watching television or "seeing" one of the stories she and Goldie shared, but the horror seemed to be speaking directly to her. Once, it claimed, it had been as beautiful as Goldie, the doll Bryna loved more than anything in the world.

Bryna's breathing became labored. Her nose twitched. She held the doll tighter still. What the hag said could not be true. Nothing as beautiful as Goldie could ever become as ugly as this, whatever it was. Goldie would never change.

Bryna loved the doll—had from the first moment she saw it. She had just turned four then, and the doll was half her size, its features so lifelike and beautiful they startled her. But only for a moment—until she realized it was not human. Its luminous eyes, full figure and sparkling tresses tugged at her. The doll's face had enchanted Bryna, but there was more to it than the blonde hair and blue eyes and darkly shadowed lashes; there was a timelessness in the doll's countenance, wedding all the authority and knowledge of the grown-up with all the innocence and beauty of a fairy-tale child. The doll, Bryna was convinced, could become that most impossible being: a wise, beautiful, all-knowing friend, a confidante, teacher and guide all in one. Someone who would never lose patience or become angry, who would understand everything, always.

vii

It seemed entirely natural to Bryna when the doll spoke to her. She said her name was Goldie and that she would be happy to be Bryna's special friend. Goldie said that Bryan, Bryna's father, had asked her to be "especially nice" to Bryna. This news thrilled Bryna, for her father, whom she missed to the point of despair, had died a few months earlier. Goldie's voice, so pure and full of promise, rang like crystal in Bryna's ears.

Her friend Jenny Meier, six, slim and pretty, paid no attention to any of this. The doll was hers, she claimed, and she called it Belle, which seemed terribly rude to Bryna. As Jenny sorted the doll's elaborate wardrobe, pridefully calling attention to the silk underclothing and cosmetic kit, she kept a wary eye on the younger girl, who seemed oblivious to what she was telling her. In fact, however, Bryna heard everything Jenny was saying and was astonished that she seemed constantly to be interrupting Goldie. Goldie had just invited Bryna to pick her up, but every time she reached for the doll Jenny swatted Bryna's hand away.

"She's much too fine for you," Jenny said. "*You* need a fat, *squat* little doll with a crooked nose and black, stringy hair." Jenny giggled at the sound of the word "squat," which she had just learned, and at her cleverness, for Bryna was indeed fat and abnormally short for her age. Her nose had a hump in it, and her dark hair, no matter how often her mother brushed it, seemed irrevocably snarled.

"And *your* doll will have to limp," Jenny added smugly.

Bryna took a last, halting step, grabbed the doll by one of its ankles and jerked it off the table where Jenny was arranging its clothes. The older girl snatched back, and the doll's black satin dress ripped. Bryna clutched the doll to her chest, a determined look on her face. Jenny stepped back in horror for a moment and then, enraged, pushed one hand into Bryna's face and tugged at the doll with the other. Goldie urged Bryna to hold on.

"You're ruining her!" Jenny screamed. Bryna, one of her eyes smarting from Jenny's gougings, wailed with pain but held fast. Goldie gave her courage, telling her not to worry about the dress. It was then that the two grown-ups burst into the room. At first Mrs. Meier insisted that Jenny let Bryna hold the doll—until she noticed the torn dress. "All right, ladies," she said, "I think we'd just better put Belle away until you both learn to behave."

Bryna, however, would not relinquish her grasp. Sharon, her mother, kept apologizing to Mrs. Meier while trying to pry Bryna's fingers from the doll. Finally she whacked Bryna smartly across the bottom.

Bryna cried for hours after the doll was taken away. Nothing would console her, not even Goldie's promise that they would see each other again. Bryna's behavior, bad though it was, made such an impression on Mrs. Meier that when Jenny died a year later she gave the doll to Bryna. Bryna could remember it all very clearly, how Mrs. Meier had arrived unannounced one Sunday afternoon, tears in her eyes, the doll and its exquisite suitcase in her arms. Bryna recalled the way Mrs. Meier had hugged her, nearly choking her—and how, later, the woman had cried in Sharon's arms, repeating over and over: "You're so lucky." This was something Bryna could not understand, since it was she, not her mother, who had Goldie.

Now, at six, Bryna was more attached to Goldie than ever. She had been horrified when Sharon told her she couldn't take Goldie to school with her. Bryna knew the other children would make fun of her, because she was fat and because she limped. She needed Goldie to protect her. Sharon, however, warned that taking the doll to school would only guarantee ridicule and that, in any event, the teachers would not permit it.

Bryna knew that Sharon didn't like Goldie. She was always trying to separate them; once she had even offered to "trade" Bryna a kitten for the doll. Bryna was genuinely offended. Goldie was as dear to her as her own life. Bryna would not throw Goldie away the way Sharon had thrown Bryan away. The kitten, which Bryna ignored, died not long after Sharon brought it home, and nothing more was said about *that*. But Sharon did continue to nag Bryna to "bring home some little friends from school." Even if any of the other children had wanted to come home with her, which they didn't, Bryna did not want to share Goldie with anyone else.

After school each day, at the first opportunity, usually while she was supposed to be doing her homework, Bryna would tell Goldie everything that had happened to her that day, even though Goldie usually seemed somehow already to know. Whatever trouble Bryna encountered, Goldie knew precisely how to smooth it over. Nothing ever ruffled her.

If the teacher had been unpleasant, Goldie confidently attributed this to "lack of breeding" or "ignorance" or "female trouble." If one of the children had called Bryna names, Goldie would dismiss the offender as a "mere child," a "brat" or, if the offense had been particularly grievous, a "shit" or a "bitch." But even when Goldie used words that were "bad," Bryna noticed that she used them with dignity—so that they came out sounding perfectly ly all right. Lately, Goldie had begun calling a boy who was particularly mean a "cocksucker." Bryna was not at all clear just what that meant, but hearing Goldie say it always made her giggle and feel better. That was the wonderful thing about Goldie; she could always make Bryna feel more grown up than the other children and thus invulnerable to their attacks.

Best of all, Goldie liked to read as much as Bryna did—not the "baby books" the other children read but more adult books. It was easy to sneak them out of the place where Sharon hid them in her bedroom closet. Bryan had begun reading to Bryna when she had been only a few months old, insisting that she would understand—and he kept right on until he died. After that, Sharon read to her for a while. But it wasn't the same as it had been with Bryan. When Sharon read it was just words—without the pictures Bryan could conjure up. And Sharon was reading to her, she knew, only because of The Guilt. She often heard her mother talking to her friend Marie about The Guilt. The Guilt didn't last long, however, and neither did the reading. By then, though, Bryna could read for herself.

At school, however, Bryna received poor marks—even in reading. Sharon often scolded her for "not trying." She knew that Bryna had learned to read much younger than most children. Bryna, however, knew that she *had* tried—at first. She had wanted to read to the other children, to show them how much better at it she was than they were. But she was afraid the same ones who made fun of her for being fat and having a limp would make fun of her when she read. She tried anyway, but the words wouldn't come. Her tongue seemed to fill her entire mouth; she stuttered, and then the others *did* laugh, just as she knew they would. After that it seemed easier to do what, increasingly, was expected of her: little or nothing.

Sometimes it satisfied Bryna to see her mother disappointed by her poor marks. Other times she felt uneasy about it. But even Goldie agreed that it served Sharon right for what she had done to Bryan. Goldie seemed to know everything there was to know about Bryna's father, as much as Bryna did, in fact. Goldie was vague on what he was doing now but said he was "waiting" somewhere for her and that she was still "his little princess." Goldie agreed that Bryan was "infinitely" nicer than any of the men Sharon brought home and did things with in her bedroom sometimes all through the night. There were a lot of them; some of them called her "princess," too; she hated them, and so did Goldie.

It hurt to think too much about Bryan, but Goldie was always there to help her think about something else. At first Bryna would read *to* Goldie but before long she discovered that Goldie could read quite nicely all by herself. Far into the night sometimes, long after she was supposed to be asleep, she would listen to Goldie read out loud in her clear bell-like voice. Bryna was not afraid her mother would put a stop to this because only *she* could hear Goldie. The doll had explained that to her long ago. Sometimes, when the laughing and other sounds coming from her mother's room were particularly noisy, Bryna would ask Goldie to read even louder.

What was especially exciting about these sessions was that once Bryna started a book Goldie could invariably improve upon it. Goldie would pretend to be reading the book but actually, Bryna knew, she would make up new details, whole new episodes even, often working herself and Bryna into central roles in the story. Goldie's version was always *infinitely* better than the original. In *Goldie's* stories, Bryna was always slim, beautiful, desirable and as blonde and blue-eyed as Goldie or, for that matter, as her father. Women envied her, men "lusted" after her. Bryna wasn't completely sure what that meant, but it seemed to be what most heroines hoped for. Men invariably fought over her in these stories, but she was faithful always to her fair-haired prince, whose face and description never changed, no matter what the story.

Sometimes, not often, Bryna looked at herself in the mirror. She was thankful that Goldie could not see her—anyway, not the way the other children saw her. Goldie was the perfect friend. Well, almost.

Bryna gasped out loud in her sleep. The smelly old thing was actually daring to caress Goldie's hair. Bryna wanted desperately to wake up so that she could stop her, but struggle as she might, she could not rouse herself. She felt immobilized by some numbing, invisible obstruction, which she suddenly recognized as coldness. She was freezing.

"Lovely," the old woman exhaled, her icy breath stinking so much that Bryna held hers. "Let me come in from the cold, and I'll make her live—in you."

Bryna's first reaction was indignation. Goldie might not be human but she was certainly alive, more alive, in fact, than any human Bryna knew. Goldie was *enchanted*, more than human.

"Quite right," the old thing concurred. "Enchanted. And you can be as she is, knowing things no human knows."

Bryna was startled at having her thoughts read so accurately.

The presence spoke again. "Let me come inside you, and I will make you as lovely, wise and beautiful as she. Just like Cinderella. I know you've *imagined* you were Cinderella. Now you really can be."

Bryna began to say she was already beautiful, but even in her dreams she knew it was not so. In her dreams she had to be *transformed*, yes, "just like Cinderella."

"Yours," the presence promised, "will be beauty unchanging, power beyond anything even your exquisite imagination has dreamed of, a special gift . . ."

Bryna was flattered. She listened more intently.

"Everything Goldie is and more you will become."

But what of Goldie, Bryna wondered suddenly; if she became "all" that Goldie was, would Goldie cease to be?

Again, the old thing sensed her doubts. "No. She will live in you, and you in her—as neither of you has lived before."

Bryna still did not understand.

The presence persisted. "Soon you will reach an age when you will not be permitted to have a doll. Think about that, how difficult . . . but if Goldie is inside you, no one will know. She'll be hidden from others. Only I can bring that to pass. Only I can provide the spark. But you must hurry. We're breaking the rules, and neither of us has much time."

Bryna turned instinctively in her dream to Goldie. The doll spoke clearly and reassuringly.

"I'm tired of living in this brittle body. We might as well do what she says. That way I can share your body and go with you wherever you go. I'll be able to help you ever so much more when you get into a fix. I could tell you what to say and how to act at just the right time—or even do it for you."

Bryna was thrilled. But still she feared this other—this thing—living in her, growing in her, perhaps. It was so ugly.

"I'll be no trouble. You won't even know I'm there unless you ask for me. Just think of me as your fairy godmother, like in Cinderella, remember? Besides, there will be nothing left of what you see now. In a few moments I will be pure light—your light, stronger than anything you can imagine now. Through that light you can avoid the darkness you've already sensed lies before you."

Bryna felt a fierce coldness pierce her, stabbing through her numbness. The horror she saw now was a near mirror-image of this spectral presence, an image of herself that gnawed at her like the pain of a tooth rotten to the roots. An image of herself grown old, still squat, grotesquely wrinkled and misshapen, impoverished and alone, her mouth sunken, her darting tongue swollen and black. She saw herself drifting aimlessly down a gray street, her shabby wrap a mantle of sorrow. No detail was lost on her; she noted even the cruelly worn heel of her right shoe, reflecting her uneven gait. As she made her solitary way down the street she saw mainly the backs of others, in retreat from her.

Alone.

Shortly she found herself emerging from a tangle of bushes to stand on the brink of a precipice, the sea crashing in on rocks a dizzying distance beneath her. The water tilted at a crazy angle. Her eyes filled with burning water. The vision that engulfed her was at once vast and vastly illuminating.

Bryna knew what she must do, and she was no longer afraid. Goldie shone now like a beacon in the salty mist.

"Yes."

Bryna was astonished. Not by the word she heard and felt herself speak but by the clear, bell-like quality of her voice. She felt herself begin to thaw, drifting in a warm, blue void. She moved again in her sleep, pushing back the covers as the warmth filled her. Goldie fell from her grasp to the floor. The doll's eyes opened on impact and stuck there—staring fixedly at the ceiling.

Bryna slept.

Part One

PREPARATION

ONE

"Jesus *Christ!*"

Sharon rolled over in bed and touched Larry; fear smothered the impulse to fall back asleep. She pulled hard to get enough breath, pushing back the covers in the air-conditioned chill.

"It's her again," Larry said flatly.

Sharon heard the next scream and knocked over Larry's waterglass as she dragged herself from bed.

The house was much like the others on that street, a three-bedroom, bath-and-a-half rancher with family room, double garage and patio with built-in barbecue, a two-tone pastel mediocrity that pleased all of its occupants save one. The lawn was compulsively cut so short that it hurt to walk on it barefoot. Despite its full quota of rationed water the lawn was turning brown in the protracted September heat.

The house was in Walnut Creek, a bedroom suburb of San Francisco. Safe. Mostly white. Dull. Even Sharon, who liked it there, considered it dull. That was one of its principal virtues. For excitement, the city was near enough. "Excitement" usually consisted of shopping at the big Union Square stores, dinner in Chinatown or, on special occasions, at Julius' Castle on Telegraph Hill. Mostly, however, Sharon was content to stay in Walnut Creek. San Francisco was where it had all gone wrong, where Bryan had given himself up entirely to fright and fantasy, dragging their daughter along with him, where Sharon, for a time, had lost herself in a frantic search, conducted mainly in bed with strangers, for identity and self-worth. Sometimes, in unguarded moments, the city became a dark presence that filled the landscape of Sharon's mind, a malignant excrescence that threatened to engulf her.

Happily, Larry had been as eager as she to move out of the city. Some of their friends thought them "provincial," but before long a number of them were also refugees from the city's rising costs, escalating crime and "permissive" ways. They met most of their friends in church.

Sharon was happier than she had been in years, "despite everything," a phrase she and her best friend often jokingly

3

applied to their respective sex lives. Sharon's, after only three years with Larry, was definitely on the downhill side. Larry was having trouble with his job and usually arrived home exhausted. After yard work and dinner, there were bills to pay and mail to attend to and, often, paperwork left over from the office.

There was seldom time for sex, sometimes not even once a week. And when they did make love it was usually perfunctory, with little foreplay and less pleasure. The slightest hitch—Sharon appearing too eager, coming on too strong, for example—and Larry would lose his erection, and that, as Sharon quipped, would be "the ball game" for another week. Sharon told herself it was temporary and, in her prayers, asked God for guidance.

Sometimes she thought she was being punished for the unfaithfulness and promiscuity that had characterized her life before she had married Larry. Sometimes this seemed right and just; other times she couldn't help feeling that it was excessive. Doctors had already told her that she could never have any more children. When she had been pregnant with Bryna she had fallen down some steps, high on speed and alcohol, out with a man whose name she could not remember the next day. But she could *still* remember the awful prelude to that evening, when she had gone home to tell Bryan what she had already known for some time, that she—that they—were going to have a baby. She had held back telling him because the marriage was already becoming a shell, and she had thought of having an abortion. But then a seemingly insignificant chance encounter with a woman who had abruptly stopped Sharon on the street and asked her to hold her baby while she made a phone call changed everything. Sharon did not want to let the baby go, though of course she did not say so. When the woman took it, Sharon had run home to Bryan, to their tiny North Beach apartment, and told him that he was going to be a father.

He looked at her blankly, a boy not a man. He did not acknowledge what she had said. He spoke of other things—his book—a children's book—a convolute and baroque tale populated by grotesque creatures with whom he seemed more intimately allied than he did with anything or anyone living. He had been working on the book, already rejected by several publishers, for nearly two years. The book had so engaged his imagination and absorbed his time that the freelance magazine work with which he had previously supported them had all evaporated. They lived on Sharon's part-time secretarial salary, handouts from friends and occasional checks from Bryan's folks.

Bryan, especially when under stress, assumed the persona of one of his characters, speaking the occult language that only he and they could understand. Sometimes Sharon thought that he was trying to drive her crazy. She was sure he was too clever and cunning to be crazy himself. He was the eternal golden boy, she thought, the prince of a thousand fairy tales before whom even good fortune begged an audience. He had everything. He had come from "the best family" and had been given "the best education." No one doubted his unusual intelligence, not even the editors who rejected his perverse "opus fantasticum." His looks were astonishing, a blue-eyed, towheaded innocent with the slenderly muscled sensuality of a great dancer. He was, in his late twenties, several years older than Sharon. He had dazzled her for awhile, wielding his dreamy erudition with all the authority of a shaman, bewitching her with his imagination, drawing her deeper and deeper into his spell, making her one of his characters.

It had gotten old fast. If it hadn't been for the sex, which she once described as "supernatural," it would have gotten old even faster. It was no fun, she reflected, being in a story she didn't understand. Once the stars started to go out Sharon could see the immaturity, the selfishness and especially the fear she had overlooked before, the cycles of mania and depression, not acute, but building. She was never sure, with Bryan, what was real and what was not. It took her a long time—forever, she thought ruefully—to realize that her "indiscretions," which increased in direct relation to his withdrawal, did not pass unnoticed. Beneath the crazy faces and manic babble of his fantastic characters seethed a cauldron of jealousy, self-pity, hatred, love and fear. By the time she realized that it was *she* who was in control it was too late.

Before that, for a while anyway, it had seemed that the overwhelming reality of the baby might rescue them. Bryna arrived prematurely, by cesarean, nearly dead of toxemia. The doctors were worried that Sharon's fall, earlier in the pregnancy, might also have damaged the child. She was a pitifully tiny baby with black hair that grew right down the back of her neck, and she had a bone defect, the legacy of which, the doctors believed, would be a lifelong limp. It was touch and go for weeks, when the doctors didn't know if she would live at all. After that there was still the specter of possible brain damage. Sharon existed between guilt, disappointment and hope. But Bryan seemed ecstatic. The defects in the child that depressed Sharon sustained Bryan. That also took Sharon a long time to realize.

5

Squat, misshapen little Bryna with her dreadful hair and gnomish face fit right into her father's galaxy of grotesques. While Sharon tried—falteringly, she knew—to bring the child to realistic terms with her defects, Bryan simply banished them with the magic of his imagination. It was no contest. Bryna's loyalty to her father, even long before she could walk, was unequivocal. Bryna was far from being retarded, and her quick little mind feasted on her father's fantasies. He was undeniably her perfect prince, and because *his* was the final word and because *he* decreed it she was his "little princess, the fairest of them all."

The first "words" she ever spoke were not English but some of the tauntingly melodic gibberish that Bryan claimed was the language of his fictional kingdom. Sharon was no longer sure he really thought it was fictional.

The memories burned her like acid: having to get away from the father and daughter for a day, sometimes two or three; then the guilt; then having to go back, knowing they would punish her but having to go back anyway; the two of them shutting her out, excluding her, always whispering and laughing, heads close together, two children, fair-haired, beautiful Bryan and dark-haired, frightful little Bryna, one the cunning master, the other his eager thrall, conspiring against the nameless "them," against the world both feared, against *her*. For not loving them enough. For not being one of them. For "acting like a grown-up." For betraying them. For doing the "bad thing." For leaving them.

Bryan shot himself through the head just before Bryna's fourth birthday. He did it standing up, his eyes boring into Sharon's. Bryna clung to him, burying her face in his legs, as he pulled the trigger. Even dead he continued to reproach Sharon. For weeks, Bryna would not speak to or even acknowledge her mother.

It had been a long time and a lot of men until she met Larry, who was so understanding, so patient, so forgiving of her past; Larry, who led her back to her faith. For that she would be forever grateful. There was more to a good marriage than sex. Larry had given her a home and security. He had values. He had also, she reflected, given her two sons she loved as if they were her own. Finally—most important—he had proved a steadying influence on Bryna.

In the two years since Larry had entered their lives, Bryna had made real progress. It was an answered prayer, Sharon was sure. The girl was still too withdrawn, but her marks had improved and she had finally begun to grow taller instead of wider. Her limp was less noticeable, and even her nose had begun to find a less obtrusive place among her other, not beautiful but no longer unpleasant, features. She was still overweight, but making progress.

Sharon was disappointed that Bryna had not yet made any real friends, but at least she no longer clung to her doll. There had been times when, hearing the child speak to the doll as if it were human, Sharon had felt a tightening in her stomach, a dread. Now the doll sat on a shelf in Bryna's room gathering dust. Bryna was not close to Larry, but Sharon was sure she respected him. She was always very polite when she spoke to him.

Everything had been going so well until that summer when Bryna began having the nightmares, crying out in her sleep. Within the past two weeks it had become a nightly event—whimpers, cries, then screams. Larry, who was a fitful sleeper at best, had borne the brunt of it. He was always the first to awaken, his patience wearing thin as his exhaustion mounted. Sharon would get up and go to Bryna's room and find the girl thrashing in her sleep, her nightclothes and sheets drenched in sweat, despite the air-conditioning. A trip to the doctor revealed nothing physically wrong. Nor had Bryna been able to shed any light on what was troubling her. She could never remember her dreams.

Sharon felt the water soaking into the carpet beneath her bare feet. She shivered. Larry grabbed her hand as she slipped from the bed and squeezed it.

"I'm sorry I swore," he said.

She squeezed his hand back and moved in the darkness toward the door of their bedroom, wrapping herself in a bathrobe. In the corridor she noticed the silence. Usually Bryna kept screaming until Sharon awakened her. Apparently she had settled down this time by herself. But then Sharon heard a door opening. She hurried past the stairs that led down to the lower level, where the boys' room was, and around the corner to a longer corridor at the end of which was Bryna's room.

Sharon snapped on the hall light and stopped. What she saw both frightened and repelled her, but she could neither cry out nor retreat.

Bryna was standing at the end of the corridor, naked, her body shiny with sweat and patchy with red, as if afflicted by a heat rash. The girl's face was also blotched, her eyes puffy and fixed. Her stance was still; she seemed to be in a trance. Her mouth and jaw worked for some moments before she could make the words come out. Her tongue darted out, and her head jerked forward as she struggled to speak. When she did speak, her voice was hoarse and constricted. She looked straight at Sharon.

"You're all going to die. You and Larry, Dave and Robbie, all of you. You're all going to burn up. This house is going to burn up. You're going to do it. You're going to start it. . . ."

The shock sent pain, unbearable had it lasted more than a few seconds, through Sharon's lower back. She had experienced the same thing when Bryan shot himself. She was not aware of having walked the length of the corridor, but she found herself shaking Bryna, furiously, uncontrollably.

"Stop it! You're being wicked! Don't say such things!" Sharon's rage, once ignited, grew. The girl's flesh was cold to the touch, when it should have been hot; her eyes, though bloodshot, were, in their centers, like black ice. Sharon felt a wave of revulsion pass through her; she shivered as though she had just come face to face with a spider or closed her hand around a garden slug in the dark. She wanted to smash it. A million submerged frustrations and fears welled up to the surface. Bryna seemed to be looking right through her, not hearing or not wanting to hear what she was saying.

Sharon slapped her hard. And then again. Larry had to pull her away.

Sharon, scrambling eggs, heard Larry shift his chair back tentatively and looked over her shoulder. She caught his grimace, though whether it was from the last of his coffee or *The Chronicle* she wasn't sure. Robbie and Dave were at the table with him, shovelling down cereal, exchanging glances, conspirators enjoying some private joke. Dave acted like he was going to catapult some cereal at Robbie, right off the end of his spoon, but Larry stopped him with a scowl. Dave then aimed the spoon at Larry for a moment. Both he and Robbie broke up.

Larry stood up, unamused, shook some crumbs from the newspaper and walked over to Sharon. "Gotta run."

She turned half toward him, holding the spatula off to the side. He kissed her lightly on the lips. Their eyes met for a moment, exchanging concern.

At the door he turned and spoke to Robbie and Dave. "I want both of you cleaning up that mess in the garage when I get home tonight."

"Yes, dad," Dave said.

"Yeeees, dad," Robbie mimicked, "and don't forget Dave's new bike."

Dave looked menacingly at Robbie.

When Larry was gone, Sharon served the eggs. "You two had better hurry; you'll be late. I hope you got that assignment done, Robbie."

Robbie looked evasive. "Where's butter-balloon?"

Sharon looked at him sharply.

"Jeez, Robbie," Dave said, curling his lip.

"You brown-noser," Robbie retorted, "you call her that yourself when mom and dad aren't around."

"She's staying home today. She's not feeling so well."

"Some people get all the breaks," Robbie said tiredly. He was about to say more but something unfamiliar in Sharon's look silenced him.

When the boys had gone, Sharon poured herself a cup of coffee and, for once, wished that Larry had not taken the paper with him. She started to clear the table, then stopped and turned on the small TV Larry had installed for her, high up on a shelf at one end of the kitchen. She tuned, as usual, to a morning talk show. An author was on discussing genetic counselling and birth defects. As Sharon filled the dishwasher she tried to follow along, but her mind kept drifting. She turned the TV off, then turned it back on without the sound. Several times she started toward Bryna's room; each time she stopped.

When she had looked in on the girl earlier and found her still sleeping, dark circles under her eyes, she decided not to disturb her. It was important that she talk to Bryna, that she find out what was troubling her, but she was dreading it.

Sharon had talked to Larry about it. She could not let Bryna go to school—not after what had happened, not without talking. She had hidden it from Larry as best she could, but her guilt was strong. She was disturbed as much by what she had experienced in herself as by what she had seen—or failed to see—in Bryna.

Sharon kept remembering some dreams she had had over and over again when Bryna was still in diapers and there was so much trouble with Bryan. The baby was constantly making demands, always crying at the wrong time. Sharon felt perpetually exhausted, and in her dreams she would punish Bryna, beating and pummeling her mercilessly. She had confided in a friend who had laughed it off, saying it was a healthy way of letting off steam. Sharon had not been so sure.

She both waited for and feared Bryna's waking. The silence pressed in on her. She thought of turning the TV sound on again, but she was afraid Bryna might call out and she wouldn't hear her. There was a sudden, sharp noise in the living room. Sharon jumped, then shook herself, feeling silly. It was the mail coming through the slot in the front door.

There was only one personal item—a letter from her mother. Sharon tilted her head back and shut her eyes for a moment. She decided not to read the letter, not right away. Another harangue from her mother was the last thing she needed right now. Lillian could not understand her daughter's decision, "after all this time," as she kept putting it, to convert to Catholicism, Larry's faith. There was no doubt about it. Lillian would prefer that Sharon remain a "heathen," which is what she had called her when she lived with Bryan. As far as Sharon was concerned there was only one God, and she had hoped, naively she realized now, that her mother would be joyful that she had found her way back to Him, no matter what faith she chose.

Lillian, after the death of Sharon's father, had taken up her neglected religion with a fervor, Sharon once commented, that suggested she was substituting piety for sex. Sharon remembered the revival meetings of her childhood held in the big tents out on the edge of Dallas. She remembered how Lillian would prod her and push her until she, too, would step forward, go up and "get right with the Lord." She remembered how the big preacher, screaming and shouting, his breath stinking of alcohol, picked her up and held her and thanked the Lord for sending her to "get the Ghost."

She remembered the church services where there had been so much talk of blood and fire and the Holy Spirit, and people speaking in tongues. She remembered how frightened she had been when Lillian fell down beside her during one of these services, fell with a real thud, her eyes rolled back, kicking and jerking and muttering incoherently, how she cried for people to help and how they all just laughed and jumped around them, shouting crazily. She remembered months when she wouldn't have to go to church at all—and then the sudden, manic "catching up."

After she left home, Sharon was completely turned off religion and regarded herself as an atheist. Then, through Larry, she found her "way back," as she put it. She wanted to find something to respect in her mother's faith, and so was thrilled when Larry told her that even some Catholics had begun to acknowledge baptism in the Holy Spirit, that, following in the footsteps of a band of students and professors at Notre Dame and Duquesne universities, they had begun to receive this baptism and that

10

they, too, spoke in the "tongues" that Sharon had once been so ashamed of.

Sharon wrote her mother about this, but Lillian would have none of her efforts at religious reconciliation. The "new charismatics," as the Catholic Pentecostals called themselves, were, Lillian declared, "false prophets," and she quoted scripture damning them to death. Lillian's letters were freighted with scripture. This one, judging by its heft, Sharon decided, was no exception. She put it aside.

Sharon felt one of her sick headaches coming on; she tended to get them on overcast days when the sun would nearly—but not quite—break through. The glare through the windows bothered her so much that she went around the house pulling the blinds. It was not yet nine-thirty, and she had no energy at all. She had slept very little the night before. Sharon slumped on the living room sofa. She tried to blot everything from her mind.

It was nearly eleven when she awoke. She was angry with herself. Bryna would certainly be awake by now. Sharon half expected to find her in the kitchen. For once she wouldn't be unhappy if she caught Bryna stuffing herself with cookies or spooning peanut butter on a banana, Bryna's idea of a good breakfast. But she wasn't there.

"Bryna?" Sharon called out softly, fearful of the sound of her own voice. No answer. She looked next in the sunroom, but she wasn't there either. Nor was she in the bathroom. Sharon started reluctantly for the girl's room. What she had not wanted to consider was that Bryna might be afraid to come out. Sharon could not shake her shame. Nor her dread.

"Bryna?" she called out again, as she started down the corridor. She noticed immediately that the door to Bryna's room was now closed, though it had been slightly ajar when she had visited it earlier that morning.

"Bryna?" Sharon knocked on the door softly, then louder. No answer. Sharon's dread was replaced by something more compelling. She pushed the door open with far more force than was required, nearly falling into the room.

Something was wrong. Where she had expected to find hurt and disorder, she found precisely the opposite. Where everything had been a mess in the room only a couple of hours earlier, everything was now neat and tidy. Even the bed was made, and Bryna, smartly dressed, was sitting on it with one of her schoolbooks open before her. And there was Bryna's smile; that, in particular, was wrong. In shame or grief, fear or guilt, even

11

recrimination, Sharon might have found an opening. But here there was nowhere to begin.

"My goodness," Sharon said. "How in the world did you . . . ?" Was this the girl's way of trying to make up for last night? Sharon was painfully aware that she had never really talked to her daughter, not about anything important. Whenever things seemed to be coming to a head, one or the other of them would take evasive action. For a long time it had seemed the best way. Now Sharon realized it had merely been the easiest. Time and again she had let Bryna slip away from her. Too often they were like strangers being polite to one another in order to avoid any real interaction.

It was happening again. And in the face of all this "normalcy," Sharon had no idea how or where to begin. Was it possible that Bryna had no memory whatever of what had happened the night before? Sharon both hoped and feared that this was the case.

"I'd like to have breakfast now, mother. And then I think I should go to school. I don't know why you let me sleep; I feel fine."

"Honey, I . . ."

"I'm really hungry, mother. I promise just to have some cereal and a peach."

Sharon couldn't immediately identify what it was, but there was something about the room that had changed, not just its tidiness. Her eyes focused on the doll. It was the dress! For more than a year the doll had sat on the shelf wearing the same blue dress. Now it was attired in its best white satin. Its delicate string of pearls was around its neck, and its makeup had been freshly and lavishly applied.

Sharon felt cold. After a moment she realized the girl was waiting for a reply. "Yes," she said, "go ahead." Another moment passed before she realized Bryna was watching her, waiting for her.

Sharon parked in front of the school. She watched Bryna walk up the sidewalk. Always watching, apprehensively, guiltily—always hoping. Hoping Bryna was growing taller, thinner, happier. Hoping she was limping less. Hoping she wasn't hoping too much. Sharon watched. Yes, she was definitely getting better. It wasn't just wishful thinking. The limp was less noticeable. And Bryna's dress, the one that was usually reserved for special occasions and so hadn't been worn in some time, was decidedly in need of taking in. Lurking somewhere inside there, Sharon was convinced, was a very pretty girl. Now if only she could convince Bryna of that.

Sharon felt a little better as she drove home. But back in the house doubt assailed her again. She felt she *must* go to Bryna's room, but she hesitated. She knew how she would have hated it, at Bryna's age, if *her* mother had snooped in *her* room. But then she felt she was simply evading her responsibility again, and she went. Immediately she felt guilty. Goldie, it seemed to her, watched her every move with reproach. Sharon was not sure what she was looking for. She picked Goldie up and examined her, noting how curiously changed she seemed with this makeup. There was no longer any hint of innocence.

In the closet Sharon found the doll's little hangers bare. More alarming, a number of Bryna's dresses were missing, too. Next Sharon noticed the gap between two boxes where Bryna's suitcase had been. Sharon felt her mouth go dry. She looked around the room frantically and then dropped to her knees alongside Bryna's bed. She lifted the spread and looked underneath. There were the suitcases, both Bryna's and the doll's. Sharon opened them but did not disturb their contents. She stared at them for a few moments and then slid them back into place, just as she had found them.

"It's the only way, honey," Sharon said that night. "Don't you see? I've got to catch her in the act of running away. Then maybe it will all come out, and we can really talk."

Larry looked doubtful. "I still say we should just march in there and confront her with those suitcases. She can't very well deny them."

"Don't count on it. She can be..." Sharon paused. She wanted to say "tricky," but she felt that was unfair. "It's just that she's so... she has a way of bottling everything up, hiding things even from herself. I didn't realize until today just how much she's been holding back. All this time I thought she was getting better...."

"She *has* gotten better."

"On the surface, yes. And what improvement there's been is due to you, Larry. I'm the one who's failed her."

Larry frowned, shaking his head impatiently.

"It's true. It goes way back to Bryan. I know that never really got resolved, her blaming me, blaming herself. I just never could deal with it; it was too painful. But I've *got* to have it out with her now, Larry. My God, you heard what she said last night; and now this."

13

Larry looked unhappy. The mere mention of Bryan, she knew, was enough to darken his mood. Once he had found a picture of Bryan she had saved, hidden away among some of her things, and had sulked for days before she learned why.

Sharon was sure Bryna would try to leave shortly after she thought everyone had fallen asleep. She decided to station herself in the darkness on the living room sofa where she could watch both the front entrance and the passageway leading to the kitchen and back door. She had no sooner settled down there, with blanket and pillow, than she realized she might fall asleep before Bryna tried to leave. The thought so unnerved her that she almost went and told Larry that she had reconsidered, that they should confront Bryna now.

Then she remembered that both the front and back doors had double locks. Because the doors were equipped with chains, they never used the extra locks, which could be engaged, both from the inside and the outside, only by key. Sharon had to hunt for several minutes but finally found the extra keys in a utility drawer. After she'd double-locked both doors, she put the keys in the pocket of her housecoat and was about to resume her vigil when she remembered the garage door. It operated by an electric eye. Sharon went to the switch box in the hall closet and, scanning down Larry's neat labels, tripped the switch that supplied current to the door.

There were the windows, of course, but most of them could not be opened; they were of the energy-saving double-layer construction. The few small windows that could be opened were screened; any attempt to remove the screens would activate the burglar-alarm system Larry had installed.

Sharon sank back onto the sofa, confident she had not forgotten anything. More than an hour passed. Sharon filled the time rehearsing what she planned to do and say. She would take Bryna quietly outside where they could talk on the steps or back porch. She would try to make her understand why she had left Bryan and then gone back to him, over and over again. She would try to make her realize how complicated love could be. She would very gently try to make Bryna see her side of it. She let her head rest against the pillow, remembering.

It was nearly three in the morning when she awoke. She sat up so abruptly her head hurt. She blinked hard, trying to focus on the luminous dial of her watch. As quietly as possible she checked each door and then tiptoed to Bryna's room, her heart pounding wildly. There was no way the girl could get out, she was sure, but panic gnawed at her anyway.

Bryna's door was as she had left it, open a few inches. Sharon pushed it lightly and looked in, holding her breath. She closed her eyes in thanks for a moment. In the dim light she could see Bryna asleep on her side, her mouth hanging open slightly. Sharon felt a tenderness envelop her. She wanted to hold Bryna in her arms and tell her how much she loved her. The suitcases, she noticed, were nowhere in evidence.

After the moment of relief had subsided Sharon felt annoyed with herself. Now she couldn't be sure what had happened. Had Bryna abandoned her plan before she even went to bed? Or had she perhaps tried to get out and found the way blocked?

Sharon considered going back to bed with Larry, but he would awaken and she didn't want that. She went back to the sofa. There was nothing more to do now but sleep. She took a cigarette from the box on the coffee table next to the sofa and lit it. She was surprised how pleasant it made her feel. More potent on an empty stomach, she thought. She drifted gently. Perhaps Larry was right. A baby was what they needed. Another girl, a little sister for Bryna, some lifetime cement for their marriage. They could adopt.

"Fucking Christ! What in the . . ."

The man with the axe stepped back. He had swung the heavy blade against the door and it had come back dripping red. The man felt his stomach flip-flop.

"God Almighty!" the man next to him shouted. "Get those medics over here!" Another man rushed over and started hacking at the door higher up. It fell open, and black, foul-smelling smoke gushed out. One of the firemen rushed into the smoke and almost immediately staggered back dragging an inert figure, a man, his hand nearly severed where the axe had struck it.

"He was gone anyway," one of the medics said. "The smoke got him."

"If he got that far, why the hell didn't he get out?"

A minute later the garage door was axed open and two smaller figures were dragged out onto the lawn.

"I think one of them's still alive," a fireman shouted. Neighbors who had gathered to watch tried to press in closer. Uniformed men pushed them back.

"That's Robbie," a woman called out.

Though obviously burned badly, Robbie sat up abruptly. He looked apprehensive, expectant. Perhaps it was hearing his name called out; perhaps he simply didn't know what he was doing.

15

But he did not look in the direction of the voice that called his name. He looked the other way, toward the hedge.

His scream reached above the gathering rumble of fire and unnerved even the medics who followed his glance with anticipated dread.

"Jesus!" someone said hoarsely.

Bryna had moved out of the shadows of the hedge. She appeared unhurt physically, but her eyes, unblinking, reflected horror. Her mouth moved slowly, as she took a halting step closer to Robbie. She held Goldie in one arm, the doll's suitcase in the other. No sound came from her moving lips. Robbie slumped back.

Bryna slept. The large, rawboned woman sitting stiffly on the chair next to her bed read to herself from a small, thick book which she held in both hands. A man came in and introduced himself, apologizing for the intrusion. He offered his hand, but the woman did not take it.

"Perhaps we should speak outside," he said.

"No. She's asleep. I want to be here when she wakes up. I'm her only kin."

"Of course; you're her grandmother? They told me you'd be here. I know you've already been told some of the details."

The man looked at the woman expectantly. She said nothing.

"The doors were all double-locked. Your daughter's husband was at the front door; he died of smoke inhalation. The two boys tried to get through the garage at the lower level. That was one of those automatic doors. The boys had turned the switch on in the garage, but the juice, the current, ma'am, had been turned off at the main, the switch box. Do you see what I'm saying?"

"That's what they told me," the woman said impassively. "I guess she killed them."

"Well, we're not exactly saying that, not for sure." The man paused, embarrassed. "I'm afraid though it's looking that way. Do you know why she might have done it?"

The woman said nothing.

The man talked to fill the silence. "They sifted through everything out there. They found her in the living room. The keys were by her. Their neighbors said they never used those extra locks. It was around three in the morning when it started."

The woman glanced down at her book. The man nodded at Bryna.

"The girl there, she got out through a window at the end of the hall. The neighbors heard the burglar alarm and saw the smoke. The funny thing is, she had her suitcase all packed. And the doll's suitcase, too. And, of course, the doll itself," he added, nodding toward the doll which one of the nurses had placed on a shelf next to Bryna's bed. "She had all that stuff with her when we found her out on the lawn. We figured she had to have known."

Again the man waited, and again the woman said nothing.

"At first she couldn't talk; fear I guess, and maybe the smoke. Then we got it out of her." He opened a notepad. "She said: 'She told me to pack and wear my best things. That we were going on a trip.' When she woke up and there was smoke everywhere she knew she had to get out. I suppose her first thought was to get her toy, and then she remembered the suitcases, too. She said she tried to shout, to warn the others but she'd already lost her voice. The smoke was pretty thick in there."

The man stopped again, unnerved by the woman's apparent disinterest. "Then she told us when she got outside she began to remember. She said she had told her what was going to happen, the fire I mean. She'd told her this a day or so before while the girl was sleeping or dreaming. She was vague on that. We figured her mother had come to her and thinking she was asleep had unburdened herself of whatever it was. . . . It looked like she wanted her daughter to get out of it alive. We figured maybe she was planning to get out with her, just the two of them. The others, the two boys, we understand . . . they weren't hers?"

"They were his."

The man nodded. He looked at his notes. "The girl, she said, 'I don't want to talk to her anymore.' And then she just clammed up. She seemed to feel . . . she seemed to blame her mother all right; we have to say that. That's the worst of it. She wouldn't even use her name. She'd just say 'her' or 'she.'"

The man waited. The woman looked at him. At his throat. He wondered if there was something on his collar.

"It's sinful," the woman said, her jaw setting.

The man was about to say again that they couldn't absolutely prove it was her daughter's fault.

"It's sinful for a man to decorate hisself like that."

"Ma'am?"

"That thing you got around your neck."

The man flushed, realizing the woman was talking about the medallion he was wearing. For the first time he was fully aware of the severity of the woman's appearance, the old-fashioned, plain black dress and shoes. No makeup or jewelry. The book she was holding, he noticed, was the Bible. He closed his notepad.

17

"I'll be going now, ma'am."

She got up from her chair and watched him walk down the corridor.

One of the nurse's aides helped them put Bryna's things into the back of Lillian's old car.

"You're a lucky girl to have such a beautiful doll. Isn't this the prettiest thing?" The young woman turned to Lillian, whose attempt at a smile looked more like a grimace.

As they drove away, Bryna, in the back seat, said, "What about Robbie?"

"He's dead."

Bryna said nothing. Through the tears, which were not just for Robbie, but for all of them, especially Sharon, Bryna caught glimpses of Lillian watching her in the rearview mirror, her brow tightly knit.

"He wasn't kin," the old woman said after a while. And then nothing. They drove for hours across barren, flat land, stopping only for gas and food, which Lillian bought in a grocery store. They ate it in silence. Despite the heat, Lillian would permit the windows to be rolled down only a crack.

Bryna felt utterly alone. The voice that had been her constant companion for so long was gone. After the fire she told it to go away and never come back. She wasn't sorry. She would scream and never stop screaming if she ever heard the voice again, she told herself. The voice had said she could suit herself and was gone. Just like that.

Bryna glanced at Goldie, sitting next to her. For a long time she had told herself that the voice belonged to Goldie, even though it no longer came from the doll but from deep within herself. But lately the voice had begun to speak harshly to her, bossing and directing like a cranky grown-up. During the fire it had even cursed her, screaming at her to get out of the house when she wanted to stay and try to warn the others. Goldie, the Goldie she had known before, would never talk to her like that. Besides, Goldie was just a doll.

Bryna knew that now. But the doll was at least a familiar object, one she had loved and set aside when the voice entered her. Perhaps she could love the doll again. Perhaps Goldie could live again. Bryna slipped her hand around the doll's supple arm. She remembered what it had been like before. . . . More tears slid from her eyes.

"Hold the Bible I gave you, dear."

18

Bryna jumped. Lillian's scowling eyes were reflected in the rearview mirror.

Somewhere near Los Angeles Lillian turned on the car radio and picked up a religious station where a man droned on and on in a singsong voice. At the end of each sentence the man would gasp: "ah-UH!" The station faded in and out, accentuating the monotonous rhythm of it. Bryna had trouble keeping her eyes open. She was desperately afraid of falling asleep, and each time she would start to nod off she would fight her way back, invariably finding Lillian's eyes boring into her in the mirror.

Finally, the stifling heat, the motion of the car and the radio overwhelmed her. Soon she began to dream that she was flying, the air cool and wonderful, rushing past her, her long blonde hair flowing behind her. That was how she saw herself in the dream, with beautiful, long blonde hair. Like Goldie's.

Bryna awakened with a start. Lillian had rolled down her window, and the air was rushing back into Bryna's face. Lillian had one hand on the steering wheel and had just reached back with the other to take Goldie.

Bryna gasped and snatched at Goldie's hair as the doll whisked from her side.

"Let go!" Lillian commanded, pulling hard. "Filthy harlot doll!"

Bryna yanked back, and Lillian, losing control for a moment, swerved into the next lane, narrowly missing another car. The angry driver, headed the same way on the freeway, came alongside, mouthing obscenities, holding up his middle finger at Lillian. The old woman, furious, ripped at Goldie again, and some of the hair came loose in Bryna's hand before the woman hurled the doll out the window, shouting "Abomination!"

Bryna could not believe what was happening. She looked back and saw Goldie bounce up against the front of a car, her head flying in one direction, her body in another. The driver of the car honked, enraged. Lillian rolled up the window.

It wasn't until nearly a minute later that Bryna realized she was holding some of the doll's hair in her hand. She looked to see if the old woman had noticed, then quickly slipped it into the Bible.

In the small hot room assigned her in her grandmother's house, Bryna discovered with some surprise that she had placed the hair at the page marked by the Bible's black ribbon. She held the strands of golden hair gently between her fingers and then

19

brushed them against her lips. Goldie's face blossomed in her imagination, blotting out everything else. But only for a moment. Abruptly, a tiny red spot erupted on Goldie's face. It grew and pulsated angrily. Bryna shook herself, startled. The doll's face dissolved.

Bryna found herself staring at the open Bible that still lay on her lap. Someone, using a red-ink pen, had placed a large dot alongside one of the verses of Leviticus. Bryna read:

"A man also or woman that hath a familiar spirit, or that is a wizard, shall surely be put to death: they shall stone them with stones; their blood *shall be* upon them."

TWO

The buzzing sound grew louder. Bryna moved restlessly, neither asleep nor awake. Sometimes the buzz sounded almost like a voice, speaking at very high speed, excited, aroused.

Then Bryna saw it. It *was* a bee! A magnificent bumblebee hovering over an exquisite pink flower. Every time the bee dipped into the center of the flower Bryna felt herself tingle pleasantly all over. The bee buried itself in the oozing clear fluid, and the buzzing sound gave way to licking, lapping, sighing sounds. Suddenly Bryna could taste the nectar, too. It was as if she were no longer the flower but had now become the bee, hungrily engorging herself.

Abruptly, the supply of golden fluid dried up. A moment later deep red liquid began gushing up out of the center of the flower, drowning the bee. Bryna felt her lips close over the edge of the flower, straining to drink as much of the red liquid as possible.

It tasted like . . . Bryna sat up in bed, the taste of blood in her mouth. She felt the sticky substance rapidly drying on her lips and fingers. She felt short of breath, hot, dizzy. She had to see. She got to her feet, walking unevenly in the dark, feeling her way around the other beds, down the dormitory corridor and through the swinging door into the blinding white-ceramic brightness of the lavatory. Her reflection leapt at her from the row of mirrors above the sinks. She was horrified to find herself naked, her face, throat, breasts and lower abdomen smeared with red. Her sweat turned cold as her hands slid down her body, down to where it was still damp between her legs.

So, it had finally begun. She had read about it, years ago, and had seen some of the girls, many younger than herself. She had wondered why she was so slow. She had not really cared much. In this place she cared little about anything. There was nothing for her here. Well, there was the rat, but sometimes even he was surly. She recalled the time she had stolen some raw meat from the kitchen for him, at great peril to herself, and how, in his impatience to get at the stuff he had bitten her finger, raising a terrible infection. If he were here now, she thought, he would climb her legs and bury himself in her, to get at the blood. She shuddered, but in fact the idea did not really displease her. She wondered why she had eaten her own blood; surely it was a sin. That thought did not displease her, either.

"You *are* a fright!"

Bryna whirled around, but there was no one there.

"Look at me when I talk to you!" The voice, that of a woman, seemed to come now from the direction of the sinks. Bryna turned again, the smell of her own perspiration burning her nostrils. In each of the mirrors now was the image of a woman, the most beautiful woman Bryna had ever seen. Her hair was shimmering, long, wavy and blonde, her eyes, a luminous blue, her brows darkly shadowed. Her figure, clad in white satin, was full and exquisitely formed.

Bryna looked over her shoulder again but still there was no one there.

"You silly thing. Look at me!"

Bryna turned again to the mirrors to find the woman scowling at her. "I've been here all along; waiting. My God, how I've waited! Just my luck to pick a stubborn, balky thing like . . . but never mind. And stop shaking like a bloody toad! Here, maybe you'd rather see yourself, then."

Bryna blinked as the image dissolved and her own replaced it. But the voice remained. "A pretty sight, hah! Look at yourself. A *pig* has a better figure." The voice took on a mocking tone. "My, you've really done well for yourself without me, haven't you? If you hadn't been such a little fool you'd be shy all this blubber right now. Cinderella, indeed. Cinderella Mozzarella!"

The image of the woman materialized again. Her eyes cruelly canvassed Bryna's body. The girl tried to cover herself with her arms, staring miserably into the mirror. She could barely get the words out.

"Wh . . . who are you?"

The mirror image started to speak, then stopped, holding up a warning hand.

21

"Hurry, someone is coming," the voice said. "Hide yourself in one of the stalls. We'll talk more in due course."

Bryna watched the figure disappear and her own reflection replace it in the row of mirrors. She heard footsteps, shook herself, and ran into the nearest toilet. She closed the door, sat down and pressed her knees to her chest. No one came in. Bryna began to feel very foolish and decided she had imagined all of it—all except the blood she had come to wash away.

The Overseer, stiffly attired in black, leaned out from where he was standing behind his desk and peered disconsolately down on the courtyard below. Cracking concrete and scruffy patches of renegade grass glowered back at him. There was still so much to do before the Elders made their inspection.

". . . and so when Sister Thelma told us about an opening here, I drove right out," the corpulent little man said, dabbing his face with a yellow handkerchief. "I felt the Spirit had spoken. . . ."

The Overseer eyed the man who had come to apply for a teaching position with the same sour countenance he turned on all flesh. He wondered what vices the man's girth concealed. What weaknesses squirmed behind all this nervous sweating?

The Overseer's glare was so intense the man stopped speaking. He peered at the wall off to one side, pretending to read the words that were framed there, though they were already as familiar to him as his own warts:

Christ is our commander, we know no defeat,
We've sounded the trumpet that ne'er calls retreat,
Then onward, right onward at His blest command,
Clear the way, we are coming, the fire-baptized band.

"This is a school for girls," the Overseer said; of course, the applicant knew this. The Overseer glanced out the window again. He squinted to make out the figure hurrying as best it could across the courtyard. A short, pudgy figure wearing glasses. Even from this range uncomely. The figure's lumpish shape and limping gait gave her away. The Overseer had known her grandmother well. When the old woman died he had personally administered her estate, most of which had gone to the church.

The Overseer pushed his long, white teeth up against his tightly drawn lips. Three times he had laid hands on the girl; three times she had resisted the Spirit; the limp persisted. Wretched girl! She was a black mark on the school; when she had arrived there at age ten there had been possibilities, but with each year—the Overseer guessed she must now be fourteen, almost fifteen—she had grown more gross, more dull. The girl's file had often crossed the Overseer's desk, and for good reason; she had not yet been able to pass beyond the seventh grade.

The girl paused, unaware she was being watched. She looked over her shoulder and then ran into the forbidden gymnasium.

"They're not all angels," the Overseer said, looking briefly back at the other man. Below him he next saw appear an old woman with a heavy cane. She looked about warily and then moved toward the gymnasium entrance, as well.

"You know what I mean?" the Overseer asked. His voice was barely audible. He waited a moment and then turned around, propping himself on both arms against the desk, leaning out toward the applicant, openly leering.

The fat man looked uncertain, swallowed and then smiled back, displaying uneven teeth and complicit imperfection.

The Overseer snapped like a sprung trap, standing bolt upright:

"Ye are of your father the devil, and the lusts of your father ye will do! He was a murderer from the beginning, and abode not in the truth, because there is no truth in him! When he speaketh a lie, he speaketh of his own: for he is a liar and the father of it!"

"Bryna! Bryna Carr!"

Bryna trembled, her momentary amazement at finding herself in this forbidden place overwhelmed by fear. A new realization was rising in her and with it a new horror. It would happen here. She would have to witness it without the comfort and closeness of others. There would be no one to say she hadn't done it.

Bryna began to cry, but there were no tears. Her chest heaved, her white skin grew even paler against the close-cropped, almost boyish black hair and the dark blue of her heavy school uniform; the muscles in her face contracted and expanded, projecting terror. Her green eyes fixed on the three concrete steps not five feet from her. She began backing slowly away from them, oblivious now to the stench of mothballs that leapt up out of the rusting urinals that lined the wall behind her.

The obscene sketches all around her were now indecipherable blurs. Only the steps, glowing yellow-green like the tile walls in the dim light that filtered through a few opaque panes of glass, remained in focus.

"Bryna, I know you're in there! Come out at once!" The creaky voice struggled with itself, but its rage could not be contained. "Damn you!"

There was a high-pitched, angry sound as a nail was wrenched from wood. Sister Eudell was using her heavy cane to pry loose the few boards Bryna had only minutes before slipped between. The boards had gone up across the door hurriedly, shortly after the basement, in what years before had been a boys' gym, was opened for renovation. The Fire Baptized Holiness School for Girls was expanding. The Overseer himself had inspected the decaying boys' lavatory and, tight-lipped, had written the order demanding that it be boarded up until the workmen, busy in another part of the building, could get to it.

Bryna had thought she might be safe there, but it had been difficult, particularly with her bulky profile, to squeeze between the boards, and her shirt had snagged on the rough wood. The sound of pursuing footsteps halted her effort to retrieve the telltale fabric, and she retreated down the concrete steps into the strange place.

There was another scream of nails ripping loose. Bryna could hear the labored breathing of the old woman as she stooped down to climb through the space she had made. Bryna continued to move away from the steps, her head moving from side to side, her jaw working involuntarily, and though she repeated over and over, "It isn't my fault," all that came from her lips was an erratic hum.

Abruptly, Sister Eudell was there, a tall, hulking figure in black, brandishing the heavy cane that she was never without, her gray, malproportioned face contorted in rage, her eyes darting into every corner of the gloom, searching. Suddenly Bryna was seeing through the teacher's eyes, feeling with the old woman's body. At first all was darkness, then, as the teacher's rheumy eyes adjusted, settling first on adolescent hieroglyphics, drawings of crudely exaggerated breasts and penises and words Bryna had not previously understood, the girl felt her private place tighten and her chest burn. A current of nausea ripped through her, and she saw herself as the woman saw her—backing up against the stained urinal, her head jerking, her mouth twisted in a horrible rictus, humming insanely, eyes bugging, fixed. She felt her stomach convulse, and then saw the red spill soundlessly from her mouth, saw it as Sister Eudell saw it, vomiting "blood," which, in reality, was the beet soup she had eaten in the cafeteria at lunch.

"Say-*tan*! Say-*tan*!" Sister Eudell screamed, raising her cane, jolting Bryna back to reality, enabling her to see through her own eyes as the old woman lurched forward, missing the first step, stumbling, then falling straight forward, seemingly filling the

24

whole room, arms outstretched, cane hurtling out in front of her. She screamed as she fell, her eyes fixed on Bryna. As her chin smashed into the tile floor there was a dull, sickening sound, as if something had snapped deep inside her.

Bryna pressed so hard against the urinal that she feared the wall behind her might collapse. Sister Eudell was flat on her stomach, her arms still outstretched, her head tilted back on her chin, her eyes open, unmoving, staring straight at Bryna. Blood spilled in slow, rhythmic gushes from her mouth.

With strength she thought she could never muster, Bryna pushed herself away from the urinal, staggered past the awful figure on the floor and ran up the steps, screaming at last, into the arms of an alarmed young man.

The Deaconess, her eyes small and reptilian, sunk deep in a seamless oval of fat, told Sister Tressy she would not tolerate any more tears. The Overseer stood by impassively.

The Deaconess spoke again. "I want you to tell me *precisely* and without the blubbering—is that clear?—exactly what happened. I want you to tell it again in the Overseer's presence."

Sister Tressy fought to compose herself, hunching her shoulders repeatedly as if that would shake off the horror. "Sister Eudell stepped out for just a minute to . . . to, you know," Sister Tressy said, glancing uncomfortably at the Overseer, "and when she came back it was on the blackboard, the words I told you, they're still there, they . . ."

"Just tell us what they said."

"They said," Sister Tressy continued, swallowing hard, "they said, 'Bryna Carr says Sister Eudell is going to break her neck today.' Sister's name was misspelled, like I told you, and . . ."

The Deaconess waved her hand impatiently. "Are you daft? We don't care about the spelling!" Her eyes narrowed until they nearly disappeared. "This was *before*? *Before* it happened?"

"Yes, I . . ."

"How do you know that?"

"I heard them. I heard Sister Eudell shout. She shouted: 'Bryna, come back here!' She was in the hall, and my room is just across the way. I stepped out and saw Bryna running away. Sister told me to watch her class, and she ran after Bryna. When I went into Sister Eudell's room, it was there, the words, I mean, on the blackboard. They were all staring at the words. Some of them were laughing. I sent Mary Kay Biddinger down the hall to fetch Sister Lavonda, she's so strong, and . . ."

The Deaconess held her hand up, signaling silence. She pushed a button on the aging desk intercom and said, "Send in Sister Lavonda now."

Sister Lavonda entered, carrying a small cardboard box. Her face betrayed no emotion. The Deaconess asked her to relate what had happened.

"Of course. I found Sister Eudell gone. On the blackboard were the words..."

"Yes, yes, go on."

"I asked who had written them. No one would speak, so I took Mary Fulford by the ears and shook her, and she said that Connie Crawford had written them. Connie began to cry and admitted it. She said Bryna Carr had told her this, that Sister Eudell was going to break her neck this very day. She said Bryna had whispered this to her just after lunch, that Bryna was acting oddly. She asked Connie not to tell but that a voice had spoken to her and she was sure it had spoken the truth. Connie likes to be the center of attention, she's the prettiest, too pretty for her own good, and everyone wants to be her friend. So when Sister Eudell stepped out for a few minutes, Connie went to the blackboard and wrote the words there. Bryna had dozed off, which isn't at all uncommon—I know from having had her in my own class—but the other girls' laughter woke her up. She stumbled up to the blackboard and was about to erase the words when Sister Eudell came in. Bryna ran right past her, out the door, guilty as sin, and Sister went after her."

The Deaconess paged through Bryna's file. "She was receiving even worse marks than usual in Sister Eudell's class. Was the girl bad-tempered?"

Both Sister Tressy and Sister Lavonda said she was withdrawn.

"An unhealthiness Sister Eudell wouldn't tolerate, unlike some others, perhaps," the Deaconess said. "But go on; then what happened?"

"The workman found them," Sister Lavonda said. "Arnie Dunn. He heard the noise when Sister pulled the boards loose. He looked in just after she fell. He says she fell."

The Deaconess used the intercom again. "Send in Arnold Dunn."

The obviously shaken young man entered.

"Now, Arnold, Arnie," the Deaconess said, smiling briefly for the first time, exposing small teeth with little spaces between them, "would you tell us what you saw. The exact sequence."

The young man shifted his weight from one foot to the other. "Well, I heard this commotion, like somethin' bein' ripped up. I was workin' on the stairs just above there. So I went down and I seen somebody goin' into that old . . . uh . . . restroom, you know, and I saw those boards we put up was ripped down. So I went in real quiet, 'cause I wasn't sure. . . ."

"We understand."

"And I saw Sister and this girl. . . ."

"Where was the girl?"

"She was back up against the wall, and Sister was . . . was on the floor. I heard her fall just after she yelled."

"What did she yell?"

Arnold flushed. Anger—perhaps recalling some of his own teachers—gave him courage to speak up. "It was like she was crazy. She was screamin' 'Satan! Satan!' The girl ran right into me tryin' to get out of there. What did she do anyway? Why was Sister so mad?"

"It was a prank," the Deaconess said. "Something Bryna did in class. Sister was old. She took these things too hard." The woman paused. "The girl, you say, was nowhere near Sister when she fell?"

Arnold looked shocked. "No! Nowhere near! You don't think she pushed her?"

The Deaconess smiled again. "Nothing of the sort. It's just that when something like this happens, you have to touch all bases. And if there was any doubt, you've dispelled it. You've done a good deed being so quick to the scene."

Arnold looked pleased with himself. The Deaconess thanked him and asked him not to speak of the incident again, "so as not to upset the girls or give encouragement to our enemies." When he was gone she similarly instructed the two teachers not to speak of the matter again, but to erase the offending words from the blackboard and inform Sister Eudell's class that their teacher had so severely beaten Bryna that the Deaconess, who endorsed the punishment but not its severity, had assigned Sister Eudell to duties outside the school. As for Bryna, the girls were to be told she had been expelled to the oft-maligned state reformatory.

When Sister Tressy had been dismissed, the Deaconess turned to Sister Lavonda and, glancing at the box in her hands, said, "All right. Tell Reverend the rest of it."

Sister Lavonda, mindful that she mustn't display her pride, tried to sound humble as she said, looking at the Overseer, "It seemed to me *obvious,* as it would to *anyone,* that there was something very, *very* wrong with this child. When Sister Eudell's class had been removed to another room I held Connie Crawford back and questioned her *sharply.* It seemed she was one of the few Bryna Carr ever talked to. I asked her if she'd observed *anything* peculiar in the girl. She said nothing in particular—except," Sister Lavonda paused, looking happily at the box in her hands, "*except* that she made a pet of sorts out of, as Connie put it, 'a nasty old rat.' Connie caught her feeding the rat one night when the other girls in that ward were asleep. Bryna threatened to turn the rat on her if she told. Connie told me its whereabouts—back in the wall behind the west-wing laundry. There's a hole there. It was easy enough to lure it out with a little raw meat."

The Overseer scowled at the box and with an impatient gesture indicated that Sister Lavonda was to open it. The Overseer peered in and then cautiously lifted out the limp but still-warm rodent. Its head was bloody.

"I hit it with a Purex bottle."

When the Overseer's eyes met Sister Lavonda's her smile disappeared as quickly as it had materialized. He let the animal sink back down and took the box from her. He nodded, and the Deaconess told Sister Lavonda she could go.

Alone with the Overseer, the Deaconess picked up Bryna's file once again and said, "You may not recall what her grandmother told us, the circumstances under which she came to us, the fire started by her mother. . . ."

"Yes, yes," the Overseer said, waving his hand. "Sorcery breeds sorcery. There were devils here I should have grappled with long ago. The memory of that sainted woman, her grandmother, held me back when it should have spurred me on. God forgive me my tardiness. We must now be unsparing. Where is she?"

"In the sick hall. She was hysterical. Nurse has her sedated."

"Good," the man said, his heavy brows tensed, "the evil in her will be sluggish."

The Deaconess noticed the droplets of sweat on the Overseer's chin. He had come prepared from his own office, after an initial recitation there of what had happened. He took his black bag and the cardboard box, and they walked through the Deaconess' outer office, down the dimly lit corridor and up the steps to the infirmary.

The Deaconess knocked twice on the door. A panel slid open, a face peered out, the panel closed. A nurse in starched white hospital habit opened the door and admitted them. The place appeared empty.

"I've moved the other girls back to their own beds as you instructed. She's up there." The nurse nodded to a curtained area accessible by a ramp. The room had once been a small auditorium, and the raised, curtained area had been a low stage. Now it was used to separate those with more serious or persistent illnesses from the less afflicted.

The Overseer led the way. At the top of the ramp he parted the curtain. Directly in front of him was the old metal gurney. On it was Bryna, strapped down, on her back, apparently asleep. The Overseer glanced inquiringly at the nurse.

"She's had an injection, Reverend. She won't wake up for a while."

The Overseer braced himself, muttering in a strange tongue, then leaned over Bryna and, sticking out one long finger, prodded her in the chest. He quickly pulled back his finger and saw that it was stained with red. He sniffed, his lip curling. Then he looked upward, sniffing the air. Bryna stirred in her drugged sleep, mumbling something incomprehensible.

The Overseer drew back quickly. "Undress her," he said to the nurse. Then turning to the Deaconess: "Bring Brother Bob and Sister Ruth." He opened his bulky black bag as the nurse struggled with Bryna's clothing. By the time he had placed candles on the floor in a circle around the gurney the others had arrived.

"You've been informed?"

The two newcomers nodded solemnly, staring at the naked girl.

Brother Bob spoke. "What demon is it, Reverend?"

"One of the devil's daughters."

Sister Ruth instantly recited scripture: "And it came to pass, when Joram saw Jehu, that he said, Is it peace, Jehu? And he answered, What peace, so long as the whoredoms of thy mother Jezebel and her witchcrafts are many?"

"Yea, Sister, you speak well," the Overseer said. The woman fell to her knees, her head jerking as she prayed in a low mumble. "Leave us now," he instructed the nurse. "Turn out the lights as you go and set the lock and let no one disturb us, no matter what sounds issue."

When the nurse had gone, Brother Bob spoke again: "A witch, then?"

The Overseer did not speak but drew the rat from its cardboard crypt and held it up in the candlelight over Bryna's inert figure.

"Her familiar?"

"I believe it so. Sister Lavonda killed it."

"May the Lord have mercy on the child's soul."

"May God smite her this hour if she does not renounce and

29

abandon her foul spirit," the Overseer corrected, placing the rat between Bryna's small breasts.

Sister Ruth's voice rose again: "Because of the multitude of the whoredoms of the well-favored harlot, the mistress of witchcrafts, that selleth nations through her whoredoms and families through her witchcrafts."

"Take your stand there, Brother. On your knees, next to your sister. Prepare, for it *will* come out and it *will* tempt you. Beware! Be strong! The Ghost be with you!"

Brother Bob and Sister Ruth kneeled on either side of the gurney, beneath Bryna's shoulders. The Deaconess stood at Bryna's head, facing the Overseer, who positioned himself at Bryna's feet. The Deaconess clutched a white wooden cross which she gripped in both hands, holding it directly over the girl's face. The Overseer held a stick of dynamite, from the supply that was used in the "baptism of the fire" and which on special occasions, was actually detonated on the denomination's retreat on the Texas plain, as prescribed in the old teachings of the church. God had declared that those who were one with the Spirit could withstand even the explosions of Hell. Some of the great early evangelists, the Overseer had heard—and having heard, believed—had held exploding sticks of dynamite in both hands and come away unscathed. Only the wicked could be harmed by the fire.

Brother Bob and Sister Ruth were now praying in tongues, their voices rising and falling in odd harmony with one another. Occasionally they would throw their heads back and their eyes would open, rolling upward.

"Thou shall not suffer a witch to live!" the Overseer shouted. "By this Holy Ghost oil may our Lord God grant those assembled in this holy purpose protection from this polluted thing!" He sprinkled oil from a large vial liberally over Bryna's nude body.

"I command you, o foul and sluttish spirit! Come out!" He spoke again for a few moments in tongues. Then, "I command you in the name of our Lord; yea, in the name of the Holy Ghost! Come out and show yourself! Die! Unloose your grip on God's child and our holy house! The Lord God commands you through me his humble servant! I will cut off witchcrafts out of thine hand, and thou shalt have no more soothsayers!"

The Overseer sprinkled more oil over Bryna's body, anointing the battered rat, as well.

"Out! Out!" he screamed. "I'll blow you back to Hell, you

filthy whore!" At this the others spoke more wildly in tongues, all but the Deaconess who stood gripping the cross as if it were her lifeline, her eyes and jaw tightly shut. Her whole upper body trembled with the strain.

The Overseer burst out of a long peal of tongues with "Praise God! Praise God for the Holy Ghost that fills up!" He filled his lungs with air and raised both arms, holding the stick of dynamite over Bryna's body.

"Praise God for the blood that cleans up! Praise God for the dynamite that blows up!"

At this the Deaconess abruptly opened her eyes, dropped the cross and took the stick of dynamite the Overseer thrust at her.

"Now!" he shouted.

The Deaconess retracted Bryna's chin so that her mouth fell open and, trembling, stuck the butt of the dynamite into the girl's mouth. Impossible though it seemed, the veins stood out in the Deaconess' fat neck.

"Deep! Deep, Sister, deep!" the Overseer commanded. "If it doesn't come out now, we'll blow it the Hell out!"

The Deaconess thrust and immediately Bryna began to gag.

"I feel it, I feel her! Oh, Jesus, Jesus," Brother Bob wailed, rolling onto his side on the floor, clutching his groin. "She's got me, she's got hold of me!"

"Be strong, Brother! Pray!" the Overseer ordered. "We're going to kill it! We've frightened it! It's coming out! It's coming!"

Bryna thrashed about on the table, fighting, unconscious though she was, against the thing that was cutting off her air. Her head jerked from side to side and she strained against the leather straps that confined her to the gurney.

"Hold, Sister, hold!" the Overseer shouted at the Deaconess who struggled to keep the stick of dynamite in Bryna's mouth.

Sister Ruth fell straight back onto the floor, her eyes rolling, her body convulsing. The backs of her heels hammered the floor in a frenzied staccato. "uhAhuhAhuhAh," she cried.

"In the name of the Holy Ghost, I command you die!" the Overseer shouted, glowering at the invisible.

Bryna's face suddenly began to turn blue. The gagging ceased.

"Withdraw!" the Overseer commanded. "The thing has gone back in and is strangling her from inside!"

The Deaconess pulled the dynamite out of Bryna's mouth. Sweat was pouring into the woman's eyes. She blinked frantically. Brother Bob and Sister Ruth continued to roll about on the floor, but their voices subsided.

"They're weakening," the Overseer said. "We must hurry." He leaned over Bryna's body again, holding a candle close to her skin, searching.

"See!" he said, after a few moments, sucking in his breath. "There!" He held the flame of the candle close to a reddish-brown pigment, just on the lip of the girl's vagina. "The Devil's mark! It is with such that Satan seals his covenants." He knelt quickly to his black bag and withdrew from it a long, white box. From that, in turn, he extracted a silver needle nine inches in length.

"This is a willful spirit. We must kill it where it roots—within. We go *there,*" he said, pointing with the needle to the mole, "straight into evil."

The Deaconess could only stare at the forbidding instrument. Her tongue darted along her lower lip. The thrashings and mutterings of the two on the floor were now considerably diminished.

"It's vanquishing them. We have no time to lose." The Overseer knelt again to the floor and pushed the heavy needle down through the flame of one of the candles and into the wax so that it stood upright, the flame shooting up its shaft. As the fire purified it, he shut his eyes and prayed out loud in tongues.

Only the Deaconess saw the movement and the sudden flush of color that perfused Bryna's body, so that her skin began to glow pink and then almost red in the candlelight. The girl's body began to strain again against the straps that held her to the wheeled table. Soon the straining became almost rythmical, hips rising and falling and twisting. And though her arms were strapped down, her hands were sufficiently free to caress and squeeze her thighs. As she writhed in this fashion the rat bounced from between her breasts, down her body and onto her lower abdomen. One of Bryna's hands closed around the body of the rat and slid it to the mouth of her vagina.

The Deaconess, still clutching the dynamite, fell back a step in horror as a cunning smile began to form on Bryna's lips. The girl, her eyes still closed, pushed the head of the rat between her legs. Blood began to flow there, though whether it was Bryna's or the rat's, the Deaconess could not be sure. The girl began to undulate more obscenely than before, her mouth falling open as she thrust the rat deeper up into her. Suddenly there was blood on the girl's lips.

The Deaconess wanted to scream, "Ye shall not eat anything with the blood: neither shall ye use enchantment," but the words would not roll off her tongue. She was truly speechless with horror. No longer conscious of what she was doing, the woman began edging around the table, fearful of making any rapid movement, lest the demon seize her. She moved instinctively toward the Overseer.

At the foot of the table, just above the kneeling Overseer, the Deaconess stopped, her attention riveted on the rat, whose head and neck were now completely buried in the girl. The abomination pulled her like a magnet. She leaned in closer, unable to help herself, uncertain that what she was seeing was real. What happened next made the Deaconess feel as if there were a million worms in her belly squirming to get out. She saw the hind haunches of the rat suddenly kick and tense frantically. The rat was alive! It pulled itself out of Bryna, shook itself, staggered, turned and leapt into the darkness, narrowly missing the Deaconess.

Just as the woman began to feel her legs give way beneath her, the Overseer, his prayers reaching a fever pitch, opened his eyes, firmly gripped the glowing hot needle between his bare fingers and then turned and hurtled to his feet in a paroxysm of pain and piety. There he found himself face to face with the collapsing Deaconess, nearly crashing into her. He felt himself suddenly relieved of the pain in his fingers.

The Deaconess' eyes, which had begun to close, abruptly opened wider—much wider than the Overseer would have ever thought possible. The woman stared straight at him, and her mouth moved slightly as if she were about to say something. Then her eyes rolled upward, and she fell silently backward onto the floor in a dead faint, a red· stain beginning to form on her white habit around the needle that had just penetrated deep into her lower abdomen.

Brother Bob, still tossing sluggishly about on the floor, was the first to hear it. He squinted out of the corner of his eye toward the supine Deaconess.

"Holy God!" he shouted, suddenly very much alive. He scrambled to his feet, using the legs of the gurney for support as he hoisted himself. Sister Ruth, startled by the sound of the man's voice, did likewise, grabbing the other side of the gurney to pull herself up. The sudden movement released the gurney's worn brake and gently propelled the wheeled table toward the ramp.

No one noticed. Or cared.

"The dynamite!" Brother Bob screamed. Its fuse had fallen into one of the flames of the candles when the Deaconess collapsed. It was sizzling now like a rattlesnake.

Brother Bob, Sister Ruth and the Overseer stared at it dumbly, paralyzed.

The gurney bearing Bryna passed through the curtain and down the ramp, gathering speed. It was nearly at the end of the ward when it crashed into the metal frame of a bed and upended. The explosion came a second later.

THREE

"We have a new girl with us today, class," Miss Lionel beamed, looking up from the drearily mimeographed piece of paper headed "Home Room Announcements—Monday, October 18, 1972." These announcements, together with an accompanying and variable assortment of forms, questionnaires, nostrums, harangues, pep talks and occasional panegyrics, constituted the holy writ of Central High as it was passed down to each teacher from The Office first thing daily. A bright red asterisk alerted Miss Lionel to the fact that the new girl had been assigned to her homeroom.

Miss Lionel surveyed the sea of faces, eagerly seeking out the new addition. She loved teaching despite the fact that in twenty years of it she had not yet found her "special student," the one who would "go on to great things" and, in a *Time* cover article or *New Yorker* profile, would recall, across all those sweet-sacrificing years, the teacher "without whom none of this would have been possible" or at least, "to whom, for her warm guidance and tireless ass-kicking I shall forever be in debt." She thought: "God bless you, Miss Lionel, wherever the hell you are."

Hope springs eternal in the proud teacher's breast. Miss Lionel's breasts were large and still proud. She was no longer precisely in her prime, but since there were a lot of people who hadn't noticed she wasn't about to behave accordingly.

oh

Bryna could feel the teacher's energy slump, could see herself, as if for the first time, through Miss Lionel's eyes: white, round, pasty face, zits, ugly, reddish-brown, framed glasses with lenses so thick you could see circles in them, long, unevenly cut, greasy black hair that concealed much of her face, "prominent" nose.

Dressed in dowdy, dark hand-me-downs that concealed as much
of her body as possible. Short, wide...

like a brick shit house
maybe it's glandular
god, i feel sorry
can you dig that, man?
yeah, with a steamshovel

It came at her like a foul wind, had been coming at her ever
since she walked down the corridor and into Miss Lionel's room.
She had been the last one, except for Miss Lionel herself. Heads
all turned slowly when she came in until the entire class was
looking at her, and she could see it, feel it, hear it, the shock, the
revulsion, the pity, hear their whispers, hear their thoughts, see
the nudges, the smirks.

Bryna's heart hammered against her chest; she was acutely
aware that until the teacher arrived she was going to be the
center of attention. She had squeezed into an empty desk at the
back of the room, painfully aware of the considerable effort this
simple act entailed. The desk clamped her like a vise. A boy
sitting across from her watched with arrogant good looks, gauging her progress with stifled snickering, nudging the girl whose
frizzy red hair and blue eye makeup Bryna had vaguely noticed
when she first entered the room.

"Jesus," the girl whispered, as Bryna let her full weight settle
into the desk.

Then Miss Lionel had come in, and all eyes, for a moment at
least, were on the teacher, who quickly skimmed the daily
announcements, discovering the new pupil. It was only on the
inside, Bryna knew, that the teacher's warm smile withered. On
the outside she was still beaming; she'd had practice. Bryna
dreaded what would happen next. Miss Lionel would now ask
her to say a few words about herself "...so we can all get to
know you."

The palms of Bryna's hands were sweating; her mouth was
instantly as dry as a reptile's skin. She knew her voice would
tremble, and she knew she was expected to rise when she spoke.
She could easily imagine the desk coming up with her, a grotesque extension of herself, her squat legs supporting it. Already,
she could tell, her hesitation was making the teacher nervous.
Miss Lionel was lifting the first page of the daily announcements
and was examining an attached copy of Bryna's entrance form,
marked "confidential." Bryna could make out very clearly what
she was focusing on: *Height: 5'4". Weight: 174 lb.*

oh god why did i do it why did i let her make me do it i was better off before

Bryna shifted miserably in her desk. The words just weren't going to come. Miss Lionel, she could see, had sensed her predicament.

"Well, let's see now," the teacher said brightly. "It's Bryna, isn't it? Bryna Borchers from . . . no, I see it's Bryna *Carr*. The Borchers are your . . ."—she had gone too far not to say it, supposed it wouldn't do any harm anyway—". . . foster parents. And you've come all the way from Dallas, Texas. Isn't that interesting, class? I wonder how Bryna's going to like our Montana winters. Perhaps some other time Bryna will tell us a little about Texas, and . . ."—*I.Q. Stanford Binet 162*—". . . . and . . ."

Bryna could feel the teacher's eyes boring into the part on the top of her head. She dared not look up. Her thumb traced the tiny letters someone had carved in the wood of her desk

fuck

and she wondered why she had let her give her the answers; now they would all expect so much of her. She could feel Miss Lionel's shocked delight.

"Bryna may look like an overnourished rutabaga on the outside but inside, my lamebrained lovelies, she's a genuine twenty-four karat sparkler with a one sixty-two I.Q.! A genuine near-genius, frogs! Sentinel High, eat your hearts out! We're going to cream you in the next Brain Bowl!"

Bryna felt herself flushing despite the fact that she knew she had only imagined Miss Lionel saying this.

The teacher had *thought* some of this, but what she actually was saying was: ". . . and Bryna, before coming here to Central attended the Fire Baptized . . ." Miss Lionel stopped abruptly and, hoping to avoid further embarrassing disclosures, read rapidly ahead, learning—with growing indignation—how Bryna had been held back in the seventh grade, her "true potential" undiscovered until an "incident" forced the closing of the school, and the girls, many of them orphans, were given over to state authorities, psychologically and academically reevaluated and, where possible, assigned foster families. The Borchers, Miss Lionel quickly noted, had several other foster children

mercenaries but then someone has to do it

and had only recently assumed custody of Bryna, now sixteen. She had attended a special rehabilitative school for more than a year before being placed in a foster home. The Borchers had moved to Montana, where Mr. Borchers, the teacher learned from the confidential report, had been offered work in the "forest industry."

out at that stinking pulp mill

". . . yes," Miss Lionel continued, "attended, I see here, a private school for girls."

But "private" couldn't erase "Fire Baptized." Bryna felt forty sets of eyes surveying her anew. The heavy black dress suddenly bespoke more than poverty or concealment. Bryna was acutely aware of the snickering commotion in the next row of seats. It was the arrogant, dark-haired boy and the girl with the frizzy hair and the makeup.

Suddenly Bryna could feel the boy, feel his heat—and then his flesh—pressing against her, holding her down on the ground. He was naked. His smile was cruel.

"Tony," she heard herself say, her voice gorged with desire. "Oh, Tony, you really know women."

Bryna shook herself, horrified at what she had imagined.

"Tony." It was Miss Lionel's voice this time, real enough. "Sit straight ahead please. And Elizabeth, shut your mouth; I wouldn't want your brains to fall out."

The red-haired girl looked dour as she was spoken to; it was a line Miss Lionel had used often enough before, but it still got a few chuckles.

Then another voice was heard, quiet but still quite clear:

"Not that that would make a very big mess."

Bryna looked up just long enough to see the look of surprise on Miss Lionel's face, a surprise that soon yielded to an involuntary smile. Bryna looked back down. Out of the shocked silence erupted a few nervous giggles followed by a general guffaw. Bryna could feel the heat of the red-haired girl's glower.

The bell rang, the signal to proceed to the first class of the day. Bryna was the last to file out. Miss Lionel smiled at her.

"I see that you'll be in my English class later on. I'm delighted." The teacher beamed again. "And Bryna, I'd like to thank you for telling us so much about yourself."

Bryna wondered for a moment if she was being sarcastic. Then she understood. She tried her best to return the teacher's smile.

P.E. was the worst. Nadine—that's what all the girls called her—ran things with crisp, military efficiency. Calling roll, she used only last names.

"Borchers."

"Here," Bryna said in a small voice.

37

"Borchers!"

"Here," Bryna repeated, louder.

Nadine looked up from her clipboard, taking in all of Bryna. "New girl," she muttered, penciling something on her chart. She looked Bryna over again, noting her orange gym trunks, taken from the boys' stock, the only ones large enough. Most of the girls wore white.

"P.E. is three times a week," Nadine lectured Bryna: "Physical fitness is every day of your life. Report to the office here in the gym after class, and I'll give you the whole program. I'm required to tell you these extra programs are optional. So is good health; it's your choice. You'll find a wide variety of sports and other activities to select from."

"Wrestling," someone said. There were titters.

"Ballet." It was Elizabeth—Liz—the girl with frizzy hair. More laughter.

Nadine blew her whistle, finished roll and shouted: "Form up!"

Sixty girls, groaning in unison, fell into familiar ranks across one half of the gym floor.

"Borchers! There!"

Bryna took the designated place and tried to keep up as the P.E. teacher, barking cadence, led the group through a strenuous set of calisthenics. Bryna's side began to ache almost at once; soon she was dripping with sweat. Her feet and ankles hurt so badly she wanted to drop to her knees. It was impossible to keep up.

"One two three four, get your butts off the floor! C'mon, Borchers, move that thing!"

beauty unchanging, power beyond

The words made no sense, yet seemed somehow familiar, perhaps another taunt. Bryna began to feel dizzy. Her head ached and her stomach hurt. She wanted to sink to the floor and go to sleep, but the whistle jarred her back to reality.

"Laps!" Nadine commanded, and the girls immediately began running single file around the perimeter of the gym. Bryna quickly found herself at the end of the line and then at the head of it, momentarily, as the first girl caught up with her and the circle closed.

Nadine moved into the center of the gym, moving in small circles, monitoring the progress of her charges.

"Step it up! Let's haul ass!"

The girls responded gleefully, hooting. Bryna was no longer a part of the action, but an obstacle. She kept bumping into the others. She was staggering. Everything around her became soft, indistinct. Voices and laughter blurred until they were just a buzz. Bryna felt as though she were falling through the air in slow motion, turning over and over. The other girls were falling, too, but more rapidly, it seemed. She slumped to her knees and then to the floor. Far off in the distance she heard a whistle. After that there was only darkness and silence.

When the light started to come back it was a muted glow, and standing against it, blotting out most of it, was a dark figure—a man, Bryna decided. He was moving toward her. The light expanded around him, gradually illuminating his features. He seemed alarmed, then relieved. He was happy to see her. She could tell that he loved her and that whatever it was that had stood between them was gone now. They could finally share each other.

Bryna felt that she should feel joyous, but she did not. The man reached out to touch her, but she could not feel his fingers on her face. She could see what was happening, but it was as if she were no longer in her body. She seemed to be watching this man—and herself—from some distance, invisible, watching as the dark-haired young man with the deep-set, steel-blue eyes reached out to her, calling her by name, tenderly touching her long, black hair. She was beautiful now, slender with full breasts and flawless skin. The man who loved her was painfully handsome.

He spoke to her: "Bryna, I thought..."

She heard herself answer: "He's dead. I killed him."

Bryna felt herself straining, fighting against something invisible, wanting more than anything to come out of the shadows, to show herself. But why and to whom? She felt frustrated, afraid. Then she saw her slim, beautiful self fall into the man's arms, murmuring, "Niko, hold me, please just hold me, Niko, Niko."

As the man's arms closed around her, Bryna felt the empty darkness close in again. She felt cold and then pain. A pain that stabbed through her nostrils and exploded in the back of her head.

"Uhhhh!"

Bryna sat up with a start.

"Easy, easy," the voice soothed. It sounded familiar. Then the face came into focus and the eyes, too. She felt sure she had seen them before.

She looked around confused, wondering what she was doing on the floor. And what was this boy doing holding the back of her head with one hand and pushing something that reeked of ammonia up under her nose with the other?

"You passed out. Everything's okay now," he said, his eyes full of concern.

Bryna looked up. The P.E. teacher was staring down at her projecting an unspoken mixture of relief and anger.

"Okay, Borchers, you'd better sit this one out in the office. Nick will help you."

nick?

Bryna looked at the boy again. Why did she feel that she knew him?

In Nadine's small office, stuffed with the paraphernalia of girls' intramural and varsity sports, the walls papered with newspaper clippings of memorable wins and losses, Bryna looked carefully at Nick for the first time. He was wearing nothing but gym shorts. He fidgeted with Nadine's coffee maker, his back to her where she sat in the hard wooden chair in front of Nadine's desk.

Nick had a lean, long body with broad shoulders. His hair was black and curly. Bryna marveled at his slender waist. His arms and legs would have seemed skinny had it not been for their sinewy contours. His skin was dark, as if lightly tanned, and seemingly flawless. Bryna saw her own skin, sickly white; she thought of the acne that had afflicted even her back lately and felt a wave of self-revulsion.

He glanced over his shoulder. "I think you could use some coffee," he said, "if I can get this thing to work."

In profile his nose was straight and strong. Bryna had seen a picture of a Greek statue in a magazine once. His nose was like that. His eyes were deep-set and an almost metallic gray-blue.

"I think I got it now," he said. "It's heating." He turned around and folded his arms over his smooth chest. He leaned back against the shelf behind Nadine's desk and looked at Bryna, his legs spread apart. He smiled at her and she looked quickly away. She pretended to adjust her glasses.

"At least you didn't break those," he said.

She didn't know what to say.

"I'm in your homeroom. I thought what you said about Liz Lowry was really great. You better be careful, though; she can play rough."

As Nick leaned over to put the coffee on Nadine's desk in front of her, she felt the warmth of his body and could see how rich and dark the hair was high up on his legs. A slightly musky, fernlike fragrance filled her nostrils. She felt herself drift. Then suddenly she saw herself standing close to him, her hand touching him.

no stop stop stop

40

Bryna shook her head, and the vision vanished.

"Are you all right?"

Bryna reached for the coffee, her hand shaking. "Yes, I . . . I mean, I still feel weak. I'm not used to the exercise."

"I know. Nadine can be pretty tough. She's even stricter than Mr. Miles, the varsity basketball coach."

Bryna swallowed some scalding coffee. She was afraid to look at Nick.

"I'm on the team," Nick said, not boastfully, just matter of factly. "I help out over here sometimes on my study halls. I was just cleaning out the whirlpool when Nadine yelled for help."

Bryna drank the rest of the coffee. She couldn't look at Nick but knew that he was looking at her. Nadine came in.

"Okay, Borchers. You feeling okay now? I can see that Doctor Andrianos has taken good care of you. Back to the pits, Nick. I'll take it from here."

"See you later," Nick said, smiling at Bryna.

Nadine wrote something on a slip of paper and told her to take it to the main office. It was for a physical examination. Meanwhile, she was exempted from P.E.

After school, Bryna walked east along Eddy Avenue, toward the university. The fall air was crisp, and Bryna was glad of her long socks and heavy clothing. The breeze that sluiced down out of Hell Gate Canyon smelled of pine trees and high places—glaciers, perhaps, Bryna thought. The mountains to the north were already dusted with white—the first snow Bryna had ever seen.

Missoula was small, only about 50,000 people, but it seemed much larger, creeping up and down a maze of canyons, flattening out for miles along the Clark Fork River. Highways reached out of the center of town like spokes on a wheel, neon glittering along each of them. Bryna preferred the old downtown with its quaint brick buildings, two ancient train depots, cobblestone streets and bridges that seemed to be everywhere.

She liked walking by herself—away from the voices and the feelings that flooded in from outside when she was with others. It had begun soon after the woman—"Sabra" she called herself— first appeared to her that night at the religious school, the night she had first menstruated. And it had grown ever since. Sometimes the feelings confused and embarrassed her, even frightened her. Sometimes she got her own thoughts and feelings confused with those of others.

The sex feelings were particularly bothersome. There were more of them all the time. Bryna burned with shame and guilt at

41

the mere thought of what she had felt when she was with Nick—and earlier with the other boy, Tony.

When similar things had happened earlier Sabra—sometimes just a voice, sometimes an image in the mirror—had explained: "You're simply picking up *their* thoughts, *their* feelings. It's nothing to worry about." But Bryna could not imagine Nick thinking or feeling such things, certainly not about her. Sabra, she felt, was not telling her everything. She was beginning to feel angry.

As she walked along Eddy, her feet drifting effortlessly through the thick, dry leaves from the oaks and maples that lined the streets in this district, Bryna admired the old houses. With their pitched roofs, gingerbread, cupolas and turrets, many of them reminded her of the houses she had loved so much in San Francisco. Daylight was rapidly fading, and Bryna warmed herself by the glow of the old chandeliers she could see through some of the windows.

At the edge of the university Bryna turned down the street that led to the river. A small black car was parked near the curb. There was a heavy-set man in it with thinning black hair and a moustache.

why is he staring at me like that?

Bryna looked up and down the street, but it was deserted. The man seemed to be scowling at her. Bryna looked at him, her apprehension growing. She was afraid to look away. The man opened the door and started to get out. Bryna ran toward the river.

"What . . . wait a minute!" the man shouted.

At the corner Bryna looked back and saw the car beginning to pull away from the curb, coming toward her. She ran faster, up the ramp and onto the long bridge. The wind was stronger now and colder. Bryna was glad because she was sweating hard. She could scarcely believe she was able to run the entire length of the bridge but, in fact, she still had breath enough to take advantage of the green light at Broadway. She dashed to the other side and only then permitted herself to walk, looking frequently back over her shoulder.

She turned down Pine. A few blocks ahead she could see the old Federal Building and the library. People were milling about. She began to feel foolish. After all, the man hadn't really done anything. She slowed down, amazed at how far she had run and how little her limp had hindered her. She stepped into an intersection, and a small black car squealed to a halt inches from her. The man with thinning black hair stared out at her. She froze as the car door swung open. A smile formed on the man's lips, but his eyes were like stone. His pants were pulled down and his hand was in his lap. Another car approached, distracting the man. Bryna dashed into the street where the other car, the driver honking angrily, swerved to avoid hitting her. Bryna looked back and saw the black car pulling quickly away, in another direction.

After that she kept running, down Orange Street and through the underpass that delivered her to Missoula's "Northside," a maze of vacant lots, crumbling graveyards, rutted streets and ramshackle houses squeezed between warehouses, the railroad tracks and the interstate highway.

Not until she could see the Borchers' house did Bryna chance another backward glance. There was no one there. The street behind her was empty. She hurried up the old wooden steps of the house the Borchers rented, stopping to catch her breath in the sagging, enclosed porch before going in. She wondered if the man was still watching somewhere out there, if he knew now where she lived.

Bryna opened the front door cautiously, hoping to pass unseen up the steps to her tiny room. The house, despite its cracking linoleum, naked bulbs, creaky plumbing and mildew—it filled the air everywhere, crept into Bryna's clothes, broadcasting her poverty—seemed almost friendly for once. There was a child bawling somewhere in the back of the house and two others shouting at it. Even over this din Bryna could hear Walter Borchers berating his wife in the kitchen. He worked the night shift at the mill and had obviously just arisen in a foul mood.

"There musta bin half that chicken left when I looked in there this mornin'," he carped.

"Wasn't none of 'em took it while I was watchin'," she said tiredly.

"It was *her* I tell ya. Christ, she eats like a sow with a double litter."

Bryna shut the voices out and started up the stairs. Her legs suddenly felt like rubber from all the exertion. Her room was in an unfinished part of the attic, bare two-by-fours framing open spaces that led to dusty crevices under the roof. But it had a door with a latch, and it was hers alone. The five other kids, all younger, shared two rooms.

Bryna shivered in her sweat-soaked clothes. She would have liked to take a bath, but it wasn't her turn. There would be complaints about "wasting hot water." She looked at herself in the cracked mirror attached to the ancient bureau. Her face was still flushed, and her hair was matted with sweat. She wrinkled her nose at what she saw. She wished that Sabra would come. She often did materialize—just when Bryna needed her. It had been Sabra—she pronounced it "SAY-bra"—not the teachers at the rehabilitative school who had taught her to read again, who had given her the examples and created the illustrations in her mind that had made her, as one of her teachers put it, "an overnight sensation" in math; it was Sabra who told her what was going to happen—before it happened. It was Sabra who had guided her through the I.Q. test, supplying many of the answers, rescuing her from what Sabra had called a "snakepit for the mentally retarded."

Bryna experienced a pang of guilt—and fear—at having been angry with Sabra. With that I.Q. score and that smart-aleck comment she'd made in Miss Lionel's homeroom to live up to, she had reached a point of no return. If Sabra were to abandon her now . . . She remembered with real terror the long dying silence through all those years after the fire. Sabra—no matter how mysterious and sometimes frightening—was the only companion she had.

She had to be careful, she knew. The same fears that she harbored about the fire sprang up again after the incident at the religious school—the fear that she or Sabra or both of them had somehow *caused* what was foreseen to occur. It was this fear that had compelled Bryna to first shut out and then, for a while, even to deny the existence of Sabra.

When the fear arose again Sabra had raged at Bryna.

"You flatter yourself," she had scolded, "imagining that you—or I through you—could influence what you call the future. What will happen *will* happen, and there's nothing any of us can do about it. Where I come from the realization that time is an illusion is as trite as your knowledge that water is wet. All things *are* all the time."

Bryna remembered how exasperated Sabra had become at that point: "Time! What a fraud! It shackles minds, cripples them, denies access to the whole world of being, commits mankind to a narrow, linear existence, like plow horses with blinders. People do happen along who, through accident, cosmic design or providential visitation, *do* see through the blinders, but then, often as not, because time is so relentless a dictator, they decide they must be crazy or hallucinating. They believe so strongly that they *cannot* know what they think has not yet happened that they explain their heretical foresight by imagining that they are somehow *personally* fulfilling their prophecies!

"Such are the arrogant, self-serving delusions of the so-called rational mind, the cerebral cortex, that overrated piece of tissue at the top of your brain which was designed to serve the imagination but instead has enslaved it. What was supposed to be the accounting office in a vast temple of sensation, creativity and experience has instead become a charnel house from which reason exerts its deadly hegemony over the life force, the vastness, beauty and unruly vitality of which terrifies the accountants."

Bryna always came away from these harangues stunned—and more convinced than ever of Sabra's potent reality. And though she had read about the functioning of the brain, it was inconceivable to Bryna that she could herself ever think, much less *utter* such things.

Bryna pulled her clammy sweater up over her head. When she pulled it off she was startled to find Sabra staring back at her from the mirror, her lovely breasts bare.

"There's something I want to show you," Sabra said. "Take off your bra."

Bryna hesitated, self-conscious.

"Come on, I know you as well as myself."

Bryna took off the bra Mrs. Borchers had given her. It was already too small.

"Now touch yourself. Go ahead. Touch your breasts."

Bryna did as she was bidden, noting with astonishment how each of her movements was copied exactly by the other—so that, the more she watched, the more it seemed the beautiful image in the mirror *was* her. After a while it was impossible for her to tell whether she or the figure in the mirror was initiating the movements. Bryna marveled at the smoothness and beauty of the skin that now seemed to be her own, at the fullness of her breasts, especially at the slenderness of her waist and the shapely firmness of her thighs. She tossed her head and felt her long, golden hair caress her shoulders. She stared into "her" blue eyes, bluer than any she had ever seen before.

"You will be like this—exactly like this," Sabra promised. "Sooner than you think. But you must do exactly as I tell you. You will follow the diet that I give you; you will exercise according to my plan. I will tolerate no lapses. In the next few days you will buy the necessary exercise equipment, running shoes and so on. Later you will get the wig, the contacts, the proper makeup and clothing."

i have no money

"When are you going to learn to trust me? The money will be there, don't worry. Now we must go one step further. Now you will not only feel through my image but *exist* through my mind. You will have no recollection of this when you return; that is forbidden. But, in fact, in this new state you will live entirely in me, experiencing the world, that vast portion of it that is presently denied you. It is in this altered state, this other plane, that you may seek refuge whenever you wish, whenever, for example, you encounter a situation you cannot or do not want to cope with; you have only to release yourself to me. . . ."

how do i get back?

Bryna vaguely sensed the other's irritation. Sabra, Bryna had discovered, did not like questions. She had never really explained who she was, where she had come from or how it was possible for her to exist in Bryna's body. Sometimes it occurred to Bryna, Sabra might exist only in her *mind,* but no sooner would that thought occur than Bryna would reject it. There were words, thoughts, *feelings* that Bryna could not or *would* not believe were her own.

"Your subconscious governs that," Sabra said. "So long as you wish to maintain your own identity you will always return to yourself, as soon as the danger passes. Of course, if you wish you may state exactly how long I am to be in control."

Sabra paused. She seemed to be looking out of the mirror toward the unfinished, open part of the attic. "For example: see, way back there under the eaves, there's a piece of thick rope. Let's imagine that it is a snake, and that you have to kill it or it will kill you. Do you understand?"

Bryna shuddered at the thought of the snake.

yes

"Well, since I have had plenty of experience with deadly snakes I imagine this might be one of those instances where it would be useful for you to turn the body—temporarily—over to me. It's really rather easy. Of course it helps if you're motivated. Look again at the rope. You see? It's moving now. See how thick and long it is. Its coils are really quite lovely in their own way, don't you think?"

Bryna stiffened. The rope was moving, and it was no longer a rope. She could hear the serpent's dry skin slithering slowly across the dusty planks, moving toward her, into the light.

Sabra's tone was urgent. "Hurry, then, imagine that you are in the water, in a great body of water. You are thrashing about in it, struggling to keep your head above the waves which grow more turbulent with each passing second. You are struggling but you can't stay above the waves. You're swallowing water, choking on it. You can't stay up any longer. You are being drawn under. . . ."

Bryna saw the tongue of the snake dart out at her through the waves that seemed to be engulfing her. She let herself sink away from it, holding her breath until her lungs felt like they would burst. Bryna looked up from beneath the water as she sank deeper and deeper. She could see Sabra just above the surface, her face staring down at her, twisted out of focus.

"Stop fighting! Let go! Trust me! I'll breathe for you!"

Bryna opened her mouth. Immediately she felt air filling her lungs, and then it seemed as if she were free-floating through a cool, blue-green, objectless space.

She sat up on the rug in the middle of Bryna's room and looked at her toes. *Mine,* she exulted. She wiggled them, then got to her feet. It felt *so good.* It had been so long. This was the only world *she* wanted to experience.

fuck the cosmos

She looked at herself in Bryna's mirror and laughed out loud. She wondered if any of the others could see her. Were they laughing? No doubt, she thought, but only on the outside.

Of course, there were the rules; you could never get away from those. She looked askance at the rope under the eaves. Well, she'd get to that soon enough. She peered closer into the mirror, then yanked one of the bureau drawers open and looked at Bryna's things.

junk junk junk

She grabbed two red barrettes Mrs. Borchers had given to Bryna to keep the hair out of her eyes (of course, she had never used them) and deftly pinned up the back and sides of her hair.

my god those cheeks no wonder she hides them

Still, she thought the neck not bad, and the bones, she could tell the bones were all in the right places. Once the fat started to recede . . . She looked up abruptly, recalling that Bryna had found a tube of lipstick on the street several days before and had stuck it under the mattress; not that she'd ever had the nerve to use it. She quickly retrieved it from its hiding place and, back at the mirror, spread her lips for the application.

ghastly shade

She put it on thick, accentuating the pout, amusing herself. Then she rapidly applied a dollop to each cheek, looked at it for a moment and then gleefully rubbed it in. She still needed . . . yes, she looked around, trying to remember where she'd seen it. There, where an old chimney passed through the attic floor and on up through the roof. Some of the bricks were loose, and soot oozed from it. She went over and dabbed two of her fingers in it.

47

Then, at the mirror, she applied it to the corners and lids of her eyes. The saucy change this effected delighted her.

Tart, she thought. *Strumpet, trollop, chippie, whore.*

Music filled her ears, and she began to shake with the sensual rhythm of it, watching herself in the mirror, feeling her tits vibrate.

She began to snap her fingers and move her hips. She shut her eyes and mouthed the words that were going through her mind, twisting and grimacing with pleasure.

She wanted to shout, to feel the vibration in her throat. But she stopped herself, remembering the others, downstairs. The exertion of the dance had started her perspiring, and she could smell herself. Pleasant as that was under the circumstances, something far more pleasurable popped into her mind.

a bath! oh god yes, water!

She unlatched the door, opened it a crack and listened. The TV was blaring. As usual at this late afternoon hour they were all watching a *Gunsmoke* rerun, hollering at each other periodically to shut up. With a minimum of concentration she could tell that the way to the bathroom was clear. The only one likely to have to use it, she sensed, was Walter Borchers himself, and she guessed he'd wait until the program was over and he had downed a couple more beers.

She hurried to the tiny closet and, surveying Bryna's three drab dresses with disgust, took the plaid rummage-sale bathrobe from its hook and put it on.

The bathroom was off a dark corridor, next to a bedroom, near the back of the house on the main floor. Getting there unseen was easy enough. She looked into the bathroom, her excitement growing, then took a couple more steps and poked her head into the bedroom. On a stand by the bed was a paperback book. She snatched it, giggling at its cover art—a fair-haired, big-breasted woman pressed up against a lone tree atop a hill, a dark-haired man on his knees before her, his anguished face half buried in the elaborate folds of her low-cut gown. As she started out of the room with it, she sensed something else, smelled it. In the closet on a hook were Mr. Borcher's overhauls, the ones he wore to work each night. She reached into the bib pocket and plucked out a pack of Camels and some matches.

In the bathroom she started the water, taking the precaution of opening the tap only a third of the way. She put a large sponge under the stream of water to further muffle the noise. In the mirror over the sink she smiled again at her impromptu makeup job and then opened the medicine cabinet, standing on tiptoe to reach up to the top shelf, where she knew Mrs. Borchers had deposited a small envelope.

bubblebath!

Even its sleazy scent pleased her as she spilled its contents into the hot water and watched it foam up toward her. She let her bathrobe fall to the floor and then expertly knocked a cigarette out of its pack and lit up. She inhaled deeply and immediately started coughing, covering her face with a towel to hide the sound.

it's been a long time

She pulled on the cigarette more gently. When the bubbles threatened to spill over the edge of the tub she stepped in. "Oh God," she whispered, shutting her eyes for a moment as she sank down into the soap and water. She leaned back in the tub, luxuriating in it for several minutes, blowing smoke into the bubbles that popped all around her chin. At length she let out a long, satisfied sigh. Then she sat up a bit, lit another cigarette, which she held continuously between her lips, and damply opened the paperback novel.

She had been reading for about ten minutes; she was just beginning to think that she was pressing her luck when suddenly it ran out. Someone was coming.

shit

She knew that it was Walter Borchers. There was nothing she could do. The lock on the door didn't work. She couldn't help giggling, anticipating the look on his face. She decided to deadpan it. Just as the door opened, she turned a page, pretending to be totally absorbed in the book. She let some smoke slither out the corner of her mouth. Her "eyeliner," she was sure, had begun to run in the humidity above the tub.

Walter Borchers' hand quickly let go of the belt buckle he had already begun to loosen. His jaw slackened. He stood there dumbly, the girl's seeming unawareness of him as unnerving as her appearance. She glanced at him just briefly, as if these were the most routine circumstances in which to be thus encountered. She howled inwardly but managed to keep a straight face as she resumed reading. He was a lean, raw-boned man who always seemed to need a shave. His characteristic smirk and swagger were momentarily displaced by this surprise. She could begin to feel his cheeks heating up and sensed his confusion, a mixture of incredulity, embarrassment and anger that finally resolved itself in opportunistic lust.

"Well, well, wellll," he said softly, shutting the door behind him. "Look what *we* have here. Look at 'er puttin' on airs, painted

49

up like a common hoor. Little Miss Prim and Proper's true colors are comin' out now, are they? What happen, they slip you some of that *dope* at school?" He looked at her cigarette suspiciously, then at the pack of Camels on the chair next to the tub. He reached over and grabbed them.

"Thievin' little bitch," he said. She continued to read. He grabbed a handful of her hair and twisted her head around so that she had to look at him.

"Pretendin' I ain't here? Yeah, well, we'll see about that." He grabbed the cigarette out of her mouth and tossed it into the water. Most of the bubbles had evaporated by now and he could see her body clearly enough. She felt the stir between his legs.

rutting pig

She decided an apprehensive look was in order.

It served its purpose. He released her hair, leering down at her. "I ain't gonna tell," he said. "We'll work somethin' out. Meanwhile, I come in here for a purpose." He grinned, turned his back to her, unbuckled his belt and stood in front of the stool.

As he relieved himself she suddenly saw his double slumped over the foot of the tub, one hand dangling under the water, touching her leg, the other thrown back at an awkward angle. His mouth was hanging open, his eyes set in a dead stare. Blood dripped from his nose and mouth into the water. His tongue was clenched between his teeth, and a wisp of blue, evil-smelling smoke rose from the top of his head. His face was turning purple. She took all this in with calm interest.

When he was done, Walter Borchers hiked up his pants and turned to the girl. "Yer little secret's safe with me—fer the time being."

She decided just the hint of a smile was in order. She could feel his excitement grow.

"You've got five minutes to git yer ass out of here," he said. "I'll keep 'em away that long." He paused at the door and looked back one more time.

The moment he left she slid down in the tub and pushed her foot contemptuously up into the face of his transfixed double. The phantom figure fell away from the tub, hitting the floor with a final thud only she could hear.

Seconds later, as she dried herself, taking care not to touch the figure sprawled across the floor, she realized she would have to put on some of Bryna's clothes and make a quick trip to the pay phone at the corner.

Bryna sat up on the rug, aware first of an unfamiliar scent and second of her nakedness. A moment later she saw the thick length of rope tied into a knot only feet from her. It looked harmless enough now. She remembered what it had looked like before and what Sabra had asked her to do. She remembered the water, the feeling that she was drowning, Sabra shouting at her, breathing for her—and then nothing at all.

She climbed to her feet, feeling a little dizzy. In the mirror her own image accosted her. She pulled back her hair to see if she had changed in any way, but there was nothing, except that her hair, especially in the back, was damp and her lips and cheeks burned, as if she had rubbed them very hard. Then she noticed her school notebook was open on the dresser, and on the page facing her were the words:

"Gave you a bath; you needed it. Love, S."

And below that:

"P.S.: Watch out for Walter; I think he has the hots for you."

Bryna felt confused and agitated. As usual in such circumstances her thoughts turned to food. Her mouth began to water as she moved toward the bed. She needed a better hiding place, she knew.

please god let it still be there

She had had to conceal it in a hurry, just before going to school. She had meant only to take a slice of it, but then she had sensed someone getting up and had grabbed the whole thing and hidden it in a paper bag under her bed. She squatted down with difficulty and sighed relief at the sight of the bag, partially soaked through now with grease.

She licked her lips, and her heart beat faster. She thrust her hand into the bag and lifted out the plump chicken. She gasped not with pleasure but with horror. It didn't seem possible. It had been fine that morning. Now it was alive with white, pus-colored worms. She stared at the chicken stupidly for a moment and then hurled it with all her strength into the dark, unfinished part of the attic, a shudder going through her as she envisioned the cat finding it there and licking it clean.

Two of the worms stuck to her hand. She leapt to her feet, brushed at them frantically and when they fell to the floor stomped on them, shaking uncontrollably, her face white, her lips quivering.

Sometime in the night Bryna stirred, half awake, and discovered the word "hegemony" slithering slowly through her mind, and though it moved like a fanged serpent it seemed lovely all the same.

FOUR

"You're worse than a baby. You have nothing to feel guilty about. It's like I told you; the money is for drugs. *Bad* drugs. You'll be doing some dippy kids a favor taking it."

but what if somebody sees me?

"Nobody's going to see you unless you stand around here all day with your finger up your ass. Now *move*. Do what I told you."

Bryna went over and sat down on the edge of the brick planter that wrapped around the corner of what proclaimed itself, in large gold letters, to be The Law Building.

"That's right," Sabra said. "Now slide a little to the left. Good. Now wait a minute until this nice young man goes by. He's going to be a lawyer someday; an asshole profession in my view, but to each his own. He's a friendly sort, you see; he smiling at you—beautiful smile—wondering what a young thing like you, a veritable squinting little gnome in a revolting polka dot dress

why do all the fat dresses come in polka dot?

and please don't interrupt me is doing way over here on campus at 7:45 a.m. All right. Now reach back behind you into the shrubbery, under the leaves; just a little to the right. There you've got it. Nobody's looking. Just put it into the bag with your lunch."

Bryna could see the money through the clear plastic bag bound with rubber bands. She put it into the brown bag and hurried away. After school that day she bought all the things Sabra had listed.

Bryna's hunger gnawed at her day and night. There was scarcely a moment's respite. It was especially hard in the beginning. Killingly hard. Bryna would see someone sipping a milkshake in a passing car, just a fleeting glance, and her mouth would flood with saliva, her stomach contract, her head ache. Sabra's list of "allowables" was cruelly circumspect: carrots and a few other vegetables, plain yogurt, hot cereal, an occasional egg, very little meat, bread without butter, one glass of milk a day, no dessert, only the smallest portions of Mrs. Borcher's endless casseroles.

Bryna often took some of the money left over from the plastic envelope to school with her, for the express purpose of making forbidden food purchases. Just having the money with her, in case she absolutely could not resist, made her feel more secure. The desire was always there, but it was seldom consummated. Bryna would be on the verge of entering a restaurant or store when abruptly she would notice someone inside pointing at her, laughing at her, or so she was convinced.

One day, after wolfing down her spartan bag lunch in an empty classroom, the hunger these trifles excited in her was so intense she resolved to get some "real food" at any cost. There was a delicatessen several blocks from school frequented mostly by downtown business people. Bryna had often passed it going to and from school; more than once she had tortured herself standing outside watching lovely pieces of red meat turning slowly, cooking over an electric flame in the window of the establishment. On this occasion she did not pause to worship at this altar but burst boldly through the doors of the temple, lest, in a moment of reflection, her nerve fail her or she glimpse something untoward.

Inside, the sights, smells and even the sounds made her senses lurch and ache. Her nose burned and itched, overburdened by this hazard of olfactory fortunes. Her stomach sang psalms. Her hands opened and closed. Her eyes alternately glazed over and zoomed in on things with enormous clarity. She sweated. The display cases bulged with REAL FOOD. Pastrami. Huge roasts of beef. Barbecued chickens. Whole turkeys. Crabs in chips of ice. Heaps of creamy mashed potatoes. Rich gravies. Sausages, sourdough bread, cheesecake, custard, lox, paté, pickled pigs' feet, herring and chives in cream sauce, buckets of butter, smoked eel and fish, clams on the half shell, calamary, Black Forest cake, apple pie, borscht, enormous sandwiches, a cauldron of creamed corn . . .

oh god

Bryna felt dizzy. She fumbled for some money and moved closer to the long display case, squeezing between the adults. There didn't seem to be any sort of line; some clamored and shouted, others just pointed. You were at the mercy of the white-hatted men behind the case. Bryna put her hands up against the glass, swallowing hard. She would have put her nose up against it, too, had she dared. She held a $10 bill.

Then it began to happen. It started with the creamed corn.

The soupy mixture began to churn and bubble. Then it stopped, and just as Bryna thought she had imagined the sudden movement a long insectile appurtenance popped up from beneath the surface followed by a large, brown, armored head, from which two bulging eyes protruded from stalks. Next the crabs and lobsters all started moving, advancing slowly toward the glass.

no please please it's not fair

Bryna watched, her nails digging into the palms of her hands, as the men in white hats passed mouldy bread, shells full of green, pulsating slime, little paper buckets full of deadly pale eels that squirmed and slithered and pigs' feet that suddenly sprouted coarse black hair and soft, warty protuberances across the counter. She could feel the cold sweat gathering on her chin and brow as one of the men turned to peer down at her, his mouth stretching into a broad grin.

"And for you, duchess?"

A green speck between the man's teeth began to wriggle.

goddamn you it's all a lie a lie a lie you can't stop me this time

"One of those." Bryna pointed quickly at one of the gargantuan sandwiches.

"Excellent choice," the man beamed.

Bryna saw the man reaching for the sandwich but dared not watch any more. She focused on a spot above the food which she could, nonetheless, feel writhing and vibrating all around her. It made her itch and shiver at the same time.

The man wrapped the sandwich in a bag and said, "You pay down there."

As Bryna walked toward the checkout turnstile the package in her hand began to move, gently at first, then more violently, squirming between her fingers. She clenched her teeth and held the package tighter. Outside, in the bright light of early afternoon her confidence—and her hunger—came rushing back.

you're not going to trick me anymore

Bryna could not wait. She spotted a narrow alley off the main street and hurried down it toward a dark cul-de-sac cluttered with garbage cans. She wanted no one to see her. She wanted only to stuff the sandwich down her throat as quickly as possible. The contents of the bag had begun to move again. It stretched a bit, then narrowed and thickened like a piece of living, muscular flesh. Bryna began to shake, clammy with sweat in the chill fall air. A ripple of nausea snaked through her.

not this time goddamn it not this time

She swallowed hard, her lips twitching. She paused one more moment and then thrust her hand into the bag and pulled its contents free. Before she focused on it she felt it, its cold leathery texture, its sickening "give." Then she saw it, a huge, puffy lizard, its neck engorged, its red-brown eyes menacing.

Bryna swallowed again, her whole body shaking, her face frozen in a determined grimace. She held the squirming thing tightly in both hands. She screamed inwardly.

not real not real not real

Bryna opened her mouth wide, preparing to bite. The reptile opened its mouth at the same time, revealing sharp fangs. A bloody red and then a putrid yellow substance spilled from its mouth. Bryna tightened her grip, and it hissed at her, its forked tongue darting out. She shut her eyes hard, threw her head forward and bit down with tremendous force. A sharp stabbing pain pierced both her tongue and the roof of her mouth. Bryna gasped, pushed the thing away from her face and spit blood. As she ran from the alley she did not look back to see the scattered remains of the sandwich and the large pointed toothpick that had held it together, tipped now in blood.

It wouldn't have mattered if she had. Her appetite was spoiled for days after that—not so much because of the superficial wound as from the recollection of the reptile. Indeed, the memory of its texture against her lips and of her teeth sinking into it could induce nausea at a moment's notice.

Bryna also learned quickly enough the perils of an undisciplined attitude toward the exercise program Sabra prescribed. Each morning she was required to arise at five-thirty and begin her stretching and breathing exercises. At first Sabra told her each move to make, chastising her when she cheated or didn't quite stretch, kick, bend or reach far enough. Days passed sometimes when the only evidence of Sabra's presence were these occasional admonishments. As fall advanced into winter Bryna had to work harder to keep warm while exercising in the poorly insulated and stingily heated house, particularly since Sabra insisted these warmups be done "unencumbered"—in the nude.

Promptly at six, Bryna would retrieve her running things from their hiding place in the attic, dress and prepare to steal out of the house. On particularly cold mornings she wore a ski mask and mittens. During the first few weeks, while the weather was still relatively warm, Bryna was instructed to alternate walking and running. The sessions in the beginning were short but still agonizing. Bryna found it difficult to believe she had run as far as she had the day the man in the black car had pursued her. Now each step required maximum willpower. Her calves and thighs ached unrelentingly, but this was nothing compared to the pain in her lungs, particularly after she had run nine or ten minutes. No sooner would she begin to feel comfortable running a given distance than Sabra would demand more, always more.

Bryna dared not think about the dark. If it had not been for Sabra's voice, usually reassuring and businesslike on these occasions, she would not have braved the early morning black at all. But Sabra was there, like a light:

"Turn right here. Watch out for that hole. Ignore the dog; he's chained."

Later, when the snow came, Bryna learned quickly enough how to manage on ice and hardpack. When the snow was deep Sabra would guide her to the streets that the early morning snowplow crew had tended first. She learned also to be unmindful of the slush; her nylon shoes and socks would dry again by the next morning.

The trouble was mostly in the beginning. Sometimes Bryna could not stand the thought of getting up in the dark and cold. Then Sabra's melodious voice would become a strident screech and sometimes a painful roar that would not relent until Bryna leapt to her feet, rubbing her ears, gasping for breath.

One morning Bryna simply couldn't find the energy to keep running. The monotony and the pain of it were so overpowering she simply dug in her heels and started walking. Sabra swore at her over and over again, but Bryna pretended not to hear.

"Okay. Suit yourself," Sabra said at last.

At first Bryna felt victorious. Then the silence began to unnerve her. Still, she was not ready to resume running. The novelty of having her own way and of resting her lungs was, momentarily at least, too rewarding. She charted her own course. As she approached a circle of light projected by an ominously buzzing street light, Bryna thought she sensed some movement in the shadows just beyond the light. She slowed and then stopped. She was sure there was something ahead—something bad.

little slut

Bryna felt a current of terror wiggle up her spine.

i've been watching you; i'll stick it in you this time

The man stepped into the light, a few yards from her. It was the same man who had chased her before. The man in the car. His face seemed more haggard this time. His mouth hung slightly open, and he was beginning to grin. Bryna felt her scalp contract, as if it were snapping to attention, and she turned and ran. It wasn't until she was sure she could go no further that she stopped, clutching her ribs. She turned and looked back. No one. Bryna was too relieved to wonder if she had only imagined the man.

As the weeks passed Bryna began to discover in the mirror all the reinforcement she needed to continue the diet and exercise program. The results, at first miniscule and grudging, were soon accruing rapidly and dramatically. Bryna weighed herself once a week, always wearing exactly the same clothes, on the scales at Woolworth's on Higgins Avenue. By Christmas she had lost 25 pounds and grown a full inch. She was beginning, for the first time, to like what she saw of herself in the mirror. She discovered curves and angles she never thought possible—and the promise of more to come. Her breasts had finally assumed shapes independent of the receding bulk of her torso. Her skin, both on her face and back, had largely cleared up. Her color had improved, and she felt more energetic than she ever had before.

Still, she took care, more care than ever in fact, to hide herself behind the thick glasses and the hair that obscured either side of her face. When it seemed that her dresses were beginning to hang noticeably limp she began wearing extra clothing under them, a sweater on top, some insulated underwear on the bottom. The length of her dresses and her long socks concealed the padding.

She padded herself out of fear—fear that if the other kids knew what she was doing she would attract more attention to herself, fear that she might still fail and then seem even more ridiculous, fear of the vulnerability that would come of letting others know that she cared how she looked. And there was one thing more, an idea that had assumed only the vaguest conscious shape, the idea that someday she would emerge, as if by magic, in one stroke, slim and beautiful.

they'll be sorry

But it was an idea too sweet—and impossible, yet—even to acknowledge.

After the incident in gym Bryna was permanently exempted from P.E. Thus she could hide her body. Not so her mind. After a while she no longer tried. Sabra insisted that she excel in all of her classes; it was essential, she declared, "if we're ever going to get out of this godforsaken place." Bryna loved the mountains, but Sabra spoke scathingly of the hinterlands and longingly of California—their target destination. Sabra told Bryna she must win a scholarship and attend college in Los Angeles. After word of her I.Q. leaked out, there was no going back. The attention frightened Bryna at first. Gradually, however, knowing Sabra was there to back her up, Bryna began to take pleasure in having others, particularly those who disliked her, envy her something.

Bryna read—everything. She could as easily assimilate Socrates or Solzhenitsyn as Jackie Susanne. She could read Bertrand Russell and Harold Robbins in the same day or even the same hour without any sign of literary dyspepsia. She loved the library job Miss Lionel gave her—sorting and stacking books, filling out overdue forms and so on. Bryna looked up and read everything she could find on psychic phenomena and "spirit possession." She was fascinated by Jane Roberts' *Seth Speaks* and wondered if Seth and other such spirit guides ever thought and talked in private, the way Sabra did. In any event, it was vastly reassuring to her to read about others who, without being regarded as raving mad, harbored apparently benign entities who claimed to come from other, albeit generally vague places, times, dimensions. Beginning with the fairy tales and fantasies of her childhood, including those Bryan had created specifically for her, Bryna had been aware of and even receptive to the idea of such entities. But the books of Jane Roberts, Carlos Castaneda and others were presented as *fact*, and that made them all the more compelling.

Sometimes in her most private thoughts Bryna wished Sabra could be more—she recognized it was an odd word to use in this context, but it conveyed her longing—more *conventional*. Sabra's conversations with her were liberally sprinkled with words like "douchebag" (Sabra's favorite appellation for a testy civics teacher Bryna nonetheless managed to charm with her apparent humility and soaring—Sabra-inspired—prose on essay tests). Sabra had nothing but contempt for authority and decorum, however, and Bryna dared not voice her objections. Nor had she yet found the courage to have it out with Sabra over the "sex things." She had gradually come to the conclusion that Sabra was at least partially responsible for the sexual hallucinations, that they were expressions of Sabra's desires. This conclusion both frightened and reassured Bryna—frightened her because Sabra shared her body, reassured her because it meant she, at least, was not herself responsible for these feelings and visions.

The problem was particularly acute where Nick was concerned. Bryna felt herself drawn to Nick, which in itself was unusual, for she scarcely felt drawn to anyone. Even more remarkable, Nick seemed drawn to her. She had no doubt, however, that he was interested in her—and she in him—only as a friend. It was

Sabra, she was sure, who envisioned something more intense. Whenever she was with Nick, Bryna could feel Sabra's presence, though she was always silent during these encounters. Bryna could tell she was there by the glow in her breasts and by the pleasurable but disturbing—disturbing *because* pleasurable—sensations further down. Sometimes images formed that Bryna had to fight desperately to extinguish.

Mostly she and Nick talked about books and philosophy. Nick would often come into the school library after basketball practice expressly to talk with Bryna. The other girls, for whom the quiet, studious athlete with the gentle manner and handsome face had long been an unattainable goal, watched with amazed consternation. Bryna often felt she had known Nick for years—and that she would know him for the rest of her life.

During Christmas holiday, Nick surprised Bryna by showing up at the Borchers. It was a bright, clear, very cold day. There was already a foot of snow on the ground. Bryna was in her room reading the last of the books Miss Lionel had loaned her from her personal library, a novel by Ford Madox Ford called *The Good Soldier*, a wonderfully unusual book unlike any other Bryna had read, for in this one, she discovered, it was impossible to believe or trust the narrator, difficult to distinguish between appearance and reality; it was a novel, as the introduction noted, "like a hall of mirrors, so constructed that, while one is always looking straight ahead at a perfectly solid surface, one is made to contemplate not the bright surface itself, but the bewildering maze of past circumstances and future consequences that—somewhat falsely—it contains."

Bryna jumped. Someone—Walter Borchers—had hoarsely shouted her name from the bottom of the stairs. He had been home for several days with the flu. Bryna had prayed that he would get better soon because in another two days Mrs. Borchers and the other children were going to "grandma's" for several days, including Christmas, leaving Bryna behind to "tend Walt" if he was not well enough to accompany them. Bryna did not savor the idea of going to grandma's with the rest of them, but she savored less the prospect of several days—and nights—alone with her foster father. For some time now, she was convinced, he had been looking at her with more than paternal interest. A foreboding was growing in her, even though Sabra, when asked, would say only that she was in no danger. Bryna felt, distinctly, that Sabra was holding something back.

watch out for walter

"You got somebody here to see ya!"

Bryna felt her heart race. No one had ever called on her. She didn't want to see anyone—least of all here.

nick

Bryna was certain. She could feel his presence, even "see" him, waiting out on the cold front porch just beyond the partially opened door. And she could feel Walter Borchers' eyes sweeping suspiciously over the boy, reaching his inevitable conclusion.

little slut is puttin' out

Bryna shouted back. "I'm coming." She put on her heavy coat, grabbed a pile of books in mittened hands and hurried toward the stairs. Her only thought was to get Nick away as quickly as possible. At the bottom of the stairs she could see Walter in his rumpled plaid bathrobe, cigarette in hand. He was waiting by the front door.

"You got yerself a Mr. *Nick* here to see ya," he said, as Bryna went down the stairs. He opened his eyes wider, too show his surprise, and exhaled some smoke.

Suddenly his eyes froze in place, dead; his face purpled, as if he'd been strangled, and blood trickled from his nose. Bryna stumbled on the steps but caught herself. When she looked up again the man's face was normal.

"Don't fall all over yerself; he ain't gonna run away." Bryna saw him turn to Nick, still invisible beyond the door, laughing at his little joke. Then he stepped back, pressing up against the wall, still holding the door open with one hand, acting as if Bryna were leading a stampede.

Bryna slipped by him. "I . . . I have to return these books to Miss Lionel," she blurted to no one in particular and started out through the porch.

Nick, nodding uncomfortably at Walter, went after her.

Bryna felt as if she were acting stupidly, but what else could she do? She hurried down the icy steps to the walk.

Nick caught up with her. "I'm sorry if I came at a bad time."

She said nothing. It was so cold her nostrils pinched together when she inhaled.

"That was a little weird back there."

"It's *always* a little weird back there," she said, glancing up at Nick.

He smiled at her, making himself even more handsome.

It was impossible, even for Bryna, not to smile back.

"Hey," he said, "you're going to freeze your ears." He pulled his stocking cap off his head and pushed it down onto Bryna's.

"Either you're getting taller or I'm getting shorter," he added.

"It's just these clunky overshoes," Bryna lied.

They walked in silence for a while, and then Nick said: "I knew which street you lived on; that was all you'd ever tell me. I asked down at the store, and they told me which house."

Bryna lifted her books up higher. Nick reached over and took some of them.

"Wow, there's some heavy stuff here, ten pounds at least," Nick joked.

"Miss Lionel . . ."

"You like her, don't you?"

Bryna nodded.

"Who else do you like?"

Bryna felt herself blushing; she hoped the blood the cold had already summoned to her cheeks would conceal it. She hated reacting this way—shy, bumbling, inept. She silently cursed herself. What could Nick possibly see in her? She knew he was waiting for an answer.

"I don't think much about it," she said feebly. Bryna braced herself for his next question.

"Well, I was wondering whether you liked *me*? Sometimes it's hard to tell whether you want to talk or not. Like right now."

Bryna forced herself to look at him for a moment. Her thoughts were churning. How could *anyone*, let alone someone like Nick, like someone as repulsive as herself, she wondered.

"Do you want to go to Miss Lionel's? I have to return these books to her." Well, it was some sort of answer.

Nick smiled, and they walked in silence for some time, each trying to think of something to say.

"Shit."

Bryna startled even herself. The word, however unpromising, brightened things a bit. Nick, who Bryna felt had begun to dispair, was looking at her with alert interest.

"I forgot," Bryna blurted. "Miss Lionel isn't home today." In her panic to get Nick away from the house, the fact that the teacher had left town for several days had slipped her mind. They had already walked through the business district and over the bridge and were approaching the university area where Miss Lionel lived. The temperature was several degrees below zero. Bryna was freezing and had been counting on the imminent warmth of Miss Lionel's house. It was Sunday afternoon, and all the downtown stores were closed. There was nothing to do but head back to the Borchers—alone. It was a long way to go without first warming up somewhere. Nick seemed to be thinking the same thing. There was a look of uncertainty in his eyes. He had some idea but he hesitated. Then:

"We can go to my place. It's only about six blocks off that way."

Bryna sensed the conflict in him. She looked at him, and it came to her.

his mother

"It's all right," she said. "I can make it back."

"C'mon." He grabbed her hand and pulled her, then let go when she followed.

While they walked, Nick said, "To tell the truth, I'm about as eager to have you meet my mother as you were to have me meet your foster father. She's . . ."

Bryna could feel the pain. "Really," she said, "I'll survive."

"You'll freeze, you mean. C'mon. She's bad sometimes, but . . . it's just that since my father died, she . . . well, even before to some extent. My sister got married and she . . . I'm all she's got now, at home, and . . ."

Bryna felt miserable. She cleared her throat but couldn't say anything.

"I guess it's just not enough. Anyway, she'll probably be sleeping."

The house was a single-story affair, not imposing but freshly painted and well-maintained. Bryna could see Nick busying himself about the place, keeping everything in good repair, hoping that if he nailed down one more loose shingle or added one more coat of paint it finally *would* be enough.

"Niko?"

niko?

The voice came from the back of the house as they entered. The sudden warmth made Bryna dizzy.

"Niko!"

"My mother, I'll be right back."

"Who are you talking to out there?"

The voice was faint, but Bryna could hear the fear in it. She tried not to listen, but she could hear them. And she could already "see" the woman propped up in bed, could see her as she had been all that afternoon, propped up against several fat pillows, book open, unread, in her lap, drifting, laughing, whispering sometimes, crying a little, sliding, warm, dreaming. Bryna could feel the narcotic.

bzzzzzzzzzzz

She could float on the lazy, lifting lies. Her mind clouded, as it used to after she had eaten too many pastries.

"Of course, of course, I have to get up. I *have* to. If you have a guest I *have* to be sociable. But you *never* have guests, Niko. I . . ."

"Really, mom, you don't have to get up. We just came in to warm up a little."

"I . . . where are my . . . ? Oh, Niko, you should give me some warning when you . . ."

"C'mon, Kate. It's nothing to get excited about; Bryna and I just . . ."

"*Bryna*? You mean you brought a *girl* home? Oh, my hair, I . . . Niko, I look *awful*! How could you . . . ?"

Bryna could feel the flutter, the anger, especially the fear. She tried to concentrate on the pictures over the mantle. She stepped nearer to see them better. One picture in particular attracted her. A handsome, confident man with Nick's nose and hair but heavier set. He stood with his arm around a slender, almost frail woman. The woman was very beautiful, younger than the man. Though she was smiling she seemed

even then

frightened, overwhelmed in the presence of so much vitality.

Bryna turned, for the wounded fluttering was all around her now. The woman, much older now, was standing there at the other end of the room, her eyes darting wildly about, searching. She was wearing a quilted housecoat weighted at the hem and cuffs with fur. The garment somehow hung crookedly on her. Her hair, faded auburn, stuck out on one side where she had tried to fluff it up. There was powder on her face. Her eyes, dark and hollow, met Bryna's.

"Oh! You were so still I didn't see you." The woman's hands began to move erratically. Bryna knew—knew without even thinking it—that the woman would be relieved once she realized how ugly she was. For now, however, she realized only that her son had brought a girl home.

"This is Bryna," Nick was saying. "I mentioned her before. Central's resident genius."

"*Genius*?" Mrs. Andrianos looked quite forlorn.

"The smartest kid in class," Nick explained, smiling at Bryna. Nick put his arm around his mother. "Bryna, this is Kate."

Bryna nodded, not knowing what to say.

Suddenly the woman was all flutters again, shaking Nick's arm from her shoulders. "So!" she said, as if she had just comprehended something. "Well! This is a surprise! Well, we're honored, indeed! The *smartest* kid . . . oh, forgive me! Niko, that's your fault; you shouldn't call *anybody* kid. The smartest *girl* in the class! My!

Well. Niko! Really! Be a gentleman! Get Bertha something! I'd offer you a scotch or, well, this is the Christmas season, isn't it, perhaps a *grog*. I always thought that was such a funny word, *grog*! Niko's father *loved* his *grog*, especially this time of year, do you remember, Niko, remember your father . . . ?"

The woman's face fell for a moment, then she looked at Bryna again, smiling. "*Do* sit down, Miss . . . ?"

"Carr," Bryna said. She was beginning to sweat. It had all come to her in a flash, what she had "seen" the day she fainted in the gym—a dream suddenly illuminated. The man who had reached out for her was Nick—Niko? But what did it mean? She could not begin to think with this woman's emotions flooding her mind.

"Miss *Carr*! Well, yes, but surely we needn't stand on formality, need we? *Do* sit down. As I say, I'd offer you a scotch or even a *grog*, though heaven knows I think I've lost the recipe by now; Niko do you have any idea . . . ?"

Nick looked unhappily at Bryna, whose mouth was beginning to tremble. "I'll get you some hot cider."

"Oh, that's the spirit! That's the spirit!" his mother said. Nick went to the kitchen, and the woman hurried over to a cabinet and poured herself a drink. "No ice, of course, but, well, you should never *bruise* good scotch with ice, my father always used to say. I never really understood that, but well, somehow I do. I do! So!" She sat down on the sofa alongside Bryna, quite near.

Bryna shifted uncomfortably, hoping Nick would hurry. Bryna could see into the woman's eyes now, could see how shiny they were.

"The *smartest* girl in class!" The woman threw her head back, watching Bryna, and downed half a tumbler of scotch, her free hand darting out to touch the girl, then quickly drawing back.

"Niko's just like his father," she said, her hands trembling now. "He admires brains. *Brains*! That's what it takes to get a head. A *head*! You get it, I'm sure, being the smartest . . . Niko's father used to say that, his little joke, he really did. Brains this, brains that. I'm afraid I never quite measured up. I never finished high school; my mother was very ill and . . . well, that doesn't interest you. A dropout you call them now. I was . . . but, it's *you* we want to talk about, isn't it? You *young* people! You've got it all before you! I suppose you'll be going to some university far away. Niko wants to go to the university. Already they're offering him athletic scholarships, you know, some of them *far* away. I suppose both of you . . ."

The woman stopped. Bryna could feel the woman's fear mixing with her own.

"I was never really smart enough for Niko's father. I used to embarrass him. I suppose that's why he... I suppose both of you will be going off, that you want him to go with you...."

The woman emptied her glass.

"Niko's father, you know, they said he was dead, but we don't know. *We don't know!* He just... he was just *gone!* And most of the money was gone, too. Maybe he just got tired of us."

Bryna felt the woman's hand gripping hers, nails beginning to dig in painfully. Bryna stared into the woman's eyes, afraid now to look away.

"Tired of *me!* He always said I was stupid. I don't want Niko to... I don't want to lose him, too. You've got to... you can't take him, too!"

The woman's eyes began to dissolve as Bryna looked into them. Gaping holes replaced them. The flesh of the woman's face peeled away, layer by layer, until only the skull remained. The teeth moved, but Bryna could not hear anything. The hand was still digging into hers, but when she looked it, too, was nothing but bone. Bryna tried to pull her hand away but could not.

help me help me

The teeth were opening and closing rapidly now, clattering like a trick set of false teeth. The woman moved closer to her, a skeleton in a housecoat and faded red wig, at least it seemed to be a wig because it abruptly slid off the smooth skull and fell at Bryna's feet. The teeth seemed to be snapping at her now.

get me home get me home

The teeth suddenly seemed longer and sharper than they had moments earlier.

now

Bryna felt herself losing consciousness, gasping for breath.

"You must *not* take Niko away!" The woman shouted into the girl's face, shaking her.

The girl calmly pulled herself free and slapped the woman sharply across the face.

The woman instantly fell silent, staring at the girl. She blinked. Then she seemed for the first time to really see the girl.

"I... I'm so sorry, I..." She began crying. "I'm so ashamed. I get carried away... I..."

"Just be quiet now," the girl said flatly. "Don't talk. You'll be better in a few minutes." Holding the woman in her arms, she could see Nick standing in the living room entrance with a mug of steaming cider. She knew he had seen her slap his mother.

"You'd better get her some coffee," she said. Nick looked at her for another astonished moment, then turned and went back into the kitchen.

A few minutes later the girl watched while the woman drank the coffee, insisting that she drink all of it. Then she asked Nick to help her get his mother back to her bed. There, holding the woman's hand, the girl said:

"No one's going to take Nick . . . Niko away from you. He'll be with you for the rest of your life."

The woman squeezed her hand, tears running down her face.

"I believe you, I believe you."

Nick sat down on the edge of the bed and embraced his mother.

"I'm going now," the girl said.

Nick looked up. "If I can get the car started I'll drive you."

"No, you should be here now. I'll call a taxi. I saw the phone."

Nick started to protest.

"Don't worry," she said, "I've got money. You stay here."

The boy looked at her, his grief, gratitude and astonishment evident. The girl reached across the bed and touched his hand, then left the room.

Outside the cabdriver repeated the address.

"That's right."

The man looked at her. "You're crazy being out on a day like this. It's headed for twenty-five below."

"I had to visit a friend. She's dying."

"Sorry to hear it. How long's she have?"

"A few more months."

The man pulled cautiously away from the curb so as not to spin out on the ice. He lit a cigarette as they turned onto Higgins.

"Can you spare one of those?"

The cabbie looked at the girl in the rearview mirror. "Yeah, I guess. Jeez, you kids today. But better you're smokin' this than that other stuff."

When they pulled up outside the house, she could see Walter Borchers glancing out the window, doing a double take as he saw her peel off some bills to pay the driver, casually flick the butt of her cigarette into a snowdrift and start up the walk. Inside he watched her go up the steps toward Bryna's room. She smiled to herself and let her hips roll provocatively.

*   *   *

It was the day before Christmas. Bryna awakened from a dream in which she had seen herself sleeping in a silk-canopied bed in a room that, like her own, was tucked under the eaves. But the dream room had a large dormer window that overlooked a tree-lined street, a thick, pale-green carpet, real closets and wallpaper that looked like a field of tall, waving grass. Here and there a bird fluttered or a bee buzzed, and up near the ceiling, in the summer-blue sky, was a wisp of cloud. On the other side of the room was an antique desk and a large bookshelf full of tantalizing tomes that begged Bryna to read them at once.

Upon waking, Bryna realized that just such a room existed—the guest room at Miss Lionel's house, a house which, with its steeply pitched roof, gables and many-paned windows, Bryna loved as much as the room itself. The first time she saw it, when Miss Lionel gave her a tour of the tidy, two-story house filled with an oddly felicitous mix of antiques and abstracts, she experienced a surge of real happiness and comfort, as if she had come to a place she had always loved and to which she had somehow always belonged.

The warm reverberations of the dream were quickly damped in the realization that by nightfall she would be alone with Walter Borchers.

At noon, amidst a great commotion, Mrs. Borchers loaded the other kids into the family station wagon and prepared to leave for her mother's. Mr. Borchers, whose illness had taken a dramatically displayed turn for the worse during the night, saw his wife off, sniffling and coughing into a dirty handkerchief.

Bryna, in her room, could hear the farewells.

"You see you stay in bed and keep warm. Bryna'll see to ya. Bryna! Bryna!"

Bryna opened her door and looked down the stairs blankly.

"You see to Walter, now, y'hear? And don't forget that laundry and the floors. I don't wanna come back to no pigsty now."

"Yes, ma'am."

The woman looked at Bryna distrustfully. Then she turned her cheek, and her husband pecked it. The moment the door closed behind the woman, Walter shot a grin up the stairs. Bryna quickly drew back into her room, closed and latched the door. For several moments she stood there, her pulse racing. But then she heard a clatter in the kitchen and the television coming on. She took a deep breath and quickly got into her outdoor clothes. It had warmed up considerably but was still nippy. As quietly as possible she edged down the stairs and slipped outside.

Downtown she browsed through the shops, happy for the throng of last-minute Christmas shoppers. The sales clerks were too harried to pay her any heed. At the Mercantile, Bryna looked at dresses, coats and costume jewelry and lingered for some time at the long cosmetics bar, wanting but not daring to try some of the samples. She watched smartly dressed women and girls making purchases, talking animatedly among themselves. She could easily imagine them, gathered around Christmas trees, watching their loved ones open packages containing the gifts they were buying now.

She could just as easily recall one of her earliest Christmases with Sharon and Bryan. There were packages under the tree, all kinds of them. The special one that was just from Bryan was the best of all—a red "Eskimo suit" with a big fur-trimmed parka. Bryna could recall with absolute clarity how thrilled she was as she climbed into the suit and how Bryan, laughing at how cute he said she looked, bounced her over his head and carried her outside, over Sharon's protestations, "to build an igloo." They had to imagine it because there wasn't any snow, but it had worked out just fine. It had all seemed so real. It was a big, beautiful igloo you could actually crawl into and, once inside, stand up in without difficulty. Bryna could remember Bryan getting down on his hands and knees to show her how to get in, once they finished building it. Sharon, of course, hadn't even been able to see it—or claimed she couldn't. She was always like that. Sometimes she even walked right through the igloo, which made Bryna very angry. She and Bryan always took great care to walk around it, even when spring came. Bryan said it took a long time for solid ice to melt. Bryna remembered the very last of it melting in the new grass.

my little princess

Bryna felt a tightening in her throat and hurried out of the store.

Later she visited the book stores along Higgins Avenue. It was dark when she came out of the last one, nearly six o'clock. She still had some of the money left and decided to get something to eat. She went to the counter at the old Palace Hotel and, without too much difficulty, resisted the blintzes and strudel. Instead she ordered a pan-fried trout, hot tea and some cottage cheese. She knew better than to touch the mashed potatoes and rich gravy that came with the dinner.

Afterwards she wandered back down Higgins, toward the river. *Fantasia* was playing at the Wilma Theater. Bryna had often peered through the large glass windows of the old place, amazed by the enormous crystal chandelier in the lobby. She decided to go in.

It was nearly eleven when, having viewed the feature twice, Bryna left the theater. She decided that by now Walter Borchers would either be asleep or, more likely, out drinking and gambling with some of his cronies. He was not likely to miss an opportunity to make the most of his wife's absence. Bryna walked north along Orange, through the dreaded underpass and past a church. She could hear the spirited singing inside. She stopped a moment and listened. She shuddered involuntarily, memories of her grandmother and the church school washing over her like acid.

christmas

The holiday recalled only pain. She had long ceased to be a believer. She hurried down the snow-packed street until the Borchers house, the main floor only partially lighted, loomed ahead. She slowed down, then stopped. She concentrated hard. She felt certain the place was empty but looked through the windows where she could before entering. Inside, she moved stealthily from room to room. In the bathroom she found evidence that Walter had shaved—there was a mess in the sink, and a bottle of after-shave lotion was sitting open on the back of the toilet. He had taken a bath, as well. The sides of the tub were visibly gritty.

Bryna looked at the mess with both disgust and relief. She was certain now he would not be back until very late, if at all, and if he did return he would be too drunk to

to what?

Bryna was not sure what she was afraid of, but she *was* afraid.

She took the scrub brush from behind the toilet and the Comet and went to work. She noticed that a small radio that was usually kept in the kitchen had been plugged in and placed on a towel shelf over the tub. She recalled that Mr. Borchers often moved the radio into the bathroom so that he could listen to sports or news while taking his long baths. She was going to unplug it because the cord was in her way but then decided some music would make her work go more quickly. She had to search for a station that was not playing Christmas music.

When she was finished the bathroom looked so inviting she decided to take a bath herself. Her long day out had left her chilled. She went upstairs to her room and peeled off her various layers of clothing, surprised, as she always was, no matter how often she looked, at her reflection. Her figure—she marvelled that she had one—was becoming more shapely each day. Her breasts, freed of their bulky restraints, became objects of fascination.

69

She always felt it might yet all be an illusion—easily preserved since there was no one else to see her.

She put on her bathrobe and went down and filled the tub. She turned the radio on again, softly as before so that she would hear if anybody came in. The music made her feel good. She leaned back, resting her head on a folded towel. The hot water and the exertion of the long day made her drowsy.

She sat up so quickly the towel slid into the water behind her. She could hear him or *feel* him, she wasn't sure which. Her mind raced, trying to catch up. The bath water was almost cold. The radio was still on, but the station she had been listening to had apparently signed off the air. All that issued now from the radio was a buzz and an occasional angry sputter of static.

Fear clutched at Bryna's throat, making it difficult to breathe. She snapped her head around and looked at the door. It began to open. She wanted to scream but no sound would come. The door opened wide, and he was there. His face was florid, his eyes bloodshot. One of his shirttails was sticking out. He reeked of rancid smoke and whiskey. He grinned at her, coughed out of control, staggered in and grinned again.

"Yeah," he said, slurring his words, "I *know* you want it." His eyes bored into her breasts and he laughed drunkenly. She instinctively covered herself with her arms wondering if she could possibly fight her way past him. Her panic was so overwhelming she did not even think of Sabra.

He took another step toward her, unbuckling his pants.

"Goddam you look good," he said. His pants dropped around his ankles. He pulled down his shorts, breathing hard. "Yer gonna like it."

Bryna felt a sick chill grab her.

"Yer gonna like it," he repeated.

Bryna was frozen, unable to act, except to brace her hands against either edge of the tub.

He lunged, falling toward her when his ankles tangled in his pants. Bryna sprang from the tub, as if she had been shot from a gun. She heard a crackle and then a dull pop and saw smoke rising from Walter Borchers' head where it hung, vibrating, over the foot of the tub. One of his arms was in the water. One horror marched after another as Bryna watched the man being electrocuted, a low, mortal stridor briefly escaping his lips, his eyes bugging, his face turning blue and then purple as the current from the radio he had knocked into the water when he fell across the power cord arced through his brain. The current stiffened him so that he was propped up against the tub like a board. Blood dripped from the man's nose.

Bryna couldn't move for some time. She stood there, staring at the man until, abruptly, his body slumped, all movement in him ceased and only the water lived.

FIVE

Bryna, only half awake, turned on her side in the canopied bed, pulled the down comforter up around her shoulders, and shut her eyes.

"There. See how cozy you are. No need for you to go out on a night like this. I'll find out where they're leaving it. I shouldn't need the body for more than an hour. You *do* agree we need the money?"

yes

"Fine. Just relax now. That's it. You're in the water. Feel it? It's getting deep..."

"George. *George*."

The man opened his eyes. He could see his wife in the shadows, in bed next to him, holding the phone.

"It's for you. A woman. She says it's urgent."

"Christ! What time is it?"

"Nearly three a.m."

"Who in hell...?"

"She won't identify herself. She says it's faculty business."

The man took the phone. "Yes? Who is this?"

"A concerned citizen, George. You may recall we spoke once before, a few months ago."

"What? I don't..."

"About the child, the fat little girl you fancied."

The man stiffened. He looked briefly at his wife, feeling her curiosity. "Oh, oh yes," he said, his mouth dry. "Couldn't we discuss it in the morning?"

"I'm afraid not. It will really have to be attended to right now."

"I see. Well, just a minute." He covered the mouthpiece and spoke to his wife. "It's one of the graduate assistants. The one I told you was so paranoid. This may take a little while. I think I'd better take this in the study."

71

"Hold on," he said, speaking into the phone again.

"I'll be right here."

In the study the man picked up the extension. He hesitated. He was sure his wife was listening, that she'd expect him to let her listen. "Estelle? You can hang up now. I've got it." He waited for the angry click.

"Why are you doing this?" He spoke in a low, urgent voice that betrayed both his fear and his anger. "I gave you the money."

"That was months ago. You're behind on your payments."

The man's temples began to throb. He tried to make sense of the voice—so calm, reassured, threatening. An adult voice, he was sure of that. It was insane. This couldn't really be happening, but it was.

"Payments? Payments! You said nothing about payments!"

"Well, you didn't say you'd be back for more, either, George. There are no freebies in this world, George, you should know that. The little girl tells me you've been following her again, exposing yourself, that you chased her while she was on her morning jog , , ,"

"That's a lie!" The man caught himself and, nearly choking on his rage, whispered hoarsely into the phone: "There was only that one time in the car, months ago. . . ."

"That's not what she tells *me*, George," the voice, implacable as ever, interrupted. "She tells *me* quite a different story."

"This is ridiculous! I'm an English professor at the university. Who'd take her word over mine? I won't be blackmailed again, goddamn you."

"*Who* would believe the child? Your wife for one, I imagine, when the girl tells the authorities about the odd way your prick curves sharply to the left when it's hard and how you've got a little moon-shaped scar on your left cheek; that's ass to you, George."

"What! How could she . . . ?"

"Indeed, George, how *could* she—unless you showed her?"

"She couldn't have seen. . . . Who are you? How could you . . . ?" Fear strangled the man for a moment so that he could no longer speak.

"The child's mother, of course," the voice said, a smirk in it.

The man felt the flesh creep along the back of his shoulders and neck.

"*Mother*. What kind of mother . . . ?"

"A practical one, George, just a very practical one."

"You . . ." The man's voice broke. "You're inhuman, you're . . ."

"Don't call *me* names, you hypocritical bag of shit. I'm not

72

going to argue with you. Here's what you're going to do, so listen and, as they say in the kind of novels you look down your pompous nose at, listen good."

"Of course, there are other ways to get money," Sabra said, "but this way we're doing some good. This is your second chance to sabotage a bad drug deal. Just walk up and..."

Bryna reached into the mailbox in front of the vacant house. Her fingers quickly found the thick envelope and closed around it. Later that same day she bought the dress, underclothing and various accessories Sabra helped her pick out. "Everything but the glass slippers," Sabra quipped. "Shoes will have to do." Then she bought the long, blonde wig made of real human hair she'd been looking at for weeks. Her last stop was a place called Optical Illusion. She had seen an ad for it promising "same-day service on many contact-lens prescriptions." After the optometrist examined her, Bryna, not wanting to appear frivolous, first ordered a pair of regular contacts and then, with some embarrassment, asked about the "cosmetic lenses" that had been mentioned in the ad—those that were designed to change eye color.

"Yes," the optometrist said. "I don't see any reason why you couldn't wear those." He showed her the available colors. There were two shades of blue. One of these was extraordinarily intense. "Effervescent," the man called it—"yet natural; there are a few people who really do have eyes this color." Bryna selected this shade.

It was not necessary to elaborately conceal her new purchases in her room at Miss Lionel's, but she did keep them out of sight. The teacher scrupulously respected her privacy, knowing that she had enjoyed so little of it elsewhere. Bryna was very fond of Miss Lionel; it was wonderful living in the teacher's home. After Walter Borchers' death Miss Lionel had moved quickly to secure custody of Bryna, easy enough under the circumstances. Already she was acting as if Bryna were more than just a temporary charge. She spoke constantly of helping Bryna with college and had already written to her cousin, a full professor at UCLA, to inquire about scholarship and admission forms.

Bryna undressed in front of the full-length mirror attached to her closet door. She had grown two inches in the past several months and was now five feet seven inches. Her weight was down to a hundred and twenty-eight pounds, and she was determined to lose another five. Sometimes—often—she lingered over her reflection for an hour or more, studying herself with the help of a hand mirror from every angle.

Tonight, however, she quickly slipped into a pair of the panties she had bought for her "sister," recalling the salesclerk's promise that "because they're cut high on the sides they give a girl a leggier look." It was a scanty satin thing, and the color was "morning-after rose." Her legs, beautifully smooth since Miss Lionel had given her an electric razor, did look longer, she decided. Next she strapped on the matching bra, pleased at the way it lifted her breasts.

what size is your sister?

36 C

Bryna put on the wig, its loose, natural curls falling down to her shoulders. After that she applied the contacts, able now to tolerate them for several hours at a time. The effect was as electrifying as always, instantly investing her with a luscious, magnetic intensity that almost frightened her. Next were the cosmetics she had been experimenting with for some time. With Sabra advising her she had finally found precisely the blend of eye shadows that best suited her, subtly applied over delicately outlined lids. She used a blue-black mascara to accent her lashes and a rouge called Midnight Wind to enhance her cheeks. For her mouth she preferred a pale plum lipstick called Deliverance. She had bleached her eyebrows—but, for contrast, not quite so light as her wig. Each day, for concealment, she darkened them again with an eyebrow pencil.

She put on the dress last, always afraid she would smudge it with cosmetics. It was a costly, clingy white satin shift secured at the shoulders with delicate ribbons and snugly gathered at the waist. The neck, a plunging V, revealed a good deal of her breasts. For shoes she had selected open-toed heels with ankle straps.

When she was dressed, Bryna opened a box and took from it a gold choker accented with tiny emeralds. Neither the emeralds nor the gold were real, of course, but the effect was stunning nevertheless. She put the choker on and then added the matching earrings she had purchased the same day she had had her ears pierced.

As she studied the final effect in the mirror, Bryna thought how much she looked like Sabra—or at least like Sabra as she had presented herself on several occasions. It was difficult to believe that all of this had happened, and indeed, Bryna would not fully believe it until she saw herself thus reflected, not in a mirror but in the eyes of another person.

She tried to decide what "type" of blonde she was. She had seen a magazine advertisement once that categorized the "species." She decided that she looked neither "dumb" nor "wholesome." She was neither Olivia Newton-John nor Goldie Hawn. That left "cool," "brainy," "society," "sexy," "sexy-feline" and "bitchy." Bryna didn't know who Ce Zee Guest, Jan Cushing, Mary Wells Lawrence and Jane Trahey were but decided she might look a little like Catherine Deneuve ("cool blonde"), a little like Harlow and Monroe ("sexy blonde"), possibly more like Bardot ("sexy feline"). The ad did not identify any of the "bitchy blondes," but Bryna, the more she looked at her strange new self, imagined, perhaps even felt, a certain potential for plain ruthlessness welling up from

where?

Power. It was an odd sensation. Bryna felt as if something inside her, hitherto unmoved and thus unnoticed, had abruptly shifted just enough so that she no longer seemed to be precisely in register with herself and her surroundings. She looked with new wonder and apprehension at herself. Her reflection stared haughtily back at her and then, unmistakably, right through her—as if she did not exist at all. Bryna felt cold.

She hurriedly took off the wig and stripped, letting her clothes fall in a heap on the floor. She did not hang them up until she had removed the contacts and every trace of makeup. Then, though the hour was late, she put on all of her own clothes, including the padding. Only then did she permit herself to look again into the mirror.

Shortly after moving into Miss Lionel's house Bryna was drafted into Brain Bowl, a competition in which opposing teams of students sought to out-answer each other. Before long Bryna, much to her embarrassment, was made captain of her team. Miss Lionel was thrilled, promising this would help Bryna "get into a good college." Sabra concurred.

Sabra unfailingly whispered the answers to Bryna, often before the moderator had even completed the question. Bryna felt guilt along with her embarrassment; it seemed like cheating, but Sabra would have none of it, insisting that "if you have three arms you don't tie one of them behind your back, especially if your opponents choose to believe that third arms—or eyes—are impossible and nonexistent."

Because they were made largely superfluous by their new captain's near-infallibility, Bryna's teammates were, at first, a bit put out. But soon they simply sat back and observed, awe-stricken. Miss Lionel, Brain Bowl adviser, referred to Bryna as a "phenomenon," and Nick, who often came by the auditorium to watch, began calling Bryna "our secret weapon." And in the expanding world of Brain Bowl she was precisely that, effortlessly dispatching first the championship team of the other Missoula high school and then, in quick succession, all the championship teams of the neighboring towns.

In time, much to her surprise, Bryna found that she began to enjoy winning. The anger, the frustration, the respect she evoked in her opponents subtly massaged her. This enjoyment, which shocked her at first and which, for a while, she hid from herself, she now hid from others, or tried to; in fact, however, her apparent uncaring attitude in the embrace of victory made her seem only that much more formidable in the eyes of her already devastated opponents.

At the end of April Nick invited Bryna to the prom.

She was stunned. They were alone in the library after school. She pretended to be utterly absorbed by a filing error. He was waiting for an answer. She could feel his thoughts as if they were his hands—gentle, loving, faultless. He really did admire her—for her mind, she kept telling herself. But she knew that it was more than that—and this shocked and frightened her. There was a stranger in her that Nick could see, and it wasn't the slender, beautiful blonde. It was Bryna, fat and dumpy, myopic and disheveled and yet, somehow, inexplicably, impossibly, desirable.

In her mind, the incongruous thought assumed the shape of a spider, making erratic, evasive digressions as it scurried, panic-stricken across the floor. Bryna divined its course and, moving one step ahead, ground her heel into it.

Sabra was screaming at her. "*Yes*. Yes, yes, yes. You know you want to go, that you want to show off your new body, see their faces, sense their envy, claim what's yours. And I know exactly how you can do it, and no one will know it's you. It will be like magic!"

Nick was beginning to look worried. Bryna glanced up at him from the file cards.

"I . . . all right," she blurted, her color rising. "But I . . . I can't dance very well."

Nick beamed. "You'll be fine. You'll see." He put his hand on hers.

In Miss Lionel's private library were a number of books on Eastern religion and philosophy. Bryna began reading these in the spring. She was particularly fascinated by a book about a cult called Tantra. Some of the color plates arrested her, depicting men and women in explicit and sometimes bizarre modes of sexual intercourse. There were photographs of ancient sculptures fashioned in brass, gold, sandstone and human bone.

In most of the pictures the figures were youthful and beautiful. One gilded couple sat locked in intercourse, their bodies so perfectly matched that, at first glance, they appeared to be one person. This was by design, Bryna soon learned from her reading, for Tantra, a school of both yogic and Buddhist philosophies, taught that sexual union, practiced according to a variety of prescribed rituals, was one of the most powerful tools available to man in his quest for cosmic enlightenment and unity. Other plates illustrated couples in standing and reclining positions of intercourse, and some depicted groups of individuals interpenetrating one another in all manner of ways with their penises, fingers, tongues and even toes.

Bryna found all of this unsettling. She had little use for religion as she had known it, but Tantra seemed an extreme and alien alternative, though from her reading she soon learned that it was still practiced today and was regarded as an important and valid philosophy by many scholars.

Bryna's fascination became even more intense when she discovered, among the illustrations of the book, one of a serpent coiled around a stone which resembled the male organ. The text confirmed that this resemblance was intended. The serpent was said to represent the *kundalini*, a cosmic force that could be aroused through sexual ritual and which, in turn, if properly channeled, could give rise to various supernatural powers.

Bryna quickly looked at the other illustrations. There were several in which The Goddess, the central figure in Tantra, assumed a grotesque persona, taking on a monstrous aspect with four arms, demented eyes, lolling tongue, fanglike teeth and discolored complexion, and with a vagina that was like a gaping wound. In some of the pictures she wore parts of human bodies about her neck and carried the severed head of a male. Often she was depicted having intercourse, squatting obscenely over the supine, corpselike figure of a man who seemed dead save for that obviously living portion of his anatomy that could be seen penetrating her. Sometimes the goddess was smeared with blood and was carrying a large evil-looking saber or flaying knife.

Bryna shuddered. Again, she turned to the text, which explained that The Goddess has two faces: one benign, one horrific. The Goddess, Bryna read, is both man's creator and his destroyer. One Tantric ritual involved The Goddess, in her killing role, as "Kali the Black One," conducting an orgy in a field of corpses.

Bryna was not completely sure why, but she did not want Miss Lionel to know that she was reading these books; it was as if the knowledge she was absorbing from them was too private and personal to share with another, even with Miss Lionel. Bryna felt herself to be somehow in the process of illicit discovery. She found herself sneaking the books, including one called *Serpent Power*, to her room after Miss Lionel had gone to bed and then placing them back in their proper niches after each reading. She knew they must be very special to Miss Lionel, for they were signed inside: "With love, Nestor."

Sabra, by her conspicuous silence during these covert sessions, seemed ominously near.

Bryna did not tell anyone that Nick had invited her to the prom. She knew that Miss Lionel would only fuss and worry about what she was going to wear. Nor did Miss Lionel ever mention the prom to Bryna, for, of course, she was certain that no one had invited her to go and, in any event, the prom did not loom large in Miss Lionel's world. What *did* loom large for Miss Lionel was the fact, known only to herself and a few other teachers, that Bryna was to be the valedictorian of her graduating class. Though Bryna herself had not yet been told this, the teacher had forwarded this intelligence, along with Bryna's completed college entrance exams and a clipping from the local paper on Bryna's Brain Bowl prowess, to her cousin at UCLA, Nestor Bagehot.

As prom night approached, Bryna found herself climbing in and out of her new clothes and wig with obsessive frequency. There were moments when, looking at her new self in the mirror, she felt she could go through with it without any major difficulty, when she actually believed she was or *could be* that girl in the mirror. But it was one thing to *look* the part, another to act it; she knew that she would need Sabra's help.

The day arrived—a mild Saturday in mid-May. "The plan," as Sabra called it, began to go into effect. Getting her things into the girls' locker room proved simple enough. She knew the prom committee would be decorating the gym most of the day. The gymnasium was in a large annex to the school, and there were entrances at two different levels. One of the entrances, along the side, was midway between the main floor, where the dance would take place, and the lavatories and shower rooms at the lowest level. Bryna, carrying a large shopping bag, used this entrance. She did as Sabra instructed, waiting until Sabra indicated it was safe to step by an occupied office along the corridor through which she had to pass. She paused again before passing the place where the wide stairs led up to the main floor, for Sabra indicated someone was there. Nevertheless, it took only a few minutes to pass unseen into the shower room, where she sequestered the clothing, cosmetics, wig and contacts in an empty locker before slipping out the same way she had entered.

Bryna was spared having to concoct a story by which she could absent herself that evening when Miss Lionel announced she was planning to take in a double bill of Bergman films at the local art theater. She invited Bryna to join her.

"I think I'd better stay in," Bryna said. "I'd like to try to finish the Proust tonight."

Miss Lionel looked more than placated. Bryna knew that Miss Lionel, though she had personally never been able to finish Proust's immense and difficult *Remembrance of Things Past*, regarded him as the greatest writer of all time. She was thrilled that her ward seemed to be gobbling him up like a box of bonbons. Bryna knew that Miss Lionel would not worry any more about her that evening; nor would she disturb her when she got home from the movies. For Miss Lionel, the act of reading great literature was almost as sacred as writing it. It demanded the utmost in concentration and calm.

Once alone in the house Bryna's nervousness began to mount. She was frightened, and she knew she was frightened. For a while she thought about dropping "the plan" and simply going as herself, her familiar, safe, fat self, sticking it out no matter how awkward and ugly she felt, no matter how much the others might turn their faces, whisper and laugh.

She undressed and showered, looking at herself in the mirror when she was done. There was an alternative.

i could go like this

But that wasn't right either, it seemed. That would only be halfway. And everyone would know who she was—and even though she might be beautiful without her wig and the contacts they would laugh at her for surprising them this way, for taking herself so seriously.

who does she think she is? cinderella?

Besides, she had only one dress that would fit this shape—and it was in a locker beneath the dance floor.

Bryna noticed that she was beginning to spot. Her period was just starting. She inserted a tampon and started dressing. She dressed as she usually did, carefully concealing the padding

79

under long black stockings and, this time, a high-necked dress with long, puffy sleeves. Miss Lionel had given it to her. It wasn't haute couture by any means, but it was at least some improvement over Bryna's customary dress. It was blue-gray in color. Bryna hated it precisely because it *did* lighten her look just a little. With her all-or-nothing ideal, advertising a *little* improvement was worse than exhibiting none at all. She wore the dress only out of consideration for Nick.

Bryna finished dressing with more than half an hour to spare. The time dragged wretchedly. Sabra chattered at her, trying, Bryna knew, to make the time pass faster. As the tension and fear mounted, she tried desperately to think of some way to back out. Sabra, avoiding the scolding tone she sometimes employed, spoke soothingly, assuring her everything was going to work out fine.

"All you have to do is get through the front door of the place and excuse yourself. It's expected. Girls always have to check their hair, powder their noses first thing. If you still don't think you can do it, I'll take it from there if you like..."

Bryna had heard all of this at least a dozen times. It still didn't keep her from jumping or her heart from racing when the doorbell rang.

"Hey man! How ya doin'?"

Matt Connor grinned in through the open car window on Nick's side. Bryna knew Matt only as one of the guys who hung out with Tony, Liz Lowry's boyfriend. He had the same arrogant, sneering quality that Bryna detested in Tony. She felt herself recoil a little as Matt looked at her contemplatively for a moment, chewing on something, trying to figure what she was doing with Nick.

"Hey, how ya doin', Brynie?"

Bryna barely nodded. She could smell the alcohol on Matt's breath. Matt had his hand on Nick's shoulder.

"I got some far-out shit here, man. You wanna score some dyna-mighty hash? Maybe a few 'ludes for you and the little lady later on?" Matt winked across at Bryna. She could feel Nick's embarrassment—for her.

"Look, Matt," Nick said, lifting the other's hand from his shoulder, "why don't you just...?"

"Hey, man, it's cool. I know when I'm not wanted. I was just tryin' to score a lousy twenty bucks. Look, I got some meth that'll blow..."

"Flake off," Nick said, starting to roll up the window.

Matt moved away, toward the front of the car, then leaned over the hood and flashed them the peace sign, slowly dropping his first finger so that only the middle one stood obscenely at attention. Nick, cursing, started to open his door, but Bryna restrained him. Matt held up both hands, like it was all a joke. His date, a girl Bryna had never seen before, leaned over and looked in at Bryna contemptuously.

As Matt and his date walked arm in arm toward the gym, Bryna could hear the girl ask Matt:

what rock did he find her under?

Inside, things were even worse. Streamers, some of them shiny strips of colored foil, drifted around the periphery of the dance floor and all through the elevated areas where the band played and couples sat at small, round tables sipping punch—and watching. Bryna felt all eyes were on her when she and Nick entered, though there were other couples in front of them. Every whisper, every glance, every chance smile Bryna felt was aimed at her. Her mouth was very dry, and her palms and forehead had begun to sweat. Her stomach was beginning to churn.

"Nick, I . . ."

"Are you all right?"

"I . . . just excuse me for a minute." Bryna broke away from him and hurried toward the stairs that would lead to the lavatories. At the moment she could not even think about the locker room. A babble of laughing voices filled her head; she dared look at no one. In the lavatory several girls were lined up along the mirrors adjusting their hair and makeup, talking. She sensed a lull in the conversation as she entered but, again, dared not look. She went straight to the back and into one of the stalls, the one nearest the door that led to the locker room. She waited for Sabra's signal, then quickly went through the door at the back of the lavatory, into the corridor and down the steps to the girls' locker room.

Inside, not daring to turn on the light, she felt her way along the wall, counting the lockers until she found the one in which she had hidden her things. First she took out the small flashlight she had left there and then quickly undressed. She took out the new things and put the old in their place. She took the bag of cosmetics over to the mirror above a short row of sinks.

For the next several minutes she worked without thinking, repeating movements she had made dozens of times before. Once the makeup was applied she put on her new panties and bra and slipped into the white dress and shoes. Then she added the wig, necklace, earrings and bracelets. Only then did she pause to look at herself in the eerie yellow light. She was surprised to find herself dressed. She seemed to have lost all sense of time, unsure whether a moment or an hour—or even more—had passed. She felt a chill.

nick is waiting for me. they're all waiting.

"The contacts."

Bryna heard the words, but where they came from did not register. The fear was back.

i can't do it i can't

Her fingers trembled so that it took her twice as long as usual to get the lenses into her eyes. She shone the light on the upper part of her dress so that, in the mirror, she could see the exposed curves of her breasts. Her face was in darkness. She tried to imagine herself beyond the door of the locker room, in the lavatory, on the stairs, stepping on to the dance floor, finding Nick. Her legs felt weak. It was all simply unimaginable.

She angled the flashlight up a little so that her eyes were reflected in the mirror. The effect was startling. The light, bouncing off only the high points of her face, left dark hollows around what seemed to be independently suspended pools of expanding, luminous blue. She let herself sink into it.

She and Bryna had previously agreed upon a name for the "new girl."

sabrina

Sabra chuckled, picked up the flashlight where it had fallen to the floor and examined herself carefully in the mirror. She looked critically at her hair, her eyes, her lips, shone the light down onto her breasts and grimaced. She set the flashlight down, quickly loosened the straps of the gown and peeled the front of it away from her body. Just as quickly she removed the offending bra and then pulled the dress back into place. Her nipples nudged provocatively into the soft satin, clearly outlined in the rich, white material.

She stepped back a few paces and then, holding the flashlight again, walked toward the mirror, watching herself. There was still something wrong. She smiled, recognizing what it was. She bent over, took off her shoes and, shimmying the shift up along her thighs, deftly peeled off her panties. Again, she took a few steps backward and then advanced toward the mirror, a smile of satisfaction on her lips as she observed the way the dress clung to her.

She replaced her shoes and put the cosmetics and flashlight back into the locker after first removing from it a small, folded piece of paper. This she took with her. In the passageway between the locker room and the lavatory she paused to concentrate, waiting for the right moment to step through the door, when it was possible for her to enter out of sight of the several girls who were now in the room.

On the edge of the dance floor, Sabra stopped a girl and asked for Nick. The girl looked at her startled and then, embarrassed, stepped back, looking across the floor. "I saw him a few minutes ago. Yeah, there he is, sitting at that table, looking this way."

"The good-looking one with black hair, sitting alone?"

The other girl nodded, unable to keep her eyes off Sabra's plunging neckline. Her thought came through loud and clear:

she's not wearing a bra

As Sabra made her way across the dance floor toward Nick, she "heard" that same thought over and over. And others.

no bra
yeah ain't you glad?
who's the lucky guy?

She basked in the attention she knew she was attracting. As she approached Nick he glanced at her, then away. He looked worried and tense and kept watching the stairway that led to the lavatories. Sabra felt almost angry.

"Nick?" Sabra popped a quick, worried smile. "Nick Andrianos?" She could hear the excited whispers all around her.

Nick stood up. "Yeah? Yes."

"Hi, I'm Sabrina... Randolph. I... may I sit down? I think people are looking at us."

somebody said he came with bryna carr

bryna! are you kidding? he's obviously with her, whoever she is

"Uh, sure," Nick said, "but I'm waiting..."

"I know. Bryna told me."

Nick sat down, looking mystified. "Is she all right?"

wow, she oughta be illegal and i oughta be in prison

i think it's disgusting. she doesn't have a thing on under that dress

"Yes, yes, fine. I mean, well, she was pretty sick there for a while, throwing up and all. I just happened to be there and..."

Nick paled. "Where is she now? I better help."

"Just hold on," Sabra said, reaching across the table to briefly put her hand reassuringly on Nick's. "I'm trying to tell you. She didn't want to make a big scene, so she left by the side entrance. My date, well, actually he's my cousin if you can believe it—Danny Weurthmiller? You probably know him? He was waiting

83

for me in the corridor, you know, and she was, well, she was so sick and embarrassed. She was going to leave anyway. I thought the least I could do was to get Danny to give her a ride home. She didn't want you to see her like that."

Nick looked at her, stunned. "Thanks," he said. "I better get over to her place and . . ."

"Hold it," Sabra said, grabbing his sleeve as he started to get up. "She asked me to give you this."

He sank back down and took the note she handed him. He read it to himself:

nick i'm sorry. i got very sick. it had ,nothing to do with you. something i ate. i just need to go home, rest and be alone. i'll talk to you tomorrow. bryna.

Nick recognized Bryna's handwriting right away. She sometimes lent him her class notes. He looked at the piece of paper miserably.

"So it looks like we're both stranded for the moment," Sabra said. "I hate to ask this, but would you mind staying here with me until Danny . . . ?"

"Oh, sure," he said, embarrassed at not already having offered. "I want to thank you. You've been great helping out like this. I just wish she'd have let me . . ."

Sabrina smiled tolerantly. "Wow, you really don't understand girls, do you? I mean, when a girl's sick like that the last person she wants to be seen by is her guy." Sabra found that the extra color in Nick's face made him even more attractive. "She seems like a really nice person. You know, this could have happened to anybody."

Nick could only nod and stare at his empty punch glass. A full one, intended for Bryna, remained untouched.

"May I?"

Nick nodded, and Sabra drank the punch, watching Nick over the top of the glass.

"Hey, it could be worse," she said. "Let's make the most of it. Wanna dance?"

Nick hesitated, looking toward the door again.

"Oh, c'mon." She took his hand and got up. It was a slow one, and nearly everyone was dancing. Gradually she moved in closer until her entire body was touching his. She was sensitive to every movement, every contour of his body. She felt more alive, more energized in his arms than she had in ages. She let his natural electricity flow into her, from the ripple of lean muscle along his ribcage and thighs, through the momentary tensing of stomach muscles, through the tips of his fingers, out of his solar plexus, into her now firm nipples.

"Dan's your cousin, you say?"

"Yes. I'm from Seattle. Our school is out already. I'm just visiting here. Danny is such a bookworm; when I heard there was a prom and he wasn't going I decided to do some missionary work. I made him go. To tell you the truth, I think he was glad to have an excuse to leave. Talk about a fish out of water."

The warm, fernlike odor of Nick's sex filled Sabra's nostrils. It made her feel wonderful. If only Nick would relax a little. Over his shoulder she noticed Matt Connor eyeing her, a drugged grin on his face. She smiled at him invitingly, careful that Nick didn't see.

The music stopped and then started again almost instantly, a reprise of the same number that had obviously been so popular. Matt's hand was on Nick's shoulder, his eyes on Sabra. Nick looked irritated and uncertain.

"It's all right," Sabra said, smiling up at Nick with just a hint of long suffering. "I'll see you after this one." She glanced at Matt's date, who was staring back at her with open hostility.

"Oh, yeah," Matt said, "this is my old lady, Tina." He looked at Nick. "I'm sure she'd be *dee*-lighted, old buddy." He pulled Sabra away and into his arms.

After the introductions, Matt said, "I thought Mr. Clean came with the Black Widow."

"If you mean Bryna, you're right, but she got sick, and my date took her home. Danny Weurthmiller."

"You came with *that* turkey?"

"Tell me about it," Sabra laughed. "Well, he's my cousin. It was charity."

"So you're sorta on the loose now?"

"You might say so." She smiled up at him and moved in closer. He was dark like Nick but his features were more blunt, his body more heavily muscled but less defined.

"Oh, god," he moaned, as she thrust her pelvis up against his. "You're so fucking beautiful."

Her fingers explored the bulges in his blazer pocket. "Got any goodies in here for Sabrina?"

"Whatever you want, baby!"

She pulled a couple of capsules out of his pocket and looked at them.

"'ludes, man," Matt said. "Two of 'em in each one of those capsules. Easier to slip into something."

"One ought to do," Sabra said, tucking the capsule into the ribbon of her corsage. "Maybe I can pay you somehow—after the dance."

"Plenty more where that came from." He held her tighter, kissing her neck.

The kiss, the whispers, the passionate way they were slowly grinding against each other was attracting attention, though Sabra was careful to keep out of Nick's sight. One set of eyes she did not hide from were Tony's. She found them studying her just as Matt started to suck on her neck. He was dancing with Liz, who was obviously aware of Tony's ill-concealed distraction. Tony's look was unsmiling, arrogantly intense. Sabra returned the look with equal intensity, then looked away as if he no longer interested her. But slowly she maneuvered Matt closer to where Tony and Liz were, aware of Tony but never looking at him.

When they were very close she whispered to Matt: "There's a boy just behind us who keeps staring at us. I think he must know you." Matt turned awkwardly around.

"Tony! Hey, babe, how ya doin'?"

Tony nodded at Matt and looked again at Sabra. Liz was looking, too, projecting pure hate. Sabra returned Tony's look, ignoring Liz. The music stopped.

"Thanks for the dance, Matt," Sabra said. "Oh, there's Nick." She smiled at Matt and started away. "Catch you later," she said, and then glanced briefly at Tony, who stared back.

caught

Nick led her off the dance floor, toward the tables.

"Were you supposed to meet Dan anywhere in particular? I haven't seen him."

"Hey, you're still not having a good time are you? Look, I have to be honest with you. I'm not at all sure Danny will be back at all; he felt so out of place it would be just like the jerk to leave me stranded. So if you want to leave I'll go, too, because neither one of us can very well stay here without dates."

He hesitated. "I don't mind staying, if you . . ."

She knew he wanted to leave. "Great," she said. "I mean we might as well enjoy ourselves now that we're here."

"There's a table."

"Great. You grab it and I'll get us something to drink." She started off before he could protest. It was simple enough to covertly empty the capsule into his drink. She stirred it with a swizzle stick and set it down on the table with a smile. He sipped on it. A new number, a fast one, started up.

"This is one of my favorites," Sabra said. "Oh, please, Nick. I don't want to miss this one."

"Sure," he said without enthusiasm.

"C'mon, then, bottoms up." They both drained their glasses and moved onto the dance floor. Sabra let the heavy beat of the music resonate through her body, until she was perfectly attuned to the rhythm. Nick danced spiritlessly in the beginning, but as the drug began its disinhibitory magic he was infected by his partner's driving energy. As they locked together, untouching, Nick laughed spontaneously. Sabra felt him yield utterly to the concentrated abandon of the music, both within and without. They were so good that as the music died a few of the couples next to them hooted and whistled in their direction.

Later they began mixing. It was Sabra's idea. "We have to be democratic and spread it around." Nick was malleable, in the full grip of the drug. His behavior wasn't sleazy like Matt's, but he felt looser than he ever had before. Sabra had no difficulty dancing with the good-looking, dark-haired types she fancied, culling several from the crowd, those most likely to fit into her plan, playing one off against the other, finally concentrating on five of them, pretending to prefer only the one she was with, giving him intimate little be-patient looks when one of the others cut in to dance with her, building tension, talking to each about how the others annoyed her, enjoying the alarm that was growing among the dates of the five, the talk that was spreading—and through it all occasionally smiling or waving at Nick, who invariably smiled and waved back.

Tony was the last to get in the game. By then it was after midnight. He had been watching Sabra all the while, trying, she knew, to impress her, possibly intimidate her with his malevolent reserve, awe her with his macho restraint. And, of course, there was Liz, holding him back, glowering at the new girl.

Sabra was dancing with Matt when she decided to make her move. "Why don't you ask Liz to dance?"

"I hate that bitch."

"Yeah, but there's something I wanna tell Tony."

"What?" He looked at her suspiciously.

"Just what a prick he is, the way he's been staring at me all night. I'm gonna get him hot and then let him have it."

"Jesus," Matt said, choking on his own laughter, wheezing. He was starting to get messy. "Sure, man, sure. You couldn't screw a nicer dude." He laughed again and then moved unevenly toward the other couple. Liz watched coldly as they approached.

Sabra smiled faintly at the other girl.

move over bitch

"She's all yours, man," Matt laughed, giving Sabra a little push toward Tony. "Hey, Liz, how 'bout a good time for a change?"

Sabra felt Liz seethe as she moved off in Tony's arms. He said nothing.

"So what's up?" Sabra asked, pointedly pressing her hips up tighter against his. "Not much I see." She felt his arms tense. She gave him a sarcastic, winsome little smile, reading his thought:

fucking cocktease

"So are you going to piss or get off the pot?" she said, leaning her head against his shoulder.

"You really think you're hot shit, don't you?"

"Hot enough to handle anything you can put out."

He snorted, "Prove it."

She looked up at him. "You're the one who's going to have to prove it," she said.

"Any time."

"Meet me outside in ten minutes, in the parking lot. You'll see me leave." She could feel him getting hard. "That is if you have the balls to ditch that tacky number you're with."

"Yeah?" he said. "What about Nick? You're with him, right?"

"I do what I want. Besides, if he comes after me, you ought to be able to handle him."

"I'll be there."

The next dance was with Nick. The drug was wearing off, she could tell. He was tenser than he had been. In the middle of the dance Sabra stiffened.

"What's wrong?"

"I don't know. I feel kind of... I think I better get some air. Gosh, first Bryna, now me."

She broke away from Nick and started quickly across the floor, toward the exit. It took Nick several moments to gather his wits and start after her.

"Hey, wait a minute!"

Sabra walked faster. She knew that heads were turning, that it appeared they had had a fight. She sensed the astonishment of several of the girls as their dates, whose eyes had been on her for some time, abruptly stopped dancing and started toward the exit, as well, saying something about having to talk to Nick.

Sabra started running, trying to avoid bumping into the other dancers. Nick, she knew, was right behind her, followed by the others to whom she had made promises—they were all in pursuit, elbowing across the crowded floor, raising tempers, curiosity and general confusion in their wake. Outside, in the fresh air, Sabra waited only a moment until Nick burst through the heavy double doors.

"Hurry," she said frantically, grabbing Nick's arm, tugging at him. "We've got to get away! They're after us!"

"Who... what...?"

"I'll explain later! C'mon!"

Her apparent panic seized him, and he sprinted after her, weaving through the parked cars toward his Chevy. Behind them the doors burst open again, and first Tony, then Matt and two others were there, cursing and shoving each other. As Nick unlocked the car Sabra waved across the lot at them, smiling, careful not to let Nick see. Nick couldn't hear what Tony was saying, but Sabra could:

the bitch conned all of us. let's get her.

As Nick slotted the souped-up '57 into reverse, the others scrambled for their cars, their dates spilling out of the gym after them. Nick squealed through the lot, narrowly missing Matt Connor, who screamed, "We're gonna get you, cunt!"

Nick peeled onto South Higgins and headed toward the mountain. There was a straight stretch of about two miles through a rundown business section before the road curved up Pattee Canyon.

"What the fuck's going on?" Nick said hoarsely. In his rearview mirror he could see one of the other cars gaining on him, darting dangerously around slower traffic in no-pass zones.

"Just stand on it, goddamn it," Sabra commanded. "If they catch us we're dead."

Nick ran a red light, sending another car into the curb. He looked back, but it appeared no real damage had been done.

"Jesus Christ," he whispered. "We're going to be dead even if they don't."

"That's Tony! He's gaining on us!" Sabra cried. "Faster, faster!"

Nick looked over at her as if she were demented, but, in fact, he did what she suggested. He heard a siren and saw a cop car pulling out of the A & W parking lot, squealing in right behind Tony.

"Don't stop!" Sabra screamed. It soon became evident that Tony had no intention of stopping, either.

Nick was looking into his rearview mirror when Sabra shouted, "Left, left!"

Nick glanced back down and realized he was about to miss the sharp turn up the mountain. He smoked his brakes, then let the

Chevy spin free up Pattee Canyon Drive, skidding dangerously near a huge construction pit between the forks of the road. Tony made the corner, too, but the cop snagged into the barricade at the lip of the pit, teetered and then nudged straight over the edge, nosediving into a big pile of sand.

As they gained altitude, winding up above the lighted construction site, Sabra could look down and see the cruiser buried up to its windshield in sand, stuck there at a forty-five degree angle. She had to stifle a laugh. The cop was sticking his head out the window, cursing, apparently all right.

Above the Farviews residential area the road narrowed. There were frequent breaks in the pavement. The road climbed tortuously through the woods, occasionally leveling off along a meadow or pasture. Over the hills and around the curves the lights of the pursuing cars played a deadly game of peekaboo.

Sabra wailed, "If they catch us they'll . . . Nick, they're going to rape me."

"Rape you!" Nick, his knuckles white against the steering wheel, sounded genuinely shocked. "What did you . . . ?"

"Oh, sure," Sabra said, sounding bitter. "Blame me! You're all the same! A guy can make any kind of crack to a girl, paw her, do anything. But if a girl tries to have a good time she's a slut, fair game, 'asking for it,' that's the phrase isn't it? Just because I was friendly, they . . . Tony and Matt and some of the others came on to me, I mean *really* came on. Matt called me a cocktease and . . ."

"*Matt*," Nick said angrily. "Look, I'm sorry, I didn't mean anything. I just couldn't figure out . . ." His rearview mirror suddenly picked up two sets of headlights. "Christ, we're in for it now."

Sabra looked back to see another car overtaking Tony, nearly forcing him off the road. She smiled faintly in the shadows. She knew who was driving the other car.

"What I was afraid of," Nick muttered. "That's Andy Letellier's Mustang; no way we're gonna outrun that. He's been working on it every night for a year."

Nick had to slow for most of the curves, but the Mustang screamed through all of them, nearly wiping out each time.

"He must be polluted," Nick growled. "I've never seen him so out of control."

On the next straight stretch the Mustang pulled up within a couple feet of the Chevy and then charged forward, ramming it. Nick dared not even look back, but cursed and gunned the Chevy up a steep stretch.

The Mustang swung over into the passing lane, going uphill, pulled even with them and started squeezing to the right, forcing the Chevy over, blowing up gravel.

"Idiots!" Nick raved, unable to believe what was happening. He looked over furiously at the other car for a second and was shocked to see only female faces staring back at him, shouting obscenities, grinning with excitement. Only Liz, who was driving, was staring grimly ahead.

A large break in the pavement on the left side of the road forced Liz to drop back in behind Nick. She began creeping up on him again as they neared the crest of the old highway. Sabra, who had been watching the road raptly, calmly counting to herself, abruptly screamed:

"Watch out! Move left!"

Nick was so startled he did exactly what she commanded, thinking she had seen something he hadn't. As they topped the grade, Liz shot by on the right, exploding off a series of deep chuck holes on her side of the road. The Mustang shot off the highway, ripped through a fence and careered through a boulder-strewn field.

"Holy shit! We better stop."

"No!" Sabra cried. "They're all right. No one was killed."

Nick looked at her, trembling as much with rage as fear. "How the fuck do you know?"

"The same way I knew those holes were coming up, just over the top of the hill. Just trust me. They're all right. Besides, the others are coming up right behind them. If there's any problem, they'll . . ."

"Yeah, and they aren't alone," Nick said. "It looks like we really bought the farm." They could both now hear the faint wail of police sirens.

"Not yet," Sabra said. "We're going to get out of this. Just do what I tell you." There were lights in the rearview mirror again. "They're still after us. Step on it."

The other cars continued to gain. The only time they were out of sight was when the road curved.

"It's no use. We might as well pull over."

"No!" Sabra shouted. "Right after the next series of curves, there's a dirt road to the left. Take it."

"How the hell do you know? You said you'd never been here before!"

"Just do what I tell you. Slow down a little. We're coming up on it. There!"

They spun off the pavement onto the dirt track, chattering

across its washboard corrugations. As they disappeared into the woods they heard one of the other cars roar by on the main road and, then, a second later, heard the tortured utterance of its brakes.

"They're on to us," Nick said forlornly. A few seconds later the lights of another car confirmed his fear. Around the next bend they saw what appeared to be an overgrown driveway, leading off the dirt road. The trees were so thick they could not see where it led.

"Pull in there," Sabra ordered. The Chevy thumped onto the narrow drive and shuddered across something neither of them had seen.

"Cattle guard," Nick said. They entered what appeared to be a small clearing now overgrown with tall grass. Nick immediately cut his lights and crept to a stop, though he let the engine idle. A second later a car barrelled by on the dirt road, and then another.

"It's working," Nick said. "They didn't see us." They could hear a third car approaching.

Sabra could feel Nick holding his breath.

"Oh!" she cried suddenly, lurching forward, as if startled. She purposely hit the horn in the process. Nick jumped.

"What the . . . !"

"I. . . I thought I saw something up by those trees."

"There's nothing out there but a few stray cows," Nick said angrily, looking back over his shoulder. "Oh, Christ . . ."

"Oh, god, they heard!" Sabra wailed. "They're coming back! We're trapped!"

Nick let the Chevy glide ahead, to the edge of the clearing, which he now realized was an abandoned parking area. Under a half moon, which had just emerged from behind clouds, they could make out an old church, its walls gray with age, its windows shattered, on a small hill just above them.

"We've still got legs," Nick said. "C'mon. Get out!"

Nick took Sabra's hand and half led her, half dragged her up the hillside toward the church. A car, its gears grinding, thrashed into the parking lot. Its lights caught them. The driver—Sabra remembered him only as "Frenchy," a big, rawboned half-breed Indian with straight, black hair, sharp, mean features and a large, sensual mouth—jumped out of the car. Somebody else got out of the car—Andy Letellier—and shouted at them.

"We've got you now, you scuzzy bitch!"

Nick stopped and turned to face them. "Are you fucking crazy!" His voice was hoarse with emotion.

"Butt out Andrianos! This is between us and her. You think your dick's the only one she diddled? She cockteased every guy she could."

Two other cars hurtled into the lot. The first stopped short, and the second rammed into it hard. There was a moment of complete silence and then a dull boom. The rear of the car that had been hit exploded into flame. The other car quickly backed away and pulled over to the side. Matt stumbled out of the burning car, muttering to himself. Tony, driving the car that had hit him, came running over, furious.

"Fucking idiot! I oughta total you! You damn near put me through the glass."

"Hey, man, hey," Matt said, "I'm the one who oughta be bitchin'. I don't even got that thing paid for."

"Cool it!" Andy screamed. "It's that cunt's fault. Come on, they're getting away!"

With the arrival of the others, Nick and Sabra had started up the hill again, hurrying toward the church, clearly visible in the eerie light of the burning automobile. There was an old graveyard in front of the church, the fence around it broken down, grass and weeds thriving all through it.

"Through here," Nick said, "and up to those woods."

They were halfway through the cemetery, dodging headstones, when Sabra cried out and sank down.

"My ankle! Oh God! I twisted it! I can't run!"

"You've got to!"

Sabra saw Andy and the Indian coming through the fence. Nick reached down and tried to force her to her feet. She cried out again and fell back into the grass.

"It's no use. Just get away, leave me!"

Nick responded as she knew he would, placing himself between her and the others, fists clenched.

"Back off, Andrianos, or you're gonna be singing soprano."

Nick swung at Andy, clipping him on the jaw. The Indian moved around behind him, immobilizing him with a hammerlock while Andy hit him in the stomach. Nick groaned and sank to his knees. The Indian held him there, kneeling on the backs of his lower legs. By the time Tony and Matt got there Andy already had his coat off and was dropping his pants. Sabra squirmed back in the grass, clutching at it with her hands, staring at Andy who was peeling off his shirt, exposing skin that seemed almost red in the light of the flaming car.

"Are you out of your minds?" Nick gasped, still fighting for breath. "You're all fucking crazy. Rape's a felony..."

93

"Shut him up," Tony said, his eyes on Sabra. Matt took Andy's shirt and roughly stuffed part of it in Nick's mouth, then pulled the loose ends around tight behind the Indian so that Nick's head was pinned back against Frenchy's chest. Blood trickled out of Nick's mouth where the fabric cut into the corner of his lip. Every time he struggled Matt yanked viciously on his makeshift bridle, hooting wildly, as if he were riding a bucking horse.

Sabra could feel everything, their energy, all of it—directed at her. Every time a muscle tightened in one of them or a nerve fired, she felt it. She could feel Nick's rage and pain, taste his blood; she could feel the lust rising all around her, hotter and brighter than the burning automobile.

Tony stepped around behind her and forced her shoulders down flat on the grass. He pinned her arms down under his knees. Andy, his pants and shorts down around his ankles, fell breathlessly between her legs, his eyes wild. He put his hands between her breasts and ripped the dress open; he kept on ripping until she was naked. She felt the shock of her beauty jolt them, momentarily intimidate them, felt Andy's need to make her dirty, deserving of defilement. As he bent over her, close enough now for her to feel his heat, she opened her mouth slightly and let her tongue slide across her teeth. Only Andy and Tony saw it.

"Yeah, you want it, you know you do," Andy muttered.

As they took their turns with her, Sabra could see herself through Nick's eyes, which were focused now on her feet, not wanting to see what he could not prevent. She realized that her shoes were still on. Slowly, as Nick watched, she squeezed her legs around Frenchy's and, putting the toe of one foot against the heel of the other, pried off both shoes and kicked them aside. Then she curled her toes to potentiate the pleasure that was building in her. Nick's shock coursed through her, heightening the pleasure with its added energy.

Matt hooted. "Yeah! All *right*! This ain't no rape, man!"

Nick stopped struggling, drained, and Matt loosened his grip on the makeshift harness.

When it was over, Sabra felt the grass again and realized where she was.

"She's all yours, man," one of them said, letting Nick go. They laughed and started for their cars. After they'd gone, Sabra looked up at Nick. She could tell he was a lost cause—for now.

"I guess we better go, too," she said matter of factly. "I can tell you're in no mood to have a good time, though for a while I had high hopes I was saving the best for last."

Even after all they had been through his color rose.

He looked away and muttered something about getting her a blanket from his car.

It was nearly four a.m. when they got back to town and he let her out, still wrapped in his blanket, in front of Danny Weurthmiller's house. For the first time in hours he thought—guiltily—of Bryna and wondered if she was all right.

Sabra, before she got out of the car, leaned over and kissed Nick on the cheek. She felt him recoil. She smiled at him, got out and, peering back in through the open window, said, "I'll catch you later."

She waited until he was out of sight and then slipped into the alley behind the Weurthmiller house.

get ready danny boy you're gonna have some questions to answer tomorrow

She laughed softly to herself and started toward Miss Lionel's only a few blocks away. She took the key she had hidden under the back steps and let herself in when she got there. Her whole body was still tingling, charged with sensation. Even the feel of the carpet under her bare feet imparted pleasure as she padded into Bryna's room from the bathroom, where she quietly cleaned herself as best she could.

A flame that had, at best, only flickered for more time than she cared to remember, now leapt along the entire wick of her being. She stood before the mirror in Bryna's room, naked, gently stroking her breasts, her abdomen, her thighs, tasting the pleasures of the evening all over again, feeling the (she smiled to herself, recalling words Bryna had read in one of the texts on Tantra)

male principle
swollen with reverence
desperately seeking the same light it had ignited within her.

SIX

Bryna awoke, bathed in sweat. She could not remember what she had been dreaming but she knew that it had not been pleasant.

"Are you all right in there?" It was Miss Lionel, knocking at her door. "It's after noon."

"Yes, I read most of the night."

"Ah, the Proust," Miss Lionel said outside the closed door. She sounded uncertain. "There was some sort of stain in the sink. It looked like blood . . ."

Bryna instinctively looked at her hands and then, pushing the covers back, quickly scanned her nude body. She noticed some bruises.

"I cut myself last night. Just a finger on the edge of some paper."

blood

"Ugh, one of those. Well, listen. This is my Sunday afternoon to answer phones at the crisis center. I'll be back around five. Can you manage?"

"Yes, thanks. Don't worry about me."

Bryna listened to the teacher's receding footsteps and then swung over onto the edge of the bed. She looked at and probed the black and blue marks on her arms and thighs. She noticed that both of her breasts were also very tender and that one of her nipples was swollen. When she stood up she ached all over. Bryna shook herself, trying to clear her head.

nick

She felt dizzy with the contradiction of her emotion. She felt simultaneously that she must see Nick at once and that she must never see him again. She tried to remember what had happened, but beyond the excursion into the girls' locker room she could recall nothing at all.

blood

Tony's face—a leer. The image presented itself so fleetingly she was not sure she had really seen it. She felt dizzy and sat back down on the edge of the bed for a few moments. Shortly her eyes focused on what seemed to be a piece of notepaper propped up against the mirror on the bureau. She got up and walked slowly, stiffly toward it. It was folded in half. She opened it with trembling hand and immediately recognized Sabra's handwriting, which in contrast to her own childish scrawl was beautifully confident and flowing. She read the note twice:

"Sabrina" was a great success, the belle of the ball, all eyes on her red with lust, green with envy. Nick handled per plan and gallant to the end. That's his blanket folded up at the foot of your bed. (All very innocent: dress had a little accident at the pizza parlor after the prom; Nick to the

rescue.) I'd be here to tell you all about it myself, but I need
a little rest, too. Wonderful evening.

Your servant,
Sabra

P.S.: "What does not kill me makes me stronger." —Nietzsche.
Try to keep things in *that* perspective.

Bryna stared at the blanket, unable to bring herself just yet to
touch it. She felt cold and went to the closet. The open-toed
heels were there on the floor where they had carelessly been
tossed. Bryna picked one of them up. It was badly scuffed and
there was dried mud and grass sticking to it. The wig was in a
heap in the back of the closet. The dress was nowhere to be
seen. Bryna even looked under the bed for it.
a little accident
Bryna looked at the blanket and immediately saw what appeared
to be an automobile in flames, eerily lighting an old graveyard.
She shook her head, dispelling the vision and, trembling, picked
up the folded blanket. She let it fall open. It was dark in color
but not so dark that a large spot near one edge was not visible.
Bryna looked at the spot closely. It seemed to be dried blood.
She dropped it and sat down on the edge of the bed, trying not
to think of anything at all.

Some minutes passed, until the chill recalled her and she
quickly dressed in some of her old things, padding herself as
usual. Her glance fell onto a college calculus workbook Miss
Lionel had given her after the teacher discovered that her charge
was getting perfect marks in Algebra II without ever opening her
textbook. Bryna sat at her window desk and rapidly dispatched
exercise after exercise, trying to crowd her mind with figures.

It was nearly three when she looked up abruptly. Too late.
Nick, unsmiling, had already seen her through the window. She
couldn't pretend not to be at home.

When she opened the door downstairs it seemed to her that
even though he appeared to be looking directly into her eyes he
was actually looking at her
shoes
This disturbed her, and she avoided his eyes as best she could.

"I'm sorry about last night," he said. "Can I come in?"

"I . . . I have some things I have to do."

"Are you mad at me?"

"No," Bryna said, looking up at him for a moment, not

97

wanting to hurt him. The moment their eyes made contact she saw it with sickening clarity: Nick pinned back in the graveyard up above the burning car, watching with shock and revulsion, watching the shoes on the otherwise bare legs, each shoe coming off in turn, saw it all in a stabbing sliver of a second. She looked around, past, through Nick, anywhere but at him, barely hearing his words through the babble in her head.

what rock did he find her under?

"Everything went crazy after you left..."

danny is such a bookworm

"Weurthmiller claims never to have heard of her.... She said he took you home. Did he?"

somebody said he came with bryna carr are you kidding i think it's disgusting

"Well, *did* he?"

"What? I... no, it wasn't Danny. I walked home."

"None of this makes any sense."

she doesn't have a thing on under that dress yeah ain't you glad

"...this chase up Pattee Canyon... Liz and some of the other girls smashed up... in the hospital...."

prove it meet me outside in ten minutes

"...I can't even tell you what they... I tried to help her, I mean when I still thought she wanted me to...."

you're all fucking crazy rape's a felony

"When you saw her, when you got sick, what did she say to you?"

this ain't no rape man

"Nothing... just that she'd give you the note."

"Are you okay now?"

she's all yours man the best for last

"I... I still don't feel so good."

Bryna suddenly saw her father's face, as tearful and devastated as it had been that day when he confronted Sharon with her infidelities that last, fatal time. Even worse than the inconsolable grief was the implacable righteousness that replaced it. In her vision she saw herself rushing toward him, limping badly.

it wasn't me it wasn't me i'm still your

Bryna hurried but her father, as if he were on some sort of invisible conveyor belt that reached into merciless infinity, receded backward from her faster and faster, finally becoming only a tiny black dot in the uncharted distance out of which emanated an icy sorrow through which her last dying words echoed hollowly:

little girl little girl little girl

"Is there anything I can do?" Nick asked.

Bryna looked into his eyes once more, unable to help herself, before she slammed the door.

i'll catch you later

Upstairs in her room, Bryna paced wildly about. She switched on the desk radio and turned the volume up painfully high. Rock music blared at her. She pressed her fists up against her temples for a few moments and then saw herself across the room, reflected in the bureau mirror. She walked toward it purposefully, her fists clenched. She stopped in front of the mirror and stared into it.

come out goddamn you come out show yourself

She waited for her features to soften, for her hair to fall golden about her shoulders, but only her own dark visage stared back at her, taunting. Her face contorted with rage. Her hand closed around a heavy cologne bottle. She pulled it back and smashed it against the mirror, hammering at it furiously, glass flying in all directions, her reflection scattering in fragments at her feet.

The radio switched off. Bryna whirled around, her face still twisted with rage, and stared at it. Its light was still glowing, but no sound issued from it, not for several seconds. Then, a voice came from it:

"Tune in again tomorrow, for another tumultuous episode. Will Bryna put the pieces back together again, will she finally learn how to stop overreacting?" A wickedly satirical peal of organ music pumped up out of the radio.

Bryna, recovering from her shock, took a threatening step toward the radio, still wielding the heavy bottle.

"Come any closer," a high, nasal voice shrilled, "and I'll spit feminine hygiene spray commercials all over you!"

Bryna stopped and looked around, trying to find something heavier to smash the radio with.

"What! Not even a little smile for Sabra?" the radio voice said. "I thought you were beginning to develop a sense of humor."

Bryna snatched a heavy, boot-shaped piece of driftwood Miss Lionel had found at Flathead Lake.

i'll kill you

"Honestly, this is going a little far, don't you think, Bryna?"

Bryna rushed toward the radio. As she was about to smash it with the driftwood the regular programming screamed at her. She held the heavy piece of wood over the radio for a few moments, trembling, then dropped it and angrily switched the radio off.

"You really *are* being silly."

99

Bryna whirled around again. This time the voice was coming from a stuffed, toy duck Bryna had found while cleaning the basement. Miss Lionel had sheepishly admitted that it had been hers as a child. Bryna had dusted it off and put it on the floor in the corner of her room. On the green carpet, beneath the summery wallpaper, the creature seemed right at home. Bryna liked its frazzled look, the daffy way its eyes pointed in different directions, the forlorn way its red little tongue stuck out. She had named it Albert. Bryna spoke to Albert sometimes, but he had never talked back.

Now he was not only speaking; he seemed to be mocking her, letting Sabra use him. Sabra's words rolled off the duck's tongue with a reedy quality.

"If you'll just settle down, we can discuss this rationally."

Bryna hurtled herself across the room, fell to her knees and began ripping at the duck with her bare hands.

"Awwwk! Awwwwwk!"

The thing struggled, hissed and squawked with pain. The stuffing, when it began to fly, looked like real down and feathers.

"Please! Please! You're killing me!" the tortured duck voice protested.

Bryna lunged for its neck with her teeth, biting and ripping. When she'd made a new hole there she yanked with her fingers, trying to open it up wider. Then she went at it again with her teeth, pulling with her fingers at the same time. The head began to rip away from the body, though it was still connected by threads and fibers that abruptly assumed the reality of exposed muscles, tendons and veins. The smell and taste of raw flesh filled Bryna's nose and mouth. She could taste and feel blood trickling down the corner of her mouth.

She leapt up and dropped the writhing, mutilated creature. Its pathetic legs churned the air, its eyes rolled and it sounded like a phonograph record that was grinding to a premature halt:

"Actions have consequences."

All movement ceased, but the eyes remained open, freezing their reproach. Bryna stood trembling over the dead thing, horrified.

"*Now* perhaps we can begin."

Bryna turned quickly around, at first feeling relief. The anger—realizing she had been tricked—returned quickly enough, though it was somewhat defused now. The voice now seemed to emanate from beneath and behind things, its position constantly changing. Bryna moved slowly toward it, picking things up, brushing things aside, hoping to surprise it, knowing that she could not, yet feeling the need to occupy herself, to move, to show some sign of resistance. But she listened.

"As you've seen, you can't kill something without making a mess. Killing me would leave you in a real mess, almost like killing yourself. As our late, departed Albert says, 'Actions have consequences.' Like the agreement we made so very long ago. That was an agreement you freely entered into, and quite wisely, if I may say so. Think back. You needed me as much as I needed you. Nothing has changed. Kill me and, at best, all you'll have left is something you fear more than death itself. That shuffling, vacant shell. I don't have to show you again, do I? No, I thought not. It's there in your mind, just a wink away."

The voice seemed now to come from up near the light fixture on the ceiling.

"Ours is a remarkable symbiosis."

Bryna felt a new surge of hostility rising in her.

i didn't want it, not what happened

"You did and you didn't. Be honest: you *did* want to get revenge on Liz and the others, to show them up; you did want to be admired and even desired. You've always wanted to be beautiful, to live up to Bryan's image of you. Now you've got that. But did you think it was all going to be free? What did you take me for? And don't tell me you bought that fairy godmother crap. No, of course not; deep down you *knew* that I wanted something, too, that I had to have something. What it was only becomes evident now. Agreements like this aren't made in a day; they're organic. I had to show you, convince you I could deliver before I could collect my first payment.

"And now that you know what it is that I require, you needn't feel any guilt, any shame. My desires and needs are not *your* desires and needs; we merely share the same body. I admit that for a while I hoped that we might be kindred spirits—that would have made it so much easier— hoped that I could bring out that capacity in you, that capacity for being . . . worshipped, lifted, energized . . . but you've already read about that. . . ."

the kundalini

"Yes, the *kundalini;* that's part of it. It is not my place to apprise you of the details; you will intuit many of them anyway. Suffice it to say that without the satisfaction of these needs you will harbor a mere shell. Indeed, without the sacred renewal of these energies through ritualized sexual union we will disintegrate together—a shell within a shell, for I will no longer have the power to give you the intuition you require to fulfill the rest of your dreams, the power, the fame, the fortune, the glamour

101

that will come to you. In due course, sooner than you think, the rich, the powerful, the glamorous will flock to you, a celebrity in your own right, a star guiding the stars.

"The body is the key. It must be beautiful, not only to fulfill your dreams, but also in order to provide me with a vehicle worthy of and capable of holding my devotees. The body is the transformer through which will arise the *siddhis*, about which you have also read, those supernatural powers that are the product of an aroused and healthy *kundalini*; those are the powers that will make the rest of your dreams come real. But you need know nothing of this process if it disturbs you; it's just a matter of logistics, to begin with, perhaps, a time-sharing schedule that . . ."

no

Bryna had listened to Sabra with interest and some measure of relief. But she did not want to be swept away too easily; she was still angry and she needed time to think, to sort things out.

"It's really so silly to waste any more time. I've bared my soul to you; what more . . . ?"

no! i'm not ready

"It'll be a cold day in hell when you are."

shut up goddamn it just shut up i have to think

Bryna waited. Moments reached into minutes. Nothing. Anger was displaced by a barely sensible apprehension as she busied herself sweeping up the shattered glass and the remains of the stuffed animal. She started out of the room with the bag of detritus, then stopped and went back to the closet. She picked up the shoes and threw them in the bag, then got the jewelry and what remained of the cosmetics and did the same. She hesitated a moment and then got the wig and stuffed it into the bag. She trembled as she carried it all downstairs to the garbage bin in the alley.

Bryna stopped exercising; she gained weight rapidly, eating whatever she liked. When she wasn't eating, she was thinking about eating. She no longer spoke up in class. She had trouble comprehending questions that were put to her. She saw little, felt less. Sabra was silent.

Miss Lionel was openly concerned. Bryna responded unenthusiastically to the announcement that she had been selected valedictorian. She made no apparent effort to prepare an address. She was equally unresponsive when Miss Lionel showed her the letter admitting her to UCLA in the fall, with financial assistance. What further alarmed Miss Lionel was the fact that the light no longer shone beneath Bryna's bedroom door far into the night. In fact, when the girl wasn't eating she seemed to be sleeping. Each night after dinner, forgetting or ignoring her household duties, such as doing the dishes, Bryna would heavily mount the steps to her room, absorbed in her own thoughts. At least Miss Lionel hoped that it was thought that Bryna was absorbed in; there was an increasingly vacant look about her.

Then, a week before graduation, Nick's mother died—of what was officially characterized an accidental drug overdose. It was generally assumed by those who knew her, however, that she had committed suicide. Bryna's class sent a card and flowers. Bryna noted the time and date of the funeral among the obituaries in the paper and waited outside Nick's house, just down the street, in the shadow of a tree. She was embarrassed and miserable but felt she had to be there. She waited a long time. Classes had already let out, and graduation was only three days away.

Finally a car pulled up in front of Nick's house. A man in a suit and a woman wearing a veil got out of the front seat. Bryna stepped deeper into the shadow. She could not hear the words, but the man seemed to be arguing with the woman. The back door of the car opened, and Nick, also in a dark suit, got out.

Bryna was immediately seized by his evident grief. The man and the woman went into the house. Nick, alone, stood motionless outside, staring at the lawn and flowers. Then he glanced down the block, past Bryna. She wanted to step out of the shadows but could not. Her heart pounded at the prospect of discovery, though discovery of what she was not sure. Nick went inside. Bryna lingered a few moments more, wanting to fill the chill emptiness he left behind, chastened by his grief.

what does not kill me makes me stronger

Bryna waited until Miss Lionel was asleep and then carried several of the books on Tantra up to her room. Bryna reread these books quickly, then slowly puzzled over certain passages. She read again of the sexual ritual that was supposed to impart certain supernatural powers, overwhelm restricting convention, and achieve the cosmic goal of "oneness." The ritual was said to be most potent if The Goddess assumed a wanton, prostitute-like attitude, giving herself to a series of male "worshippers" who celebrate life in the face of death. Thus, the ritual she read about, was described as occurring amidst corpses and flaming funeral pyres.

Bryna shuddered, recalling the cemetery and the burning car. But somehow she felt better than she had in days. If there was meaning and purpose, design,

ritual

if it had all been

necessary

then perhaps . . . She caught herself, again not wanting to be swayed too easily. The mystery and drama of Tantra fascinated her, but the fascination must always be—she groped in her thoughts for the proper word and found it:

academic.

"Kundalini rising," she read in *The Tantric Way*, "in the language of modern science, means the activation of vast dormant areas of the brain." The arousal of *kundalini*, which was further defined as the "coiled and dormant cosmic power" represented by the serpent, was said to give rise to various supernatural powers called *siddhis*. These included the ability to become infinitely small or large, to enter or leave the body at will and to possess supernormal sight and hearing, enabling one to see or hear into the thoughts and dreams of others, into the past and into the future. It was noted that the *siddhis* were only an incidental result of an aroused *kundalini*, that they were not always present and that they should never be regarded as ends in themselves, lest the Tantric aspirant lose sight of the real goal— cosmic oneness.

The *kundalini*, Bryna gathered, was the raw human fuel one needed to lift oneself into a higher state of consciousness. It could be mobilized, in part, through various meditative techniques, the repetition of mantras, special yogic breathing exercises and the like, but most effective of all was the *asana*, the ritual in which sex, the most basic fuel of all, was used to ignite the *kundalini*.

Enlightenment, in the Tantric vision, was to be obtained not through the denial of the senses, as so many theologies insisted, but through their fervid exploitation. The grosser the pleasure, in fact, the better, it seemed, for the idea was not only to abandon oneself to the physical and sexual matrices of creation but also, in so doing, to separate oneself from the narrow conventions of society, which create the illusion of petty individual identity and importance and thus are the real obstacles that stand between the seeker and his or her selflessness.

Bryna began to drift toward sleep, pondering the rift between the Tantric fundamentalists and the latter-day revisionists. Both schools, it seemed, prescribed marathon sexual rituals, sometimes with the use of drugs and alcohol, but the revisionists forbade the male to ejaculate in the female, and the female was forbidden to experience orgasm in the normal sense. Instead, complicated and seemingly supernatural techniques were described whereby both the male and female sexual climaxes could be turned inward for further self-illumination. The other, apparently older, school detected in this a crypto-puritanism that it scorned.

One modern-day interpreter of the fundamental school insisted that in *asana*, the body was meant to be "pumped like a laser" for as long as possible, building up sexual tension and energy—energy which was then to be released, at the last possible moment, "in a blinding shot." Another traditionalist spoke of the "male seed... ultimately" being "ejaculated into the woman's responding yoni, as if it were an offering of sacred oil being poured into an altar fire."

Sabra, Bryna had no doubt, was a fundamentalist.

The banner emblazoned across the back of the stage, just above the risers, on which was proudly perched the Central High Class of '73, proclaimed:

NE QUID NIMIS

And under it, the translation:

"Not Anything in Excess"

Such was the motto that had been foisted upon the class by the graduation committee, whose adviser was, as usual, Miss Sullivan, the Latin teacher.

The band, in the orchestra pit beneath the stage, had already done its opening numbers: "The Star Spangled Banner," the school song and then the processional march that had carried the graduating class, shuffling like an army of automatons, from the back of the auditorium down the aisle between several hundred parents and spectators, through the forest of flowers and up the steps onto the stage where each member took his or her preappointed place on the risers behind the podium, between the flag, on the one hand, and the commencement dignitaries, spread across five folding chairs, on the other.

These dignitaries were the Reverend Father McClatchy, who had given the invocation; Mr. Ramsey, the superintendent; Mr. Clifford, the principal; and Bradley ("Big Bill") Bromholm, lieutenant governor of the state, and Mrs. Bromholm. The lieutenant governor was the commencement speaker. He was currently popular among many of the voters for his hard-line anticrime stance and, in particular, for his recent statement, widely reported in the press, that "drug pushers should not be prosecuted, they should be executed."

Bryna was seated on the lowest riser, directly behind the speaker's ample backside. Her golden valedictory tassle contrasted with the dark blue of the others. The speaker boasted that "ours are the most privileged, richest, smartest, best-fed, best-dressed, best-educated, best-looking bunch of kids anywhere in the world."

The speaker won himself tumultuous applause time and again—both by scaling the platitudinous peaks of national pride and by descending into the deep valleys where he warned of moral, social and economic decay. Bryna's head was swimming. Soon there were only the diplomas to be handed out, and then she, left alone on the stage with the dignitaries, was to rise and give the valedictory address. Miss Sullivan had supplied her with a number of "helpful hints," such as "keep it short and upbeat, remember the ones who aren't smart enough to go to college, and smile, smile, smile." She had also given her a tattered copy of *Famous Valedictory Addresses*, copyrighted *circa* 1930, and a selection of "appropriate" Latin phrases "to dress it up a bit." Bryna had stayed up the whole night struggling with it. The best she had been able to come up with was a scrawled two-page pastiche of

drivel

lifted from the musty Sullivan source materials.

As names were called by the principal, students filed off the risers and down past the podium where the superintendent handed out the diplomas, spread out on a small table. Each student then left the stage and took a reserved seat in the front of the auditorium. Bryna knew that she was to receive her diploma last, give her address and then go down the steps off the stage and continue down the aisle, the others falling in behind her for the recessional march out of the building.

"All very dignified," as Miss Sullivan had put it.

As the ranks dwindled around her, Bryna began to doubt that she could even get to her feet in a dignified manner, let alone actually deliver the pompous speech she had pasted together in an apparent fog. Her thinking processes seemed only now to be reawakening, after a prolonged sleep, or something almost like sleep. Only now was she sensible enough to feel the full force of the panic that was building in her.

106

She tried desperately to recall the short speech she literally had tucked away up the sleeve of her graduation gown. It would be better to say something, no matter how inane, than nothing at all.

. . . and so as some of us prepare to matriculate in colleges and universities all across the land, others, more eager to thrust themselves into the body politic, intend to put their inner resources into more practical and immediately rewarding places . . .

Bryna could not imagine herself uttering these words.

. . . the boys and the girls, tomorrow, the men and the women, your sons and your daughters, plunging in, at once wise and naive, with eyes open and hearts on their sleeves . . .

As the last row filed past her, Bryna felt as if someone had stuffed cotton in her mouth.

semper paratus. always prepared

No, what she had prepared was just too awful. And so, she reflected, was she. Since going off her diet she had gained back twenty pounds, her face was broken out, her hair had never been oilier and she had a big cold sore, getting bigger by the second, blooming out of the corner of her mouth.

i can't do it i can't, please help me

Suddenly, it was as if someone had just turned on the sound. The *buzz*, the background noise was back. Voices, thoughts, rose up out of the din. Bryna could feel Miss Lionel's pride swelling somewhere out there, about fifteen rows back from the front, but of course Miss Lionel could not see her face at that moment. The principal, glancing back at her, nodding encouragement, as the last few came forward for their diplomas, could. And he obviously read her discomfort. The lieutenant governor's wife was looking at her, too, her face a mask of smiles, behind which:

my god such a fat little thing and scared to death, too. bill's a hard act to follow.

Bryna had no time to ponder the return of the voices. She heard the principal call her name, and everyone on the stage turned to look at her.

please, please help me

"Oh, sure, *now* you want me. What am I supposed to say to these assholes?"

Bryna was on her feet, trying to move forward. Her tongue seemed to fill her mouth, and the limp was back with a vengeance. The dignitaries, all of them, appeared to be smirking.

say whatever you want

Bryna stumbled and fell toward the podium, gasping for breath in the blue silence.

Sabra caught herself on the podium, much to the principal's relief, though her curse, "tripped on the bloody gown," carried weakly over the P.A. system. There was light laughter. Sabra received the diploma from the superintendent and, taking her place behind the podium, surveyed first the dignitaries and then the assembled.

"Well," she said, smiling faintly, "this is an unexpected honor." The crowd looked blankly back at her, only a tiny current of unease troubling the air. "Let's see. Oh, yes, first a few jokes to break the ice." She paused, then theatrically lifted her arm and pulled out the scrawled notes, producing some scattered, nervous laughter. "I just happen to have a few on me." She glanced briefly down at Miss Sullivan, who was scowling. Sabra turned the notes in all directions, as if having difficulty making out her own writing.

"Oh, I think I found one," she said, pretending to read: "What's blue and has wheels?" She waited for a moment, then, exhibiting bogus puzzlement, looked back at the paper, turning it in search of the answer. She squinted, pretending again to read: "The sky. I lied about the wheels." The laughter, more general, halted when she added: "That pretty well sums up what we learn in high school, doesn't it?" She felt the dignitaries stiffen. A low murmur rose up from the assembled.

"Here's another one. How do they separate the men from the boys in North Dakota?" Once more she played her game, pretending to have difficulty finding the answer amongst the notes. "Ah, here it is: with a bucket of cold water."

The principal flinched. Arlene Buckholtz, one of the graduating seniors, unleashed her shrill, slightly hysterical laugh, famous in movie theaters all over town. People generally laughed louder at Arlene's laugh than at the situations that occasioned it. But now there was more murmur than mirth in the crowd. Sabra could hear the principal whispering to the superintendent.

"Just one more," she said, wasting no time. "How come birds fly upside down over Missoula?" She turned the notepaper, ostensibly to read the answer: "Because it's not worth a shit." She presented a poker face and shrugged apologetically.

Arlene Buckholtz did her number again, totally out of control now. The sound was lost in a sea of gasps. Mrs. Bromholm reddened, Father McClatchy glowered at her, and Mr. Ramsey rose from his chair and took a step toward the podium.

"Hold it, class," Sabra said, holding up a be-patient hand. "The super wants something." She put her hand over the microphone so the audience wouldn't hear the man's voice, then turned to look at Mr. Ramsey.

"All right, Bryna," he said, trying to control himself, "why don't you just step off stage, just step back behind the curtain"— he gestured with his thumb—"and everything will be all right. We'll just . . ."

Sabra held up her hand to silence him and leaned into the microphone to address the audience. "It seems the super wants to be excused for a few minutes, but I'm afraid he'll just have to tie a knot in it and wait until recess like the rest of us."

Arlene let it rip, louder than ever this time. A number of people, families and older couples, got up and started to leave. A portly man, shepherding his wife and two children out of the auditorium, paused to look back at the stage, indignantly.

"If this is what our tax dollars are contributing to," he shouted, "there's going to be some changes in the next legislature." Others, getting to their feet, applauded.

Sabra shouted over the noise, through the microphone: "As Einstein said: 'Great spirits have always encountered violent opposition from mediocre minds.'"

At that, the superintendent started quickly toward the podium. The principal, too, jumped to his feet.

"Hold it right there!" Sabra commanded, turning to face Mr. Ramsey. "Take one more step and I'll be forced to tell all these nice people just what it was you *really* were doing at 9:30 last Friday night, when you told your wife you were at the office working on the budget. Where is your wife, anyway?" She scanned the audience quickly. "Oh, yes, I see her out there, such a lovely lady when she isn't soused, but then who can blame her? She's always alone. You work on that budget much more and you just might get it pregnant."

The superintendent swallowed hard, hesitated and then turned abruptly and left the stage. The crowd appeared stunned. Only the man who had spoken out a moment earlier continued to leave, ushering his family out with him.

"You with the stuffed shirt!" Sabra shouted after him. "When you get home you horny hypocrite, be sure to show your wife the interesting pictures you keep hidden down in that nifty little wine cellar you're so proud of. Show her those magazines, too. I'm sure she'll find the one called *Lolita in Chains* most illuminating."

The man reddened; his wife looked at him incredulously. Sabra could hear clearly enough her shocked whisper:

how does she know we have a wine cellar?

Other questions, Sabra knew, would follow. Meanwhile, Father McClatchy had just crossed himself and was now muttering Latin, as he rose to leave, hurrying after the politician and his wife.

"Oh, for Christsake," she groaned. "Look at that will you. I'm surprised he hasn't dropped to his knees, but I guess they're pretty sore. He spends so much time down there in front of his altar . . . boys."

Father McClatchy's eyes opened wide. He stared at Sabra for a moment with apparent fear, then got to his feet and hurried after the politician and his wife, who were making a rapid exit.

"There goes Church and State," Sabra quipped. "Look at them run. I guess Big Bill's afraid that if he stays around any longer something else might slip out—like some of those illegal campaign funds he's been laundering through that dummy corporation called Canines Unlimited."

The principal, who had also been about to make his retreat, now sank back into his seat, carefully avoiding eye contact with the valedictorian. Others, who were standing in the audience, were uncertain what to do, fearful that if they tried to leave they, too, would be singled out. Sabra scanned the faces of the malcontents, ready to pounce. A photographer from the local newspaper, who had come prepared to sleep through another boring commencement exercise, was frantically snapping pictures of all the activity, looking, by the expression on his face, as if he thought he'd died and gone to heaven.

Just then Mr. Ramsey and Miss Sullivan scrambled to the orchestra pit, and a moment later the recessional march commenced. Miss Sullivan then turned to the graduating class, herding them wildly into the aisle. The band was playing much too loud and much too fast. Everyone was out of step.

Sabra shouted into the microphone, reading Bryna's stilted prose. Then, halfway through, she crumpled up the notes, tossed them over her shoulder and, with a satisfied curl of her lips, started down the steps of the stage to take up the rear. As she made her way down the aisle, she turned her head only once, to give Miss Lionel, whose smile of disbelief now appeared permanent-pressed on her face, the thumbs-up sign.

Outside, on the grass, some of the kids stared at Sabra with fear, envy, awe and disgust, in various combinations; some were simply bewildered, unable to figure out what had happened. Still others, however, milled around her, whooping and shouting, thrilled by her performance, demanding she tell them how she

110

knew the things she had disclosed with such apparent accuracy. Even one of the local newspaper reporters chased her outside, pen and notepad in hand.

"Is Canines Unlimited for real?" the reporter asked.

"Check it out for yourself. It's in Helena," she said.

The reporter shook his head, as if he couldn't believe any of this, yet could not afford to ignore it, either.

"That's all I have to say. Nick, will you give me a ride home?"

The kids squeezed up against the car. Sabra smiled and waved as they pulled cautiously out of the parking lot. As they drove toward Miss Lionel's, Nick kept glancing over at Sabra, a I-don't-believe-this-is-happening smile on his face.

"I think I'm dreaming," he said. Sabra knew that he was struggling to place her voice, so much fuller, stronger and more confident than Bryna's.

"I care very much for you," Sabra said, putting her hand on his for a moment. "I'm leaving for Los Angeles in a few days. I want you to come with me."

He looked into her eyes; it had to be a joke, and yet he knew she meant it.

"I need you, Nick," she said matter of factly. "You're a part of my plan."

"Los Angeles? What would we . . . what would *I* do?"

"We'll both go to school."

Nick shook his head, laughing a little. No matter how preposterous the whole thing seemed, he realized suddenly that he would do anything she suggested. There was nothing to keep him here—not anymore.

"How do we live?" he asked. "I mean, I heard about your scholarship but . . ."

"You'll work for me."

"So what are you going to do—give famous valedictory addresses?"

They both laughed.

"No," she said. "I'm going to be a psychic, and we're going to get very rich."

Nick pulled up in front of Miss Lionel's house, asking a thousand questions about what had happened.

"Look," Sabra said, "I'm really tired after all the excitement. Let's talk over the details tomorrow."

They looked at each other for a moment. This time Nick put his hand on Sabra's. "That was really one far-out performance, Bryna." For the first time in days he had forgotten about his mother.

Sabra squeezed his hand, leaned over, kissed him lightly on the lips and got out of the car, saying, "I'll catch you later."

The words echoed through Nick's mind. He sat there alone for several minutes, staring at the house, numb with discovery.

Bryna had only to look into Miss Lionel's eyes to know what had happened; Sabra, in any event, had already told her. Miss Lionel could only shake her head for the longest time, saying things like: "I don't know whether I should laugh or cry." Thinking things like:

there's no accounting for genius but good lord!

"The looks on their faces, Bryna! It was..." Miss Lionel chuckled, then turned serious. "Bryna, what you have is a... a special gift. I mean I can only assume by the guilt that was written all over their faces that what you said was true. They'd have taken your diploma away otherwise. A gift like this, Bryna, it's something you have to use in a... a very careful way. It's obvious that you've been bottling things up for a very long time and today... today the dam broke. Now you've got to learn to channel your emotions, your insights in a more constructive way. You've got to..."

Bryna managed easily enough to look contrite during Miss Lionel's kindly lecture; she *felt* contrite. She also sensed that Miss Lionel was more thrilled than angry or upset. At length, the teacher spoke of the "enormous opportunities" there would be in Los Angeles "to explore and develop your psychic talents, with the proper guidance." Miss Lionel said that her cousin, the UCLA professor, would be eager to help. "He's so open to things like this."

Suddenly Miss Lionel stopped talking and looked at Bryna with something akin to shock.

"You... you can tell exactly what I'm thinking at any given time, can't you?"

Bryna looked down, feeling the teacher's discomfort, her first little inner tremble of fear.

"What number am I thinking of?"

nine four no three three

"Three. And before that nine and four."

Bryna felt the teacher's chill, her nakedness.

"Bryna! That's incredible!"

"I can't tell everything," Bryna said, still looking away. "I have to see the person or..."

"Now what number am I thinking of?"

And so on. Bryna passively played the game for several

112

minutes while her mind reached deeper, deeper down into the teacher's thoughts, to where thoughts, not yet formed, were assembled, to where Miss Lionel was preparing to think

it will be better when she's out of here.

Bryna felt sad.

i want to be normal

"You want beauty, money, power, respect. 'Normal' is mediocre."

Bryna, in bed, stared into the darkness.

i don't want a voice rattling around in my head all the time—ever. i don't want to have to worry about "seeing" things or "hearing" things other people don't see and hear. i can't live like that. and i don't want . . . i don't want to see or hear you, either

"But you still want everything I can give you."

Bryna could not help herself.

yes

Sabra sighed. "It would be nice if, just once, one of your kind could enter into an honest relationship with one of my kind, without all the guilt, fear, loathing, hocus pocus and subterfuge. But, what the hell . . . I think we can work something out so that you can have your cake and eat it, too. You can go into one of those dumb trances everyone expects of people who have 'spirit guides.' That's the only time I'll come through; you won't even have to hear me. You can use automatic writing—that's an old favorite—or someone, Nick perhaps, can take down what I say. You'll just be the vehicle. You needn't take any responsibility for what I say, at all. It's dumb, but it's good theater; it ought to be good for business."

how will i go into this trance?

"That's simple. You already know how. But we'll work something out that will look dramatic."

and you won't ever bother me again?

"Bother! You have a lot to learn about gratitude. But, no, I won't *bother* you as long as you live up to your end of the bargain and take care of the body."

what do you mean?

"Well, naturally, if you stuff yourself the way you have the last couple weeks, quit exercising and let the body go to hell, you're going to hear from me. The body has to be kept in top form."

how often do you want the . . . the body, and how do i know you won't hurt me . . . it?

"We'll work out a schedule that will be convenient for both of us; I can be reasonable. The schedule will change as circumstances warrant, but bear in mind that you benefit, as well, from my use of the body. I have to keep the batteries charged if you want to be a psychic. As for any harm that will come to the body, naturally, it would be counterproductive for me to intentionally harm it in any way; it's the only body I have, too. Anyway, you'll be in an excellent position to monitor things. If you're dissatisfied at any point, you can always keep the keys, so to speak."

what if somebody finds out that you and i are the same . . . i mean that we share the same body?

"Well, I'll just have to see to it that they don't, won't I? I'll expect to be held accountable for any indiscretion that would—how should I put it?—give you away."

we aren't the same

"We know that, of course, but others aren't going to be quite as perceptive, are they? No, I'm going to have to be careful and I will be. Of course, you're going to have to cooperate, and you're going to have to realize that I'm a person, too; I have my rights and I have to have a life of my own, particularly since you're cutting me out of yours. I'm not one of those silly ghosts who are content to hang around in two-story houses going bump in the night, conjuring up gobs of green goo, attracting flies, persuading pubescent girls to masturbate with crosses and bark like dogs. Neither am I content to become one of those armchair gasbags who spout nonsense about Atlantis, the soul, the gods, reincarnation elves, angels, peyote and all that other dreary drivel. You aren't the only one who's graduated.

"And in addition to whatever time is routinely allotted me I'll expect an occasional weekend, an annual vacation, a budget for clothes and other necessities, a salary, a medical plan, a percentage of the take, all of this subject to renegotiation as our income grows. In the beginning, as far as privacy goes, I won't demand much more than my own closet; later I'll want my own room, eventually my own quarters. And why not? You'll have no less."

Bryna drifted. She wasn't sure whether she dreamed or merely imagined the big house with all of the strange-looking artifacts. She could see herself meditating, waiting for something or somebody in a darkened room. In another part of the house, which was very handsome indeed, she could see Nick—only now she called him "Niko"—greeting a beautiful, glamorously dressed woman, obviously anxious to see her. But the lavishly appointed room into which Niko ushered the woman—Bryna recognized her now as a famous film actress—was *full* of beautiful, glamorously dressed people, *all* obviously anxious to see her.

Bryna thought how striking Niko looked in the expensive Italian suit she had just bought him.

After awhile, Bryna heard Sabra's voice again, though it was softer now, intimate. She wondered if she had been talking all along.

"Of course, both of us must guard against those who would monopolize the body. Marriage, in that respect, is risky; pregnancy could put us in real peril, as well—a nasty business, anyway. And what you mortals call Love, with a capital L, well, I don't think I have to tell you, Love is fatal."

Bryna slept soundly.

Part Two

LIFE (AND LOVE)

ONE

He was almost fifty but he still had the body of a boy. He was particularly mindful of that just now. He looked at his bare skin in the full-length mirror. The lights that mushroomed along its chrome periphery—like those around a makeup mirror—amused him, only these were of the soft pink, almost peach, slice of the spectrum favored by those for whom no scalpel or chemical blush could ever utterly reverse what his mother had been fond of calling the "raptures of time." These were not the white-hot lights he braved, indeed, *insisted* upon in dressing rooms around the world.

As he stood naked before the mirror, now only remotely stimulated by the other set of eyes that recorded his image, eyes that were at once deceived and, he had no doubt, deceiving, he noted with satisfaction that the lights' cosmetic glow could add nothing to the now permanent tan he had accumulated, curried and ultimately hoarded across nearly four decades of public life.

He glanced only briefly at his face, its features familiar to millions but obscured now by the expertly crafted black wig and the black beard. Only the eyes, slate-blue as alpine water, and the teeth—"Mormon teeth," one reviewer had called them—were his own.

"Hey, Joe," the boy said, sensing the man's moodshift, his voice still cocked for sex, "you got any more smokes?"

His name was not Joe, but many of them called him that, not out of naïveté but with a playful cynicism reserved for Americans. The man turned and surveyed the boy's face, realizing suddenly that the "boy," though he looked sixteen, was probably in his twenties and perhaps had a wife and children. Many of them did. The boy's naked insouciance in these circumstances bespoke a power, a distance, that engaged the man's imagination, frightened and challenged him somehow. He felt a rush of energy, the fuel he needed to possess and control the boy, if only for a few more moments, to reassure himself that everything that mattered about the boy was present here, in this room, now, *his*.

The man was asleep when the phone rang. At first he thought that it was the boy and he was annoyed, but then he recalled that he had not given the boy—nor any of the others he had met at the bars—the last name under which he was registered at the hotel. But if it wasn't one of them, he asked himself, who could it be? He had taken elaborate precautions as always. No one, not even his personal manager, had any idea where he was; he had always insisted on privacy, the right to get away from time to time, to "return to anonymity," as he put it. His wife, Julie, and the family had always accepted this unquestionably; so, of course, had their retainers. There were directors who complained occasionally, but never too loudly where so bankable a talent was in the balance.

The man looked at his watch. It couldn't be room service, either. Not at this hour. It had to be a wrong number. He lifted the receiver peevishly.

"Mr. Landers? Sorry, sir, to disturb you at this hour, but it's long distance. They say it's urgent."

Shock and fear made the man's nostrils flare. He had registered in the hotel under the name Nathan Landers, one of several he used on such trips, each with convincing passports and other I.D. to support it. Was it possible that there was another Landers registered at the hotel? Yes, that must be it, he thought, certain he had made no slips; still, his heart pounded fiercely.

"I think there's been a mistake," he said.

"No mistake," a long-distance voice cut in. "Thank you, operator; this is the party I want to talk to."

"Go ahead, Los Angeles," the operator said, ringing off.

"So, Jimmy," the voice from Los Angeles said evenly, "was the kid a good fuck?"

James Raymond slumped to the bed, still holding the phone to his ear, unable to respond. There was *no way*, he kept telling himself. No way at all the boy could have found out. He always took care to travel with only one set of identification, in this case that of Nathan Landers, a name in no way connected to his own. And the disguise, the disguises had never failed him. The closest to failing they'd ever come was that time he'd picked up some rough trade on Market Street in San Francisco and the kid had said to him that if he'd bleach his hair he might look "a little" like James Raymond. But that had been years ago, and this was safe, faraway Bangkok, not risky San Francisco.

"Your secret is safe with us," the voice said in a tone that was intended to soothe. "We're in the business of keeping secrets. Of course, like every worthwhile business, we operate on the profit principle. . . ."

120

It was a woman's voice, these merciless modulations, a voice, his experience as an actor told him, that was expertly disguised.

Marissa Salomon was furious. George, her producer-husband, had promised her the lead in his new TV docudrama, a role she could finally sink her teeth into. Instead he had given it to a British actress, a woman twice her age who had made her mark on Broadway years before, the type they called a "serious actress." Marissa was sick of playing what *she* and the tabloids called "jiggle queen" roles. She had appeared in several movies and now even "starred" in her own TV series. She was top box office, but she was still, she reflected bitterly, "all boobs and no brains," the butt of endless jokes. Sometimes, after she'd had too much to drink, she saw herself as a tragic figure, another Jayne Mansfield, another Marilyn.

George had sworn up and down that he had fought for her for the part but that the "money men" wouldn't go for her. Marissa had another drink and hated herself for hating George; she knew how hard he had worked for her, how much faith he had in her, but, dammit, faith wasn't going to be enough. She still felt he'd let her down. She'd tried so hard with the acting lessons he'd paid for, she'd tried so hard to be a good wife to him, even though he was twenty years older than she, to be a good mother to the two children. . . . She was crying now in the gloom of her Pajaro Dunes beach house. *Her* house. She had paid for it with her own money. A place to get away, to be alone.

After the blowup over the role, the bitter words, she had driven here, fast, recklessly even, in her baby blue Rolls. She pulled the blinds, fighting back the tears, expecting to see a magnificent sunset over the Pacific. But even that was over now, and she felt cheated again. As often happened when she was in one of these states, her hands began to explore her body, compulsively seeking reconfirmation of her beauty. And she *was* beautiful. Exceptionally so. "A perfect twenty," a writer had quipped, explaining: "ten on each side."

Marissa undressed quickly, her hands caressing her breasts, belly and thighs with growing intensity. She stared out the window at the ocean, at the frothy lips of the surf breaking in the shallows, glowing white in the near darkness. As she reached orgasm she felt some of the bitterness and frustration subside. She shut her eyes and felt her heart pounding in her ears, in sync, she imagined, with the surf. She did not hear the door open behind her. She slid open the glass door in front of her and, catching the sea breeze, which seemed to her suddenly so real, so *pure,* so much of what life was really about, she was seized for a moment by the impulse to run headlong, naked, across the sand and into the surf, there to swim far, far out into the sea.

It was a boozy, romantic impulse that died the moment her feet touched the sand. She had expected it to be still warm from the sun but it was already cold and somehow hostile. She shivered a little and turned to go back in. The only light in the house was coming from the hall, just enough to tell Marissa that something was changed in the large living room where she had been drinking the past half hour. The first little shock of fear resonated along her lower jaw, and her teeth would have chattered had she not tensed the muscles in her face. There was something—somebody—cooly surveying her from the couch.

At first, paralyzed by terror, the actress could only think: *this is wrong; there shouldn't be anyone there.* But as her eyes focused on the man—she could now see his moustache and the hair on his nude chest—she realized there was something that went beyond merely "wrong." The man was unreal somehow and thus all the more horrifying. His head and facial features were bulbous, his moustache and chest hair painted on. She stepped closer, unable to help herself, hanging on the hope that if she could only turn on a light everything would be all right again.

Another step and she saw the rest of him—of *it*—the hideous caricature of the male organ, pointing at her like an accusation. Trembling, she leaned over, intending to turn on one of the lights at the end of the couch when she heard the sliding door close behind her. She felt as if she were drowning as she wheeled around. Her scream died as quickly as the knife entered her heart.

A few days after James Raymond returned to Taos to inform his family that, on advice of his principal accountant, he would quietly give his five thousand acre ranch there, complete with its own golf course, chair-lift equipped skiing mountain, two hundred head of prize cattle, forty thoroughbred horses and twenty-four room, solar-heated adobe casa "to a charitable organization for tax purposes," Bryna Carr, standing at her study window, was regarding the Golden Gate Bridge with a proprietary air.

The dead vine surrounding the window did not disturb Bryna. Its woody skeleton, which still clung in tenacious and abundant patches to the northern, windswept wall of the massive stone Seacliff mansion, imparted to the house, Bryna had long since decided, an insulating eminence that was decidedly superior to any quantity of mutable green matter. Niko, of course, disagreed; he called it a "vampire vine," a parasite which, having leeched the house of its life blood, had finally starved itself—or nearly so. Bryna had no doubt that Niko envisioned the vine's furthest metastases gradually insinuating their way through some accommodating and now complicit chink in the old manse's armor, penetrating the interior, their hooks moistening and swelling, sharpening, pulsing messages to the awakening rear-guard, keening with hunger.

Bryna shook herself impatiently, aware that she was once again confusing her own imaginings with those of another. "Projection—you're a master of it," Dr. Hevesey, her psychiatrist often told her. "It's an especially onerous burden for a psychic," the doctor would continue. "When you 'read' a person you're always fearful that perhaps *you* wrote the book, that you predestine through the power of suggestion as much as you precognize, that you people the psychic landscape with your own bogeymen, give them life in the lives of others—where they oughtn't to be."

Bryna stopped herself again, before she could put more words in her psychiatrist's mouth, not that Naomi Hevesey hadn't said *some* of that. Her thoughts returned to the house. Niko disliked it simply because he thought it overly grand, sterile, unfriendly. Bryna, at times, felt the same way, but she was not about to abandon the place. In fact, she had no intention of *ever* giving it up. Apart from the fact, by no means insignificant to her, that it was an excellent investment, a standout even in an assemblage of extraordinary homes, coveted not only for its size and somber grandeur but also for its enviable perch on the very precipice of Seacliff, the house, through her possession of it, anchored her, provided a sense of place such as she had never enjoyed before.

Even as Bryna reflected on Niko's disapproval of the house, she felt a sudden surge of warmth for her friend. She knew that Niko ultimately forgave her all her "excesses," as he called them, recognizing as he did that she was merely trying to compensate for her underprivileged childhood—all those years after the fire that killed her mother, her stepfather and stepbrothers, all those times she could now scarcely bring herself to speak of, those years with her grandmother, the religious school and the foster homes. There was not a day that Bryna did not feel the deprivation of those bygone times; her response, all too often she knew, was to try to dispel the depression and fear those memories birthed by *buying* something.

She remembered how appalled Niko had been when, with her first burst of success as a psychic, she had rushed out and purchased an enormous freezer—big enough for a grand hotel—and filled it to overflowing with the finest cuts of meat and the plumpest fowl far more than she, particularly with her strict diet, could ever consume before it would freezer-burn and have to be thrown out. Niko's shock had passed into concern and sadness when he realized she needed all that food not to feed herself but to feel safe and secure. He had almost cried for her, she remembered, when she told him the story of the chicken carcasses she used to keep under her bed at the Borchers'. Then one day they loaded up the car with frozen meat and drove through the skid-row district handing out frozen imported pheasant and forty-dollar roasts to startled derelicts, laughing together over Bryna's folly like two schoolchildren.

Bryna stood a few moments longer at the window surveying the surging green waters of the bay and, beyond them, the Marin headlands, Pt. Bolinas and, ethereally outlined in the distant north, Pt. Reyes. To the east was the lush crescent of Baker's beach, where Niko sometimes jogged. To the west were the vertiginous cliffs and windsculpted wilds of Land's End, where lovers of all persuasions, most of them strangers meeting one another there for the first and last time, cruised one another, it seemed to Bryna, like tumid sharks, making pass after pass in the relatively open areas until the right elements, a mystery of phosphorescence and pheromones she supposed, conspired to pair them for quick and furtive, but often observed, release in the shadows. Occasionally, the release was of another quality and more lasting. Neither murder nor suicide was a stranger to Land's End.

Above all this, but hidden from Bryna's present view, was the cooly surreal Palace of the Legion of Honor. Below, far below, was the surf, crashing upon rocks the size of locomotives. And beyond all was the Pacific Ocean, cold and deep here, shark-infested, stirred by powerful, deceiving currents and killing riptides, generating sudden, impenetrable fogs. This was no place for father-knows-best cottages. The house, *her* house, fit squarely here, reflecting its surroundings—arrogant, cold, violent. Bryna had taken the responsibility of decorating and furnishing the interior of the house with great seriousness, determined to err, if at all, on the side of darkness.

Finished, the house looked something like a museum, though a highly specialized one, devoted entirely to the artifacts of Tantrism. Here, at last, Bryna found a use for the subject she had studied at UCLA with so many mixed emotions—anthropology. It wasn't that this particular subject bored her—they *all*, at least singly, failed to satisfy her. Concentrating on one subject, she feared she was missing out on all others. She changed majors so many times that she was in peril of completing none.

She had hoped to find herself in one subject or another, to be able finally to say: "Philosophy is my passion;" "I live for music;" or "My life would be meaningless without mathematics." She envied to the extent of experiencing physical pain those who could convincingly profess to joy in the pursuit of particular knowledge. The study of Tantrism did provide some partial solace, however at odds this study might seem to those who detected in her a peculiar emotional vacuum that nothing seemed capable of filling.

That Bryna Carr should be fascinated by the occult sensuality of an ancient religious philosophy that had trendy and, to some, bizarre manifestations in the present age seemed to those few who knew her well, but perhaps not well enough, odd. The public, treated to generally unrevealing interviews with her and descriptions of her house was equally puzzled—and titillated. To some extent, Bryna's fascination with Tantrism insulated her against the gossip that she was—sexually—a very cold fish. Except that, as those who paid close attention noted, it was Sabra, not Bryna, who was truly interested in Tantra, or so Bryna said in the few passing references she ever made, publicly, about her "spirit guide." Bryna's interest in Tantrism was thus presented as something "academic."

She had been guided in her study of Tantrism by Nestor Bagehot, a professor of anthropology at UCLA and a self-acknowledged master of the occult. Leaving the window, Bryna glanced at the small photo of Nestor and herself that she kept on her desk. Niko had taken it the day she—and Niko, too, for that matter—had graduated from college, four years earlier. The photo was small, but there was nothing small about Nestor Bagehot. He was of average height but, as he put it himself, of "heroic girth." He carried his solid weight well, however, under a mane of graying, wiry hair and a fierce, still black beard. His dark, penetrating eyes were set under a prominent, aggressive brow that sprouted a belligerent-looking wart just above his left eye, the same eye that seemed always to be open just perceptibly wider than its mate.

At fifty-five, Nestor Bagehot still had a reputation for bedding his most beautiful students. Highly cerebral as well as overtly physical, his was a charisma that few could resist, either in the bedroom or the academic boardroom. He generally had his way. Bryna knew that he found her beautiful. He had told her so quite

125

bluntly not long after they first met, adding even that he would have "ravished" her "ceaselessly" had she evinced even the slightest desire for him. She remembered still the touch of his lips upon her forehead the day he told her this. It was the only way he would ever permit himself to kiss her, given her reserve. Had she had it in her power to return the passion he professed for her she would have given all to command its presence. But beyond that one declaration he never pressed or pursued her, confiding, "There are places even I know not to tread."

It was Nestor who had accompanied her to India and Nepal in search of the Tantric art that now distinguished the interior of the house, "punctuating it with terror," one reporter had written. Representations of the Tantric "dual goddess"—known both as Sakti, goddess of creation and bliss, and as Kali, the black one, holding the severed heads and genitalia of her victims, all of them male—abounded, some in oil, some in metal and stone. Serpents coiled around phallic-shaped stones, mushrooms and swords, representing the power of *Kundalini* rising, of ascendant psychic and sexual powers, sprang up everywhere, as did couples, trios and groups locked in all manner and mode of ritual sexual intercourse. In immortal slabs of stone and metal the female genitalia, spread open as in "prehistoric *Penthouse* centerfolds," to borrow another reporter's vivid description, were graphically tendered, offered up as the "ultimate ground of reverence."

Of all her pieces, Bryna most prized an eight-foot-tall bronze sculpture depicting the goddess as "the Void." This piece was situated in the corridor that ran the length of the uppermost floor of the mansion, set in a carefully lighted recess halfway down its length, accorded all the sanctity of an altar, one which was dramatically visible from the bottom of the wide stairs that led up to it from the second floor of the house.

The priceless piece was strikingly anthropomorphic—a tall reflecting glass to which were attached arms, legs, even ears. The mirror-being appeared to be seated on a massive base, just above which began the legs, which were bent at the knees, with bare feet planted squarely on the floor. Higher up along the rectangular frame of the eight-foot-tall mirror protruded the large arms, outstretched, fingers wide, as if prepared to grab the unwary. Near the top of the frame were the ears. Two brass rings suspended in front of the mirror, dangling on wires from the framing at the top, formed oddly shifting eyes. Over the frame, but affixed to it, was a high, ornate crest.

Bryna remembered the day Nestor had led her to it, to where it had gathered dust for decades in an impoverished museum in

Kandy, in the interior highlands of Sri Lanka. It had been mislabelled and misunderstood. But even then it took some hefty bribes to secure its passage out of the country, apart from a not insubstantial purchase price. Nestor, Bryna recalled, had been even more excited than she by the acquisition, but then he was a practicing tantrika, and she was not. She had known this almost from the beginning—that the rituals she studied with such abstract absorption, insulated from their astonishing reality by the brittle dryness of old texts which, for her, *were* the reality, or all she wanted of it, had all been *lived*, not on the page, but in the flesh, by Nestor Bagehot.

She could not forget the night she had arrived, unannounced, at Nestor's weekend retreat in Marin County, a stone and glass aerie perched high atop one of the headlands.

Bryna was still in college at the time. It was during spring break. Nestor was in Marin working on a book. Niko was in Baja with friends. Suddenly depressed, Bryna had gotten into her car and started driving north.

It had been nearly three in the morning when she had arrived, only to find the parking lot behind Nestor's aerie full of cars. As she approached the side entrance, light—violet light—flickered out at her from the front of the house; it was a warm evening, and the sliding doors leading to the large deck at the front of the house were apparently open. Sounds—moaning—reached Bryna's ears. As she drew nearer it became evident that the moaning was actually chanting. Bryna smelled the incense and realized, with a tightening in her stomach, that a collective Tantric *asana*, a group coupling, a protracted, sensual eucharist, was in progress. She stopped, again ready to retreat, but something once more compelled her to move closer to the house, to a small window where she could see, unobstructed, the naked couples sitting on the floor in a circle, each in the *padmasana* lotus position, each male adept with his individual goddess, his *sakti*, to his left.

She knew precisely what she was witnessing, knew the meaning of the chant.

So 'ham.

"I am He."

Sa 'ham.

"I am She."

The striving for existential unity through the merging of the male and female principles. Unity aimed at extinguishing the ego, pride, destructive illusion. Bryna knew all the words. But it was not the words that held her, at once fascinated and horrified, unable to move or even to think beyond the present moment.

She could only watch, hypnotized. Watch their bodies, their swollen parts so appallingly real, so far removed from their stone and bronze effigies. Watch the faces, their eyes in distant bliss, their jaws moving, in the passage of the chant.

In the center of this human *chakra* was a man—his face painted with black and red stripes—who was obviously the *chakresvara*, the *chakra* leader. He was stretched out full-length, facing the floor, holding himself above it on the tips of his toes and fingers, as if in a protracted push-up. Bryna knew that his *sakti* was beneath him. She knew also by the new chant what was transpiring. It was one of the mantras of *linga* worship. The woman was fellating the *chakresvara*. The man's head reared upward and then extended far back, his mouth opening and his eyes rolling with the sensation he was experiencing. Bryna recoiled with shock as she realized the *chakresvara* was her mentor, Nestor Bagehot.

As Nestor's body plunged heavily, back and forth above the girl, his eyes seemed to lunge at Bryna, drawing nearer with each pelvic thrust. She felt a tightness at the top of her head, a flash of heat bursting upward from the pit of her. She felt dizzy. With a wrenching effort she twisted herself free of Nestor's gaze. Bryna ran, stumbling, to the car and, forgetting everything but the need to get away, drove recklessly back down the mountain.

Bryna shook herself, banishing, at least for the moment, the memory of that night, a night never spoken of, either by herself or by Nestor. Her phone buzzed. That would be Niko. She lifted the receiver.

"Sorry to bother you," he said. "Can you make room today for James Raymond? He says it's an emergency."

This was supposed to be a day free of work, but it obviously wasn't going to work out that way. While Bryna waited for the film star to arrive, she reread the newspaper account of Marissa Salomon's death.

The bizarre crime had generated international headlines. It was but the latest in what had come to be known as the "celebrity murders." A series of well-known personalities had been slain in the past year, each found in a pose mockingly suggestive of some phase of his or her career. The murderer obviously had a macabre sense of humor.

Top country-western singer Pike Subic, who got his start on the Grand Ol' Opry with his melodic "hog calls," had been found on his California ranch partially eaten by his own prize pigs. The police determined, however, that he had been drugged before being thrown into the pigs' feeding trough. Mary Frampton, a well-known pin-up girl from the forties, who had lately settled into a life of conservative politics, becoming national news again by winning a seat in the U.S. Congress, was found garrishly made up in her Orange County home, dressed only in black stockings and garter belts, drowned in a bubblebath. From the marks around her neck it was safely assumed that someone had given her a helping hand. Alec Kvinner, a director whose films were obsessively concerned with the paradoxes and tyrannies of time, was found in a bell tower of the Tijuana church where he had been filming his latest opus. Though the actual cause of death was a heart attack, he, like Subic, had been drugged. Then he had been deposited in the bell tower, where he was deafened by the protracted, festive bells of Christmas Eve. He was found with the blood still dripping from his nose and ears, his heart as shattered as his eardrums.

Bryna finished reading. Salomon, one of the screen's reigning sex symbols, had been found in bed in her beach house with a lewd, $29.94 male blow-up doll hunched over her, as if in the act of sex, one of its lifeless hands on the actress' equally lifeless breasts. The star's eyes were closed, her lips parted in a caricature of orgasmic ecstasy. When the police pulled back the sheets they found one of the doll's hands glued to the knife that was sunk deep in her chest.

Bryna hunched her shoulders with distaste, dropping the newspaper, which in reporting on Salomon's death, also recapped the previous killings. Still, Bryna was pleased that the authorities had finally expressed interest in having her assist them in their attempts—so far completely fruitless—to find her murderer. That Marissa Salomon had once consulted Bryna was a coincidence, she thought it better not to tell the police. Though she was loath to admit it even to herself, Bryna was wearying of her present psychic practice, developing something akin to contempt for many of her wealthy and privileged clients, whose credulous infatuation with the occult and paranormal made her work uninspirationally easy and, in the end, somehow, it seemed to her, cheap.

Now that she had attained the imprimatur of wealth, she yearned for the approval of those powerful scientific skeptics who yet relegated all matters psychic to the pages of the tabloids and the realm of the suspect. This was why the work she was doing at the Spectrum Research Institute was so important to her. She was sick of all the charlatanry, the unsubstantiated claims, the endless ambiguities that had plagued poorly conceived and underfunded psychic research for decades. At last she had the opportunity, she believed, to prove the reality of at least some psi phenomena and to do so in a setting and under circumstances that would command respect. She knew that it was owing directly to her new work at Spectrum that the homicide department had been emboldened to seek her help.

Bryna believed, without benefit or need of psychic intuition, that her career was at a crucial turning point. If all went well she would soon become, she told herself, an instrument of science, rather than an entertainer and a counselor of the rich. She was no sooner lifted by this thought than the phone again summoned her. As she raised the receiver, knowing that her client, the idol of millions, the man who had led a stampede of other stars to her years earlier, had arrived, she felt almost hostile toward James Raymond.

TWO

Bryna no longer greeted her clients before their readings. Too often they began reciting their troubles before she had properly gone into trance, thus blurring the validity of the reading. Besides, it was unseemly for oracles to indulge in small talk. Bryna did not even sit in the same room with her clients. In the beginning, she had simply gone into trance and let Sabra speak through her. This proved unacceptable, however, as, on several occasions, Sabra had proved too scathingly frank; thereafter, Bryna silenced her "guide" for good and resorted, instead, to having Sabra communicate through her via automatic writing. This, too, proved difficult, as it was often impossible for Bryna's hand to keep up with Sabra's outpourings.

It was Sabra herself who finally proposed the set-up that Bryna now employed, much to the fascination of the press. "Looks like something out of a science-fiction set or a NASA lab," one article exclaimed. Apart from the waiting room, ordinary enough, except for the portentousness of the great foyer space and its Tantric artifacts, the business of being psychic was carried out in three small chambers on the first floor of the mansion. One of these, directly accessible through the foyer, was the "receiving room," where the client was seated before a computerized console that contained a typewriter keyboard, a built-in microphone, a printer affixed to a word processor and a large television screen that could display whatever was typed or received on the word processor, as well as the image of Bryna in trance. Clients could type or verbally introduce their questions into the system, baring their innermost fears and concerns in the soundproof, dimly lighted, plush confines of their electronic chamber, feeling rather like they were in the confessional booths of the next century. Bryna was situated, during these sessions, in the "transmitting room." There, in trance, Sabra's responses to the clients' questions flowed through her. Niko, in the adjacent "editing module," received what Bryna typed and had the opportunity to delete or edit passages that might in raw form shock, frighten or offend the clients. Nothing was transmitted to the screen in the receiving room until it had been monitored by Niko.

This arrangement pleased Bryna, not only because it conveyed an aura of scientific legitimacy to the proceedings, but also because it protected her, by storing the whole of each encounter, in the system's computer memory, from misrepresentation and possible litigation later on. It also enabled her to easily quantify her successes and failures. And, most important from Bryna's standpoint, it minimized Sabra's presence in her life, a presence that she still feared as much as she depended upon.

Though at first Bryna, in the interests of building a following, had traded upon the exoticness of having a "spirit guide," more recently she had begun to downplay this. She was learning that "spirits," of any description, were not popular in "respectable" scientific circles. Sabra, she knew, was an acute embarrassment to Dr. Manning at Spectrum; he had begun hinting that "she"— Sabra—might be an impediment to future funding. In a frank, private conversation, Samuel Manning had urged Bryna to "take responsibility" for her own gift. In short, she knew, he was asking her to renounce Sabra as an unconscious fabrication, a trick of her own mind. The conversation had so filled Bryna with inner conflict that she had become physically ill and had been unable to work for days afterward. Dr. Manning had no idea how strong a position Sabra commanded, and Bryna was terrified that he would find out what, so far, only Niko, Nestor Bagehot and Naomi Hevesey, her psychiatrist, knew.

These troubled thoughts occupied Bryna's mind as she sat, waiting, in the transmitting room. Niko was already in place in the editing module. Bryna could see him through the small, soundproof window that connected their two chambers. He smiled at her, that special smile he reserved, without even knowing it, for her. It hurt her, this love he had for her, knowing that she could not return it. With Nestor it was difficult enough, but at least Nestor was capable of loving many. Niko could love only her.

Sometimes Bryna resented Niko for the very qualities that endeared him to her—his honesty, his loyalty, even his physical beauty. If only there had been some logical reason for her not to love so desirable a man as Niko Andrianos she might have preserved the illusion—she could think of no other word for it—that she might be capable of loving someone, *anyone*, someday. If he had a single flaw, she reflected bitterly, it was perhaps his poor judgment or ill luck in choosing her as the object of his love.

Bryna returned Niko's smile, revealing nothing of this in her expression. There was no need to go over it again. They'd had it all out many times. Frustration, years before, had finally overcome Niko's native shyness. It had happened toward the end of their first year in college. They'd been living together, sharing the same apartment, and it had finally become too much for him to keep to himself any longer. He confessed his feelings for her. She knew already, of course. It was difficult. She had tried, going so far as to let him kiss her, to touch her, but his touch, in this context was suddenly frightening, threatening. She had literally run from him, shutting herself away in her own room, disgusted by her actions and in anguish over the hurt she was inflicting on her friend—but unable to do otherwise. Yet, when he had moved out of the apartment, declaring that he could stand the sexual frustration no longer, it was she who had begged him to come back, knowing that he could not refuse, wounding him more deeply yet by insisting that she would not blame him if he brought other girls to their shared quarters. Ultimately, he had done exactly that, partly to test her, she knew, partly for release. Bryna had dared not encourage his feelings for her by even the slightest simulation of jealousy and thus ended up, by her apparent indifference, only hurting him more. The conviction that he would never really leave her, based on the fact that the psychic practice they had built together was just too lucrative to walk away from, made it possible for her to countenance his sexual adventures with equanimity. But that she should enjoy such security in view of his predicament added considerably to her already large burden of guilt, a burden she sought to ease by continually increasing his salary and giving him greater responsibility for her business affairs.

It seemed to Bryna that she and Niko had always been together. It had taken him a while, after he found out about Sabra—to feel comfortable around her. But, gradually, he came

132

to share Bryna's conviction that Sabra was, indeed, a separate entity and not merely the product of "split personality." The Bryna he idealized was just too different from the Sabra he came to know through his role as intermediary, too different for them ever to be the same or even part of the same whole, in his perception of things. And, of course, he could never forget his evening with Sabra, the night of the prom. Whenever he had doubts, whenever it seemed that Sabra was imaginary, Niko thought of that night at the cemetery, and all doubts evaporated. Bryna and Sabra, so far as he was concerned, could *not* be one and the same.

Niko argued that Bryna had beauty, talent and even psychic insight independent of Sabra, that, in many ways, Sabra was, in his view, as parasitic as the vine that clutched the Seacliff mansion. Though such arguments were flattering they were also frightening to Bryna. There were talents and capacities that Bryna wanted no part of, and those, she was convinced, were Sabra's province.

Niko and Bryna had been together eight years now, more than that, counting high school. They had gone to Los Angeles together, embarked on a seemingly impossible adventure. At first they had lived with Nestor Bagehot, Miss Lionel's cousin. Nestor had embraced both of them as if they were his own children. Niko had never become as fond of the older man as Bryna had, but they had all lived happily enough together. Nestor, living so close to her, had discovered her secret—that Sabra was more than merely a disembodied "spirit," but they seldom spoke of Bryna's arrangement with the other, and the professor made no judgments as to the "reality" or "unreality" of the situation. Instead, he worked to make Bryna feel better about what was happening by assisting her in her study of Tantrism.

It was Nestor, moreover, who helped Bryna get started—giving public readings in a small nightclub, a gathering spot for devotees of the occult. He had also persuaded friends of his in the press to pay heed; from there her career had burgeoned. Word of mouth confirmed her as a talented psychic. James Raymond had been her first "big" client; after that she could not keep up with the demand.

A year after she and Niko graduated—he in business administration—they left L.A. for San Francisco, a move that miffed and mystified many of Bryna's clients, most of whom, nonetheless, began making regular pilgrimages north. There had been no question about Niko accompanying her. He acted as her personal business manager as well as her "psychic editor." At social gatherings, Niko was also usually her companion. If Bryna was seen in public, Niko was almost always seen with her. She did have interests, however, that he did not share, Tantra, for one, her interest in weaponry and martial arts, for another. For relaxation, Bryna often target practiced; she had her own rifle range in the basement of the big house. She was also accomplished in archery and with knives. She had more than a passing interest in karate.

Niko, only half jokingly, called these Bryna's "criminal pastimes" and said he could not understand her interest in them. Dr. Hevesey could—or said she could. "With your emotions, especially your sexual emotions locked up the way they are, these pursuits give you a physical outlet. They also give you a feeling of individuality and help you compensate for the feeling of weakness which is the natural consequence of your belief that you are in the grip of a much more powerful personality."

Bryna glanced at Niko through the small window that separated them. He was putting a new disc in the computer. He was casually dressed in neat blue jeans, the tightness of which defined the muscularity of his thighs. He was wearing an equally tight red T-shirt which revealed the taut contours of his chest and belly. The red looked good on him with his curly black hair. She admired him—all of him. But there it ended, leaving her feeling inadequate and incomplete as always.

She remembered that first time she had seen him—in the high school gym. She recalled the dream sequence that had occurred when she'd fainted on the gym floor that day. Those dream images often haunted her still. She could not forget how accurately she had foreseen Niko, not the boy she had yet to lay eyes on, but Niko the man, as he looked now, years later. On the stage of her unconscious she had fallen into Niko's arms, murmuring, "He's dead. I killed him." And then she had awakened to find herself seeing Niko for the first conscious time.

i killed him

The celebrity murders flashed through her mind, jolting her.

who? killed who?

Niko gave her the thumbs-up signal. They were ready to begin. Bryna concentrated, trying to feel nothing.

Niko saw Bryna's neck stiffen, her head jerk upward and her eyes open wide, frozen. The sight of this, even though by now thoroughly familiar to him, never ceased to frighten him. It was as if, he thought, an electrical current passed through Bryna's body and charged her. Sometimes her arms jerked, too, and then remained rigid; movements, when they occurred, were mechanical. Sabra was near, if not already present, waiting to be summoned.

In the dim, blue-lit ambience of her shielded module, Bryna looked, it seemed to Niko, like an electronic marionette. Yet he thought her still lovely, her skin even paler than normal against the thick black hair that would have curled tightly around her head but for the weighty length that made luxuriant ebony rivulets of it instead, wild black water that rushed into the shadows between her shoulders. He particularly liked the way she wore her hair on this occasion, a black, daggerlike barrette holding it back on one side to expose the entire proud jawline, earlobe supporting a milky white glass globe and the long, graceful neck encircled by an intricately beaded macrame choker that had at its apex a tiny serpent's head with eyes of the same milky glass.

Bryna's own eyes appeared to be lignite under carefully darkened brows and naturally long lashes, but they were actually a dark green. Her nose was prominent and slightly bent; with her high cheekbones and high forehead it suited her. Her full breasts did not, or so she often thought—without justification in Niko's view. Though at times she could look haughty and remote, the same magnetism of her eyes that could menace could never fail but to attract, and the soft fullness of her mouth and the youthful smoothness of her skin betrayed a certain vulnerability. She was attractive by any standard, but to Niko she was stunning.

Niko pushed a button and typed the letters SABRA, which instantly appeared on the screens in each of the three chambers. Sabra "spoke" now through Bryna's rapidly moving fingers:

Who is it this time? Oh, my God, not him again. He's an open book. Why is he spending his money here? He needs a fortune cookie, not a psychic.

Niko glanced briefly through the glass aperture at Bryna, her face and upper body still immobile, her eyes on her screen, looking at the image of James Raymond. Her fingers were poised over the keyboard, momentarily frozen. Niko, who had transmitted none of the above to Raymond, flashed the STAND BY signal on the receiving-room screen and then addressed himself once again to Sabra:

Mr. Raymond is a very important client. We have a commitment to him. We have payments to make.

Sabra, through Bryna:

Don't hand me that crap. I should have such payments. I

135

should live so well. For that matter, I should *look* so well.
Niko, you look better every day. Sleep with me just once
and I promise you'll never regret it. It's not like sleeping
with an ordinary woman. It's like nothing you've ever
known. Try me.

Niko:

We've been over this a hundred times. The answer is no.
Can we get back to the client?

Sabra:

Did you think I was serious, eunuch? You're as frigid as she
is. Me sleep with the likes of you? It is to laugh, dear
friends. Look. Look, Niko, I'm laughing at you.

Niko, quickly punching the pause control, blotting out Bryna's
image on Raymond's screen, looked up from the editing console
and through the window to see Bryna's body turned awkwardly
toward him, her mouth soundlessly opening and closing in a
tortured caricature of laughter. Niko felt himself flush with rage
and fear. He turned back to his keyboard, typing furiously:

Stop it, goddamn you. You're hurting her. You agreed never
to do this.

He watched intently as Bryna slowly, mechanically resumed
her previous position. Soon her fingers began to move across the
keyboard again:

You really should try to develop a sense of humor, Niko.
And loosen up a little for Christsake. You're almost as
gloomy as she is. You're wasting it, babycakes.

Niko:

About the client. Can we get on with it?

Sabra:

All work and no play. Okay. It's very simple. He's going
to ask me who's blackmailing him. Go ahead.

Niko pushed another button. The word "begin" appeared on
Raymond's screen. The actor began typing immediately:

Someone is blackmailing me. Who?

Niko activated the "STAND BY" message again while Sabra
began to respond:

You notice he didn't ask *why* someone is blackmailing him.
He sleeps with boys. Big deal. Well, I can almost sympathize
with him. My God, that wife of his. If you could see the
horrors gravity has worked on that woman's tits.

Niko:

Could you just answer his question, please?

Sabra:

Clare Friedkin.

Clare Friedkin. My God, Niko thought, Friedkin was Hollywood's premier gossip columnist. Also its most ruthless. At least, that was her reputation. She was known for her enduring loyalties *and* her undying grudges. Her wealth was said to exceed that of many of the international stars. Was this a new wrinkle in her career or something she'd been up to for years? Niko transmitted Sabra's answer to James Raymond's screen. He watched the actor's face on his own screen, gauging the depth of his shock at this news. He could see that it was considerable. The actor's hands were trembling when he began typing again:

How did she find out?

Sabra:

She has a network of private investigators. One of them followed you. It was simple. She thought something might turn up, and it did.

Raymond:

How much more will she try to take me for?

Sabra:

Everything you're worth.

Raymond:

How can I stop her?

Sabra:

She's got a weak heart. It ought to be easy to...

Niko deleted this, replacing Sabra's last response with:

That's up to you. I urge you to be prudent.

Niko watched the muscles in the actor's face writhe with hate. The man hesitated, as if he might ask something else, then rose and left, nearly stumbling in his haste.

Niko:

Anything else?

Sabra:

Just this. Before you stick me back in my coffin, why don't you do what you've always wanted to do? She doesn't have to know. I'll even pretend I'm her. I'll do the whole vestal virgin bit. We'll assume the missionary position, of course, and you'll have trouble getting in, and I'll whimper a little but I'll be brave because I've read all those magazine articles about what to do and how to react and you'll kiss me tenderly, reassuring me, and then you'll kiss me madly as you lose yourself, ravishing me equally with your hot tongue and impossibly huge...

Niko (overriding):

Time to sign off.

Sabra:

The truth scares the shit out of you doesn't it? When are you finally going to get it through your head that she's already taken?

Niko:

By *you?* I don't have to be told that.

Sabra:

By her father, my dear man, by her *father.* When are you going to face it?

THREE

She shrugged, and the fur slid silently onto the carpet. She let her long blonde hair with its rich wave caress her back as she rubbed her head against first one shoulder and then the other, watching herself in the mirrored walls, momentarily pleased by her naked reflection before discovering—and frowning at—a small red mark just below her right breast.

"You beast," she said with mock petulance. "You bit me too hard. There'll be hell to pay for this; nothing escapes her notice. It's gotten even to where she's complaining she can still *taste* the cigarettes, for Christsake, even though I make it a point never to smoke for *two* fucking hours before I cash in my chips. And the *mouthwash!* She even bitched about that. First it's 'too mediciney,' then it's 'too sweet.' Said she prefers baking soda. That suits me fine. If I ever see another bottle of Scope I'll puke. Mouthwash is decidedly against my religion. Next she'll insist I start *flossing!*"

She threw her head back again, shut her eyes and took a deep breath. "God, listen to me. I never used to let her get under my skin, if you'll pardon the expression. Well, forget it." She peered back into the cavernous closet, pushed a button on the wall and watched her wardrobe glide by, revolving on a concealed track.

"I've got acres of dresses in here, and I swear there isn't anything I want to wear tonight."

"What's tonight?"

"Just a little dinner with Bruno."

"Bruno? I didn't think you fucked the help."

"I *always* fuck the help, dear man. What's help *for* if not for that?"

138

A laugh erupted from somewhere deep inside the man, though his lips did not appear to move.

"I still have so much to learn," he apologized, reaching out from the bed to stroke the firm flesh of the woman's inner thigh. He let the ball of his thumb tease the playful nerves of her perineum. He watched her face, gauging her response. Her blue eyes narrowed and she buried her hands in his hair, pulling him forward, into her pubic hair. His tongue darted into her. It knew its way, and she moaned, tightening her grip on him. When she began to come he knew not to stop but instead redoubled his efforts, deftly fellating her swollen clitoris, lifting her from one peak of sensation to another.

When she at last released him and fell to the bed, weak from pleasure, he instantly mounted her, penetrating hungrily, drawing sensation from her while building his own until he could withstand no longer and came.

"Twice in one hour," she said, as he rolled off her. "You're as good as ever, professor."

Nestor Bagehot sat on the foot of the bed and peered into the small, blossom-shaped pool sunk in imported tile across the room. He gathered himself with just a hint of weariness and walked to the edge of the water. He activated a switch recessed in the floor, and the surface of the water came instantly to life, churned by jets of air that created pulsating, sybaritic currents. He dropped into the cauldron and adjusted the temperature as silent, invisible fans sucked the humidity from the air.

"A sinfully indecent invention," he muttered. His eyes focused again on the woman. "Eight years ago, when you revealed yourself to me for the first time," he said, "I had no idea it would end in this." His eyes took in the whole room.

"End? I don't intend to *end* for a very, *very* long time."

"Come to this, I mean," he amended. "This place—and *you*, the uncrowned and thus all the more dangerous empress of Laurel Canyon, envied by the stars for your anonymous power, for your *un*public ways, for the ability to be in it and yet above it all, something none of them, not the most idolized, can afford. Envied and feared for your mystery, Madame Sabrina Kherashkov Jouhaux. Sabra to your intimates, of course, and to some you profitably suffer to imagine themselves your intimates.

"Yes," Bagehot continued, enjoying the sound of his own voice, "how is it the latest story goes, the one the gossip columnists have pooled from what I have no doubt are your own carefully choreographed leaks? French father—well, that we've known for some time—but now a Russian mother, hence *two* fortunes, you clever woman, one squirreled out of Russia with the fall of the Czar betwixt the aristocratic thighs of grandmama Kherashkov, wisely invested in countries without taxes and bequeathed, at her majority, to the beauteous surviving Kherashkov who, until she was freed of the burden, lived dutifully with her bewidowered French father in Cambodia, whence came the other, it now seems not-so-respectable fortune. Daddy, I'm now hearing, was in the poppy business. What was it Clare Friedkin said in her column only the other day?"

Standing in the vapors at the shallow end of the pool, Bagehot stared at the ceiling for a moment, prompting his memory. "Yes," he said, smiling faintly again. "Which Laurel Canyon casa, the envy of even Tinsel Town's goldenest glitterati, was built by money made in heroin traffic? Watch this space for more on the house that smack built." Bagehot looked at Sabra again, adding, "You may have gone too far with that one. Friedkin's curiosity, once piqued, knows no rational bounds. Besides, she's already got it in for you. She abhors a mystery the way nature abhors a vacuum. I'm afraid you're becoming too visible."

"Mmmm," Sabra said. "Well, I thought by confiding—only to a dear and trusted friend, of course—that there was something dark and evil in my background, for which I was blameless, naturally, no one would wonder any longer why I reveal so little about myself. I hadn't counted on Friedkin bulldogging it to death. She's already got her private dicks on my tail."

Bagehot looked concerned. "You're one step ahead of her, I trust?"

"Of course," she snapped, irritated by his doubt. "She'll be neutralized any time now. I told Raymond that it's Friedkin who's blackmailing him."

Bagehot's eyes widened. "A stroke of... but then you know that. Still, I can't help worrying a bit about Raymond himself. We've never worked with any of Bryna's clients in the past."

"Which was damned foolish—not to, I mean."

"Yes, but what's she going to think if suddenly all her clients come to her saying they're being blackmailed? For that matter, what are *they* going to think? If they find out there are others they'll *have* to suspect her. After all, who knows more about them...?"

"We don't blackmail *all* of them, dear man. We have to be *selective*."

"But we've been doing fine, and we haven't had to touch any of her clients. Why start now?"

"Simple. She has some of the fattest cats in the business in her appointment books. It's criminal to let them get away, particularly since we know so much about them already. Besides, I like the idea. There's a certain perversity about it that rings true."

"And you think Raymond will . . . ?"

"Yes; he's plotting his final payment right now. Friedkin should be getting it any day."

"It couldn't happen to a lovelier lady."

Sabra looked suddenly weary.

"What is it?" said Bagehot. "You think there might be a catch."

"With Friedkin? No. It's something else. I've been sensing it for some time now. I can't quite pin it down."

"Perhaps," Bagehot said, "it's this business with the police that bothers you, her new search for respectability, helping solve those murders. Maybe you're afraid all this do-gooding for free is going to cut into profits?"

Sabra looked irritated again, and uncharacteristically, confused. "Those murders, hmmm . . . I don't know what it is. I just keep feeling something is going to happen, and I can't understand why I can't get a fix on it. It's *her.* It must be. Something is changing or is going to change."

"You're just tired, overworked," Bagehot said. "Besides Raymond we've taken on three new clients in the last month. I know how that kind of research wears on you. And I know what your night life is like. Nobody can keep up with you. Why don't you demand a week and take an unscheduled vacation?"

Sabra seemed lost in her own thoughts. She reached down and picked up the fur, pressing its soft deadness to her body. "No," she said. "I have to be watchful now. Change is not always necessarily bad; my kind know that change is a time for seizing new opportunities."

"And you, my dear," Bagehot said, stepping out of the pool, droplets of water clinging to the heavily matted hair that covered most of his body, "are the ultimate opportunist."

"Thank you," she said, smiling at him.

"Furthermore," he added, "tired or not, you've never looked more lovely than you do right now. There isn't a woman in Hollywood who could carry on like you do and not look twenty years older than she should."

"Ah, but you forget," Sabra said, "I'm good—every other day. *She* maintains the body. *I* use it." She laughed, a little ruefully, remembering how difficult it had been to "train" balky Bryna, alternately tantalizing her with images of what she *could* be if only she would cooperate and horrifying her with the vision of what she *would* be, if she didn't.

"Dynamite body." The words kept echoing through Ethan Kendal's mind as he deftly guided his new BMW through the lacunae of late-afternoon traffic on the Hollywood Freeway. George Sanders had said it twice, the words spurting out of him as if expelled by some great inner pressure, some intolerable torment. It was the sort of thing the critics would say no one else could get. The odd, almost quirky but terribly *true* sort of thing the bereaved husband of a newly murdered actress, a woman young enough to be his daughter, would *think* and, perhaps even in the presence of an Ethan Kendal, *say*. And he *did* say it.

As Ethan drove he forwarded and reversed the small tape recorder with his free hand until he found the place again, where George Sanders said: "God, oh Jesus, Marissa was, I don't know. They think, you know, she was just what *they* saw every week on the tube, but she was, she was more, a mother, a wife, oh god, she was great, an intellectual, really, an intellectual behind all that, you know, and that body, just the most *dy*namite body and . . .

And then he had let it all out, the most intimate details of their life, desperately trying to make Ethan—and thus the world—understand how much *he* had lost, trying to reclaim completely in death what he had been forced to share, with now obvious resentment, in life. There was something almost like hatred in his voice when he said of his late wife's following: "They lost a laugh; I lost, oh, Christ, I lost . . ." The man's voice broke, and Ethan switched off the tape.

Ethan anticipated playing some of the tape for his agent, teasing her with a little of it later that evening. He knew she would be excited. The book was proceeding better even than he had hoped. Several chapters, covering most of the earlier murders, were now complete, at least in first draft. His agent was ecstatic over the copy; more important, so was Ethan's publisher. The editor in chief himself had called the work to date "masterful," telephoning Ethan in San Francisco from his New York office to add "this one will not only win you the Pulitzer Prize but also the top slot on the best-seller lists for months to come," an obvious reference to Ethan's earlier, critically acclaimed but commercially marginal books, two of them novels and one a chronicle of disillusionment and lost innocence written during his stint as an intelligence officer in Vietnam, an effort that won him the Pulitzer Prize.

His present book had been inspired by what was known as the "nonfiction novel," or "faction," as some labeled it, a child of the new journalism, an excursion *through* the discernible facts into another dimension, one projected by what was known but ultimately contained only by the intuition and within the imagination of the reporter-novelist. In this instance Ethan Kendal had charged himself with the task not only of knowing as much as he could about each celebrated murder victim, his or her innermost thoughts and dreams, his or her final breaths, but also, by virtue of this painstaking re-creation of events, moments and emotions, all leading directly to the null space of death, of conjuring the presence of the murderer himself—or herself—of projecting, through the interference patterns of all the known data, a dark and elusive image that would at last cohere in holographic depth and clarity under the laserlike illumination of his craft. The book was to be as much a portrait of the unseen murderer as of the victims themselves.

So far, all who had read excerpts of the book agreed that the murderer, in Ethan's prose, seemed chillingly near at hand, almost as real and identifiable as the victims. The publisher declared that Kendal's book would make all previous work in the same ground-breaking area—Capote's and Mailer's efforts, for example—seem passé.

There was some concern, of course, about what would happen if the murderer were apprehended before the book was published. The publisher was gambling—the advance against royalties had been considerable—that this would not happen. But even if it did Ethan would still be in an excellent position—perhaps the best position—to incorporate what would become known about the murderer into his book, perhaps even reflecting on where he had been right and where he had been wrong. Either way, a best-seller of some staying power seemed an excellent possibility.

Ethan played part of the tape again, listening not only to each word, but to each divergent modulation, listening for a pattern, waiting for the signal, listening to his own utterances, monitoring even more sensitively his own silences—each wielded like a weapon, *forcing* disclosure. Ethan Kendal knew that he was no better than most reporters when it came to knowing what to ask, but he was quite certain that he was without equal when it came to knowing when to ask—when to say—*nothing* at all. And having mastered that he had also learned how to react—or not react—when the words began to come, desperately unfolding around the bloody silence, trying to staunch its flow. When George Sanders' voice had suddenly pitched slightly higher, for example, Ethan had become almost catatonic, staring directly into the other man's eyes, where the panic and rage and loss were all pooling, ready to overflow.

Ethan swung onto the Harbor Freeway, headed toward Pasadena and his agent's rented bungalow. She didn't actually live *in* Pasadena but close enough to sustain a few jokes. Ethan knew she had her eye on a place in Beverly Hills. "Your book is going to pay for it," she often said, not entirely joking. Ethan decided he would take her to dinner in celebration of the Sanders' interview.

At the same time that Madame Jouhaux and her swarthy companion Bruno were washing down their truffle paté with wine bottled decades earlier, Ethan Kendal and his agent were, in a nearby establishment, contemplating the double-digit appetizers that would launch their meal. Meanwhile, Lieutenant Albert Brazil, hundreds of miles to the north, was complaining to his wife that while her wheat-soy varnishkas might save him from an early grave—"and the starving millions from the profligacy of the meat eaters"—he nonetheless would require "a peanut butter and jam on white" if he were expected not to visit the local MacDonald's at the end of Haight Street before the night was over.

Mrs. Brazil looked at her husband accusingly. "It wouldn't surprise me," she said, genuinely outraged. "God, the thought of anyone, let alone my own husband, setting foot inside one of those places." She shuddered, also genuinely. "That's probably why you're so pale all the time." She waved the huge cucumber she had been slicing over the sink at him. "It's no wonder you can't lose that extra weight—and your physical's only a month away—stuffing yourself with all that shit. Those hamburgers are full of female hormones; if you keep eating them you're going to have tits, which is all I need right now."

Lieutenant Brazil walked over to the sink, pushed his wife against the wall and stopped her talking by covering her mouth with his. She struggled as his hand crept up her leg and began unfastening her blue jeans. She tried to push him away, beating him on the back with the cucumber.

"I'm not against meat per se," she said, "just *dead* meat." She flicked his crotch as she pushed past him to the sink.

Brazil slumped visibly, smiled wryly and shook his head, still staring into the wall. "That's what I get for marrying a kid—dirty talk, vegetables, no mercy."

Mrs. Brazil—at twenty-four, younger than her husband by eighteen years—softened. "I'm sorry. I wasn't really referring to last night. It wasn't your fault, although I still don't think a little ginseng would hurt."

Brazil said the same thing he had in bed the night before, only now a little more defensively. "It's this damned case. They're busting my balls. They want me to come up with something before L.A. does, and to hell with the fact that we've only had one and they've had what now...? I dunno. Half a dozen."

"Half a dozen *what?*"

"Murders. We've just had the one. The Salomon broad."

"*Woman.*"

"Woman. Right. Whatever. I don't know why we should take it, anyway. Pajaro Dunes. Christ, that must be a hundred miles and a million bucks from here. They keep a Pacific Heights address for the servants." He sat down at the kitchen table, frowned at the half-eaten varnishkas, which were the leftover Tuesday-night specials at his wife's The Real Thing restaurant on San Francisco's Haight Street. He opened his battered old black briefcase, the unstreamlined kind, and pulled out Bryna Carr's book, *The Psychic Within,* a combination of very sketchy autobiography and how-to-be-psychic advice, consisting mainly of meditation exercises, with references to Tantric philosophy.

"I can't make shit from shinola out of most of this," Brazil said wearily, his long brown hair hanging down and brushing the open pages of the book. He had done a stint as an undercover cop, and now his wife wouldn't let him cut his hair.

"Bryna Carr?" Mrs. Brazil said, squinting at the book.

"You heard of her?"

"Yeah. The psychic, of course. Hey, wait a minute. Don't tell me."

"So what? Harry wants this case solved *yesterday;* okay, I resort to magic."

"No need to be defensive. I think this is the best idea the cops have had since . . . sorry, I can't think of another good idea the cops have had."

Bryna paused only for a moment to turn and look back into the mirror of the Void. The body was hers again, and everything appeared in order, though there was a scent that annoyed her; it had been meant, she supposed, to mask the odor of cigarette smoke that clung to her hair. At one time she had insisted that

Sabra shower before returning the body, but the other had tastes in soap and shampoo that were not at all to Bryna's liking, and she had always ended up showering the body again anyway, once she had repossessed it.

Bryna opened the top of her bathrobe, the same that Sabra always wrapped the body in, the same that Bryna always wore to the Void at the appointed hour. She looked at herself in the mirror again and immediately noticed the small red mark below her right breast, though Sabra had made a careless effort to conceal it with body makeup. She noticed also a roughness on the side of her throat. She felt, rather than looked at, herself further down, her jaw setting as she felt the tenderness there.

Bryna closed her robe in the dimly lit corridor. She turned to go down the stairs, then stopped and hesitatingly pushed against the mirror with one hand—not to see if she could get back into the concealed room but to make sure that she could *not*. She had no idea how to open the concealed combination lock; nor did she want to know. Bryna had no knowledge, at least no conscious knowledge, of what lay beyond the door; Sabra, in possession of the body, had decorated it herself. Bryna knew only that the room was there and that the mirror somehow opened into it. Whenever it was time to relinquish the body she would go alone to the Void, stare at herself until her own image would begin to dissolve and she would find herself going into trance. She had no memory of actually going into the forbidden chamber. Nor did she believe that, in fact, *she*, Bryna, had ever entered the room. Only Sabra was permitted to enter it. If there were things that needed cleaning or changing in the room, she assumed that Sabra took care of that.

Bryna *was* aware of the fact that there was a second entrance to the room. That had all been worked out in the beginning. Bryna had insisted that no one see Sabra coming and going. Sabra promised all this would be taken care of, and Niko, who had scouted ahead for the proper house, had told her of the old service elevator that went from a now concealed subbasement up the back of the house. The shaft was concealed and now served only Sabra's secret room.

The subbasement itself was accessible not only from the house proper, provided you knew the way, but also from a subterranean passageway that led to a garage on the side street to the west, well below the main entrance to the old mansion. It was here that Sabra kept an automobile—most recently, Niko had observed—a black Porsche 928.

146

"A little excessive," he had grumbled to Bryna, "considering she only uses it to go to and from the airport."

Bryna had never even been to the subbasement and had no desire to go there. For that matter, she did not want to hear about Sabra's car, either, and constantly discouraged Niko from "checking up on her," as he put it. He had once proposed following Sabra to Los Angeles—where they assumed she lived, since it was for that reason that Bryna had left L.A. years earlier. This proposal had so upset Bryna that she had burst into tears and made Niko promise never to do such a thing.

Bryna went down the stairs to her study. It was nearly three a.m. but she knew she would have to buzz Niko, whose apartment was in the main basement, which is where he preferred to be, or he would come up. He insisted upon both "checking in" and "checking out" the body, making sure that Sabra did not use more than her allotted time, typically three days each week, usually taken all at once.

Bryna picked up the house phone and buzzed Niko's room twice.

"Are you all right?"

"Yes," she said, her voice flat. "Everything is fine."

"Do you need anything?"

"Just sleep, thank you. Goodnight, Niko."

She could feel his need, waiting for something more. She put the receiver down. Her absences were easily enough explained. Niko told Bryna's clients and acquaintances that she required considerable time to herself, to meditate and—a phrase that made her flinch inwardly—"recharge her psychic batteries." She wondered to whom Sabra made *her* excuses. But then a woman like Sabra, Bryna reflected, as she stepped into the shower, could come and go as she pleased, without need of excuse.

FOUR

Samuel Manning was bald and blunt-featured, a big man with hard gray eyes. The pretty, freckled, redhead at his side was Libby Horne, Spectrum Research Institute's new director of publicity, pirated from a rival think-tank on the East Coast. Horne, though barely thirty, was known for her potent fundraising abilities. It had been her idea to bring Ethan Kendal to today's tour and demonstration, along with Lieutenant Brazil of the San Francisco Police Department's homicide division. Indeed, it had been her idea to entice the police into asking for Bryna Carr's help in the first place—something she knew Miss Carr would welcome.

Libby was pleased at how smoothly things were starting off. Kendal and Brazil, it developed, already knew each other. The writer had interviewed the officer right after the Salomon murder. The two men seemed comfortable with one another as they made the rounds with Dr. Manning.

"This is the primate unit," the researcher explained, quickly tapping a code into a small, wall-mounted keyboard next to the massive door. In response, the door slid silently open, then closed again once they stepped inside. Along one side of the windowless but blindingly bright, porcelain-white room were cages containing rhesus monkeys. Along another wall were several computers, and in the center of the room were a number of restraining chairs, in which still more monkeys were strapped in sitting positions. White-coated technicians were drilling burr holes in the skulls of two of these wide-eyed creatures.

"Jesus Christ," Brazil exhaled. "Excuse me, Miss Horne, but what in the...?"

Libby Horne smiled, deferring to Dr. Manning, who began speaking at once. "These animals are being prepared for implantation of deep-brain electrodes, which are introduced through the burr holes you now see being drilled in these anesthetized animals' skulls. Under X-ray visualization, we use these micromanipulative devices, communicating through a stereotaxic grid, to implant stainless-steel electrodes through the burr holes, sinking them into the brain to the desired depth."

"With techniques like these," Libby cut in, "functions of various brain centers have already been extensively mapped. You simply zap a few milliamps of electricity through those electrodes and *voilà!* You note and record the evoked response. Typically, if the electrode is positioned in exactly the same place in different animals, a like amount of current will evoke exactly the same response. We can get that kind of exact positioning with computer guidance. It takes very little electricity to make an animal hungry, horny, placid, aggressive, whatever you want. We can control them almost as if they were robots."

"Spooky," Brazil said, shaking his head.

"Here," Dr. Manning said, moving to another of the restraining units. "We'll give you an example. Darlene," he said, turning to one of the technicians at the computer console, "have unit seven here give us a message."

Darlene tapped a coded message into the computer, and "unit seven" immediately looked up at his visitors, as if coming out of a trance, snarled and raised the middle finger of his right hand, poking the air with it obscenely.

"Jesus," Brazil said, "that's . . . that's just . . ."

Kendal merely laughed.

"We like to use that one on visiting government officials," Horne said dryly.

"All very impressive," Ethan Kendal said at last, "but what has all this got to do with the murders, and why have you asked *me* here today?"

Libby Horne smiled or, rather, kept on smiling. "I'm sorry," she said. "I won't keep you in suspense any longer. We have a talented psychic under study here. We've already told Lieutenant Brazil about her. He's quite interested in meeting her because *we* think she might be of some help to the police in solving the celebrity murder cases."

Ethan was clearly taken off guard. His surprise showed. "I'd heard there was some psychic research going on here, but . . ." He looked quickly at Brazil, questioning.

Brazil shrugged. "Look," he said. "I'm desperate. I admit it. I'll try *anything* three times." He smiled at his own joke, then realizing his faux pas, quickly added, looking at Dr. Manning, "No offense intended, sir. It's just that this psychic stuff is new to me, and frankly there's some resistance, but . . . uh . . . well, I'm here, ready to be convinced."

"I take it you're a skeptic," Libby Horne said, turning to Ethan Kendal.

"I . . . well, it's not something I've given much thought to," Ethan said, his discomfort apparent.

"Still, I trust you'll give us the benefit of the doubt—at least for a few minutes," Dr. Manning said. "Miss Horne is going to show you a film while I prepare the psychic in question—her name is Bryna Carr, you may have heard of her—for the next part of our demonstration."

Manning excused himself while the others watched the film in a room adjacent to the primate unit. Libby watched both men while *they* watched Bryna Carr, on screen, go into trance.

"Jesus," Brazil said in a loud whisper, "that is weird. I mean, I read about it in her book, but seeing it . . ."

Kendal said nothing but stared intently at the screen.

The film—voiceover by Dr. Manning—showed Bryna predicting, with great accuracy, the precise movements of rhesus monkeys implanted with brain electrodes. Dr. Manning explained that the monkeys were randomly programmed by the computers to make various finger, hand and arm movements and to alter facial expressions in a variety of specific ways. The experimental design was such that only the computer knew which movements were scheduled.

"We could have used human subjects and merely asked them to make movements at random," Dr. Manning, speaking from the screen, explained. "But then we would not have been able to verify with complete reliability the accuracy of the predictions, for we would not have been certain of the intended movement, nor could we then have eliminated the possibility of subconscious human cueing, subtle movements giving away the intended signal, gesture or expression. We could also have asked our psychic subjects simply to predict the commands of a randomly programmed computer, as has been done in other projects, but we discovered, in pilot programs, that many psychics respond far more accurately to biological systems. Our approach is unique. . . ."

Via split-screen image, Kendal and Brazil watched Bryna Carr seated, in trance, in one room and one of the computer-controlled rhesus monkeys in another room. Each time a light flashed on a panel in front of her Bryna would assume a new facial expression or make a new gesture. The flashing light was her signal to predict, by *mimicking* before it had occurred, the next computer-controlled monkey movement or expression. The effect—seeing Bryna and the monkey make the same movements a second or two apart—was stunning, particularly when viewed on the split screen. It was also, for those watching, eerie in the extreme, for Bryna's movements, as much as the monkeys, seemed under the control of some extraneous force.

"Amazing. This is *just* amazing," Lieutenant Brazil kept repeating, as the film ended.

Libby Horne escorted the two men to another part of the building. As they walked down the corridor, Brazil chattered incessantly. Libby finally disconnected herself and glanced at Ethan who had been preternaturally quiet, absorbed in this own thoughts.

"You seem a bit shaken," she ventured, addressing Ethan.

"You're not afraid she's going to solve this whole thing before you get your book done, are you?"

Ethan looked at the woman sharply. His expression softened almost as quickly, however, and he said, "I have to admit it's a new wrinkle for me. I've never put much faith in psychic phenomena; what I just saw was impressive, on the face of it, anyway, but . . ."

"For you seeing isn't always believing?"

"Not always, no. I've seen enough to arouse my curiosity, but assuming this precognitive ability is real, how is that going to help the police solve something that has already occurred, something in the past?"

"Ah," Libby said, "well, Bryna Carr's strongest suit *is* precognition, knowing what *will* happen, but she does seem to have some ability to reconstruct past events, provided she is in close proximity to some stimulus."

"Stimulus?"

"An object, a person, anything associated with that past event."

Lieutenant Brazil stopped and abruptly snapped open his bulky brief case. "Her dress," he said matter of factly.

"What?" Ethan said.

"Well, actually it's her negligee. What she was wearing the night she was killed, or at least what she had on when they found her, Marissa Salomon's negligee." He showed Ethan its black insubstantiality.

"We're going to show it to her in trance and see what she can tell us," Libby Horne said, beaming. They went into the room where Bryna Carr was waiting, Libby and Lieutenant Brazil struggling for a moment to usher the other in first. Ethan went in last.

Bryna had been ill at ease all morning. She could feel herself perspiring. She knew that a homicide officer would be present at the demonstration, that she would be asked specifically about one or more of the murders. She also knew that the writer Ethan Kendal would be present, another of Libby's self-proclaimed "coups." If Kendal would write about Bryna Carr and, incidentally, Spectrum Research Institute, it would, she promised, "do all of us worlds of good." She kept stressing Ethan's Pulitzer Prize. Bryna, who never felt the slightest quiver in the presence of some of the entertainment world's biggest names, suddenly found herself with a classic case of stage fright. For once, she was eager to go into trance.

First, however, Dr. Manning wanted her to meet their two visitors. He did not have to stress their potential importance to her career and their research project. There were those among Dr. Manning's scientific peers, Bryna knew, who were already nitpicking his monkey experiments; no matter how clever psychic researchers were in eliminating bias and various artifacts, there were always those who would be eager to find fault.

"If physicists operated under the burden of doubt placed on paraphysicists and parapsychologists," Dr. Manning was fond of saying, "we'd still be looking for the atom and doubting its existence."

Bryna knew that Samuel Manning longed for the big splash that would finally sink his critics. The burden of his hopes lay heavily upon her shoulders as he took her arm and led her into an anteroom to meet Albert Brazil and Ethan Kendal.

Ethan's presence impacted on her like a sound wave, beyond the normal, audible range, one that comes from a great distance and from another time, seeking her, speaking only to her. When her eyes met his she was fixed by them, momentarily unable to move, their pale blue enveloping her. She sensed a turbulence in him which was, she decided, merely a reflection of her own disquiet, which he could not have failed to note. She wanted to tell him not to worry, that everything was all right, that he "merely" reminded her of someone, that he "merely" looked astonishingly like her dead father, so achingly so that for a moment she wanted to fall against him and cry, to feel his arms around her, the touch of his hand on her face, his lips. . . . She felt a stabbing sensation in her lower back, on either side. The pain was intense. She knew that it was grief and guilt and a kind of longing she did not want to think about yet. She turned away from Ethan, a movement that required an almost mechanical lurch. The pain eased a bit.

"My wife's one of your biggest fans, Miss Carr," Lieutenant Brazil was saying. "She follows you in all the papers, *The Searcher, The Investigator,* you know. . . ."

Bryna, struggling to get her bearings, realized how disappointed she was in Lieutenant Brazil. Where she had hoped for a hard-nosed skeptic she would have to win over she was presented instead with a gushing true believer. She spoke more sharply than she intended.

"No, I don't know," she said. "I never read tabloids."

"Well, I know they're a little sensational sometimes," Brazil said, slightly abashed, "but they reach the common people, millions of them. There's something to be said for that, don't you think? I mean, they get right down to the grass roots, don't they? Like I say, my wife never misses an item about you or your— what do you call her—your spirit guide. I notice there was no mention of her in the film we just saw. I thought . . ."

"I'm sure most of what you've read about this is nonsense," Manning cut in.

"Sabra, isn't it? Isn't that what you call her," Brazil persisted, as if he had not heard Manning.

Bryna began to speak, but Manning cut in.

"Sabra is just a word," the researcher said, forcing a smile, assuming a remedial tone. "Psychics are human like the rest of us, Lieutenant. But they do have the ability to use talents that remain dormant in most of us. Sometimes their minds require little tricks to help them employ those talents. It's like hypnosis induced through the invocation of some word that's been planted during a previous hypnotic session. You just say that word and you go into trance. It simplifies things. Think of 'Sabra' as a word like that. 'Sabra' is not a *she*; 'Sabra' is a mechanism employed by Miss Carr to facilitate access to the trance state in which her psychic abilities express themselves."

Brazil looked blankly at Manning for a moment. Then: "That's . . . that's very interesting, Doctor. But I did get the impression in Miss Carr's book . . ."

The research chamber was arranged rather like Bryna Carr's psychic salon. Three cubicles on a small, lighted stage, sunken rather than raised, surrounded by plush risers for easy observation by small audiences, housed the electronic equipment. Video cameras were trained on the stage. Monitors linked to the word processor permitted the audience to see both the questions and answers typed into the system. Niko was in the editing cubicle, as usual. Dr. Manning was in another, ready to ask questions. Bryna was in the third space, waiting to go into trance. Dr. Manning gave her the signal. He had already given Niko instructions to transmit Sabra's name only to Bryna's screen. He would have asked that the name not be used at all, but he had tried that in the past and nothing whatever had come through.

Bryna, acknowledging Manning's signal, looked into her screen, which emitted blue light. She felt hot, and it was difficult to concentrate. She wished that she could chant a mantra aloud to quiet her mind, to clear it, but she knew that would embarrass Dr. Manning. Bryna shut her eyes for a moment and began some of the breathing exercises she had relied upon years earlier. She pulled air into her lungs, deeper and deeper, then held. She repeated this several times, trying to obliterate the feeling that this time she would fail, that she would not be able to achieve the trance state. She repeated the breathing exercise several times until the body of water she could normally visualize in seconds at last came into inner view, its blue-black surface crashing against towering bluffs, much stormier than usual. Soon she could feel herself struggling in the water, desperate to keep her ahead above the jarring waves.

When she could struggle no longer she let herself sink into it, consciously submitting to it. Normally, at this point Sabra would begin to breathe for her, and gradually the water would calm and she would be suspended in it, aware only of the blue void and the silent breathing of the other, a rhythmic, reassuring wind that issued in and out of her. This time it was different. Bryna began distinctly to feel the water invading her lungs. She began to cough and choke. She felt caught between herself and the other—one attempting to inhale, the other trying to exhale. She thrashed in the water, trying to lift herself out of it, but by now the whirlpool had seized her and she could feel herself being dragged under, deeper and deeper, sinking in its inky darkness.

When it seemed her lungs would burst she abruptly found herself facing a man in a room. The man was holding out his hand. There was hurt in his eyes; he was telling her that he loved her. She saw herself with blonde hair and blue eyes—but the face was unmistakably her own—staring coldly at the man, a knife in her hand. The man pleaded with her. He was her father. She watched herself calmly throw back her arm and hurl the knife at him. A double-edged dagger with an ivory and ruby handle, the knife sunk deep into Bryan's chest. His eyes fixed on her, their pale, blue hurt stinging like acid, their disbelief total, searing, annihilating. The man took one step toward her and fell heavily, dead at her feet. When his eyes blinked open, frozen open in death, they were the eyes, this was the face, not of her father, but of Ethan Kendal.

Bryna watched it all on videotape later. Normally she could not stand to watch herself. The sight of herself becoming rigid, of her eyes growing large, vacant and fixated always disturbed her deeply. But this time she had to watch. Niko had tried to dissuade her, telling her that if she insisted upon seeing it she should wait at least until she was out of the hospital. But she would not listen; she told herself that somehow it was her *duty* to see it, to try to understand what had happened.

It all began as she remembered it, with the breathing. Then

suddenly she saw and heard herself choking and coughing. She saw herself clutch at her mouth and throat, saw the blood congest in her face, first red, then almost blue. She watched as she flung the glass door to her cubicle open with such force that it shattered. Her eyes were terrible as she staggered out of the cubicle and onto the stage, stumbling through the wicked shards of broken glass, stooping to pick one of them up, clutching it like a knife, blood running down its full length to drip off its sharp point. Bryna saw herself stagger toward the risers, obviously intent upon something or someone. The camera moved dizzyingly, and suddenly she saw Ethan Kendal's horrified face and herself moving toward him. Brazil was just starting to get up, as was Ethan, when she collapsed at the writer's feet.

The moment Bryna saw Ethan Kendal's face on the television screen through which the videotape was played she saw the face of her father—just the way he had looked while she was in trance. His expression flashed to her with searing clarity. She looked at her hand, mittened now in bandages. The vomit spilled from her, down the front of her hospital smock, its heat burning her breasts. Niko hurried toward her.

he's dead. i killed him.

The words flashed to her across the years and she heard herself say now what she had heard herself say then:

"Niko, hold me, please just hold me, Niko, Niko."

FIVE

James Raymond, disguised as a telephone repairman, drove the van he had rented under one of his aliases into the service entrance of Clare Friedkin's Bel Aire estate. He had been watching the house for some time. He knew that Friedkin was home and that she had a man—or, rather, a boy—with her. Carl, the muscular black houseman who had worked for Friedkin for years, met Raymond at the service entrance. Raymond had called ahead.

"It's like I say," Carl complained, eyeing the van suspiciously. "I checked all the phones. We have no problem here."

"The problem isn't *here*," Raymond said, from behind tinted glasses and a bushy brown beard. "It's further down the line; we have to check the capacitance at intermediate points. There was a power surge that could reduce the . . . takes too long to explain."

Carl still looked dubious, but the impressive set of tools and beeping portable phone unit hanging from the actor's hips persuaded him to let the man in. The moment Carl's back was turned, Raymond hit him on the head with the butt of his forty-five. The big man collapsed without a sound. Carl, Raymond knew, was Friedkin's only live-in servant; the others had left for the evening.

The actor moved stealthily up the stairs. He had been in the house before and knew his way. That was what so enraged him, the fact that Clare Friedkin, who still pretended to be his friend, was the one who was blackmailing him. He knew that she would be upstairs somewhere, probably in her bedroom with the boy. As he mounted the last riser he heard muffled voices coming from the end of the long corridor. He crept along the wall, trembling with excitement and fury. He was not sure just yet how he was going to do it, but he was certain it wasn't going to be pretty.

He listened for a moment outside the bedroom door. He could hear Friedkin's voice. He had imagined its sound for two weeks now, hating it, longing to smother it. It was all he could do to keep himself from bursting into the room at once, but he forced himself to wait, listening. The boy was with her. The door was thick, and it was difficult to hear, but it sounded as if the woman was excited. He envisioned the scene inside. Carefully, he tried the knob. It wasn't locked. He pushed the door open quietly, holding the gun in his right hand.

For a moment they didn't see him. The gossip columnist was naked, spread-eagled across the bed, her arms and feet bound and tied to its solid four posts. The slenderly muscled, dark-haired boy, about eighteen, was also naked; he stood next to the bed, cursing the columnist, striking her with a riding crop, raising three welts in rapid succession across her pendulous breasts and sagging stomach. The woman cried out with each blow, her body writhing with pleasure, her eyes opening and closing rapidly. Raymond noted the huge dildo on the bed between the woman's legs. In a flick of his eye he took in the rest of the room, a veritable torture chamber, complete with wrist manacles bolted to the walls, whips, leather face masks and a large variety of the sort of toys carried by the better-outfitted S & M boutiques.

Raymond pushed the door closed behind him with a resounding and intended thud. Friedkin opened her eyes in horror and lurched forward, straining against the ropes, panic invading every crevice of her face. The boy wheeled round still gripping the riding crop. Raymond smiled at them malevolently.

"Oh my god," Friedkin whispered. "It's . . . stop him, stop him . . . it's the murderer!" She was fairly shrieking now.

The boy, however, did nothing, immobilized by shock and fear. "Hurry, *hurry!*" Friedkin screamed. "Get him, get him before he gets us!" The boy, drained of all color, stepped back rather than forward.

As Friedkin moaned, bucking hysterically against the ropes, the boy, eyeing the intruder warily, his voice trembling, said, "I don't want any part of this. I don't know who you are and I don't care. If you want her, man, you got her," he added, throwing down the riding crop and stepping further back and away from the bed. "She's just another john to me," he said.

"You shit, you shit," Friedkin sputtered.

Raymond realized how perfect it all was. He could tie up the boy and kill Friedkin, and it would be assumed that this was just the latest in the series of celebrity murders. Raymond had followed all of the news accounts about them. He reached for the gun concealed under his belt and nodded the boy over to the wall. "Into those," he said, disguising his voice, making it deeper. The boy faced into the wall and the actor closed the manacles around his wrists and ankles.

Friedkin could only roll from side to side, her eyes bugging, her breasts heaving. Raymond bent over to pick up the riding crop, needing to strike her with something besides his fist. As he stooped down his wig slipped off and he knew he had betrayed himself.

"You," she said, sucking in her breath. "My god, *Jimmy!*"

Hearing his name uttered by her slashed at him like a knife. All the hate spilled out. He realized now that he had *wanted* her to know his true identity, so that she would know what she was dying for.

"Why?" she said. "Oh, Jimmy, *why?*"

"Why? Why?" he shouted. "You *fucking, cunting, blackmailing* slut! You ask me *why!*" He struck her across the face with the crop, then threw it aside and pointed the gun at her, his hand shaking badly.

"I'll blow your fucking brains out you blackmailing bitch!"

"Blackmail? Blackmail. I'd never . . . Jimmy, please, wait, wait. I'd never blackmail you, never, *never.* My god, we've been friends, *friends,* Jimmy, for nearly thirty years, we fought the reds together, my *god,* we worked side by side for Reagan in *three* campaigns! *Me* blackmail *you! Jimmy, Jimmy, Jimmy.* Please, *baby. Listen* to me!"

The energy of this outburst, the word, "baby," the repetition of his name, threw him off, unnerved him. "The... the boy," he stammered. "In Bangkok, the telephone call..."

"Boy? *Boy!*" Friedkin suddenly had an inkling. "The *boys!* Jimmy, for godsake, I've known about the *boys* for years. One of my men picked that up, my god, it was ten years ago, *ten years ago,* Jimmy, those trips you were always taking to Mexico. He followed you on his own. I never put him up to it, Jimmy, I told him to forget it! I told him he was *mistaken,* that if he ever repeated it to anybody he was as good as dead in the business. Blackmail *you!* Jimmy, for godsake, I *protected* you! You're a national treasure, Jimmy, I'd never do anything to..." Friedkin was sobbing now. "Jimmy, Jimmy," she blubbered, "I protected you the same way Louella protected Monty years ago."

Raymond stood by the bed, drooping now, the gun hanging limply at his side. It was true what she said about Mexico, those trips years earlier. He felt exhausted.

"Somebody's set you up," Friedkin was saying. "I'll help you, Jimmy. We'll find out *who.* You've got to trust me, let me help you."

Raymond sat down on the edge of the bed, then fell against the big woman, burying his face in her pillowy breasts, sobbing.

"Baby, *baby,*" she cooed. "*Trust* me, baby. We'll get whoever it is. That's right, baby, cry, *cry.* Get it all out." She moved her chest, caressing his face with her breasts, unable to touch him with her hands.

"It must be her," he said suddenly, raising his face. "She's the only one who could have known. How could I have...?"

"*Who,* Jimmy, *who?* Tell me; I'll put my *best* man on it."

"Bryna Carr," Jimmy said softly.

Dr. Hevesey glanced at her cheerless reflection in the mirror near the door to her office, strategically placed there so that patients who were crying or angry when they left might miraculously pull themselves together in time to present a composed and reassuring picture to those standing by in the waiting room. Dr. Hevesey flashed herself a forced smile, its egregious phoniness lightening her mood a little, thinking an "up" attitude was the least she could provide for Bryna Carr who, after all, as her most celebrated and unusual patient, had contributed something different to her placid, if lucrative, practice. In Bryna Carr, at least, she had a patient whose *business* was insight but who was, from the psychiatrist's point of view, ironically and remarkably blind to her own reality. That this apparent lack of *self*-insight might be essential to Bryna Carr's continued existence was what continually intrigued Dr. Hevesey.

It had been two years since Bryna had begun seeing the psychiatrist two and three times a week. In their time together, Dr. Hevesey reflected, she had grappled with every possibility concerning Sabra. She had become an expert on spirit possession but had always regarded that hypothesis as delusional.

She had also considered the possibility that Sabra might be fictional, a psychic prop designed to make Bryna herself more colorful. But that hypothesis, too, was soon discarded. The doctor's observations convinced her that Bryna was incapable of conscious fraud.

At the root of her patient's problem, the psychiatrist now believed, was a deep and abiding inferiority complex *imposed upon* a mind of unusual brilliance and imagination, a mind that was at vast odds with its own, conscious perception of itself. Bryna could not believe herself capable of any real imagination and so was constantly having to "find" outside "sources" for her own ingenuity. This explained the haglike dream entity that Bryna, under hypnosis, recalled from her early childhood, the doll Goldie, the voice that spoke to her, all of these ultimately coalescing in what Dr. Hevesey regarded as the hallucinatory image of Sabra, psychic spirit guide, the ultimate origin of all thoughts, imaginings, feelings, emotions that Bryna could not believe were her own.

Bryna, Dr. Hevesey knew, still saw herself very much as she had been as a child and adolescent—fat, lame, blemished, dull, doomed, though, in fact, to the objective eye, she was now slim and attractive. Sabra, Dr. Hevesey decided, was that impossible "golden princess," the seductive Cinderella Bryna's father had conjured up. Part of her was still trying to please him. In fact, Dr. Hevesey was now convinced, Bryna had subconsciously pledged herself to her dead father, pledged her virginity to him, determined to be faithful to him, to atone for her mother's sins and assuage her own guilt.

The unbridled part of Bryna's being still needed a sexual outlet, and Sabra, Dr. Hevesey reasoned, provided that outlet—with a vengeance. A classically dissociated part of Bryna's personality, Sabra could do what she liked with her body, and Bryna, so long as she consciously clung to the belief that Sabra was an

159

independent entity, could disavow any responsibility for her actions. A defense mechanism kept Bryna from remembering what Sabra did.

It was further apparent to the doctor that Bryna had invested everything unique about herself in Sabra. It was Sabra, Bryna insisted, who was psychic, not she. And indeed, whenever Sabra was not present, Bryna exhibited no extrasensory capability whatever. Yet Dr. Hevesey at no time entertained the idea of a psychiatric exorcism, an attempt to extinguish the Sabra personality, though she knew some of her colleagues would consider her remiss for not having done so. For one thing, the psychiatrist was quite certain that if she "killed" Sabra she would kill Bryna, as well, that without the nourishment of the mind and body that Sabra provided, without the emotional outlet, Bryna would either explode with frustration or simply wither away, devolving into an empty shell. Sabra, Dr. Hevesey felt, could perhaps survive without Bryna, but Bryna could never survive without Sabra; of that she was certain.

For a time, Dr. Hevesey hoped for an integration of the two personalities she perceived, but Bryna had demonstrated a disappointingly low tolerance for her other self. Indeed, she had not even yet come to seriously consider the possibility that Sabra was anything but a *real*—supernatural—entity over whom she had only restricted control. To accept Sabra as part of her own self, Dr. Hevesey realized, Bryna would have to come to grips with her own sexual and intellectual imagination and with another life which almost certainly was at shocking odds with her own. She would have to admit to "infidelities."

In the absence of either exorcism or integration, Dr. Hevesey had played it by ear. She was of that small but growing school of psychiatry that believes that "normalcy," the ability to function with minimal assistance in society, is quite often the product of distorted perception—of some "impossible" but ultimately saving idea. Delusions, illusions, even hallucinations could be useful. For Bryna, the Sabra personality represented, at least to some degree, Dr. Hevesey once wrote in her journal, "an ingenious mechanism of self-preservation, effecting an elegant accommodation of impulses and drives that might otherwise be at deadly war with one another, utterly incapacitating her."

In short, Dr. Hevesey was tolerant of Sabra and to some extent admiring of the imagination which, almost of necessity, she believed, had conceived and created her. At the same time, there was a vast difference, she recognized, between merely functioning and actually being happy and fulfilled. She wondered if Bryna, particularly now as she entered into those years when she should be most sexually and socially active, could survive on the meager slice of life she had reserved for herself.

Bryna was grateful the doctor had agreed to see her on such short notice. For an hour she talked with Dr. Hevesey about what had happened at Spectrum, how oddly she had been affected by Ethan Kendal, how she had felt "caught in some new, terrifying place" when her trance had seemingly misfired, how for the first time she had been able to remember something of what happened in the trance state, how her father, the victim of her deadly dream assault, had merged with the image of Ethan Kendal.

Bryna spoke haltingly, fearfully, yet somehow, it seemed to Dr. Hevesey, hopefully, as well. "He was so . . . from the beginning . . . from the first moment I saw him, I felt . . . it was as if my father was there, standing there, that I . . . that I had another chance . . . and then, oh, god . . . what happened . . . it was awful. . . ."

Dr. Hevesey tried to mask her excitement. She spoke gently. "Have you spoken with him, with Ethan Kendal, since it happened?"

Bryna shook her head forlornly. "I doubt that he'll dare come anywhere near me now." She looked up, brightening a little. "It wasn't simply the resemblance; it was . . . something more. I felt . . ." She stopped, embarrassed.

"Have you thought of asking Sabra about him?"

Bryna looked at the other woman sharply. "No," she said, almost vehemently. Then, embarrassed again, she said more quietly, "No, I haven't. It's . . . there's nothing to ask her."

At the end of the session, Bryna asked Dr. Hevesey to prescribe some mild tranquilizers, saying she was "jumpy" and had not been able to sleep. Dr. Hevesey, who took a dim view of most psychotropic drugs, hesitated, then complied, cautioning Bryna to "go easy on the pills."

As soon as Bryna had gone, Lou Anne buzzed.

"Nobody out here," the secretary said. "I just wanted to check in. Miss Carr seemed more agitated than usual. Anything new?"

Naomi Hevesey had been confiding in her faithful secretary for years. In fact, she often joked that Lou Anne should send her monthly bills for professional services. Such was the secretary's loyalty that the psychiatrist considered it no real breach of professional ethics to confide in her—and it did Naomi Hevesey a great deal of good. Lou Anne was *her* outlet.

"Yes, as a matter of fact there is something new. The psychic is in love, but she doesn't know it yet."

It wasn't until a week after her emergency session with Dr. Hevesey that Bryna discovered that Niko had for days been deflecting calls from Ethan Kendal. He had done this, she knew, with the best of intentions—trying to protect her from further stress—but she snapped at him anyway when she lifted the receiver one afternoon and heard Niko telling Ethan that she was indisposed. She waited until Ethan had hung up, then, her voice rising, she had ordered Niko never to take such "liberties" again. Niko's shock over this scolding was apparent, and Bryna immediately regretted the incident, but in her excitement over learning that Ethan had been trying to reach her daily she neglected to apologize.

The next day, Ethan called again, and this time she talked to him. He spoke only briefly, inviting her to dinner. She felt her heart pound ridiculously—like a schoolgirl's, she thought—as she accepted. Her readings went poorly all the rest of that day. Sabra, she could tell by Niko's expression and by a quick glance at some of the transcripts of that day's proceedings, had been in an evil temper. Bryna shrugged and hurried to get ready for that evening.

She was usually careful to look businesslike in public, fashionable but never provocative. Tonight, as she looked over the choices her wardrobe afforded, nothing pleased her. She had suddenly had enough of high necks, tweed jackets, tasteful, pleated skirts. She spotted a pale green, satiny dress with low neckline and sashed waist and quickly put it on. She piled her hair high on her head, fastening it so that only a few ringlets fell on either side of her face. Without pausing to give herself time to "come to her senses," she applied her makeup with a bit more daring than usual, added a finely crafted triple-strand gold choker, heels and a lacy wrap with full, elbow-length sleeves of a pale green that matched her dress, and only then allowed herself a lingering look in the mirror, perhaps fearing that if she looked too long she would once again become the fat, sullen child of her nightmares. If she lost her nerve now, it would be too late to change, anyway. She took one of the tranquilizers Dr. Hevesey had prescribed— already her supply was running low—and put the bottle in her clutch bag.

When the housekeeper called to say that Mr. Kendal had arrived, she went promptly downstairs, passing Niko in the hall. It wasn't until she was climbing into Ethan's BMW that she understood the combination of shock and hurt she had seen in Niko's eyes. The dress she was wearing had been a gift from him; the color, he said, suited her dark hair and green eyes. It was obvious he thought it suited other parts of her anatomy, too. She had previously tried it on only once and then put it in the back of the closet, promising Niko she would wear it "on the right occasion."

At the end of the dinner—Ethan had chosen Julius' Castle, a romantic restaurant perched amongst the trees on the edge of Telegraph Hill—Bryna realized she had eaten but not tasted her food. Ethan, no doubt hoping to help her relax, had done most of the talking. He had told her a little about his family, of his southern belle mother, overshadowed obviously by her husband, Ethan's famous father, General Nathan Edward Kendal, whose last hurrah had been the Vietnam War. Ethan spoke of his time with Army intelligence, serving under his father, "in the gung-ho days when we still thought we were there to win," of the sophisticated surveillance technologies they used to so little avail, of his growing disillusionment with the war, of his final break with the "old man," of his mother's suicide, of his writing career. It hurt Bryna to hear Ethan deprecate his earlier work.

"I read one of your novels. I thought it superb. I sensed something in it . . ."

"What was that?"

"I don't know. A longing, I guess, a desire to be in control, taking a responsible, active role instead of muddling on, letting events dictate our lives . . ." Bryna stopped, feeling self-conscious.

Ethan smiled at her quizzically. "I had no idea you'd read any of my stuff. I'm flattered."

Bryna felt her cheeks grow warm. "Actually," she blurted, "I just read it this week."

Ethan said nothing, but looked at her intently, a faint smile still on his lips.

"I . . . I felt I had to know you," Bryna said, filling the silence. "Even if I never saw you again."

Ethan put his hand on hers, and his touch seemed, for a moment, to alter Bryna's vision, to make it sharper, more perceptive. The way he looked, tall, slender, broad-shouldered, his hair the color of straw, his pale blue eyes (in Bryna's imagination these were suddenly the deceptively serene portals of a cavernous imagination), the way his lean, clean-shaven face still managed to dimple slightly when he smiled, the curve of his lips, the articulation of his long, strong fingers, his voice, his vibration, even his smell, somewhere between that of a man and a boy, perpetually young, all of these things, real or imagined, suddenly, sharply recalled Bryan. Except that Bryan was dead, Ethan alive.

"My current book," he said, "will put all that earlier stuff to shame."

Bryna, grateful that the conversation had veered away from the personal, said, "It seems an unusual topic for someone like yourself."

"Unusual? Murder? It's pretty fundamental, isn't it? My other books dealt with death, too, but there it was accidental or institutionalized death. In war, death has no morality. There's no choice involved, not really. It's all passive—the individual being acted upon by the collective consciousness or some societal directive, by chance, by accident, by the negative energy of inertia. . . ."

This time Ethan looked a little self-conscious. "Don't get me started on this," he said, "I can go on all night."

"Please," Bryna said, "I could *listen* all night."

"These murders," Ethan said, signaling for the check, "are something different. They're not at all like the killings you have, say, in war. Society, by and large, considers those okay. But the truth is those killings are, in many ways, more immoral than these murders. In war nobody, no individual, really takes responsibility. It's as if a mindless machine is pulling the trigger. We have all sorts of soothing names for that machine: democracy, communism, freedom, justice. But these murders, more than any others I've studied, seem to be the product of an individual will, actively directed. . . ."

"You mean whoever is doing them is *choosing* to do them, without motive, other than as a pure expression of active will?"

Ethan looked at Bryna with surprise. "It took me months to capsulize it that way, in my own mind," he said. "I thought *you* weren't psychic."

Bryna looked embarrassed, then puzzled.

"You see," Ethan said, "I've been doing some reading of my own lately. In fact, I just read *your* book. I was intrigued by your references to what you call your spirit guide, Sabra. You're really convinced she is the source of your psychic power?"

"I'm capable of generating my own thoughts," Bryna said. "You don't have to be psychic to be insightful on occasion."

"I'm sorry," Ethan said. "I was simply surprised by your perception of something that eluded me for some time." He studied her for a moment, weighing his words, then added: "I'm beginning to see why the police want your help."

It was the closest they had come to talking about what had happened at Spectrum, when Bryna's trance had gone all wrong and . . . She tried to smother the image. She wasn't ready yet to talk about it. She felt certain that the celebrity murders still figured somehow in her destiny, but that certainty was now more unsettling than encouraging.

"From what you've said," Bryna commented, purposely ignoring Ethan's last statement, "I gather you don't think the murderer is deranged."

"Not really. Not in the common sense. I think he—or she—perceives of all this as something of a cosmic joke, taking actors, actresses, entertainers mainly, making them perform, entertain even in death. . . ."

Bryna shuddered. "It's not human to kill in this way, everything planned, staged."

"Well, then, if it isn't human is it superhuman or subhuman? We call those who love without motive saints—superhumans. I'm not sure that makes sense. Those are some of the issues this book deals with. And, of course, I could be dead wrong. There could be quite ordinary motives for all of these murders—all cleverly disguised. But I don't see any pattern so far and believe me, I've looked for patterns. There've been times when I've wondered if it isn't some diabolically resourceful, out-of-work director staging a series of fatal set pieces, getting even with the industry. The only trouble with that hypothesis is that any director *that* clever couldn't help but be in endless demand."

"Talent is often overlooked," Bryna countered. It somehow came out sounding wrong to her ear, almost complaining.

Ethan was silent for a moment, looking at the last of his wine.

"In *The Psychic Within*," Ethan said, "I almost got the feeling that you regard Sabra as something more than just an inner voice. . . ."

"That book was written years ago, when I was still performing in clubs in Los Angeles," Bryna interrupted. "It isn't exactly anything I'm proud of. The writing is awful, and I know it."

"I'm not going to tell you the writing is going to win you a Nobel Prize," Ethan said. "Not that that should break your heart. Prizes don't sell books. I imagine you did pretty well with this. I see it's gone through several printings, which is more than you can say for any of my books. Anyway, I wasn't talking about your style; I was talking about content. I wished you had said

165

more, though, about Sabra and the whole Tantric concept. You talked about the *kundalini*, the energy that the tantrikas believe is at the base of their psychic power, the idea that that is replenished through meditation, sexual ritual, in particular..."

Ethan stopped a moment, as if considering what to say next. Bryna felt her heart pound.

"I have to admit to some confusion," he continued. "How does a Tantric *spirit* replenish itself?"

Bryna felt herself getting warm again. She hated to blush. Her eyes met Ethan's for a moment, then she quickly looked at her wine glass.

"If that question is out of line,..." Ethan began.

"There are volumes written on Tantric philosophy," Bryna said stiffly and, as she was aware, not at all to the point. "I've edited a couple of them myself. My interest in the subject is scholarly." She knew she was sounding like a prig and hated herself. "Sabra is a... something," she stumbled on, "an energy, if you want to look at it that way, that expresses itself through me when I'm in an altered state of consciousness. She... it, whatever, claims Tantra as the source of her psychic power."

Bryna stopped, thinking she was only making matters more confusing. She knew she had not answered Ethan's question, and she knew that *he* knew it.

"If the Tantric angle makes you so uncomfortable," Ethan persisted, "why did you mention it at all in the book?"

"It doesn't make me... it helps explain..."

"I'm sorry," Ethan said. "I'm not trying to probe your sex life."

"I think we should go," Bryna said, the blood stinging her cheeks.

Outside the restaurant, climbing the steps that wound up through gardens and trees to the parking lot at the base of Coit Tower, glowing luminously far above, Ethan grabbed Bryna's hand, stopping her. She halted her rapid ascent, but did not look at him.

"I'm sorry," he said, "I really am, but I have to admit, I *did* mean to probe. I've been consumed with curiosity about you from the first moment I saw you. When I read your book my imagination ran away with me. I wondered if I was going to have to compete with..."

Bryna turned and looked at him, silencing him with her pleading eyes. A thought formed in her mind, but she could not give voice to it; its mere existence was frightening enough. Ethan's arms were around her, and she fell into them. His mouth pressed against hers. She felt something shift deep inside her.

SIX

It was only a kiss, Bryna told herself the next day, but the memory of it so agitated her that she had canceled all appointments for the day, pleading illness. She asked Niko to deflect all phone calls, then kept checking with him to see who was calling. Ethan called twice that morning and was told each time that Bryna was too ill to come to the phone. Bryna's state was such by noon that she had already taken twice the prescribed number of tranquilizers for the entire day.

Late in the afternoon, pacing about her study, watching the December fog boil into the mouth of the bay, Bryna could stand it no longer. She asked Niko to put Ethan's next call through to her. It was only minutes later that he called and she answered.

"Goddamn it," he said, "what are you trying to do to me?"

"I don't..."

"You said we'd talk today."

"Not today. I don't feel..."

"Look, a week ago you tried to kill me, last night you kissed me. I think I'm due some sort of explanation. I'm coming over."

Bryna held the phone tautly for a moment. Ethan had hung up. She put down the receiver. She felt flushed, shamed by Ethan's words, miserable with the memory of the previous evening—the tears after the kiss, her inability to explain to Ethan why she was crying or what she was feeling. And yet she also felt a strange exhilaration, as if she were on the verge of some impossible discovery.

She sat down at her desk, shuffled papers, rose, paced the room, felt her thoughts and her heart pounding inside her, felt she would explode—waiting. She took yet another of the little blue pills. And still the ringing of the phone made her jump. It was Niko announcing Ethan's arrival, offering to get rid of him.

"No," Bryna said, a bit too loud, "bring him up."

She sat at her desk again, put on reading glasses she rarely wore, opened a client's file, as if she were absorbed in work. The pose seemed so patently false, however, that she immediately removed the glasses, closed the file and leapt to her feet, repositioning herself on the sofa, opening a magazine, as if demurely whiling away the minutes. This, too, struck her as ludicrous. She was on the way to the bay window behind her desk, to be found there in a contemplative, convalescent mood, when Niko rapped on the door.

"Come in," she said weakly, turning slowly around. Niko was holding the door open, Ethan standing there waiting to be invited in, obviously annoyed by the arm—Niko's—that still blocked his entrance.

"Ethan," Bryna said, her tone flat in the effort to betray no emotion.

Niko withdrew his arm. "Remember your appointment at eight-thirty," he said pointedly, glancing at Bryna before turning to go.

"Why do I get the feeling that guy doesn't like me?" Ethan asked, when they were alone.

"Niko?" Bryna said, trying to smile. "He doesn't even know you."

"I believe he's jealous," Ethan said. He took several steps into the room, until he was only a step from her. "I think he has reason to be," he added, taking the final step, pulling her into his arms.

She felt the tension of the day drain from her, drifted until his kisses became too insistent and demanded a response. She felt a new tension building and pulled herself free of him. She turned and moved to the window, looking out, trying to compose herself.

"I thought we were going to talk," she said, her voice barely audible. She peered into the fog that was rolling along the surface of the water in sensuous white curves, looking rather like downed cumulus clouds. Soon, she knew, the fog would swell up around the old house, as it did almost every afternoon this time of year, blocking her view, leaving her no choice but to face Ethan.

"All right," Ethan said briskly. "Let's talk. No, *you* talk. Tell me what happened at Spectrum last week?"

"It had nothing to do with you," she said, her tone contradicting her.

"I find that hard to believe."

"It...the trance didn't take. Something happened and I saw..." Her throat began to constrict. "I saw something that..." She felt his hand on her shoulder and broke, weeping softly. She imagined that her tears mingled with the fog, wisps of which were already billowing up around the window. She felt enveloped by it, the last tranquilizer finally taking hold. The warm pressure on her shoulder was comforting. After several moments she began again, feeling both of his hands caressing her shoulder and neck. He said nothing.

"It was... my father. I saw my father. He was telling me... telling me he loved me, begging me not to... I had a knife and I... I threw it, and he fell... when his... when I could see his eyes they weren't *his* eyes any longer. They were yours."

"What in god's name do you mean?"

She shook her head, tears still coming from her eyes, then pressed her face against his chest, unable to endure his eyes any longer. "You remind me of him so much," she sobbed.

He tilted her head gently back so that he could see her eyes again, but she shut them, and said in a tortured voice, "I always thought somehow... somehow I killed him."

Ethan waited a moment, then said, "I think you'd better tell me everything."

In the more than two hours that followed, Ethan practiced his interviewer's art, drawing Bryna out with a few carefully chosen words and expectant silences, probing the murkier recesses of her childhood and adolescence. Bryna spoke as she had never spoken to anyone before, confiding her deep and special love for her father, feelings about his death, her loneliness and self-loathing, her belief in Sabra as the source of her psychic insight, her dreams of bringing new scientific respectability to psychic research, her hopes for the project at Spectrum and her fear that she might not be able to help the police, even the fact that she had kept from the police that Marissa Salomon had once been her client, everything except her compact with Sabra.

Even as she unburdened herself of a thousand anxieties, a new and more intense fear was building in her, the fear that Ethan would discover Sabra's use of her body. It seemed to her that he had somehow already begun to suspect, that inadequately guarded comments in her book and the Tantric artifacts in which she immersed herself were giving her away. What she had filled the house with in a desperate effort to convince *herself* of the philosophical, religious and *moral* validity of Sabra's lifestyle now seemed shabby cover, indeed, each sexually explicit piece of art emitting dangerous clues of an aberration Bryna suddenly wanted above all else to conceal from Ethan Kendal.

Sometime, somewhere in the course of their encounter, Ethan had moved—and Bryna with him—to the couch. She could not remember for how long he had sat next to her, his arm around her. But suddenly she was aware that his arm *was* around her and that, in fact, he was kissing her softly on the neck. She knew a good deal of time must have passed, for the room was now in darkness, save for the dim light of a small lamp she had turned on in the late afternoon. Nor did she know for how long both of them had been silent.

As his lips found the lobe of her ear, she felt his fingertips gently press against her breast. She tried to fend off panic with speech, but no words would come. As his lips closed over hers she felt his hand cup her breast more firmly. She felt her mouth open, unbidden, and his tongue enter her. Somewhere, seemingly out of touch with her brain, she felt her hand burn and realized that it was from the heat of his flesh, that her hand was on his thigh. She seemed powerless to remove it.

From a far distance, and through the fog, she saw herself sinking back into the softness of the sofa, Ethan on the floor alongside, leaning over her, kissing her, whispering to her, touching her.

"You're so beautiful," she heard him murmur. "Relax. Just relax."

His voice was faint, adding to the feeling that she was watching, listening from a distance, disconnected from what was transpiring on the sofa. She saw the girl who looked like herself reach out and touch the handsome young man, touch him on the face, the lips, open her mouth, inviting more of his kisses, saw the man begin to unbutton her blouse, saw him pause from this place to place his hand on her leg, to let his fingers slide up under her skirt. . . .

The phone rang, louder than Bryna had ever heard it ring before, and abruptly the perception of distance evaporated and she found herself in her body, on the sofa, blinking into Ethan's eyes as if he were, for a second, a complete stranger. His hands pulled away as she stiffened, so quickly that she could not be sure where he had been touching her. Her panic was real enough now, and she had only the slightest awareness of how unbalanced she must suddenly look to Ethan, as she struggled to her feet, pushing past him.

"My god," she said, "the time . . . I . . ."

She fidgeted with the buttons of her blouse with one hand, unaware that she was doing so, and lifted the receiver with her other hand. It was Niko, as she had known it would be.

"You've got exactly two minutes," Niko said, the anger in his voice ill-concealed.

Normally, before turning the body over to Sabra, Bryna "checked out" at least ten minutes before departure, so that there would be time to discuss anything that needed to be tended to by Niko in her absence.

"I'm leaving now," Bryna said, out of breath.

She put the phone down, glanced briefly at Ethan. "I'm sorry," she said. "I have another appointment..."

"*Appointment*," he said, "is that what I am, just one of your appointments? I don't get you," he said standing up, adjusting his pants. "We were in the process of ridding you of your virginity, or so you'd have me believe, and you're worried, to the point of aborting an absolutely crucial fuck, about a goddamned *appointment?*"

"I..." Bryna knew it was hopeless. She couldn't possibly explain. She hurried from the room, leaving Ethan behind to untangle the shirt he had already removed and tossed aside.

Niko was on the landing, a scowling timekeeper. His eyes swept over her, finding in her disheveled appearance the confirmation of his fears. He watched Bryna mount the stairs that led to the Void.

Ethan moved sullenly through the suggestive murk of the bar, the humiliation he had experienced earlier in the evening endowing him with a vengeful horniness. The sullenness, he knew, proceeded from the predictability of it all—the male need to prove himself in the wake of a fiasco. A spectacular sexual fiasco. Ethan resented the mandate of his glands; the phrase "being led by the balls" flashed through his mind. Nonetheless, a good fuck, one preferably free of any pretense of something "meaningful," he told himself, loomed as the only practical antidote to the frustration and anger he was still feeling.

The swell of a woman's ass, neatly packaged in a pair of skintight jeans, caught his eye. He followed her, deeper into one of the tunnels, each of which featured recessed bars, conversational alcoves, make-out niches, freaky mirrors and imaginative lighting schemes. The tunnels, some of them dark and padded, others intermittently bright and made of transparent material, emanated spokelike from a central hub which was the main dancing and drinking area. So far he had not seen her face, but through a momentary opening in the crush of bodies he had to squeeze through as he pursued her he observed that she had an alluring figure, a small waist, perfect ass. She turned just slightly at one point, enough so that he could see the generous swell of her breasts, braless in a skintight tube top. Men were turning to look at her.

Finally she turned and paused for a moment, her eyes seeking. Her long, blonde hair was strikingly accented by the gold lamé of her tube top. Ethan was stunned by her beauty—and by something familiar about her. He was almost certain he had seen her somewhere before. She did not smile at him, but her look—for him alone, he was sure of it—was unmistakably physical, her blue eyes not quite fully open, her lips slightly parted. She let one of her arms fall carelessly in front of her, her fingers brushing against her inner thigh.

She glided from sight, like an apparition, and Ethan hurried after her. The smell of poppers filled the air. The floor here felt like it was made of sponge rubber; so did the walls. Dim lights flashed erratically, illuminating various recesses, pods and bifurcations off the main passage. Ethan could see couples in embrace, one man with his hand up the skirt of a woman, his other hand holding the popper to her nose. Another couple rubbed coke on their gums, giggled and french kissed. The music oozed from the serpentine foam walls.

The darkness was so complete at one point that Ethan had to run his hand along the wall to find his way. Suddenly he lost contact with the surface. Then his hand found something else, but he knew it wasn't the wall. It felt like a woman's breast. He quickly pulled his hand back.

"*Tu veux me baiser? Baises-moi ici maintenant. Allez viens, depeches-toi.*"

Ethan could not see the woman who had spoken this, but he was certain she must be the blonde; his fingers said gold lamé and full breast; the tone of her voice spoke the same simmering desire that inhabited the eyes and lips of the woman he had followed. For the moment he did not reflect upon the fact that she had spoken to him in French, nor upon the coincidence of his own fluency in that language. The gist—"You want to fuck me? Fuck me here, now. Come. Quickly."—overwhelmed the medium.

He felt her hand on his crotch and moved closer. He felt himself harden almost instantly. The sweet/sharp combination of opium and cannabis on her breath told him she had been smoking gonji. The odor evoked dozens of erotic memories, getting high, tricking his mind, fucking beyond the limits it normally imposed. Far beyond. He kissed her, clutching her ass with both hands, his desire enveloping him. He opened her jeans and pulled them down several inches. She was wearing nothing under them. He opened his own pants and pressed against her, but she whispered:

"*D'abord avec ta langue.*"

He obeyed her command, dropping under the pressure of her hand to his knees as she pressed herself deeper into the recessed

172

space. A red light flashed several times somewhere down the passageway, spurting enough light for Ethan to see the flawless, smooth contour of the woman's belly. She spread her legs. His desire mounted painfully. He pressed his face against her, his tongue teasing the lips of her organ before pushing into her, tasting her, massaging her inside.

He was sure she was going to come when her fingers suddenly dug into his scalp. Instead, grabbing his hair, she jerked his head back, away from her, and held him there, so that he was staring up at her just as a searing white light flashed directly overhead in the recessed space. In the eerie strobing light he saw the woman, frame by frame, grab her own hair with her free hand and pull it from her head. He felt his stomach flip-flop.

"Bryna!" he gasped, as the wig came free. "For Christsake . . ."

The woman stared hard at him for a moment, then laughed stridently. She released her grip on him, throwing his head back contemptuously. Ethan fell back into the passageway, the strobe flashed off, and for a moment he was blinded. Before he could get to his feet, the woman was gone.

Ethan nearly fell when the fresh air outside hit him. He saw the woman climbing into a black Porsche with a man she had apparently picked up on her way out of the bar. He started after them, but the dizziness caught him; the lights strobed at him again, and he saw the woman pulling the wig from her head, heard her hateful laughter pounding in his ears. He watched the car pull rapidly from the lot, forcing himself to concentrate on its license plate.

Several days later Clare Friedkin spoke breathlessly into her phone.

"We've had an incredible break!"

"You got into Carr's house?"

"Not *Carr's*. Jouhaux's! Sabrina *Jouhaux's*!"

"Jouhaux?" James Raymond asked impatiently, trying to hold his voice down as he spoke into the phone at the poolside, smiling with false serenity at his wife, who had paused to peer out at him through the glass-enclosed patio.

"I'll explain later. Let's just say I was keeping tabs on Jouhaux for other reasons. . . . I had no idea we'd come up with . . . oh, Jimmy, wait until you see these photos! And there's more, I'm sure of it; I'm going to send my man back in there. . . ."

"I don't give a fried *fuck* about Jouhaux," Raymond seethed, still smiling at his wife. "What about Carr?"

"Jimmy, just . . . please, get over here as fast as you can. You won't be sorry!"

SEVEN

Laura Malory cheerfully said good-night to the last of her assistants, wishing each of them a merry Christmas. This was the time she liked best to be alone in her big kitchen, the stage center of the Laura Malory School of Culinary Arts. As she often told her nationally syndicated TV audience, "the *only* time to bake is after the family's in bed." Christmas Eve was always a particularly exciting night for the famous cook and epicure, the one time of year when she could bake with total abandon, mindless of her own best-selling books that prohibited excesses of cholesterol, sugars, artificial color and the like. On this one night of the year she was more the sculptor and the painter than the cook. Her phantasmagoric pastries, pies and cakes would all go on display at the annual Christmas brunch at the Palace Hotel the next day, and if people actually wanted to buy and—she shuddered a little—*eat* them after the assembled had delivered the requisite oohs and ahhs then that was *their* business, and Laura Malory wasn't going to think about *that* anymore.

Laura was a midget, a circumstance which, imbuing her as it did with a certain novelty and charm, had no doubt contributed somewhat to her phenomenal success. Her kitchen was unique, equipped as it was with all sorts of little stairs and even automated lifts custom designed to boost the diminutive gourmand to the proper operating level for her various appliances, some of which were oversize even by tall-people standards. Laura seemed determined to demonstrate to all the world that the "little people," as she called her kind, could do quite nicely in even the biggest of kitchens.

It was after midnight when Laura finished her *pièce de résistance*, Santa's sleigh and all the reindeer. Or nearly finished it. She'd baked the individual parts, glued them together with a gooey pastry concoction and was now putting on the final glaze, after which she would commit it once more to her big oven, an oven big enough, she once quipped, "to bake a senator in." It *wasn't* in fact—unless the senator happened to be a

174

midget—but it was this sort of tart irreverence that had so endeared Laura to her audience.

She worked another half hour, totally involved in her handicraft, before she was finally done. She straightened up and reached for the jar of capers she always kept nearby. Capers were her passion; she ate them with her fingers, directly from the jar. She loved their tartness and ate them, in particular, whenever she was working with sweet, rich foods. The capers were like an antidote against the offending sugars. She reached—but the capers were not there. She looked frantically around the room; perched as she was on the platform next to her work table she could see everything. Somehow the capers had moved. They were now across the room on another table. She could not remember putting them there and decided she had been working too hard.

With the press of a button she lowered the platform she was on to the floor and quickly retrieved the jar, thrusting her hand into it and putting several of the little green berries in her mouth. She knew almost immediately that something was wrong. She tried to spit, but whatever it was worked very fast. Everything became very bright. The whole kitchen seemed to radiate blinding white light. Then the light whirled, picking her up and dropping her to the floor. She vaguely felt herself being lifted but she could not see by what or by whom. After that all sensation faded save for a most distressing sweetness that pervaded her entire mouth. The last thought she had was that it was suddenly becoming very, very warm.

Bryna opened the book and reread the handwritten inscription: "A mutual friend has spoken of you. I know your struggle and that which you struggle with. I know that you will triumph in *His* loving possession. My heartfelt prayers are with you this most Holy Day."

It was signed, "Ives Matlock."

Obviously *the* Ives Matlock, the internationally famed evangelist who hobnobbed with Hollywood stars, U.S. presidents and other heads of state, who presided over a television flock of millions from the charismatic pulpit of his Los Angeles "Fortress of Faith," a multimillion-dollar edifice that did, indeed, look like an old fortress, complete with turreted stone walls, moat and drawbridge.

Bryna had never met Matlock, nor did she know who the "mutual friend" he spoke of could possibly be. She focused on

175

the book itself. Matlock had written the foreword to it, but the author was a woman Bryna had never heard of named Mary Beckman. The book, apparently just published, was entitled *Earthbound!* and subtitled: *A former, famed psychic's harrowing true story of spirit possession and spiritual rescue.*

Bryna, feeling a rush of annoyance and unease, opened the book and skimmed the copy on the inner flap, stopping when she came to: ". . . story of the woman who was known to millions as Joyce Rampling, internationally known psychic, medium and best-selling authoress who, at the height of her glittering career, suffered a nervous breakdown that nearly killed her..." Bryna remembered reading, with fascination, during her senior year in college of Joyce Rampling's spectacular breakdown on a national TV talk show on which Rampling had been a frequent guest over the years.

In the middle of one of her trances, answering the questions of various celebrities present, Rampling had suddenly assumed the persona of a crude-talking man, her voice deepening dramatically. In that voice she had slandered several of the other guests on the show, growled obscenities at the host and the audience, made vulgar gestures and finally comported herself with all the subtlety of a wild animal. It ended when she fell to the stage, writhing, frothing at the mouth. Aides said she had suffered a nervous breakdown due to overwork and exhaustion; they had said she would be well again soon. But that had been several years ago, Bryna reflected, and Rampling had never been heard from again—until now.

Bryna continued reading, compelled by intense curiosity and an equal measure of dread: "... now, for the first time, Mary Beckman, the woman who, for years, called herself Joyce Rampling at the insistence of her 'spirit guide,' who called himself 'Lothmi,' reveals in shocking and illuminating detail the anatomy, both physical and mental, of evil itself, of an *earthbound* spirit, once human, trapped between this world and the next by its intransigent materialism and base animal lusts ... confesses the price she paid for her psychic power, the degradations to which she was subjected by 'Lothmi' ... *Earthbound!* interprets psychic phenomena in a frightening new light, warning of the potentially fatal, soul-shattering pitfalls ... no one can afford to ignore ... *Earthbound!* is bound to scare the Hell out of you!"

Bryna pushed the book away from her and shook herself, both chilled and disgusted. It was Christmas Day, nearly five p.m. She walked to the study's marble fireplace to warm herself. She had made the fire herself earlier that afternoon. The day before she had insisted that Niko, who had been hanging about, worried, take a few days off. He had left, disconsolately, and she had spent Christmas Eve alone.

Bryna's thoughts were, as usual, on Ethan Kendal. She had, days earlier, looked in vain for a phone listing and had since considered various ploys by which she might, with seemingly casualness, obtain his number from Libby Horne or perhaps even Lieutenant Brazil. Bryna was still angry at herself for having missed the opportunity, earlier that day, of asking Dr. Manning if he had Ethan's number. Manning had called to invite Bryna, once again, to dinner at his home. She had declined, using the same excuse by which she had isolated herself from the similar invitations of those who could not stand the thought of anyone, let alone Bryna Carr, spending Christmas alone; she was, she said, coming down with a cold.

Bryna had particularly not wanted to spend the day with Dr. Manning. She felt the weight of his concern too heavily as it was. Ever since the day she had, in trance, smashed the glass of her cubicle, cut herself and nearly attacked Ethan, her performance at Spectrum had declined disastrously. Her precognitive results with the animal-computer model had descended from a level of very high statistical significance to something in the neighborhood of mere chance. There had been no more talk of her working with the police, who were told she had fallen ill. And since her debacle with Ethan a week earlier, she had no longer been able to see clients. Fortunately, she had set aside a two-week vacation for herself, in any event, and so only a few appointments had to be canceled. Sabra, who abhorred the Christmas season, had made no fuss about the timing of this vacation when it had been scheduled months earlier.

Bryna had heard nothing from Ethan since that awful night she had nearly forgotten her commitment to Sabra; nor had there been any messages from Ethan waiting for her when she regained the use of the body a few days later. She had done her best to hide her disappointment, but Niko, she knew, sensed her desperation. She knew how difficult it must be for him. He had, for the past few days, been uncharacteristically subdued, saying little of anything. Then, the day before, when she had all but ordered him to take a brief vacation and he had packed a few things and come to say goodbye, he had suddenly embraced her, almost fiercely.

They had talked, and, for a while at least, it was almost like old times. They talked about their time together at Central High in Montana, about Miss Lionel and Brain Bowl. It started out light enough; Bryna knew Niko was trying to cheer her up and perhaps divert her from thinking about the absent Ethan, but it ended on a disturbing note, with Niko turning serious again.

"You're strong enough for anything," he'd said, clutching her arms in his strong hands, almost hurting her with his intensity. "You've got to remember that."

She had looked away then, but he had persisted. "That day, do you remember, when you came to my house in Missoula? When you met my mother? We never talked about that. But you remember, she was hysterical and you slapped her, to bring her out of it, I mean you just took charge, knew *exactly* what to do. Anybody else would have been scared out of their wits, but you . . . I think it was then I fell in love with you. . . ."

Bryna had twisted free then, not because Niko's touch repelled her but because she knew she was unworthy. She knew her words could not be other than cruel.

"It wasn't me you fell in love with then," she'd said. "It was *her. She* slapped your mother."

Niko's shock was evident before he tried to conceal it. He had moved toward Bryna again, but she turned from him. After a moment he left.

Bryna was already regretting the fact that she had banished both Niko and the housekeeper for the holiday; the utter silence, which came of the knowledge that the house was empty, increasingly oppressed Bryna. She thought of going to the basement to target practice, but she felt too shaky to make a good accounting of herself there today. She paced for a while, then walked downstairs; the foyer with its cathedral-height ceiling seemed unwelcoming. Even the huge Christmas tree Niko had trimmed failed to impart any real warmth to the cavernous space. Bryna turned on its lights anyway, since it was already dark outside. Then she stood back for a moment to regard the colors and patterns. The display of merriment seemed pitiful in the prevailing gloom, and she switched them off again. The gifts piled under the tree did not even momentarily tempt her.

Bryna stood by the large oak door that led outside and stifled an impulse to open it, knowing there was nothing out there but more gloom, fog and drizzle. Suddenly she felt more than merely alone in the large room; she felt *vulnerable*. She wondered why she had left the coziness of her study to come down here in the first place. Back in her study, Bryna stood very near the fire for several minutes, trying to dispel the cold that had penetrated so suddenly. Then she turned and faced away from the fire, her eye almost immediately falling on Joyce Rampling's book.

After a moment's hesitation, Bryna walked slowly toward it, picked it up and sitting on the sofa near the fire, began reading it. She was astonished to find that it was lucidly, even compelling written. Soon she was so engrossed in the book that she forgot entirely about having dinner and paused only once, to put a large piece of oak on the fire.

Rampling, or Beckman, as she now called herself, insisted that Lothmi, her male spirit guide, was a "soul in limbo," an "earth-bound spirit-entity who, consigned to the cold, featureless void that exists between this world and the next, amused himself, like so many of his kind, with supernatural mischief, sampling and perpetrating more of the same evils that had resulted in his present fate in the first place." Spirits like Lothmi, Beckman argued, were "field agents from Hell with no passport home."

Lothmi, at first her "prince in shining armor," Beckman wrote, graduated to become her "demon lover." In exchange for his psychic powers—a given, she claimed, in a realm where time has no meaning—she came finally to understand that she must do his bidding without hesitation or complaint. Her own lust for accep-tance and respect put her finally, she confessed, in Lothmi's power. At first he was content simply to have her, she said, describing her sexual encounters with Lothmi as "more real and intense than anything I had experienced before." With the passage of time, she continued, Lothmi wanted other women, as well. She was forced by her pact with him, she said, to enter into "what seemed on the face of it, lesbian relationships." In reality, she continued, "Lothmi was inside me, taking the dominant role." In the months just before her breakdown, Mary began seeking out and sexually abusing young girls she picked up in parks and on the streets. Finally, she confided, at Lothmi's command she sexually assaulted her own young daughter.

The horror Bryna experienced bunched in her shoulders and the back of her neck. Her eyes burned, too, and she realized, but only dimly, that she had been reading for hours in the now chill room. The large piece of oak was now only a glowing ember. Still she persisted, turning page after page, coming at last to the breakdown itself and its aftermath, to the possessed Joyce Rampling's rebirth as Mary Beckman through the exorcism of Lothmi under the auspices of Ives Matlock and his ministry. One of Matlock's pastors, Beckman explained, "discovered" her in the "incurable ward" of a mental institutition, abandoned there by the associ-ates who had previously profited by her psychic work.

As the born-again trumpets began to sound in the book,

Bryna's mind began to turn off. She found it more and more difficult to turn the pages, felt stuporous, numb.

Bryna dreamed that she was in the bell tower of an enormous, dark cathedral hopelessly trying to find the way out before the bells, already painfully loud, deafened her. When it seemed she could withstand the pain in her ears no longer, she awoke with a start, her face damp with cold perspiration. The bells she had imagined were the loud, chimelike doorbells of her own house. Someone was downstairs, ringing relentlessly.

Bryna got unsteadily to her feet, noting by the clock on her desk that it was after two a.m. A heavy wind was driving rain against the windows of her study. Bryna's first thought was that Niko, worried about her, had returned only to find himself locked out, keys misplaced. She went quickly down the stairs. She switched on the outdoor lights, covering her ears. The madly chiming bells, echoing in this large space, truly were deafening down here. Bryna peered through the one-way peephole in the door. No one was visible. Still, she thought, it was vaguely possible that someone was standing just out of her line of vision, through for what reason she could not imagine.

"Who's there?" she asked, her voice weak. There was no answer. She repeated the question, her apprehension building. Again no answer. She hesitated a moment, then turned, unable to think what to do except go back upstairs where it seemed, as it had earlier that evening, somehow safer. As she started for the stairs she felt something grip her arm tightly. All her strength momentarily rushed out of her, and she thought she would faint. Then she saw what—or, rather, *who*—it was that had seized her.

"Ethan! My god, you . . ."

He said nothing, but stood very near, still holding her.

"The door is locked!" she said, astonished, struggling to be heard over the maddening bells. "How did you get in?"

"The same way *you* did," he said, pausing before he added, "the way you came in a few nights ago."

"I don't understand," Bryna said, but as he began to speak she covered her ears, the pain in her head now overwhelming. Ethan released her, walked over to the wall, took something from his pocket, pressed it into an aperture at the bottom of the bell box, and the noise ceased, leaving only ringing silence behind.

"You seem to forget I used to be a spook," Ethan said.

Bryna noticed that he was unshaven and dissheveled, in contrast to his accustomed fastidiousness.

"I was a spy in Vietnam. Here I do the same thing in a sense, but it's called investigative reporting. In short, I've been spying on you."

Ethan's tone seemed ominously neutral to Bryna. Her fear shifted now to panic. "You have no right..." she said weakly.

Ethan stepped toward her, his jaw set; he gripped both of her arms painfully tight.

"What are you doing, breaking in here, frightening me with those bells...?"

"No right?" Ethan said, his voice under pressure now, ignoring her last question. "You cocktease me *twice* in one night, run out on me the first time, laugh in my face the second, like some demented bitch, and you say I have *no* right? You slide back the mask just long enough to mind-fuck me, to lead me on, then you run away. But you *want* me to see, you *want* me to find out. I don't know yet whether you're schizo, demented or just cruel, but I intend to find out."

"I don't know what you're talking about," Bryna said flatly, a sick feeling expanding in her stomach. "I don't want to hear any of this." She spoke without force, knowing that if she raised her voice it would crack.

"Oh, you don't?" Ethan asked, looking wild. "Maybe you'd rather *see* something instead." Holding Bryna's arm firmly with one hand, Ethan leaned over and grabbed a black satchel. He dragged this close, unsnapped it and withdrew from it a yellow envelope. He kicked the satchel out of his way and pulled Bryna across the room to a marble table. He shook the contents of the envelope free. Glossy photos of a blonde woman in various sexual poses with two muscular, dark-haired men, scattered across the top of the table, making an obscene collage.

Bryna stared for a moment, all color draining from her. Then she tried to pull free of Ethan, but he held her there.

"Recognize her?" he asked.

Bryna swept the pictures from the table with her free hand, a choking sound escaping her lips. She began to sob a moment later, her whole body shaking uncontrollably. Ethan let go of her arm, and she immediately sank, energyless, to her knees.

"Why?" she gasped. "Why did you have to...?"

"Because, god help me, I think I love you," he said.

"How could you? How could anyone?"

He touched her hair. "I want to help you. But I can't do that unless you let me."

"I...I never wanted to do it," Bryna said, still sobbing. "She...I...she makes me...."

"Get up," Ethan said gently, helping her. Pulling her to her feet he forced her to look at him. "There *is* no *she*," he said firmly. "There's only *you*."

Bryna shook her head desperately, her eyes bleary with tears. "No, you're wrong, you're wrong... I have no control over what she does, I..."

"Jesus," Ethan muttered, his frustration making him angry. "Do you really believe she's *real*? Separate from *you*?"

Bryna answered by her silence.

"Christ," Ethan whispered, pulling her to him again. "Didn't it ever occur to you that this is a split personality? Didn't the shrink you said you were seeing ever explore that with you? I mean, doesn't that make more sense than—what?—some kind of goddamned ghost?"

"She's real," Bryna said, her voice barely audible. "She makes me do it, makes me give her the body. I have to... without it, she can't..."

"Can't what?"

"Can't be psychic."

Ethan let her go. "Jesus," he said, stepping back, looking disgusted, "this has got to be the most original justification for sleeping around I've ever heard!"

Bryna looked more frightened than hurt—so much so that Ethan pulled her to him again.

"I'm sorry," he said, as she cried with her face buried in his jacket. "It's... for a while I wasn't sure. I thought maybe you were doing all of this consciously. I see now you weren't. But don't *you* see? Even when you're in this other personality, you're asking for help. Why else would you have followed me to that singles bar and exposed yourself the way you did?"

Ethan forced a few sketchy details from Bryna—about her arrangement with Sabra. Then he told her what had happened after their last encounter, admitting he had gone looking for sex to help salve his wounded ego. Then he told her the rest.

"Don't you see?" he said, "this other part of you, the part you call Sabra, that part of you followed me. At some level of consciousness you wanted me to find out about your double life so that I could help you. You took off the wig so that I could see who you were."

Bryna shook her head. "No, no," she said. "It's a trick; she's trying to trick you. I don't trust her. I..."

"Stop it," Ethan said sternly. "It's no trick. The only trick is the one you're playing on yourself. Why can't you just accept the fact that there's this other side to you and go from there?"

Bryna tried to answer but the words wouldn't come.

"All right," Ethan said, kissing her hair. "We'll talk about it—*tomorrow*. Right now we both need some rest. I'm putting you to bed. I've got something that will help you sleep."

When Bryna awoke, Ethan was asleep beside her, tucked under the sheets of her bed as if he had always belonged there. She stifled an impulse to touch his face, the dark stubble of it contrasting attractively with the blonde of his hair. He reminded her more than ever of her father, when he would emerge from his room, after days, sometimes, of locking himself away, working on his novel. He would always be excited when he came out, clutching pages of his manuscript, reading from them aloud. Bryna would always giggle at the stuff on his face, and he would respond by picking her up, kissing her and rubbing his rough face against hers.

Bryna remembered the night before with a sudden rush of shame. Ethan knew the worst and was still there—that was the miracle—but she knew he would demand that she tell him everything. She was not sure she would be able to do it. She remembered how she had pleaded with him not to leave her alone, to stay with her. He had lain down beside her, still clothed, while the drug put her to sleep. Obviously, some time later, he had undressed. His trousers were folded over a chair near the bed. She wondered if their bodies had touched in the night. The thought of this brought warmth to her cheeks. She slipped quietly from bed. She was in her long flannel nightgown, which seemed suddenly childlike.

The pictures Ethan had shown her—the pictures of Sabra—flashed before her. In panic she hurried downstairs, thinking they might still be there for someone, the housekeeper, Niko perhaps, to see. But there was no sign of them. She returned to her bedroom. Her eyes sought out and found Ethan's black satchel. She moved hesitantly toward it, stood over it a moment, reached down, pulled her hand back, then reached again.

"I burned them last night."

"Oh!" Bryna jumped.

Ethan sat up in bed and looked at her, the sheets falling to his waist, his smooth, well-defined torso bare.

"It wasn't difficult," he said, sensing the question she dared not ask. "There's quite a collection of those pictures, I'm afraid."

Bryna shot Ethan a look and then walked to the window, to stare out at the fog breaking up over the bay. She remained there for some time immobile.

Breakfast was an awkward, silent affair. Afterward, Ethan

183

suggested they go outside. It was already late morning; the fog had lifted, and the sun was shining. They walked for nearly an hour, first along the beach, then through the trails and along the cliffs of Land's End. The wind picked up in exposed places, and Ethan put his arm around Bryna's shoulders, to steady her, as they took in the view from one of the higher ledges. Then he took her hand and led her back into the trees.

The feeling that was building in Bryna, a feeling heightened by Ethan's touch, by the sensation of his hand enclosing hers, threatened to overwhelm her. As they passed a shrub-infested ravine, Bryna fought to distance herself from her emotions.

"A girl jogger was raped and murdered here not long ago," she said, her voice, as much as her words, assaulting the feeling that had been growing around them.

Then, embarrassed by this outburst, she broke away from Ethan, stopped and pretended to examine the leaves of a flowering shrub. She felt his hands on her shoulders, as he turned her toward him.

"It's been a nightmare for you, hasn't it?"

She looked into his eyes and then slowly pressed her face against his chest. "Don't leave me," she whispered. "Please don't leave me. I never thought I'd find you."

He kissed her gently on the mouth, then again, more hungrily. He took her hand and led her off the trail, through a crawl space in a wall of green. They found a natural bower, protected from the wind and the eyes of other hikers.

"We're safe enough here," he said. He kissed her, and she responded eagerly, her fears momentarily smothered by desire, a desire that, for once, seemed right in the sense that it possessed some answer, some solution, though to what she was not at all certain.

He took off his leather jacket and put it down on the ground. Dead leaves from some of the trees made the rest of their bed. Bryna lay down, her head on Ethan's jacket. He lay beside her, opening her coat, helping her out of it. If it was cold, neither of them noticed it.

She wanted to tell him, to make him believe, that for her this really was the first time. But he silenced her with kisses and with his touch. Soon all thought was consumed in the fierceness of the emotions that churned through her. She opened her mouth against his and felt his tongue enter her. He flung his shirt off and she ran her hands freely over his taut back. Kissing her, fondling her, he undressed her expertly. She felt herself glow as

184

his lips explored her throat, her breasts, his unshaven face erotically savaging her skin. As they made love, Bryna felt herself lifted, higher and higher. Then suddenly she saw herself—watched herself—in the leaves with Ethan, her head thrown back, her eyes glazed with pleasure. She was aware of Sharon, glowering at them from the shadows. Bryna didn't care.

"You never loved him anyway," she muttered.

Then Sharon was gone and forgotten, and it was just the two of them—so perfect together, it seemed. Bryna, still watching from a distance, marveled that she had ever doubted that it could be so; marveled that she had doubted herself. Ethan was perfect, and so, after all, was she.

It was only later, early the next morning, when Bryna awakened in a cold sweat, her heart pounding erratically, that she recalled the hallucinations that had accompanied her first coupling with Ethan. It was Bryan that she had seen naked on the leaves, and the woman in his arms was blonde. That was the morning after the news of Laura Malory's murder had shocked the country. The drugged midget had been basted with one of her own syrups and her mouth stuffed with sugar plums before she was baked in her big oven at 425 degrees until one of her assistants discovered her Christmas morning. Like Marissa Salomon, Laura Malory had also been one of Bryna's celebrated clients.

They had been over it a dozen times. They had talked for hours, and not without tears. Bryna had told Ethan of her earliest memories of Sabra, of her experiences at home, at the religious school and in high school, of her pact with Sabra, *everything*. She tried to recall each detail as vividly as she could, hoping by the accuracy of her recitation to make Ethan *feel* Sabra's reality. But he was having none of it.

He used what she told him of her childhood to argue that Sabra was another part of her personality, the dissociated locus of all her self-forbidden impulses and desires, for all her "impossible" talents and insights.

On the issue of Tantra, the *kundalini* and their relationship to Bryna's psychic power, Ethan was relentless. "You've invented all that, seized upon it, trying to make your other life respectable. The idea that you have to fuck everything in pants in order to tell whether the sun's going to rise tomorrow is complete shit," he said heatedly. "I'll tell you one thing, I'm not sharing you with anybody, not even a ghost. And I'm sure as hell not going to let you sleep around with every..."

She covered her ears with her hands, her anguish apparent.

"Please," she said, silencing him. "Please, oh god, please just love me and I'll do whatever you want."

EIGHT

The next week was like a dream. Not since long before Bryan died had Bryna awakened with a sense of joyful anticipation. She recalled those mornings long ago when, forgetting her limp, she would run to her parents' room, when they still slept together, to lie in her father's arms while Sharon slept—or pretended to. She had liked it even better when Bryan slept on the couch or in the room he later set aside for himself and his writing. It was like that now—to awaken each morning in Ethan's arms. They spent much of the week in bed. When they were not in bed, they were outside, walking along the beach, through the Presidio and Golden Gate Park, up and down the hills of San Francisco. Bryna ignored her answering service, except to return a call to Niko and insist that he extend his ski trip by a few days. She did not have to tell him that her mood had changed—and why. The mere tone of her voice told him all he needed to know. It hurt Bryna that her new-found happiness would be yet further cause of pain to Niko, but her regret was short-lived, for Ethan's presence mattered more than anything now.

They walked hand in hand everywhere, stopping to kiss wherevery they felt like it. At one point, standing near an antique ship at Fisherman's Wharf, they were startled to find themselves being photographed in mid-kiss by an apologetically smiling Japanese tourist, more interested in them than in the ship. He had the latest Polaroid camera and showed them the picture he had taken. He handed it first to Bryna. She laughed and took it, but her smile faded as she looked at it. Her hand trembled. Ethan quickly took it from her, then handed it back to the tourist, who now looked even more troubled than Bryna as he scrutinized the picture, trying to find the defect that had so troubled the lady.

Bryna did not tell Ethan what she had seen—that in the picture her hair was, to her eye at least, blonde. They had, at her insistence, agreed to talk about everything that week *except* Sabra and what Ethan called Bryna's "double life." Ethan had not argued, saying, "One at a time. I'll get to know *you* first." It was not much time, a week, but it was all Bryna had, a brief reprieve from something she did not want to think about.

There were moments when Ethan still seemed the investigative reporter, when he seemed to be looking for something, guiding her, subtly directing the conversation, probing, moving, shifting, trying to get at it, whatever *it*, at any given moment, was. But mostly they were easy together, teasing, playing, loving. They went to the museums, rode the cable cars, rented horses and galloped along Ocean Beach, jogged together, target practiced, even had a karate match, Bryna teaching Ethan some new moves that ended in lovemaking. At night they walked through Chinatown and North Beach, let a barker pull them into one of the area's live sex shows, a pallid imitation of the real thing, Bryna decided, sampled the city's jazz, punk rock and gay disco, rode the bumper cars at Pier 39 and dined out in notorious tourist traps for the sheer perversity of it and to help preserve the illusion of encountering the city as if for the first time, to make it as fresh to them as they were to one another.

The days passed quickly, and as the week drew to a close, dread began to concentrate in Bryna, occasionally spilling out. They were at Ethan's cottage on one such occasion—his place among the trees, along the steep Vulcan Steps. He was showing Bryna his work space, the computerized word processor with which he was writing his novel, the tools of his trade. Pages of his manuscript were everywhere.

Bryna looked around the place—a renovated Victorian with an open feeling and many windows. "This is a wonderful place. You're lucky to own it."

"Ha!" Ethan said. "A serf like me? I'm lucky to be *renting* it."

"That will all change soon. When you've finished this book you can buy a dozen of these."

Ethan looked perturbed. "I'm not so sure. It was a great idea this book but . . . I don't know. . . ."

"What do you mean? It's going to be *wonderful*. It would have to be, with you writing it."

Ethan smiled wanly.

"It needs something," he said. "Frankly I can't figure out how to end it. It needs a real bang. A new angle, something. I don't know. Maybe I've been at it so long I'm getting bored with it."

It hurt Bryna to see Ethan even remotely disconsolate. As was her habit, she assumed that if Ethan was unhappy she was somehow to blame.

"I'm afraid I haven't been much help, have I?" she said.

187

Ethan looked at her blankly.

"I mean with the police. That might have been the angle you needed."

"Hey, wait a minute," Ethan said. "I haven't given up on that, even if you have. Every time you mention your career or anything related to it, you make it sound like it's all over, that you're washed up. Is *that* the effect I'm having on you? I know we're officially not talking about it this week, but I just want you to know you're going to be better than ever, wait and see. You're going to have Lieutenant Brazil spit shining your shoes. I happen to know that the Malory murder, coming on top of the Salomon killing, has got him going in circles. He wants, he *needs* your help. I'm going to work with you, and . . ."

"What?"

Ethan hesitated, then shook his head. "Later, this is vacation time, remember?"

The thought of being part of Ethan's book had always excited Bryna. If she could do something to give him that *bang* ending . . . It would also be wonderful for her own career, she suddenly realized, feeling guilty again. *Everything*, so far, had been for her career. Helping solve the celebrity murders would put her on top. The thought that she might be using Ethan, hoping for some major role in his book, stabbed at her.

"You're going to be all right," he said.

But she was not all right. Not when she was alone. When Ethan was absent, it all seemed preposterous, all this happiness. Sometimes she wondered if she hadn't imagined it all, all the times with Ethan. Then she told herself she could not *really* be in love, not if she harbored these doubts, not if the briefest absence made her so afraid. *Not* to be in love was at once reassuring *and* terrifying. The contrariness of it all made her head spin.

When she was with Ethan it all seemed so clear. At last she had found love, and *of course* she would give up everything for love. She would choose Ethan over Sabra. But then, alone, none of it seemed so simple anymore. To love Ethan would mean denying Sabra the body; without the body, Sabra's psychic powers would fade; Bryna's career would collapse. Would Ethan, in reality, still be attracted to her if she were—Bryna groped in her thoughts for the correct word—ordinary? That, at best, she told herself, is what she would be without Sabra. So she could choose Ethan and *lose* him. Then she would have to beg Sabra to come back; perhaps that wouldn't be possible, and if it were possible it would, she knew, be on new and harsher terms.

Bryna was getting ready for the New Year's Eve party. The house was empty. She checked the time. Ethan would be by in half an hour. She was surprised at how late it was, wondering how she could have let so much time slip by. She felt cold, annoyed at herself and apprehensive. She did not like "lost time," time she couldn't account for. In the bathroom of her bedroom suite, she looked at the bottle of little blue pills. Surely she could last another half hour, but no, her hand reached for the bottle. She took two of the pills without water. She waited a few minutes and then, when she felt calmer, she began to dress. It was to be one of those "gala" big hotel ballroom affairs, complete with confetti, pointy hats, champagne and a Glen Miller-type band, the perfect conclusion to their touristy week.

Bryna put on a long gown—Ethan, she knew, would be wearing a tux—and examined herself in the mirror. She piled her hair high and looked unhappily at her face, surprised by the lines around her eyes. She disliked makeup and applied it sparingly, yet the more she put on, the more obvious the lines seemed to become. Her skin seemed suddenly gray and loose. Bryna's hand, applying powder to her cheek, began to tremble. She pulled it quickly away. The light over her makeup mirror flickered and buzzed. She decided that was it—the defective lighting, and perhaps the makeup itself. She quickly dabbed cold cream across her face and wiped the makeup off with gobs of tissue, glancing only briefly back at her reflection to make sure she had got it all.

The doorbell rang. Relieved, Bryna grabbed her wrap and hurried down the stairs. In the dim foyer, walking quickly to the door, something, some unfamiliar pattern of light detected by her peripheral vision, caused her to turn, startled, and stare into a mirrored wall panel where she was smiling grotesquely back at herself, her skin elephantine with age, her face a gargoyle caricature. In the mirror, she was heavy, squat, with deformities that were the more grotesque in the Givenchy gown which, too long for her mirror image, fell in ludicrous folds around her feet. Bryna's mouth opened in horror, and her reflection displayed a swollen, black tongue which darted obscenely at her. As Bryna tried to force herself to move, her reflection laughed silently at her, its features contorting more horribly yet in an imitation of mirth.

Bryna flung the front door open and rushed into Ethan's arms, her heart crashing inside her.

NINE

The moment had come and gone, and on the surface of things it was like any other, yet it seemed to Bryna as if, in the undercurrent of time, space had turned, warped just sufficiently to create a new beginning, a new end and a seemingly limitless expanse in-between that she could never hope to fill.

"You see," Ethan said, holding her, "it's after eight-thirty and you're still in one piece. No green slime oozing in under the doors. The house isn't caving in. Stigmata aren't breaking out on your forehead." He peered closer, to be sure. She did not even attempt a smile.

"At nine-thirty some lucky standby is going to get Madame Jouhaux's seat to Los Angeles, first class, at that. An hour later a perplexed chauffeur is going to drive a white Rolls or a long black limo back up Laurel Canyon—empty-handed. Some phone calls are going to go out. By tomorrow morning somebody may be skulking around up here, spying on us."

Bryna shuddered.

"How many know about . . . her?"

"That's what I'd like to find out," Ethan said. "That and a number of other things."

Bryna did not respond. They had already discussed this, argued about it. Ethan had made it clear that he was impatient to get on with the work of dismantling Sabra's life. It was obvious to Bryna that he was fascinated by that other existence, that he wanted to dissect it. It was his reporter's instincts, she supposed. Bryna had been adamant in her insistence that he keep hands off—at least for now. She was having enough trouble coping as it was. When Ethan proposed going back to the house in L.A. where he had found the photos and breaking in again, Bryna had panicked, making him promise not to do so. For the time being, she wanted to know nothing more of what Ethan had already discovered.

Niko knew only that Bryna had decided to resist Sabra, that, for the first time, Bryna would not relinquish her body on the schedule previously agreed upon, indeed, that she had vowed never to relinquish the body again.

"I love him," she told Niko. That was the only explanation

necessary. Niko had merely nodded, his face a mask. Thereafter his manner had become stiff, almost formal, where Bryna was concerned, more like that of a servant than a friend. As for Ethan, he spoke to him only when it was absolutely necessary.

Dr. Manning, Ethan assured Bryna, knew nothing of what Ethan had discovered, but the researcher was told that Bryna had decided to claim herself, to try to function as a psychic without her "imaginary" spirit guide. Manning was elated. He was pleased, too, by news that Bryna had agreed to see a new psychiatrist, one Ethan himself had selected—Dr. Arthur Mendelsohn. Dr. Hevesey, who had tolerated what Manning called the "Sabra fantasy," was banished with a single phone call from her replacement, followed by a brief note from Bryna herself.

Dr. Mendelsohn, the author of a provocative text on dissociated personalities, did little to hide his dismay over Dr. Hevesey's handling of Bryna's case. From his wheelchair, to which he had been confined for years, the thin, balding, hawk-featured man with the piercing dark eyes of an inquisitioner, spoke disparagingly of the "new liberals" in his profession "who think it's a lark to be crazy."

Wheeling about suddenly in his chair, fixing Bryna with his black eyes, he said, "And let's face it, you *are* crazy. Now, you think I will say, 'but then we're all a little bit crazy, aren't we?' and we'll both laugh. Well, we *aren't* all crazy—and we aren't here to laugh. Not until there's something to laugh about. You don't have to tell me. I know already. You believe yourself to be—let's not bandy words—*possessed*."

Bryna could only nod, dumbly, into the scowling countenance of her new confessor.

It was accounted a major step forward, whatever the motivation, that Bryna had "denied Sabra" by refusing, for the first time, to go into trance and "give" the body to Sabra. But against Dr. Manning's optimistic belief that this first step was the largest part of the battle, Dr. Mendelsohn insisted that the battle had only begun. Harsh steps would have to be taken to make the conscious mind aware of its duplicity. The battle would be won only when Bryna would not merely *say* she wanted to be free but when, in fact, she longed with all her *will* to be free.

"He's controversial," Ethan had said of Dr. Mendelsohn, "but he gets results, that I know. You could spend the rest of your life in standard psychiatric analysis and get nowhere—except poor and bored."

Dr. Mendelsohn believed in confronting problems head-on: "*Si vis pacem, para bellum*," he said to Bryna during their first session together. He translated for her: "If you wish peace, prepare for war." He paused, permitting himself a rare smile. "You will forgive me for spouting Latin at you from time to time. The language itself imposes discipline upon thought, something in short supply these days. The French, oddly enough, have a phrase for it: *au bout de son latin*. It means that when you run out of Latin you run out of reason."

The Latin, which the doctor had learned before abandoning his Jesuitical studies decades earlier, made an impression on Bryna, pompous though it often seemed. Various phrases kept repeating in her mind, as when the psychiatrist, discussing "spirit guides," suddenly declaimed: "*Omne ignotum pro magnifico*," following, as usual, with the translation: "Everything unknown is taken to be grand." He paused and then enlarged: "Because you cannot explain something extraordinary, such as your psychic abilities, in ordinary sensory terms your mind decided the source of all this must be something stupendous, something *super*natural. The mind is full of nonsense."

Dr. Mendelsohn examined the pills Dr. Hevesey had prescribed, muttered to himself and tossed the vials in the waste basket. "Those," he said scornfully, "are for neurotics who play at being sick. You are not playing. Here." He handed her a new prescription. "For the voices," he said. "The hallucinations." He looked at her, scowling. "With these maybe you will not try to kill anyone," he added, an obvious allusion to the incident at Spectrum.

Sabra, Dr. Mendelsohn now counselled those associated with Bryna, was *verboten*. "Even the mention of that name," he warned, "will reinforce what we wish to destroy." Bryna's work at Spectrum, in any event, had been suspended following several attempts by Dr. Manning to extract psychic information from Bryna. He had not even been able to get her to go into trance.

These failures severely depressed Bryna. Ethan and, to a lesser extent, Dr. Mendelsohn, were the only ones she could talk to about it. And her fear of Dr. Mendelsohn grew to the point where, finally, there was only Ethan she dared confide in, now that Niko had turned so cold. Try as she might, wanting above all else to please Ethan, Bryna could not convince herself that Sabra was unreal.

Ethan told her he would never stop believing in her, and she clung to that promise. Both he and Dr. Mendelsohn said she was in a period of transition, that she would perhaps get worse before she got better. Eventually, Ethan insisted, she would be able to work again. Meanwhile, Dr. Manning was attempting to appear patient, and Bryna's clients were told that she had contracted a serious infection that would require prolonged rest and isolation.

In fact, however, a day scarcely passed that Ethan did not insist Bryna take her place in the transmitting room of her psychic salon. He assumed the role of trainer, prodding her, making her go through the motions, practicing, seeking the self-confidence that he said would eventually enable her to be psychic in her own right, "better than ever." Sometimes he told her she was in "police training," getting ready to help solve the murders. He took Niko's old place in the editing room.

"The first step," he said, "is to try to get back into that place where your mind is capable of channeling the psychic energy. What you call the trance state is really just a form of self-hypnosis. You can learn that all over again." This was the idea he had alluded to earlier, that Bryna would secretly retrain herself, with his help, to be psychic.

Ethan taught her techniques he had learned during his military duty. Bryna was a good pupil and was soon able to achieve what appeared to be self-induced trance, this time without calling upon anything outside herself. When, upon awakening from her first such trance, Ethan showed her that more than half an hour had passed in what had seemed to her but a second, she was elated.

"Did I . . . ?"

"Did you say anything? Not so fast," he said. "We'll get to that. One thing at a time."

They discussed these sessions with no one except Dr. Mendelsohn. Soon Bryna began responding to Ethan's questions—typing her responses into the system while in trance. That, too, was cause for elation, at least at first. Bryna eagerly asked to see the transcripts, but Ethan refused, and in his recurring promise that things would improve, she read his disappointment in the results. She could guess by Ethan's expression that she was failing each of his simple tests—to predict the draw of a card or the roll of dice—and that, moreover, she was probably, in her childish eagerness to please him, spieling off god knows what drivel. After each of these sessions, seeing the disappointment in Ethan's face, behind all that cheerfulness, she would feel guilty at having failed him again.

When Ethan was not with her—when he was forced away to work on his book—tranquilizers were her only source of comfort. Her sessions with Dr. Mendelsohn only further unnerved her.

His psychoanalytical gibberish and "conditioning" techniques, some of which utilized shock as "negative reinforcement" left her confused and dazed. Her fear grew.

"I don't want to wait any longer," James Raymond said.

"Just a *little* longer, Jimmy," Clare Friedkin soothed.

"We've got the pictures, that's enough."

"I'd like to watch her Laurel Canyon place just a little longer. I can't understand why 'Sabrina Jouhaux' hasn't made an appearance."

"Maybe she's on to us... the missing pictures."

"Her secretary, *male*, by the way, says she's out of the country."

"Yeah. San Francisco. Damn it, we've waited long enough."

"Soon, Jimmy, *soon*."

TEN

it's time now it's time now it's time now

Ethan's parting words kept reverberating through Bryna's mind all day long, repeating like an obsessive riddle.

"You'll see," he said. "You'll get better. It's time now." Then he had kissed her and gone, flown off to Los Angeles or New York, someplace, she couldn't remember where, all that mattered was that it was *away*, away from her. It was difficult to remember anything now. Several times, frightened she was forgetting what Ethan looked like, she had seized the picture of him she kept on her desk and studied it intently, for minutes on end.

She tried to remember the expression of his face during that last moment before he had turned and gone the night before— was that possible? It seemed to her that he had been gone much longer, weeks, *years*. How had he looked during that last moment: sad? hopeful? relieved? Relieved that he was leaving? His expression had told her something, but she could no longer remember what it was.

time now time now time now.

Time for her to get better? Time for her to stop being such a burden to Ethan? Time for him to leave? Time for him to leave *her*? Time...?

Bryna shook herself angrily. There was some *reason* to be angry, she vaguely remembered, as her eyes focused on the newspaper she still held in her hands. It was the afternoon paper, in reality little better than a tabloid though it masqueraded as a serious publication. Her picture was on the front page, along with a large headline: "The Strange Case of Bryna Carr."

The story itself, except for a brief summary, was inside—in the "People" section of the newspaper, where another headline screamed: "Psychic's Bizarre Behavior." The lead paragraphs related the incident at Spectrum that had ended Bryna's participation in the research project there. It was sensationalized, quoting only unnamed "sources at Spectrum and elsewhere." The article claimed: "Miss Carr was attempting to help solve the Celebrity Murders at the time she suffered her dramatic breakdown. SFPD homicide officers were said to be present. . . . After her spectacular failure she became severely depressed, according to one of her acquaintances. . . . Her famous clients have been unable to reach her to make appointments. They are being told by Miss Carr's associates that she is ill with an infection, but it is reported that she is making almost daily visits to the offices of San Francisco psychiatrist Dr. Arthur Mendelsohn, the controversial proponent of 'aversion' therapies and . . ."

The story concluded: "Spectrum's plunge into psychic research raised eyebrows in scientific circles. Revelations that the police were similarly taking a psychic seriously is now likely to do the same."

For a few moments the hatred she felt for the perpetrators of this story, those who wrote it, those who published it, those who leaked it—some technician at Spectrum, she supposed, or perhaps that police officer, Lieutenant Brazil—cleared her mind. She bitterly resented the implication that it was somehow less than respectable for Spectrum or the police to be working with a psychic. Between the lines, it seemed to her, the story was saying she was, and had been all along, just another psychic charlatan, the proof of which was this "breakdown." She raged at the unfairness of the story, ignoring as it did all of her past successes and the high level of work she had done at Spectrum.

Dr. Manning had already telephoned, asking her to resist making any comment, saying "they're just trying to smoke you out." But it was obvious to Bryna that he feared the story would grow and that his project would be discredited. She sensed, in the tone of his voice, that she was rapidly becoming, not the vehicle of the great breakthrough in psychic research that he had hoped for, but a liability and an embarrassment.

it's time it's time it's time

Bryna ripped the paper apart and threw it into the fire. She watched the fragments of her picture curl out at her in the heat, blacken and then burst into flames.

It was after midnight when Niko found her. She might have sat there all night, had she securely closed the door to the sound-proof transmitting console. Coming in for the evening, Niko heard the staccato clatter of the computer printer. He found Bryna sitting at the word processor, her fingers still poised stiffly over the keyboard, staring vacantly into the display screen, across which flashed the same words that spilled out of the printer:

there will be more killings here

Niko surmised from the amount of paper that had already spewed out of the printer, all of it covered with the same message, that Bryna had been in trance for at least an hour. Having typed her grim prediction into the system, she had apparently, either by accident or on purpose, tripped the REPEAT button, and the machine had carried on from there. Niko released the button. The printer ceased its demonic hammering, and at the same moment all of the tension went out of Bryna's body, and she slumped forward. Niko caught her, lifted her into his arms and carried her upstairs to her bed. She awakened as he gently put her down.

She opened her eyes and said, as if she had never been asleep or in trance at all, "I'm getting better. I really am." She smiled faintly at Niko, who put a trembling finger softly to her lips.

"You see," Dr. Mendelsohn had said, "you are going to be psychic whether you like it or not; it's part of you. *You,* not some goblin. It's coming back to you, your power, and you don't need any help from the ghosts."

Now Bryna waited for Dr. Manning. Ethan talked to her.

"How does it feel to be working again?"

She smiled wanly. "I don't know yet. I don't know that I *can* work."

"It's coming back to you, Bryna. Don't fight it."

Bryna said nothing. She did not want to add her own voice to those that warred in her head. If the power was coming back and she still loved Ethan, then perhaps they were right, Sabra was a delusion. The film Ethan had burgled from the house in Los Angeles had already put the lie to Sabra's Tantra. Or had it? And

Nestor Bagehot . . . Bryna let the babble sweep by her, trying to concentrate on Ethan's touch.

He held her hand, reassuring her. "You're going to do fine."

"All right."

It was Libby Horne, poking her head out of Manning's lab. "We're ready."

Bryna looked blankly at Ethan.

"It's time," he said, and kissed her.

They went in together, and Bryna took her accustomed place at the keyboard. Manning stationed himself at the other keyboard in the adjoining glass cubicle. He glanced at Bryna through the glass and then typed: "You will now go into trance." The words appeared on Bryna's screen. The setup, as before, was like the one she used at home.

Upon receiving Dr. Manning's command, Bryna took a deep breath, and that was all. As the air escaped her lungs she froze in place, her face staring at the screen in front of her.

"Bryna," Dr. Manning typed, "can you read this?"

Bryna's fingers moved rapidly over the keyboard:

"Yes."

"You said 'there will be more killings here.' What did you mean?"

"Murders."

"Which murders?"

"The Celebrity Murders. Here. Mostly in San Francisco."

"Do you know who the murderer is?"

"No."

Mendelsohn paused a moment, then asked his next question. He, Ethan and Libby had discussed it all before they began. They had agreed upon the questions.

"Do you know who the victims will be?"

"Yes. Five."

Manning looked up through the glass to the risers, where Ethan and Libby were watching, his excitement evident.

"Five victims?"

"Yes."

"We don't want you to tell us any more now. But if we ask you again tomorrow, will you be able to tell us who the victims will be?"

"Yes."

"Will you also be able to tell us the precise day upon which each murder will occur?"

"Yes."

"Thank you, Bryna. That's all for now. We'll talk again tomorrow. You may wake up now."

Bryna opened her eyes and looked immediately at Ethan. His smile told her everything had gone well. She looked at the EEG, which confirmed she had gone into a deep trance "and with amazing rapidity," Manning observed. She looked also at the printout and shuddered.

"Five," she said softly.

"If it works," Manning said, "it's going to be the breakthrough we've all waited for. No one will ever be able to deny the validity of precognition. They'll *have* to give us our due."

"Aren't they going to say the predictions themselves precipitated the murders, that they attracted the killer, or maybe some other killer . . . ?"

"For that precise reason," Manning said, "we can't make them public. We're setting up a totally blind protocol; even *we* won't know who you name. Nobody but the computer will know. The names and dates you type into the system, out of view of any of us, will be instantly encrypted. No name will be decoded by the computer until one minute past midnight of the predicted murder date tagged to that name. We'll use independent observers and independent data banks to guard against claims of fraud. Spectrum itself will have no access to the decoding key. All we're going to know is whether any names were typed into the system—and how many. We'll get a blip on our monitoring screen for each name and date encoded. And once those codes are in place it will be impossible for anyone to delete, add to or in any way alter them."

"There's one flaw," Bryna said.

The others looked at her.

"Me," she said. "Skeptics will always be able to say there was *one* person who knew those names and dates."

"Yourself?" Manning asked. "You forget; you'll be in trance. We'll have an independent EEG confirm that the information is given in an unconscious state. That will dispose of two difficulties: one, that you were aware of the names as you gave them, and two, that you planned, that is, consciously determined in advance, which names you would provide. Of course, you *could* have names in mind, but the likelihood of those names coming through, with the conscious mind disconnected, is remote. And in any event, I seriously doubt even the most hidebound of skeptics is going to accuse you, or even your subconscious, of carrying out the murders yourself in order to ensure the accuracy of your predictions."

Dr. Manning's laughter echoed hollowly in Bryna's ears.

The next day the preparations were all made, the experts called to witness. All present were sworn to secrecy. Dr. Manning made no bones about it: if the experiment worked, if the predictions came through and were borne out by events, it would be the long-awaited breakthrough and the world would never be the same again; if it failed, the experiment would, hopefully, be only a footnote in an obscure research paper.

For Bryna, however, failure would be more than a footnote. It would, in all likelihood, mean the end of her psychic career. For a while she had thought she could give that up anyway—for Ethan. But he would not let her. So, for him, she told herself, as he whispered to her that it was time, as he kissed her, for him she would risk everything, including her sanity.

There were seven names, not five.

Part Three

DEATH (AND AFTER)

ONE

Samuel Manning's nose was purple-red, the color it assumed whenever he was angry, which, lately, was often.

"I want the source of this leak found and fired," he said, throwing the afternoon paper down on his desk.

"I can't believe it was anyone on the staff here," Libby Horne said. "Could it have been one of the observers?"

"Jesus," Manning said, "I don't know, I don't know. It's a serious breach of scientific confidentiality that . . ." His jaw set, and he shook his head.

The leak he referred to filled half the front page of the paper he had just thrown on his desk. The story, accompanied by a large photo of Bryna, was headlined: "Psychic Predicts Murder Victims," with a kicker over it announcing, "Bryna Carr: 7 Will Die." A sidebar Manning's superior had circled in red claimed: "Strange Spectrum Experiment Shrouded in Secrecy."

Manning's fist came down hard on his desk, hitting the newspaper, landing squarely on Bryna's face.

"If only there was half a chance those predictions were right it wouldn't be so bad," he complained.

"We don't know yet that they won't be," Ethan said.

"She *is* getting into trance," Libby added hopefully.

"Oh, yeah, yeah," Manning said, looking at the two of them as if they were in need of a quick education, "and look what's coming out of it. We've had her in trance here four times since the murder predictions and what have we got?" He picked up the charts that showed Bryna scoring on standard precognitive tests at levels of chance or below. "We've got *zilch*! We've got *worse* than zilch! We've got garbage. Nonsense. Babble. Like talking in her sleep."

"There's a difference," Ethan said levelly.

"Difference? What difference?"

"The trance in which she first mentioned the murders was spontaneous; these have all been induced. Maybe her feelings about the murders were so strong she couldn't keep it in. But all the rest of this; she's not ready to go back to work. . . ."

Manning sighed heavily as he sat at his desk. He rubbed his forehead, trying to ease the tension. "I don't know," he said, "it doesn't look good. And now the whole world knows about it. If those killings do start again and the right names don't come out of the computer there's going to be a new story every *fucking* time. It could go on for months, *years*."

Ethan and Libby waited in embarrassed silence. Then Manning pounded his desk again. "Jesus, what went wrong? She was doing so well, so well until . . ." His eyes, meeting Ethan's, were almost accusatory. "Is that shrink doing her any goddamn good?"

"*I* think so," Ethan said.

Manning studied his hands for a moment, considering his words. "You know," he said, more calmly. "Maybe I made a mistake. Maybe we all did. Ever since we tried to get her to take all of this on her own shoulders . . ."

"You're sorry now we decided to bump off Sabra?".

Manning bridled. "I didn't say that. It's just that . . . Sabra, what *is* Sabra anyway, just a word, but maybe an important word, a password, the key to her psychic unconscious. . . ."

"She was an embarrassment to you not long ago, as I recall," Ethan cut in. "And if you've reconsidered now because you've decided an embarrassment is better than a big hole in your next grant application, if there's ever going to *be* a next one, *I* haven't. Sabra isn't just a word, just a key, she's a sickness, a whole psychology Bryna's got to be free of. So if you think I'm going to resurrect her long enough to rescue your project, forget it. Don't even ask."

"It isn't just *our* project," Libby Horne said. "Ethan, what about *her*? It's her future, too. We might still have time to salvage something. Have you considered *her* feelings, *her* career? She has more at stake here than any of us, and, from what I understand, from what you've told us yourself, and from what little we've heard from Mendelsohn, it wasn't *our* wanting Sabra out of the picture that caused her breakdown. It was the conflict she experienced when she met you, when she fell in love. . . ."

The day before it happened, Bryna awakened feeling more tired than when she had gone to bed. As was her habit now, immediately upon awakening, she took one, sometimes two, of the "psychic energizers" Dr. Mendelsohn had prescribed. She needed those to get going. Later, if she got jittery, and she knew she would, she'd start on the neuroleptics and a little alcohol.

She was aware that the press was calling incessantly, that the police had made inquiries, that the housekeeper looked mildly disapproving whenever she ordered more food sent up, but none of that mattered a great deal. When Ethan was gone, nothing mattered at all. And he was gone now. The day stretched before her like a dull challenge, just so much time to be consumed. With television and pills she made it through to four, then Niko took her to her appointment with Dr. Mendelsohn and picked her up again afterwards.

Bryna could feel Niko's hurt and pity—or was it disgust?—as they drove back to the house. She was certain it would only be a matter of time until he moved out. Then . . .

Anxiety stabbed her. If only Ethan would marry her, then . . . then *what*? She couldn't remember. That evening she could not eat dinner. Instead, she had a drink and then another, alone in her room, washing down her pills with the booze. The dream drifted in and out of her consciousness while she vacantly watched TV. It was a dream she had been having for some days now. In it, dozens of men sexually ravished her. Most of them were strangers, but some of them she recognized as the boys who had "raped" her on Prom night in the old cemetery. They were led by Nestor Bagehot. It always began like a Tantric ritual, with chanting and incense, and then it disintegrated into an orgy, the Tantric trappings falling away, as false as the blonde wig and blue eyes that disappeared as the dream progressed. Sometimes it was Niko who was forced to watch, other times Ethan or Bryan. In the dream the other men laughed at them, and so did Bryna.

Then something caused her to focus, to force herself to see the picture in front of her. It was the eleven o'clock news, and Bryna realized then that she had been sitting there for hours, not so much killing time as *losing* it. It was a name—and now an image—that had caught her attention.

James Raymond, the actor, was being interviewed. The announcer explained that the star was in town for the shooting of a new film—a thriller in which Raymond played a maverick police officer who bucks corrupt superiors to root out criminals with top political connections, in short, a typical Raymond vehicle. A scene shot earlier that day was shown, and an account of the next day's action followed.

Bryna watched intently, despite the fact that Raymond, though one of her clients and, indeed, her first important client, had never excited her curiosity in the past. If anything, she had privately regarded him as vapid and self-centered with a simplified black-and-white view of the world. He was just another of the "beautiful people" who had built her reputation as a celebrity psychic, a reputation she had later, as she quested after scientific respectability, come to regret.

Yet Bryna now found herself poring over the man's features,

listening intently to his every word, following the camera as it recorded the events that had occurred in the filming that day. She noted the locations at which the shooting would proceed the following day and evening, and for several minutes she forgot entirely about her own difficulties.

The next morning she had forgotten all of this when Niko observed that James Raymond had been calling, wanting Bryna to join him for a drink while he was in town. Bryna evinced no interest whatever. It was one of several such invitations she shrugged off without discussion. Niko left a packet of mail and other telephone messages with her, along with an unruly stack of other unattended papers, and left her alone.

Bryna gazed at the mess on her desk—papers and mail had been accumulating for some time now—and without any evident emotion, swept them onto the floor and watched them cascade to the carpet. One paper landed face up at her feet. It was a telephone memo. On it was the time of the call, the number called from and the name James Raymond. Bryna stared at it for a moment, but did not pick it up.

Later, buoyed by two of the energizers, Bryna decided to go for a walk. She did not tell Niko or the housekeeper. They would only worry, perhaps even try to follow her. She took care to slip out of the house unseen.

It was nearly ten that evening when James Raymond was finally ready. The other actors, the lighting and film crew, the extras, the director, all of them, had been kept waiting for more than two hours.

"It's the insignia," Raymond had fumed. "The goddamned insignia," he said, holding out the blue shirt the wardrobe girl had handed him moments before. "It's sewn on crooked and in the wrong place for Christsake. What kind of production is this anyway? Every shirt I wear has got to be the same. *Exactly the same*. The insignia can't be one way today, and then another way tomorrow."

The wardrobe manager was summoned and finally the director. Nobody could detect any crookedness in the insignia, but the director, in deference to his star, pretended to perceive the defect and, with a meaningful glance, had the offending shirt carried away by a perplexed seamstress. When the shirt came back, with the insignia in nearly the same position, Raymond ignored the insignia and raved instead that the shirt was now too wrinkled to wear.

"Crawford," he lectured, naming the police officer he had

played in a series of movies now, "would never—*never*—wear this. He despises *anything* slovenly; he's as impeccable in his dress as he is in his morality."

While he waited for the shirt to be ironed, Raymond raged inwardly over Bryna Carr's refusal to answer his calls. He ached to confront her, to tell her everything he and Friedkin had found out; he savored the thought of her denials, the look on her face—he could see it clearly—when he told her about the pictures that graphically proved that Bryna Carr, psychic, and Sabrina Jouhaux, socialite, blackmailer and whore, were one and the same. She would threaten him at first, he imagined, but he was secure—as secure as those photos locked up in Friedkin's safe. First he'd get back the ranch in New Mexico, then, gradually, slowly, relentlessly, he'd go after everything she owned. *Then* he'd let Clare finish her off with innuendo, with obvious blind items. They'd let the pictures slip out of their hands. She could talk all she wanted then. Nobody would believe anything she said. It was perfect.

Almost perfect. Raymond's mood darkened again when he reflected on his partner in this. Clare Friedkin's smothering affection, bordering on possessiveness, was bad enough, but lately he had begun to suspect it wasn't all that sincere. The money to be gained from this, over and above reclaiming what he had lost to Carr, had not been of particular interest to him at first. But it obviously was of great—and growing—interest to Friedkin. She was getting pushy about the money, and Raymond didn't like it.

As the filming finally began, he put Friedkin out of his mind and concentrated on Bryna Carr instead, rehearsing his revenge again. Despite this, he never missed a move or fluffed a line. On the contrary, he was the first to note any defect in the performance of any of the other actors and to call halt to the action without so much as a signal to the director. What made this so galling to those thus preempted or upbraided was the fact that Raymond was almost always correct. Moreover, as a coproducer, as well as star of the film, Raymond's decisions tended to go unquestioned, even if they did not go unresented.

At the climax of the filming that evening, Raymond, playing the puritanical Crawford, entered Grace Cathedral, atop Nob Hill. The script called for Crawford to wait in one of the empty pews near the shadowy edge of the vast church, ostensibly listening to the boys' choir rehearsing its Christmas program. He was to wait there for the man who would deliver the payoff he secretly had no intention of accepting. When the man materialized, stepping out of the shadow of an enormous pillar, Raymond-as-Crawford recoiled with shock, recognizing the payoff man as his best friend and fellow police officer. When Crawford reluctantly reached for his gun, the other officer was, as called for in the script, ahead of him, drawing first and firing two shots just as the cymbals of the choir orchestra clashed in the background.

Raymond, true to the script, slumped forward, and the other actor fled. The choir froze in place, a tableau of rehearsed horror. The director waited for Raymond, motionless for the prescribed several seconds, to pull himself partially up before falling back down again between the pews—the first sign that he may yet have a chance to survive and the cue for the members of the choir to rush forward like angels of mercy.

The allotted seconds came and went. Everyone waited in silence, the cameras rolling. Raymond did not move. The seconds stretched into a full minute, as the director looked about nervously, wondering what lesson his temperamental star intended in all of this. A nervous giggle from somewhere in the choir fractured the stillness.

"Cut," the director said softly. "Uh, James..." No response. Then louder: "James. Could we...?" Still nothing. "James!" The director's voice was much louder than he had intended. It echoed through the cavernous space.

"Christ, that's..."

"Jesus God."

Two of the lighting crew had turned, unbidden, a stronger light on the crumpled actor. He was lying on his side, his eyes open, unblinking in the glare.

"That's real blood!"

"He's... dead!"

James Raymond made the eleven o'clock news the second night in a row.

Lieutenant Albert Brazil, spending a rare evening at home with his wife, was in that state of mind that is neither sleeping nor waking, the "theta state," or so wife, who kept up on such things, called it, pointing out that it is characterized by particular brain-wave activity notable for generating "creative *and* erotic possibilities."

"Driiift," his wife kept cooing. "Wait for the images to appear."

Brazil tried, but something had disturbed his reverie. The TV was on. That was it. The volume was down, but something the announcer had said...

"*Driiift.*"

He strained to hear. He opened one eye and then the other. It was his firm conviction that you hear better with your eyes open.

"Holy Christ."

Mrs. Brazil stopped, then looked up.

"Somebody killed James Raymond," her husband said. "Right there. Look. Somebody killed Raymond. Why haven't they called me? I gotta hear it on the news now?" Brazil pulled up his pants as he rushed for the phone.

TWO

"You think he's clean?"

"*Clean?* Christ, his dinner, his lunch, his breakfast even, they're all on the front of his shirt. Whaddaya mean *clean?*" Brazil shook his head, surveying the younger officer with disdain.

The younger man looked blank.

"You're gonna kill somebody, you don't kill somebody with the cameras rolling, with the . . . okay, you *might* if you were . . . but this guy *isn't*, he isn't that type. It would take one cool character to pull that off, and this guy's in shock. He's practically dead himself. Imagine. *Imagine*. Put yourself in his shoes for a minute. Jesus. I had to get out of there."

"You're letting him go?"

"Of *course* I'm letting him go. He was never a suspect. Jesus. Don't even say that. The guy's a basket case. A . . ."

The door swung open, and the man who had shot James Raymond staggered out, supported by two detectives. The man's eyes were swollen, unseeing. One of the officers had halfheartedly tried to clean some of the vomit from the front of the actor's shirt. The wet towel he'd used had only made the mess worse.

"I'm sorry," Brazil said to the man, who stopped and blinked at him incomprehendingly. "Your wife's waiting for you out there. We'll get you out through the side entrance, away from the press."

It was nearly one a.m. when Brazil, back in his cubbyhole office, called his wife. She answered on the third ring.

"What took you so long?"

"I was popping corn."

"Jesus."

"Who did it?"

"No idea."

"Typical."

"Shuddup."

"The director, maybe."

"No."

"An embittered key grip."

"Christ."

"Raymond's wife?"

"Out of state."

"Fingerprints?"

"None we weren't expecting."

"Okay, so tell me, inspector, who squirreled the live ammo into that thirty-eight special?"

"Don't wait up."

"Love you."

"You, too, chickyboom."

Brazil made a loud kissing sound into the phone as he hung up. At that precise moment he became aware that his boss was standing in the door of his cubicle, standing there with the malevolent patience of one who'd been standing there for some time.

"Harry, sir! I didn't hear you ... that was my wife. Y'know how they worry...."

"Save it, chickyboom. Read this."

It was a piece of wire copy, obviously just in. Brazil skimmed over it, stopped, ran a hand through his hair and started over again. It was, he noted, a four-bell bulletin tagged to the Raymond murder stories that had been ticking off the wire for two hours:

San Francisco—A scientist at the prestigious Spectrum Research Institute here announced early today that Bryna Carr, widely known as the "psychic to the stars," predicted the murder of actor James Raymond more than two weeks before the crime occurred. The scientist said she also accurately predicted the date upon which Raymond was murdered.

Dr. Samuel Manning, noted physicist turned psychic researcher, followed his stunning announcement at 12:45 this morning with an acknowledgement that Miss Carr had been the subject of an innovative psychic research project at Spectrum for some months. It had recently been rumored that Miss Carr was attempting to predict the future victims of the so-called "celebrity murderer," but this was the first

210

confirmation by a Spectrum official that the psychic had actually made such predictions.

Pressed for details, Dr. Manning said: "We will publish our results through proper channels in due course. Beyond that, I cannot comment at this time."

Spectrum director of public relations Libby Horne added, "We cannot elaborate further because the experiment is not yet complete."

There are unsubstantiated reports that Raymond was only the first of seven victims named by Bryna Carr while in a trance state. According to these reports the names were electronically encoded and locked in remote computers from which they will not emerge until after the predicted murder dates.

If these reports are true, then neither Raymond nor anyone else was aware that his death had been predicted, unless it was possible for someone to gain access to the encoded names in the computer. Spectrum officials declined to comment on this possibility.

Homicide Chief Harrison Warner refused to confirm that the police regard Raymond as the latest victim of the celebrity killer, calling this "unauthorized conjecture." He gave a terse "no comment" when asked if he was aware of Miss Carr's murder predictions.

Miss Carr herself was not available for comment early this morning. Attempts to reach her at her residence in the posh Seacliff neighborhood of San Francisco were deflected by her business manager, Niko Andrianos, who said the psychic was too ill to come to the phone. Rumors have been circulating that Miss Carr suffered a nervous breakdown recently. Those rumors have not been confirmed.

Brazil looked up at Harrison Warner, who towered over him, arms folded, the smile of a jackal enlivening the deep furrows of his face. He snatched the wire copy from his lieutenant.

"What the hell kind of squat is this psychic crap anyway? I have to learn from George you called in this Carr broad weeks ago on the Salomon case, right? I get no follow-up on that at all, right? And now I've got the press telling me we knew Raymond was going to be offed two weeks ago, and we're sitting right here when it happens with our bloody stumps up our ass. What the fuck's going on?"

"Right. To begin with, sir, when I told you I was thinking of

211

using a psychic in the Salomon case, you called it 'squat.' I guess it just didn't register with you when I told you. I observed Miss Carr once at Spectrum. She seems like a very nice lady. She had quite a reputation. So does Spectrum. I thought it might be worth a try. But then Miss Carr seemed to freak out...."

"Speak English, Brazil."

"Go bananas, you know? Ape shit. See, she was in trance and suddenly she started making funny sounds, broke the glass cubicle she was in, grabbed a piece of the glass, cut herself awful, just awful, sir, and made like she was going to stab this guy with it...."

"Hold it," Warner interrupted. "Jesus Christ, Brazil, start at the beginning."

Brazil explained the scene at Spectrum as best he could. Then he continued. "So I didn't mention it to you again, sir, because I thought maybe you were right, that it was all...uh, squat, sir. I mean it was obvious the woman was having some kind of breakdown. Something was screwing her up."

"Yeah," Warner said, "screwing her up so bad she knows James Raymond's a stiff two weeks before we do. How is that, Brazil? Can you explain that to me? I want answers, Brazil, and I want them before I have to face those press pistols tomorrow."

Bryna turned on the TV in her bedroom and saw the impressive façade of her Seacliff mansion fill the screen. The camera pulled back and she saw the clutch of reporters and cameramen Niko told her had gathered out front. Several neighbors and curious passersby mingled with the newspeople. Some of the neighbors were being interviewed. Bryna didn't know their names, and it was obvious they knew equally little about her—only what they read in the papers.

Ethan was there, at her door, a moment later. They looked at each other for a moment, then burst into smiles.

"Ethan..."

"You did it. You did it!"

He rushed to her, kissing her.

"You're a star," he said. "Hell, you're a galaxy! Did you see them outside? And it isn't just them. Manning has been getting calls from scientists all over the world, *The New York Times*, *Science Magazine*. It's everything you dreamed of. They're going to pay attention from here on, I promise you."

Bryna's smile faltered.

"What is it?"

"I just wish it didn't have to be this kind of prediction . . . somebody dying. . . ."

"I know," he said. "But it's like Manning says, there have been all kinds of accurate predictions by psychics in the past, earthquakes, all manner of things. They cause a sensation for a few days and then they're forgotten. But predicting that specific people, *important* people, will die on specific dates, that's something nobody can ignore, especially when there's more to come."

"What's going to happen now?"

"They're getting ready to give a press conference. Manning has discussed it with the top people at Spectrum. They realize they *have* to say something. Raymond's name came out of a computer in Dayton. The people there let the story out, or enough of it that Manning had to make a statement last night. Mendelsohn's here to protect you, to say you're in shock or something. They want to keep a somber face on the whole thing to avoid excess controversy."

"They're going to say there are six more?"

"Yeah. They feel they have to be up front about it now. When they confirm that there are six to go it's going to create a sensation that will dwarf what's going on now. When each of those predictions comes true, my God! It's mind-boggling what this is going to do to the skeptics."

Bryna brightened.

"It's going to destroy them," Ethan said. "Even if you never do another thing. Not that I've given up on you," he added quickly. "Just because those sessions with Manning haven't worked, you shouldn't worry. It will come back."

Bryna kissed Ethan, wanting to dampen her own doubts, level her seesawing emotions. She wanted him now with an aching immediacy.

She reached up and loosened his tie.

Ethan smiled at her. "I'm afraid Manning is going to want to see you in a minute."

"I want you," Bryna said, starting on the buttons of his shirt.

"Brazil will break in here any time now," Ethan said, his smile a grin.

"They'll wait."

As she pulled back the sheets of the bed, something caught her eye, a winking, golden something. Then she focused on it—a long, blonde hair, glimmering on the dark satin of her pillow case. She felt blood rush into her face, shook the pillow as if plumping it, then turned breathlessly to Ethan, searching his

213

eyes for evidence that he, too, had seen. Satisfied that he had not, she pulled him down onto the softness of the bed, falling back as his weight pressed against her and her mind raced somewhere, somewhere else, *where* she could not say, not until Ethan's orgasm roused her and, like someone just awakening, she fleetingly glimpsed her dream. She saw herself, a child again, hunched over an open Bible, felt the threatening heat of her grandmother's attic, felt the softness of Goldie's last locks, those strands of golden hair she had rescued when the doll was torn from her hands, saw the passage in the Bible she had been meant to see:

A man also or a woman that hath a familiar spirit, or that is a wizard, shall surely be put to death.

THREE

"And so you're telling me there's no way to get those predictions back out of the computer?"

"That's right, Lieutenant," Dr. Manning said. "Oh, there might be, but it would take a tremendous effort. It could cost hundreds of thousands of dollars and take months."

"And nobody could have tapped the computer?"

"They *could* have, Lieutenant," Manning said, barely concealing his smile. "But all of the equipment was inspected by experts from three different centers. And in any event, if someone *did* tap the computer, they'd just get that code we talked about."

"And that they couldn't decipher?"

"We used a relatively new encoding system," Manning explained. "It's the result of several breakthroughs in cryptography. It renders algorithms, all the old methods of encryption obsolete.

"Using one-way functions and keys based on large prime numbers," Manning continued, "we came up with products not even the largest computers can factor—ever. Not without knowing those prime numbers, and only the recipient computer, in this case, knows those. We don't even know which of dozens of participating computers received the encoded names, and nothing comes out of those computers until the time tags release them, one minute, in each case, after the day of the murder— that is, one minute after midnight. There's an electronic record that substantiates the precise time of transmission of the encoded

214

data, so no one can claim it was entered into the system after the fact."

He paused and then added. "It's airtight. Of course, you should talk to the independent observers. We'll give you the names of all who participated."

"There's no chance she could have been aware of the names she gave, that she wasn't really unconscious?"

"There's no chance at all. Check it out."

Brazil nodded. "There was something, as I watched the video-tape of the experiment you showed me earlier, when you asked her for the names. You said the *five* names. And then there were those blips; you said each represented a name."

"Yes."

"But there turned out to be seven, not five."

"Yes."

"There were five in rapid succession, and you all looked at each other and started talking and then a few seconds later there were two more and you all looked surprised."

"Because we'd been expecting just the five she had mentioned in trance a day earlier, as I explained."

"But what do you make of the fact there were seven? The five in one group, then the pause, then two more."

Manning looked at the police officer blankly.

"I don't make anything of it," he said. "Why should I? Perhaps the other information came to her later."

"And the pause?"

Dr. Manning laughed impatiently. "I don't see what you're getting at. Information comes through like conversation. There *will* be pauses from time to time."

"Then it doesn't seem odd to you?"

Manning shook his head.

Brazil thanked him and left. Manning watched him go. He was irritated when the officer came back a minute later.

"*Yes*, Lieutenant?"

"There wouldn't be any chance of getting her *back* into trance and asking her for those names all over again? I mean maybe just so we could protect those people?"

"I'm afraid not," Dr. Manning said. "We've tried to . . . this is confidential."

"Understand. Agreed."

"We've tried to continue our experiments with Miss Carr on a number of occasions since the murder predictions. Nothing comes through at all. She's been having some, uh, personal difficulties."

"I see. Tell me, this is maybe just a crazy idea, but would it be possible for somebody to get hold of Miss Carr and maybe somehow get that information out of her subconscious mind?"

"You don't believe she's psychic, do you, that there has to be some other angle?"

"No, no, I'm not saying that. Please. I just mean, well, we have to cover all the possibilities."

"What you suggest borders on the preposterous. If we can't get any further information out of her here I don't see how anyone else could. We've told her—and she's agreed—not to go into trance anywhere but here, and incidentally, we always have independent observers on hand now, so there's no chance of any of us trying to covertly get the information from her."

"You don't want to know then?"

"Well," Dr. Manning said, "it would . . ."

"Ruin your experiment?"

"Well, obviously, if we *knew* there would always be the possibility the results were manipulated," Manning said heatedly, "but apart from that, Lieutenant, it's been our observation that just because you *know* what's going to happen doesn't mean you can alter or prevent something from happening. On the contrary, we find the opposite; that it will happen no matter what. And if the names were to become known, well, it should be obvious, Lieutenant: any number of crackpots might come forward to fullfil the prophecy. Furthermore, we don't *assume*, despite this first success, that the others will be correct, too. We could be sued if we made those names public—sued by the people named. Imagine the anguish. . . ."

"I get your point," Brazil said. "I'm sorry, sir, it was like I said, just a wild idea."

On the day before it happened again—less than a week after James Raymond was murdered—Lieutenant Brazil spoke with Bryna Carr.

"I'm sorry," he said, brushing the hair out of his eyes. "I know what a strain this must be for you, Miss Carr. Doctor Manning, Doctor Mendelsohn, your boyfriend, also Niko . . . forget . . ."

"Andrianos."

"Yeah. Yes. A nice fellow. A little quiet maybe, on the brooding side, but . . ."

"*Please,* Lieutenant."

"Ma'am?"

"Could we get to the point, whatever that might be?"

"I'm terribly sorry. I was just about to say, Dr. Manning, all of them, they've told me what a strain this has been on you. I mean, this awful thing, this murder, and at the same time, what a *tremendous* success for you. I've spoken with all the computer fellows, all the experts. Everything checks out, Miss Carr. I mean what a success! I try to put myself in your shoes, Miss Carr. *Imagine.* Predicting something like this in a trance and then suddenly having it sprung on you, that it was correct. I mean, wow!"

Brazil shook his head, staring at Bryna, something between a smile and a grimace seizing his mouth.

"It must have been overwhelming. A *murder*! To know who was going to be murdered and exactly *when*. And yet not know it. Not know who you named. I wonder how you keep your sanity, Miss Carr?"

Brazil's technique grated on Bryna. His obsequiousness was clearly phony. More than that, Brazil suddenly struck her as pettily devious.

The headache that had been pinching her tightened its grip.

"My wife, Miss Carr, my wife—you should meet her sometime—she's completely beside herself. You can imagine. She's your *biggest* fan. What the police couldn't accomplish with all their collected resources—knowing who and when—you accomplish all by yourself. You make it tough for me at home, Miss Carr, I can tell you that."

"A mere woman, is that it, Lieutenant?" Bryna felt the pain grab her neck hard. "Why don't you cut the Columbo crap and tell me what you want to know?"

Brazil stared at her for a moment, as if shocked.

"You notice that, do you? My wife used to watch that TV program—it's not on anymore, is it? I'm a movie buff myself. The big screen. I can't get enough of the movies, especially those great old movies, those great old stars. Yourself?"

Bryna shrugged her shoulders, exasperated.

"All right, all right. The point. Right! Well, we know you were unconscious when you made those predictions, and so far as we know you haven't had any luck with your, uh, trances since then. I mean, we're keeping that to ourselves. That's nobody's business but . . . the point, the *point*, Miss Carr, is you haven't come through with anything at Spectrum. They get a big zero out of you, but maybe, just maybe, at home by yourself, say, or perhaps with your old friend Niko, uh, you know, or who knows who, you *do* get something, like those names for example. . . ."

"And then *I* go out and kill those people, right?"

"It's just that I'd be remiss if I didn't... Where were you when the murder occurred?"

This was stated so flatly, so blandly that Bryna did not comprehend for a moment.

"I was... I don't know... well, I was here, in this house. In bed by then."

"Was there anyone with you?"

Bryna looked at him dumbly.

He threw up his hands apologetically.

"No offense intended. But these days, I mean, why not?"

"There was *no* one with me," Bryna said stiffly.

"I'm sorry, Miss Carr, I'm very sorry."

"Are you trying to be funny?"

Lieutenant Brazil looked blank for a moment, then realized his second faux pas.

"Again, Lieutenant, what do you want?"

"An alibi would be useful."

"I have none."

"Please. This is all routine. In the hours before the murder, was anyone with you?"

"No... I wasn't feeling well. I spent the afternoon here in my study. Well, Niko and the housekeeper were here, in the house."

"They would have seen you leave?"

"Leave the house? I'm sure one of them would have."

"And so you didn't go out at all that day?"

"No, no I didn't," Bryna said, remembering too late that she had, in fact, taken a long walk by herself in the late afternoon. She decided to say nothing about it.

"Would you tell me a little about her?"

The change of subject was sudden and unsettling, but Bryna knew exactly who he meant by "her."

"I'm really not feeling so well," she said truthfully. "I... excuse me a moment will you." She hurried into the bathroom, shut the door behind her and took two of her tranquilizers, swallowing them without water. She looked at herself briefly in the mirror, something she rarely did now, and then went back out.

"Just a few more questions," Brazil promised.

"I don't want to talk about Sabra. I don't see what that has to do with it."

"That? I got the feeling from reading your book that you thought of Sabra as a *her*, not a *that*."

"She's a... a concept," Bryna said, confused and impatient.

"A concept?"

218

"Yes. What has this got to do with . . . I don't have to talk about any of this."

"Well, it's just that I'm fascinated, really, I mean, when you go into those trances, and this power comes through you, isn't it something like having two different personalities?"

Bryna said nothing.

"I've read some of your papers on Tantrism, Miss Carr. Fascinating, just fascinating. And you've got quite a collection here in the house. It's like a museum. I wish my wife could see this. It's just—all those costumes, masks, knives . . . all those weapons. I understand you're quite a marksman, too. Marksperson? My wife's always correcting me."

"Yes," Bryna said simply, suddenly wondering why she had been fighting the questions. She resented the implication that because she had known about Raymond's death she must have had something to do with it, but, she told herself, she had nothing to hide. Yet the anger lingered. She was angry that Brazil, that the police, rather than concede the possibility of precognition, would instead choose to suspect her. It was all so little and mean, the conventional wisdom insisting upon the conventional answers. Still, Manning and Ethan had assured her that the people who really mattered, the scientists, were taking note; they might still be skeptical, but now they were paying attention. Manning was receiving invitations to speak at scientific symposiums all over the country; Bryna herself would join him as soon as she felt well enough.

"I'd be honored, Miss Carr, if you'd show me your collection— of guns, I mean."

"Of course," Bryna said, concealing her agitation. She took the detective to the basement. He whistled when he saw the indoor rifle range, the gleaming glass cases full of revolvers, automatics, rifles.

"This is quite a deployment," he said. "I wish some of the boys could see this."

"All registered and licensed," Bryna said.

"Oh, I know, I know," Brazil said. "We checked you out." His eyes were on the thirty-eights.

"Jeez," he said absently. "Just beautiful, beautiful. And I bet . . . don't tell me, Miss Carr, each of these cabinets underneath here contains . . ." He held up his hand, then dropped to his knees and popped open the cabinet doors under the thirty-eights.

"The ammunition," he said. "All so orderly. You do it all so neat, Miss Carr." As he peered in, Bryna could not help peering

219

in after him. One box of thirty-eight shells, she immediately noticed, was pulled slightly out of its place, its cover open. One of the big shells was sticking out. Everything else was in place.

Bryna felt her heart pound.

Brazil was silent, staring into the cabinet for some seconds. It seemed almost that he was praying.

"Just beautiful," he said again. Then he stood up, brushed his hands perfunctorily and said, "It's like I say, all of this is routine. I'm really sorry I've taken so much of your time. The doc tells me you need some rest. Goodbye, Miss Carr."

Bryna did not offer to see him out. When she could no longer hear his footfalls, she dropped to her knees and looked into the ammunition cabinet. She touched the open box, started to take it out, then pulled her hand back, as if stung.

Clare Friedkin took a taxi from the airport to the Hyatt Regency Hotel at Five Embarcadero Center in San Francisco's financial district. It was well after midnight when she checked in. She had always stayed at the Stanford Court—ever since she'd heard that Jackie stayed there—but had chosen the Embarcadero Hyatt on this occasion because James Raymond had been staying there on his last—and final—visit to San Francisco.

A touch of sentiment, she thought. In fact, however, Raymond's murder had not grieved her, not, at least, for more than a pleasantly theatrical half hour and in dramatic short takes when she was with friends and acquaintances, tearfully relating how "close" she and the star had grown "in his final weeks." Actually, Friedkin admitted to herself, it was rather nice having Raymond out of the way. Now *she* could call all the shots with the Carr bitch. And the stories that she would eventually write, once she had drained, ruined and robbed Bryna Carr of all her cash and credibility, would be the more heartwrenching now that one of Carr's principal victims was dead. In fact, it would now be possible to reveal Raymond's sexual peccadilloes—the same that she would reveal she had hidden from public view for years in an effort to protect the star—but only in the course, naturally, of exposing the "viciousness" of Bryna Carr and her blackmailing phony alter ego, Sabrina Jouhaux. She might, it had occurred to her on the plane, even hint that Raymond had not been the latest victim of the celebrity murderer but a suicide, that unable to cope with the blackmail any longer, he had covertly placed the live ammunition in the gun, knowing that it would kill him.

In fact, however, Carr's prediction of Raymond's death had

unnerved her. It seemed almost too convenient that he should be disposed of in this manner and at this particular time. Convenient for Bryna Carr. Still, Friedkin could not quite believe that Carr would assume the risks of murdering someone. Still, if she was genuinely psychic, and Friedkin believed she must be, else how could she have found out about Raymond and how could she have maintained her lucrative psychic practice for so long, then there was the possibility she had found out that Raymond intended to counter her blackmail. In that case, might she not also know about Friedkin's role?

The columnist shook herself; it was not her style to be afraid. Carr couldn't know everything. No psychic did. And anyway, Raymond had been one of her clients; she'd had ample opportunity to pick things up from him over the years. Friedkin had presented no such opportunity.

Friedkin opened her address book and copied the phone number on a hotel pad. Psychic or not, Bryna Carr would have little defense against the evidence Friedkin had in her suitcase—photos of Bryna, both as herself and as Sabrina.

She thought, thank god I didn't let Jimmy take the pictures with him; the police would have them now. As a precaution against anyone scooping her, Friedkin had not duplicated the photos. There was only the one set. She had not dared even put them in her checked baggage, but had carried them on board the plane with her.

"This is for you, Jimmy," she said, smiling grimly, as she dialed the number on the pad. The fact that it was now nearly one-thirty a.m. did not bother her. Bad news was always most effectively delivered when least expected, when resistance to mental shock was at the lowest possible ebb. The number she called was unlisted. It was a secret number available only to Bryna Carr's clients.

A man answered the phone, his tone unfriendly. He demanded to know who was calling, but Friedkin would only say that she was "a friend of James Raymond with a message for Miss Carr." The ploy backfired. The man hung up, and Friedkin realized he had dismissed her as a crank caller.

Infuriated nonetheless, she called back immediately. "This is Clare Friedkin," she said quickly, "and if you hang up on me again, you'll regret it. I want to speak to Bryna Carr, and I want to speak to her now."

There was a pause, then the man said, "She's sleeping and I can't awaken her."

"Just get her up!"

"That's not possible. I have orders from her doctor not to disturb her."

"What's your name?"

"Niko Andrianos."

"All right, Mr. Andrianos. But I suggest you have Miss Carr call me here at the hotel no later than nine a.m." She gave him the number and her room extension. As she finished she heard a distinct click, as if someone had been listening in. Bryna Carr herself, no doubt. She was about to protest when Andrianos hung up.

She considered calling back again but decided against it. If she hadn't heard anything by nine she would call back then and be more explicit, *much* more explicit. In any event, this left the rest of the evening free. There were things she could do, she realized; it wasn't too late by any means. Especially not in San Francisco. She didn't have James Raymond's flair for disguises, but she had always managed when she was on the road by herself. It was time to trot out Esther Mathias.

She took the blonde wig from its case and put it on. She looked at herself in the mirror. The wig, she was convinced, made her look years younger, though she never wore it around those who knew her. It changed her appearance radically, but there was still the possibility someone might recognize her, even with the special makeup and the tinted glasses.

She took out her address book again, found the number she wanted and dialed. It was an escort service, a very discreet one she had used on previous visits. She told them what she wanted, then prepared her bath. She anticipated the look on the boy's face when he would arrive in an hour. She'd answer the door clad only in her blonde wig, spike heels, black nylons and garter belts. Maybe tonight, she decided, they'd get into some watersports. The boy would understand, if she paid him enough.

The two couples sat at a little glass table in the spectacular lobby of the Hyatt Regency Hotel, the ceiling dozens of stories away. The balconies of each floor were visible from the lobby, each stacked on top of the other, creating, in the irregular space the hotel occupied, impossible angles, dizzying illusions, just as they had been designed to do.

"This place is incredible," the young woman said, watching the ornate glass elevators climb the walls. "We haven't got anything like this in Des Moines. Hell, we haven't got anything like this in the whole state of Iowa." She laughed and took another sip of her drink, only a little embarrassed by her own tipsy exuberance.

"Forget Iowa," her husband said. "We're here to celebrate Jack's speech. That was one hell of a spiel you delivered tonight."

"It woke them up, if I do say so myself," Jack said, beaming.

"*Conventions,*" Jack's wife said, disdainfully. "This is the last one *I* ever attend."

"Oh come on," the younger man said. "Cheer up. It's over tomorrow." He raised his glass, preparing to toast his boss. "Here's to that speech, Jack."

As their glasses clinked together, they were smashed from their hands. Jack's wife, who was hit hardest, screamed in pain. All of them were knocked backward, sprawling on the floor in broken glass and blood. A blonde wig flew through the air and hit Jack in the face.

Screams mixed with shouts of horror.

"My god! What . . . !"

"Christ!"

"She's dead! She has to be!"

"Those people! They're hurt. . . ."

A security officer and a bellman rushed to the scene, pushing people back—away from the shattered table, away from the four injured conventioneers from Des Moines, away from the nude, black-gartered, grotesquely twisted body of Clare Friedkin.

FOUR

"The punk's got her gold lighter and nine hundred bucks in cash on him and you still say he had nothing to do with it?"

Brazil started to reply.

"For Christsake, they saw him, one of the other guests saw the little fuck coming out of the broad's room. . . ."

"With all due respect, sir," Brazil said quietly, "you don't take roses and a twelve-inch dildo to a murder."

"So he didn't plan it."

"More likely it's like the kid says, sir. The door was open, wide open. He went in; after all, he was expected. We've confirmed that. Nobody's there. He thinks he's dealing with a whacko, that his trip over there is wasted. He sees her purse, he decides to pay himself. Okay, *over*pay himself. As he goes out he hears the commotion below. He looks over the ledge and sees somebody has jumped; I mean that would be the natural assumption. He puts two and two together and figures it's his client. He knows this isn't going to look good if he's found in her room, so he panics. Yeah, he *looks*, he *acts* guilty, but he isn't."

"Yeah? And so where's the real murderer all this time? This murderer is maybe invisible? Is that how we explain we haven't caught him?"

"The murderer throws the lady over the balcony, ducks through the fire door and takes the stairs down a flight or two before getting the elevator. The kid, at the same time the murderer is slipping through the fire door, comes *out* of the elevator and goes directly into her room. We paced it through, the timing. All possible. The fire door was right by the spot she went over; we can tell the spot by the way the plants along the ledge there were disturbed. And ask yourself, sir, *why* would the kid do it, throw a big heavy lady like that over the ledge? He didn't need to kill her. He could have just ripped her off and walked out of there. She couldn't very well lodge a complaint under the circumstances."

"Christ, why can't anything be simple anymore? It was bad enough with the first one. Now I've got the press offering that Carr bitch my job. Did you see that cartoon in the morning paper? Christ!"

Brazil did his best to look regretful.

"And these headlines! These fucking headlines! 'Two Down! Five to Go!' Jesus! Can you believe that shit? And *we* claim the Romans were barbaric. They're making a fucking circus out of it."

"Okay, now Carr. That's where it get's a little more interesting, real interesting, I'd say," Brazil continued. "You see, sir, Friedkin's luggage had all been gone through. It looked like somebody wanted something this time; we've never seen that in any of the other celebrity killings. There was never any robbery, nothing missing. We don't know for sure there was anything missing this time, either, but we did find an empty manila envelope on the floor, and the lab boys say that envelope contained glossy photos: emulsion traces, that sort of thing. And we found this."

Brazil held out a small white piece of paper.

"So? It's from a Hyatt notepad."

"From her room. Next to the phone."

"A fucking blank piece of paper."

"Not entirely blank, sir. Look closer." He held it up to the

224

light. "There, you see the impression? It's a number, sir, a telephone number she wrote on the piece of paper directly above this one. She pressed down hard enough that . . ."

"I *understand*, Lieutenant. *Whose* number is it?"

"Bryna Carr's."

Warner looked sick for a moment.

"And the paper on which the number was actually written was missing."

"You've talked to her?"

"Yes, sir. Of course, we didn't know Friedkin was on Carr's list until after midnight. When it came out of that computer in Boston. I talked to her as soon as I could, this morning. It was a madhouse over there. The press is going crackers over this. Carr was, I don't know, she doesn't strike me as all together, and I'm afraid I didn't make matters any better when I told her about the paper with her number on it. She says she doesn't know Friedkin from Eve. I talked to her assistant, Andrianos, he was there the night she was killed, in the house, he says. Carr claims to have been out cold, on sleeping pills that whole night, and Andrianos backs her up. He says he never had any contact with Friedkin, either. But when I told Carr, Miss Carr, about the phone number, she got upset, really upset. I mean, she tried to hide it, but I could tell it upset her."

"So it upset her, Lieutenant. Big deal. We're talking about dead people here, Lieutenant. And now you're feeling sorry for this crazy . . ."

"There's something else, sir. We found out that Raymond was also trying to phone her just before he died. He'd made several efforts, but she wouldn't return his calls. One of the crew members on the film overheard him talking to Andrianos, demanding to speak with Miss Carr. Andrianos admits Raymond called several times but says Miss Carr hasn't been taking calls from anybody."

"What about a lie-detector test?"

"I mentioned it."

"And?"

"Her doctor told me to get out."

"He was there?"

"Yeah, the whole time. They said he had to be, that she's under strain. He laughed in my face when I suggested she take the test, said that they're 'twentieth-century voodoo,' his exact words. He quoted all kinds of statistics trying to tell me how unreliable they are. And he said he couldn't permit it anyway, that it would put her under too much pressure."

"Shit. Well, you can't make anybody take a lie-detector test, but I want somebody watching that place day and night, keeping a log of who comes and goes and when. And I want you to check out Manning *and* Mendelsohn, everybody around her. Andrianos. He strikes me as shifty. Her boyfriends, everybody. Anybody who has anything to gain from those predictions coming true. And get somebody on those computers. See if we can't get those names out. The commissioner has been calling every hour. I want some progress and I want it yesterday, understand?"

"Right, sir. We're also looking for links between Friedkin and Raymond; his name was in her address book, but so was half of Hollywood. As for the computer thing, I dunno. That's locked up pretty tight. Those codes appear to be airtight."

"Check it out, goddamn it. Check it out, and keep checking it out. *Nothing's* airtight except the commissioner's ass."

"Right, sir." Brazil started to go, then stopped. "Oh, one other thing, sir. The boys in pathology found out why nobody heard Friedkin scream, either before or during her fall. The killer crushed her voice box. They say it can be done with a single, well-placed blow, a good karate chop."

Harrison Warner considered this silently for a moment, his fingers involuntarily palpating his big adam's apple. Then realizing what he was doing and that Brazil was still there watching him, he quickly pulled his hand away and barked, "Get out of here, Lieutenant."

It hadn't so much been the news that Raymond and Friedkin had both tried calling her that made Bryna want to stop everything. And it wasn't that Brazil—that wretched little man—had found someone who had seen her out walking that afternoon, the day Raymond was killed, the afternoon she said she had spent entirely indoors, or that he had asked her to take a lie-detector test. Nor was it so much the weight of not being able to do anything, the sickening absence of power when she needed it most, when the attention of the world was focused upon her at last, when the opportunity she had longed for was at hand; nor was it even Niko's new wariness, though that grieved her intensely. More and more she had detected, though sometimes she thought she imagined it, a watchfulness about Ethan, a suspicion.

god not ethan too don't let him doubt me

That had begun, she thought, right after the murder predictions, when the subsequent work at Spectrum was going so badly

226

and she had asked him if they could not resume their private "practice" sessions, of the sort they'd had before the predictions, pleading that she felt so much more safe with him, desperate to regain what she had lost, what he kept telling her was coming back. He had looked at her oddly, she recalled, and pointed out that Dr. Manning had firmly instructed her *not* to go into trance except at Spectrum and with independent observers present. He had told her that she must be patient, that they must wait.

But it wasn't that, either, that made her want to withdraw inside herself, where she would see nothing, feel nothing, hear nothing, say nothing. It had begun that morning, moments before Niko told her about Friedkin dying the night before. It was an immediate sense of something wrong, something out of its proper place, something somehow familiar but now terrifying. She had been agitated by it for hours now; it produced a cold, hollow feeling, a vague nausea that threatened at any moment to intensify.

Later that afternoon the feeling drove her out into the corridor, outside her study. It was as if something was compelling her to move, to *discover*. She found herself in the gloom, looking up the broad stairway to the Void above. Its mirrored face and outstretched arms seemed to beckon at her. She felt a cold vibration jiggle down the back of her neck and lodge in her spine. She began climbing the stairs. Halfway to the top, she whirled around. There had been no sound, but there, at the foot of the stairs was Niko. He was staring up at her, his look so intense he was almost scowling.

"Last night," he said, "I couldn't sleep. I got these old books I had up there in the storeroom." He was holding two books. "I was just taking them back. The funny thing is, when I was up there, I heard something."

Bryna felt cold and stiff.

"What could you possibly have heard?" she said, her voice too loud, almost belligerent.

"I don't know. A noise. Like something falling. In there." He nodded up at the Void. "In *her* room."

It came to Bryna, filling her nostrils and then her mind. The thing that had been there now for hours, the thing that was out of place, that was wrong. It was the perfume, *her* perfume, the perfume Bryna loathed. It was on her, on her skin, enveloping her. She felt the nausea now, coming in hot spasms, felt the cold perspiration on her chin.

She limped down the stairs, pulling away like a frightened

animal when Niko tried to help her. She made it to her bedroom, dragging the leg that wouldn't work, and locked the door behind her.

FIVE

Bryna told no one about the perfume, either before or after the electroshock treatments that finally terminated several days of complete withdrawal. Dr. Mendelsohn had admitted her to a private sanatorium and administered the electroconvulsive therapy there himself. He wanted to keep her there longer, Bryna knew, but Ethan had not permitted it. Her mind had been clear enough, after the third series of shock, that she could remember now how they had argued outside her room at the sanatorium.

Their heated words came back to her, as if being played on a tape:

"She's responding, yes, but that doesn't mean she's well," Mendelsohn said.

"I want her out of here today," Ethan insisted.

"She's very sick. We can do things for her here that we can't do anywhere else."

"There's no need..."

"You think she's given up her delusion? You're blinded! So was I, for a little while. But she's lying. It's not at all uncommon. It's like a child who says his toothache has gone away, even though he's in excrutiating pain. Anything to avoid a trip to the dentist. She's trying to pretend the problem away. She's so torn between her love for you and her commitment to this delusion, a commitment that precludes love for anyone, that she's paralyzed, frozen. All she can do is try to get through the next moment with tranquilizers, booze, lies, lies she doesn't even know are lies."

"I think I can help her more than..."

"*Amor vincit omnia?*" Mendelsohn asked, sarcastically. "Love will conquer all?"

"Maybe," Ethan said. "Yeah, maybe that's right."

"Listen," Mendelsohn said, "those drugs I was working on, I think we might be able to..."

"No! I'm not going to let you use her as a guinea pig the way you used those poor yellow bastards we turned over to you in 'Nam. You forget who you're talking to."

"All right," Mendelsohn said, a menacing agreeableness in his voice. "You can take her home today. And if love isn't completely blind, you'll soon see just how confused she is. Then you'll beg me to bring her back here."

Except that she wasn't confused, not anymore, Bryna told herself. The doubts were gone now, the doubts that had so sickened her. The electroshock had cleared the air. She knew now for certain.

sabra is real

Bryna had tried to believe otherwise, to please Dr. Manning, to please Dr. Mendelsohn, to please Ethan. But it was no use trying to deceive herself any longer, she thought. And it wasn't easier this way, it *wasn't*! It wasn't a convenient cop-out, as they all implied, a subconscious ploy to have someone else take the blame. Sabra was real, and now, Bryna was convinced, Sabra was malignant. She would have to destroy her or be destroyed *by* her. She could think of only one thing to do.

Oddsmakers were taking bets on the accuracy of the remaining predictions. The tabloids were having a field day. One claimed to have "inside" knowledge of who had been named and when the "five to go" would die. Another sponsored a contest—offering one hundred thousand dollars to anyone who could guess who the next victim would be and the date upon which the killing would occur, prompting an immediate outcry from law enforcement authorities who feared a flock of self-fulfilling and fatal prophecies. The tabloid stood firm, however, stipulating that only those victims named by Bryna Carr would be counted as valid guesses.

The "respectable" media carried daily stories on the predictions, as well. Everyone who had the slightest connection with Bryna Carr was interviewed, if only to get a "no comment," which was all Nestor Bagehot, for example, would ever offer. He did not tell the press that Bryna Carr had not, for some time, answered any of his calls. Bryna was the favorite topic of many religious figures, too, the more vocal of whom generally decried her as a "false prophet" and the "Antichrist." Ives Matlock was a notable exception, for though he saw evil around her and perhaps within her, he did not see her as the source of that evil.

"I pray daily for Miss Carr and for those souls her predictions consign to death." Asked whether he believed those deaths could be prevented, he unhesitatingly replied: "Oh, yes. In Christ, *Ev-ry-thing* is *pos-sible*," adding, with calculated mystery, "I be-lieve Miss Carr is struggling *now* to save them. I be-lieve she is grap-pling with the great-est *e*-vil known to man. I cannot predict whether she will pre-*vail*, but I *know* she *can* pre-*vail*."

It was all much easier than Bryna had thought it would be—persuading Ethan. She had looked for ridicule and scorn in his words, but she had found none. She had asked him to read *Earthbound!*, the book by Mary Beckman with the foreword by Ives Matlock, and he had done so, taking the book from her, clearly surprised, looking at her with something like shock, but then he had read the book and had accounted it "well written."

"I expected it to be right off the wall," he said. "Not that I buy this idea, but..."

"I want to meet them," Bryna blurted.

And then it had all come out, amidst tears, her confession, her belief, stronger than ever now, she said, that Sabra was real, everything but those darker fears that came to her in the image of a single golden strand of hair, just the suggestion in the air of a scent she hated and feared, the sound, echoing in her mind, of something heavy falling, the terror of forgotten, obliterated hours.

"It's my only chance," she cried.

"An exorcism..."

"Oh, Ethan, please, I have to try...."

"I...god, I don't know. I have to tell you, I think Matlock's a crock; I think *religion's* a crock, but..."

"You think I'm crazy?"

"I think we're *both* crazy. If you want to meet him, if you think it will help, I'll arrange it."

No ridicule, no contempt, but there was in Ethan's tone, Bryna thought, a certain resignation. No doubt like Naomi Hevesey, she decided, he thought that if you believed in something strongly enough it might help you, whether it was a "crock" or not.

"I actually *know* Matlock," Ethan added. "I interviewed him months ago, in connection with one of the murders. Pike Subic, the country western star, was a born-again Christian. Matlock converted him; it was one of his coups." Ethan laughed, a little ruefully. "I hope you know what you're getting into."

"He helped *her*," Bryna said. "He helped Mary Beckman."

The Reverend Ives Matlock was a surprisingly short but handsome man with thick, wavy hair so blonde it appeared almost white. His eyes were, as one writer had put it, "blue as heaven." His features appeared chiseled from granite, his plenti- ful teeth slightly prognathic and white as ivory. When Bryna and

Ethan walked into the outer chamber of his enormous office in the "nerve center" of Matlock's Fortress of Faith in a suburb of Los Angeles, the evangelist materialized immediately, striding confidently from the inner office, stopping for only a moment to survey his visitors before embracing Bryna warmly.

"I *knew* you'd come *home,*" he said to her in his richly modulated, Southern-accented voice. Then he released her and seized her companion. "Brother *E*-than! *Wel*-come back."

Bryna felt overwhelmed at first. She could not but recall with revulsion the religious teachers who had inflicted so much horror upon her in her childhood. A part of her instantly hated this man; another part yearned for his approval, his forgiveness, the sanctity of his embrace.

Matlock promised them that Mary Beckman would be along soon. In the meantime, he insisted, he would give his visitors the grand tour of his vast and still expanding Fortress of Faith, a complex enclosed within massive walls that did, indeed, resemble those of an ancient fortress. Matlock spoke with enthusiasm about "the new computer center," the "advanced electronics," the "special effects, better'n anything they got at *Dis*-ney-land." His pride and joy was quite obviously the pulpit itself—an enormous stage above a "congregation hall" that could seat eight thousand people "in op-ry hall com-fort," as he put it.

The stage was equipped with "*fif*-ty mov-ing sec-tions" capable of elevating, lowering, spreading, condensing, materializing, even "*de*-materializing" special displays, soloists, whole stage sets, the orchestra, the choir, Matlock himself. Concealed lights and motion picture, laser and planetarium-style projectors could, in league with various vents connected to elaborate plumbing, produce snowstorms, lightning storms, rainstorms, thunder, the roar of cannons, puffs of smoke, ethereal clouds of every hue, images of outer space, all manner of illusions, even the smell of sulphur and brimstone and the heat of hellfire.

The elevated lectern from which Matlock preached was similarly mobile, able to sink from sight beneath the stage or to rise high above it, boosting the diminutive evangelist to heroic heights behind his rostrum. Moreover, with the press of a concealed button on a remote-control device Matlock always carried hidden in his robes, the preacher could command the thick, fortresslike walls on either side of the lectern to open and close around him, in dramatic concert with his changing moods.

"They call it '*show*-man-ship,'" Matlock said. "*I* call it *Gawd's* own mag-ic. No matter how long I live, I will *nev*-er cease to mar-vel at the won-ders of *e*-lec-tric-i-ty. I'm like a kid with a

231

brand new toy. And, lis-sen, if it makes people sit *up* and pay *at*-ten-tion to the Lord, then by *Gawd*, it's *o-kay.*" Matlock showed them the control center for the special stage effects, the remote-control devices he and a select few, the Guardians of the Fortress, carried concealed upon their persons during sermons and telecasts. "The higher up the ladder," Matlock said, smiling, "the more they get to play with."

He looked proudly around, then added: "A lot of it's *spon*-tan-e-ous. While I'm *preach*-ing, I *or*-che-strate these walls, floors, lights, sounds and visions like a *band* leader . . . like the *cap*-tain of a *foot*-ball team, you see what I mean? All of this, all of these ac-*cou*-tre-ments become ex-*ten*-sions of myself, *am*-pli-fy-ing *the word of Gawd.*" Matlock stopped, looking slightly embarrassed. "You'll forgive me my *pride*. That's the *one* sin I am *con*-tin-u-al-ly com-mit-tin'. Only last week my lit-tle daughter *Glow*-ri-a said, 'Daddy, does *Gawd* care if we're better'n *Dis*-ney?' Oh! I was *so* a-shamed. I'd been rantin' and ravin' to the 'lec-tron-ic boys I wanted *some*-thing to rival Space *Moun*-tain and . . . well, from the lips of a *babe!*"

After the tour the three returned to Matlock's office. "Well," the evangelist said, "*E*-than, what say you and me go have lunch with some of the fellas and leave the *wim*-min here to compare notes?"

Ethan shot a glance at Bryna, begging to be saved. Bryna merely smiled at him, too excited over the prospect of meeting Mary Beckman to worry much about Ethan's plight. Anyway, she had decided she liked Matlock.

"An' now that lady her-*sef*," Matlock said, speaking into his intercom, "*May*-ry Beck-man. Ruth, will ya send her in?"

When their visitors had gone, Ives Matlock and Mary Beckman sat on the big horsehide sofa, the woman's hand over the evangelist's.

"That Kendal fellow is *real in*-quis-i-tive," Matlock said. "A *real bull*-dog for *de*-tail."

"You don't think he'll try to stop her?"

"*Stop* her? Why should he? He just wants to know what *kinda* crazy we are, whether we'll turn the trick. Hell, he *wants* us to succeed."

"I don't think he believes . . ."

"*Course* not. But he's smart enough to know it's what *she* believes that counts. He doesn't care what it is, a ghost, a spirit, a *de*-lu-sion. He don't want to share her with *no-body.*"

Mary Beckman was thoughtful for a moment.

"So *spill*," Matlock said. "Did ya git it out of her?"

"*Poured* out," Mary Beckman said. "It's even worse than we thought."

"Hot *dawg*, babe, ya did it!" Matlock said, slapping Beckman on the thigh.

"It's all on tape." She picked up a remote-control device on the coffee table and pressed the playback button.

"I...I read your book." It was Bryna Carr, a tremor in her voice.

"I'm *so* pleased," Mary answered, her voice soft, yet full, reassuring, loving.

"I was moved."

"I know what you've been going through."

"Oh, god, do you? Yes, yes I think you do."

"I know how hopeless it may seem to you now, but trust me, there *is* a way out... the *only* way out."

Ives Matlock listened raptly.

"I have to do it, and I have to do it publicly."

"Tell everything?" Ethan asked.

"Yes," Bryna said, the excitement already building in her. "Mary says it's the only way. Ethan, I believe her. I feel it...."

"A classic purging of the soul—in view of millions?" Ethan asked. "If it's what you want, if you think it will help..."

"I do. Oh, Ethan, I do, I *do*!"

"Well, I'll tell you one thing. Matlock's ratings that night are going to purge his competition."

"You don't care then? You'll let me do it?"

"Of course."

"Ethan...oh, I can't tell you how much better I feel. I...Ethan, I know you're being tolerant, indulgent, but I wish you could have been there, *heard* what Mary had to say...."

"Believe me," Ethan said, as their cab headed for the airport, "I wish I had, too. Two hours with Ives Matlock and the 'fellas' isn't my idea of a great time."

"She was so... I don't know... it sounds corny I know, but the only word I can come up with is *spiritual*. She just seems so full and alive and *real*. And I could *feel* it, Ethan, how much she wants to help me."

"All hell's going to break loose when Manning hears about this. Mendelsohn, too. He'll have us both committed."

The mention of those names dispirited Bryna.

"I don't want to see either of them again," she said angrily. "There's no point in it, anyway. Not anymore."

*   *   *

A week later Bryna was alone in the "green room" with Mary Beckman. Ethan would not be in the wings, after all, but in the audience, right up front. She wanted him, she said, where she could see him—to give her courage, though out there, under the blinding lights and special effects of the Fortress of Faith, she wasn't sure she would be able to see him, after all.

"I know how peculiar you must feel right now," Mary said, putting her hand on Bryna's, caressing it. "I remember *my* night, when I was doing just what you're about to do. *Giving* myself to *Him*, renouncing what was inside me. Oh, Bryna, what you're going to experience! It's . . . it's . . ." Mary Beckman struggled for the words, her face enraptured. "You're going to experience it *all*. You'll feel a lightening, a literal *lightening* of the soul. *All* of us, *millions* of us are going to be praying for you at the precise same moment, and when Ives places his hands on your head, and all of that prayer, all of that *energy* courses through you, you're going to feel yourself lifted, *cleansed*. . . ."

Bryna heard only snatches of what Mary said now. Her mind was racing as fast as her heart. Ever since her private prayer session with Mary and Ives earlier that evening, she had already begun to feel lighter; yes, Mary's word was exactly right. *Lightening*. It sounded like *lightning*, and it came in a flash, but it was a cleansing, unburdening flash. Bryna felt herself glow, radiate with the heat of that recurring flash. She felt love, love for Mary, love for Ives, love for Ethan, love for God, love for Everyone. It scarcely seemed possible, but it was happening. She was going to be free, she told herself.

free

It was time.

The voice telling her this startled her. Suddenly there were faces, angry, shocked, desperate faces, intruding on her high. Mendelsohn, Manning, Libby Horne, even Niko. Then she heard their voices, recalled their words as they had tried to "reason" with her: heard Manning, losing all patience, finally shouting at her, saying she was throwing everything away, ruining her career, ruining *him*, destroying her one great chance to convince Science of the reality of the paranormal; heard Libby Horne begging her not to go through with it, saying she would make Spectrum a "laughingstock"; saw Niko, hanging back, saying little, but looking deeply concerned; heard Mendelsohn vituperating, muttering in Latin, scorning her, bullying her, warning her. . . .

"Bryna?"

234

Mary Beckman's face came into focus. "You'll be all right." She kissed Bryna softly on the cheek. Bryna looked at her, and the next thing she knew she was walking, with one of the associate directors, down the long corridor toward the stage. As they walked, Bryna could see Ives Matlock, behind his lectern, on TV monitors, could hear his voice through concealed speakers.

"First there was *May*-ry Beckman," Matlock shouted, as a single light shone down upon him. "Now, there's *Bry*-na Carr!"

Bryna's lightness verged on vertigo. She tightened her grip on the arm of the man who escorted her.

"You *know May*-ry's story. We've told it *here*, we've spread her message to the far *cor*-ners of this world and, I daresay, right into the *next* world and... *and* the world *be-tween* this one and the next, that *neth*-er world where *earth*-bound spirits lay in wait, *lay in wait*, friends, not always for the *weak*-est, but sometimes for the *strongest* of us!"

As the evangelist spoke, he gesticulated energetically, raising his arms straight over his head and out to the side, other times holding them close to his body, his hands concealed behind the lectern. The lighting effects changed dramatically from time to time, turning brighter, hotter, when he exclaimed loudly. The walls on either side of him glided silently toward him, then away, further altering the effects of lights, projected from both the front and the rear, as well as from over the pulpit. As a final touch, the platform beneath him lifted and lowered him, so that he seemed to grow and expand as his declamations built to a crescendo and to shrink a bit as he settled back to catch his breath.

"Yes, *May*-ry *Beck*-man, be-loved, that in-*dom*-na-ble *spir*-it, I'm *talk*-ing about her *soul*, be-loved, that *soul that could not be bro-ken*! You've *read* her book—*Earthbound*! Praise *Gawd*! It's *still* number *four* on the *Los Ange-lees* Times best-seller list! If *you* haven't read it, *your* soul is in *mor*-tal danger. You *know* what I'm *talk*-ing about. And *to*-night, beloved, praise *Gawd* in His *glow*-ry for bringin' us a-*noth*-er *May*-ry Beckman. I'm *talk*-ing, *friends*, about *Bry*-na Carr! You've *all* heard of her! *Bry*-na Carr! The in-ter-*nash*-nly known *psy*-chic *super*-star whose recent *pre*-dic-tions of *mur*-der, that's right, beloved, *mur-der*! you've *all* read about and *heard* about and *seen* on *net*-work *tee*-vee night after night. *Bry*-na Carr! That's right! She's *here*! She's *with us*! In the *For-tress* of *Faith*! Right now! *You'll see her in a minute! She coming out to talk to us! Oh, praise the Lord! All of you now! Praise the Lord! Praise Gawd! Let Him hear it!*"

The congregation went wild, screaming its praises.

Matlock's voice blasted over the din, as the lights around him began to explode and a dozen organs began to pump.

"For she is here," Matlock shouted, "*to de-liv-er her-sef to Gawd!*"

The organs roared like jets as Bryna, alone now, stepped out onto the huge stage from an entrance to the side and in front of the lectern. The throng shouted its hallelujahs as Bryna made her way toward the evangelist, who had now risen to his greatest height and, eyes shut, was holding both arms triumphantly heavenward as the walls on either side of the lectern glided silently toward him, creating a narrowing aperture of blazing white light, leaving only Matlock and Bryna visible on the stage.

Bryna, whose back was to the audience as she walked toward Matlock, suddenly stumbled. She fell forward, onto her knees and huddled there, apparently unable to get up. Matlock looked disconcerted, for this was not in the script. Then he looked more disturbed still when a murmur began to rise from the assembled, a murmur which became a gasp.

There were screams, too, and people standing and pointing at the stage, but all of this was too late. Matlock wasted precious seconds fumbling with his remote device, and then the walls were pressing against his shoulders, pinning him, holding him, his legs dangling as he kicked the lectern away from him and the platform sunk beneath the stage. Amidst screams and shouts, and the panicked bustle of stagehands, the walls crushed the life out of the Reverend Ives Matlock, while millions watched.

The sounds of breaking bones and hemorrhaging organs were amplified horribly over the public-address system. Blood came in gushes from the evangelist's mouth, nose and eyes. And then, in a series of short, sharp explosions, and bizarre bursts of light, smoke and the odor of sulphur, the entire system overloaded. Peals of shrill, distorted electronic music shrieked through enormous speakers just before all was still and the congregation was plunged into utter darkness.

SIX

"Christ!" Harrison Warner exploded. "Raymond, the actor, was trying to call Carr, the psychic, the day he died; this we know, right?" He didn't wait for an answer. "We know Friedkin was also trying to call Carr the day *she* was murdered, *right*? Friedkin, the columnist? We know she had something, pictures probably, somebody wanted. We know she and Raymond were friends, that they were in this together. Right, goddamn it? We also know that Carr, who predicted both of these deaths, didn't have a decent alibi on either occasion. Am I *right*? We also know she lied to us about not going out the day Raymond was killed, and she obviously lied about not getting a phone call from Friedkin. Right? *And* we know Carr was only *inches* from Matlock, the preacher, when, at 9:31 last night the walls crushed the bejesus out of him, *right*? Right! And you tell me we still don't have any fucking probable cause to arrest the murdering bitch? Is that *right*, Lieutenant?"

"Right, sir," Brazil said, matter of factly. "I mean right about the probable cause, sir. Right about everything else, too, sir, except we don't really know for a fact, sir, that she lied about getting a call from Friedkin. We *assume* Friedkin called the house. We also don't know about Raymond and Friedkin being friends. *Their* friends don't recall any particular friendship, though they suddenly started meeting in their, uh, last days, sir. Their friends characterize this as 'peculiar,' sir. Nobody can imagine what they had in common. . . ."

"What they had in *common*, Lieutenant, was that they were both about to get bumped off by this Carr broad!"

"And they *knew* that, sir, so they formed a club?"

Warner's jaw set, threateningly.

"Sorry, sir, but you get my point? I'm very curious as to why these two suddenly got so chummy and why they both were in such a rush to reach Carr, just before they died. So far we haven't been able to find any reason. As for Matlock, sir, we don't really know that he was murdered. We *do* know his name came out of a computer early this morning, that he was number three on Miss Carr's list. But, unless we're going to officially accept Miss Carr's predictions as proof of murder, we can't really say yet that this was a homicide."

"Oh, Christ, Lieutenant..."

"I know how you feel, sir, but the fact is, we have no weapon, no motive, no suspect...."

Warner muttered something.

"The walls closed in on the guy," Brazil continued. "We have no evidence it wasn't an accident."

"I read the report, Lieutenant. You don't have any evidence— period. The whole place could have been booby-trapped for all you know."

Brazil shrugged. "The church fathers won't talk. They slammed the door shut and won't let anybody in. It's like the devil himself is at the gate. The governing council of the church is having an emergency meeting right now...."

"*Fuck* their emergency! I want you to get a search warrant and go through that whole fucking amusement park with a fine-toothed comb. And if you find *anything* out of place, *anything* missing, like one of those remote-control units, I guess you know where I want you to look for it, don't you, Lieutenant?"

Brazil considered mentioning the difficulties that would be encountered in obtaining a search warrant to pick through the premises of a powerful church, but thought better of it. "Yes, sir," he said.

Harrison Warner looked momentarily appeased. The lines in his face deepened and regrouped, however, as his eyes fell on the morning paper he had already thrown down twice that morning. The entire front page was devoted to Matlock's spectacular demise and associated events.

"NUMBER THREE: EVANGELIST KILLED WHILE MIL-
LIONS WATCH"
    "Psychic Right Again!"
    "Hundred Trampled in Ensuing Panic; Three Die"
    "Police Still at a Loss"
    "Church Elder: 'Work of the Devil'"

Warner read aloud from one of the stories, pausing regularly to look pained, contemptuous, furious, confused. The story he selected was headlined: "Bryna Carr 'In Shock'":

... Miss Carr was taken, reportedly unconscious, from the Fortress of Faith shortly after police arrived at the chaotic

238

scene of the evangelist's grisly death. She was taken to a nearby emergency treatment center and then released in the care of writer Ethan Kendal, who identified himself to police as her fiancé. . . . Miss Carr was met at the airport in San Francisco by her psychiatrist, Arthur Mendelsohn. She staggered as she emerged from the plane and refused to answer any questions put to her, according to a police officer at the scene. Reporters who were present noted that the psychic did not seem to hear the questions they asked her. . . . Miss Carr was reported resting at her Seacliff mansion early today and was said to be under 'heavy sedation.' Not all of the details have emerged yet, but it appears that Miss Carr was on the verge of renouncing her psychic powers on the same television program that gave America, much of Europe and even some of the Far East a front-row seat to a death which Miss Carr has called murder. The coincidence of her appearance at the very death she had predicted in trance weeks earlier has left experts in the paranormal and the police baffled. . . .

"Baffled! Fucking squat!"

Brazil shifted uncomfortably under Warner's accusing glare and was relieved when the boss looked again at the paper. He watched the older man's already terrible visage assume several more degrees of terribleness.

"Manning," Warner whispered at last.

"Sir?"

"*Manning!*" Warner whacked a picture on page one of the paper with the back of his hand. "Jesus, here it is staring us in the face and . . ."

"Sir?"

Warner thrust the picture, a grainy wirephoto that showed Bryna Carr, looking catatonic, being supported by two men, one on either side of her. One of them was Ethan Kendal. The other, though partially obscured by a blurred figure in the foreground, could, Brazil decided, indeed be Samuel Manning.

Brazil tried to look reflective for a moment, then said, "So, it's Manning, sir. I mean, it could be him."

"It's him all right," Warner roared.

"Yeah, okay."

"Yeah, okay?" Warner mimicked. "Look at the dateline on that photo."

Brazil squinted: "Los Angeles. Los Angeles!"

239

Warner nodded.

"He was there, in Los Angeles. I thought he met her at the airport here."

"So he must have been in the audience when . . . or backstage, or who knows the fuck where. He had everything to gain by bumping Matlock off. And the electronics would have been a snap for a guy like him. Jesus. *Jesus!*"

"I'll question him right away, sir."

"No! No. I don't want him questioned. Not yet. I want him *watched.* Do you understand? Twenty-four hours a day. *Every* day. I want *all* of them watched. Carr, her boyfriend Kendal, the Greek, Nick whatever. You got that? All four of them. Do you understand?"

"Yes, sir. And that photo, sir; that was good work, sir."

"Get out of here, Lieutenant, before I kick you to death."

Samuel Manning, frantically pacing back and forth in his lab, was suddenly aware that his activity had commanded the undivided attention of two dozen rhesus monkeys. Normally pacing themselves, they had stopped to stare at the researcher, their faces pressed against the wire of their cages. Manning, now aware he had an audience, stopped, an odd embarrassment adding fuel to his rage.

"How you could *ever* have allowed her to go down there in the first place and get mixed up in anything as ridiculous, as *insane,* as that religious freak show, with a *faith* healer!"

Ethan looked at the other man with quiet but obvious contempt. "Some of your colleagues seem to think what you're doing is crazy, too," he said. "If there are psychics, why can't there be faith healers? Besides, nothing else was working. I figured if Matlock could *convince* her she was free of her evil spirit that was as good as—better than—anything the shrinks have been able to do for her."

"If she'd gone on that show," Manning said, "if she'd said what Matlock wanted her to say, it would have ruined her, destroyed her credibility forever. Given her state of mind, didn't you think she deserved better, a chance to think, reflect?"

"Reflect? Where? In a straitjacket, maybe? Locked up someplace, drugged? That's what you would have preferred, that's what you and Mendelsohn had in mind, isn't it?"

"I would have *talked* to her. . . ."

"You *did* talk to her. You talked *at* her, you and Mendelsohn." Manning stared at Ethan with undisguised hatred.

"For Christsake," Ethan said, "here you are worried about your goddamn reputation and so far not one word about the most amazing part of this whole thing."

Again, Manning was silent.

"Hasn't it occurred to you," Ethan went on, "that if she hadn't gone down there Matlock might not have died, that the prediction might not have come true?"

Manning blinked.

"It *has* to have occurred to you," Ethan persisted. "It was a special program, set up just for her."

"So what are you suggesting," Manning said cautiously, "that *she* was somehow responsible?"

"I'm not saying that. It's just... I don't know. It's like some kind of paradox."

"Nonsense..."

"You call the coincidence of her being there, on the very day she said he would die, 'nonsense'?"

"It's... there are any number of... perhaps the murderer knew she was trying to help the police solve these murders, that she intended to try. News of that leaked out somehow. Maybe he formulated his list at that time, choosing people close to Bryna, to defy her, to..."

"Yes," Ethan said, "I thought of that, too, but there's more. There's Raymond and Friedkin. Raymond was one of Bryna's clients; that fits your theory. But she didn't even know Friedkin...."

"Maybe *thought* she did...."

"And if he wanted to *defy* her, as you put it, once it became known that she had made these predictions, why would the killer stick to his original list. Why wouldn't he make up a new one—so that her predictions *wouldn't* come true?"

"You misunderstand," Manning said. "These things are rarely determined *consciously*. The killer, in all likelihood, was not fully aware of what he was doing when he decided to choose people close to Bryna, *if* that's what he did. It is, as you say, only a theory."

"Friedkin and Raymond were trying to blackmail her. *That* isn't theory."

"What!"

"They found out some things...."

"What things?" Manning demanded.

"It doesn't matter...."

"The police, do they...?"

"They don't know anything."

Ethan noted Manning's obvious relief.

"How did you find out?" the researcher asked. "Did she tell you?"

"Never mind how. The fact is they were doing it—and they both died."

"I wouldn't talk about this. . . ."

"Don't worry. But try to fit it into your theory, if you can. It's got me climbing the fucking walls, trying to figure it out. I can't believe she did it, but there's something crazy, some weird connection between her and the . . . like cause and effect are blurred."

"I wouldn't talk about this," Manning repeated. "It just complicates things. . . ."

"Shit!" Ethan exploded. "You've got one of the most intriguing mysteries of all time staring you in the face and all you can think about is keeping things uncomplicated."

"You don't understand, do you?" Manning said bitterly. "No, of course not. You haven't had to face them—the doubters, the skeptics, the smug bastards. I've been up against it for twenty years now, and finally we have a chance . . ." Manning fought to control his rage and frustration. "We have a chance to prove them all wrong and now . . . can't you see it? They'll seize on any excuse to dismiss this as fraud. They'd love to believe she did it, that she committed those murders, or that *I* committed them. It may take us decades to figure out what's really happened, but they're not ready for that yet, for what you call 'complications.' First we have to prove . . ."

"I've heard it before. I don't want to fight you on this, but *I* just . . ."

"If you really love her, then help us."

"I don't like the sound of that."

"Don't you see? We *have* to hospitalize her, for her own good."

"Have her under lock and key so that when the next one happens nobody will be able to say she did it, put her away so that she can't embarrass you anymore and ruin your experiment? Put her away where you can try to force her, with drugs, shock, whatever, force her to be what *you* want her to be? You really think you're all that different from Matlock—you and Mendelsohn?"

"I'm sorry you're taking this attitude, Ethan," Manning said, his tone suddenly businesslike. "I have to inform you that I intend to cooperate with Dr. Mendelsohn in every way."

"What the hell does that mean?"

"It means that I intend to support his effort to have her committed. If you cooperate, it can all be done quietly. It will look like a voluntary hospitalization—for a physical problem, or exhaustion. It would be understandable—given the stress she's been under. No one would . . ."

Ethan turned and began to leave.

"We'll get a court order. There's nothing you can do to stop us."

Ethan turned and looked at the other man until he walked away.

Two nights later the plainclothesman assigned to watch Manning radioed Lieutenant Brazil from the parking lot outside Spectrum Research Institute. "It's almost ten p.m. and he's still in there."

"His car's still there?"

"Right."

"So he's working late. Stay on it."

Brazil was watching the clock, shuffling papers. He'd be off at midnight. At ten-fifteen he got another radio call.

"It's Andrianos, sir. He's leaving the house now. Taking his Alfa. Fred's got it."

"Tell him to stay snug."

"Right."

At eleven forty-five Brazil checked with the man outside Spectrum.

"Still in there, sir. Nothing."

"Right. Stay on it."

At eleven-fifty Brazil checked the Carr residence.

"Kendal and Carr are both in there. Andrianos is still out."

"Where is he?"

There was a pause.

"Didn't Fred call in?"

"No."

"He said he'd call you directly."

"He hasn't, goddamn it. Get him."

Brazil waited, heard the other man curse.

"His unit's out, sir!"

"What!"

"No response at all, sir."

"*Shit!*"

Brazil and his replacement were still manning the radios, dispatching units in search of the missing plainclothesman, when Harrison Warner walked in at twelve-twenty a.m. His smile was sickly. He held a piece of wire copy delicately between thumb and finger. His color was worse than usual; the blotches in his

243

face looked like exotic purple islands in a sea of pale green. Warner daintily set the piece of paper in front of the two men and waited. They peered at it, turning pale themselves.

Brazil gulped, hoping that would help. The other man dropped his head to the radio desk.

The man assigned to follow Samuel Manning was shaking visibly as he showed the security guard his badge.

"What's this about?" the security man asked.

"Never mind. I have to see Manning right away."

The guard checked the register.

"He's still here. In his office, I suppose. E-wing 712. I'll call."

The plainclothesman fidgeted while the guard called, first Manning's office, then his lab. There was no answer.

"I'll try the lounge."

"*No*. Just get me to Manning's office. *Now*."

The guard looked at the cop.

"Hey, man, what's happening?"

"Just hurry."

As they approached Manning's office, passing through several "security portals," each of which was accessed by electronic code, the plainclothesman noted the TV cameras in the corridors.

"You been watching the monitors tonight?"

"Yeah, well, I mean, we watch 'em now and again. But with all this other crap nobody gets in here, unless they know all these codes. . . ."

"How many entrances?"

"Eight, man."

"Eight? Jesus."

Outside Manning's office, the cop drew his gun, signaling the alarmed guard to be silent. He stood beside the door for a moment, waved the guard back, then kicked the door as hard as he could. As it flew open, the detective dropped to his knees. The room was lighted and empty, both chambers.

"His lab, show me his lab," the cop said, a cold sweat evident on his face.

"Shit, man, you could at least tell me . . ."

"His lab," the detective insisted.

A flight up they stopped in front of a massive white metal door.

"You're not gonna kick this one down, man," the guard whispered.

"What's in there?"

"Monkeys, man, nothin' but monkeys. They give me the creeps."

"Yeah, well open it."

244

The guard tapped in the code on the panel near the door. The heavy barricade slid silently open. The two men stepped inside. The large room was dimly illuminated with blue light.

"S'posed to make 'em sleep better," the guard said. A rustling sound rose all around them.

The detective raised his gun and whirled around.

"Monkeys, man, just monkeys," the guard said, still speaking in a whisper.

As the cop's eyes adjusted to the dim light, he could see the cages that lined the walls of the gleaming white space. In the middle of the room was the stereotaxic operating apparatus. Restraining chairs were situated throughout the irregularly shaped room, some of them obscured behind computer panels and other equipment. The two men looked around from where they stood near the entrance but saw no sign of Dr. Manning. They could dimly make out some monkeys strapped in the restraining units, electrode sockets attached to their heads.

The plainclothesman moved with slow, fascinated horror toward one of the animals, which stared back at him unblinking.

"Christ, what is this?" the cop asked.

"I told you it's creepy. They got their brains wired."

Suddenly, some lights blinked at them from one of the computer panels. As if on cue, all of the animals in the restraining units opened their mouths wide in vicious snarls.

The plainclothesman, who had been peering into the stony eyes of one of the animals, jumped backward as the creature's mouth opened and its eyes turned fierce. In his fright, the cop lost his footing and fell, knocking over a screen. As he began picking himself up, cursing, his eyes fixed on a pair of human feet and legs and froze. It took him several seconds to realize that the man he was looking at, strapped into a restraining chair, his mouth opening and closing in silent snarls, his eyes wide and fierce and staring straight ahead, was Dr. Manning. He'd been there, behind the screen, all along.

The lights on another computer panel blinked, and Dr. Manning's arms shot straight out in front of him as his mouth snapped closed. The cop, still down on his haunches, scrambled backward, knocking over yet more equipment. A moan escaped him, and he was unaware that the security guard had fainted.

"Yes, sir, he was dead before midnight; that's what the lab boys tell me, sir. Technically dead. Brain dead. Those electrodes were sunk deep. Whoever did it knew something about it but was no expert. The computer put him through those movements, sir,

245

motor movements, sort of like a chicken with it's head cut off, sir. Sorry, sir. But you get my point."

Harrison Warner glanced briefly at Brazil, then back at the wall he had been staring at for some time.

"I guess that takes care of Manning, doesn't it, sir? As a suspect, I mean. And Carr and her boyfriend, they were definitely in her house. There's only the front entrances. No way out the back, sir. That leaves Andrianos. He was the only one out. Fred's radio conked out. He got preoccupied trying to fix it, and Andrianos got away. Like I said, sir, we should have him any time. For questioning. Sir? Sir!"

Warner was knocking his head against the wall. On the desk next to him was the wire copy he had shown Brazil earlier. Brazil, in desperate need of something to do, picked it up and began reading it again:

San Francisco—Psychic researcher Dr. Samuel Manning of Spectrum Research Institute is dead—if psychic Bryna Carr is correct. Manning's name emerged from a computer in Portland at 12:01 this morning, and researchers there said . . . Manning, ironically, is the man who, for a year, probed Bryna Carr's psychic abilities and then presided over the experiment in which the psychic went into trance and named seven future victims of the so-called "Celebrity Murderer." Police, shortly after midnight, refused to confirm that Manning was dead and declined all other comment. . . .

SEVEN

The morning after Manning's murder, Bryna sat up in bed and tried to scream. Nothing came out. The night Matlock was crushed to death she had cried and babbled until there was nothing left of her voice. Moreover, she had severely bitten her tongue and it was now badly swollen, making speech all the more painful. Her face, too, was swollen and discolored where she had hit it when she fell to the stage that night.

"It's Niko," she rasped.

She was soaked with sweat, and it gradually dawned on her that she had been dreaming. But it had seemed so much more than a dream. Something had happened to Niko, she was certain. She shook Ethan, and when he did not awaken she forced herself to her feet and staggered to the phone. She called Niko's apartment in the basement. There was no answer. She let it ring. Nothing.

"Ethan," she cried, "Ethan," her voice so weak it died halfway across the room. She dragged herself back to the bed and shook Ethan anew, noting by the clock that it was almost nine a.m. It wasn't like Ethan to sleep so late. It was even less like him not to awaken immediately at the mere whisper of his name. His stillness alarmed Bryna. She pulled her hands back, away from him. She stared at him, then pushed the buzzer next to her bed, summoning the nurse Ethan had hired at Dr. Mendelsohn's insistence.

The woman, an R.N., was there in less than a minute. She took in the scene with obvious distaste.

"Ethan," Bryna whispered hoarsely. "Ethan. He won't wake up."

The nurse hurried to the bed, rolled back one of Ethan's eyelids and began taking his pulse. Her officious reserve yielded to a frown. She sniffed the air. She put her face close to Ethan's. Then her eye fell on the water glass next to him on the nightstand. She sniffed that, as well.

"Barbiturates," she said firmly. "Was Mr. Kendal taking sleeping pills, too?"

Bryna looked confused.

The nurse went into the bathroom and came back with smelling salts. She held these under Ethan's nose. He began to moan.

"Mr. Kendal, wake up! Wake up!"

Ethan opened one red eye, then another.

"Wha . . . ?"

"It's all right, Mr. Kendal."

"What . . . what time is it?"

"How many pills did you take?"

"Pills?"

"Sleeping pills."

"None. I . . ."

"Well, you must have taken at least two."

"I don't under . . ." Ethan followed the nurse's eye to the water glass on the nightstand. Then he looked across the room at Bryna, whose hand was trembling at her throat. This time the nurse followed his gaze.

"Don't tell me you drank the water I gave Miss Carr?"

Ethan glanced back at the water glass next to him.

"Oh, for heaven's sakes," the nurse said irritably. "There were

247

sleeping pills dissolved in that water. You know how difficult it's been for her to sleep, the nightmares, and Dr. Mendelsohn said . . ." The nurse stopped and looked sharply at Bryna. "No wonder you look so awful this morning. I'll bet you barely slept a wink last night. How did this happen?"

Bryna looked at Ethan, frightened.

Ethan stared at her intently for a moment, then broke his gaze. "It was obviously a mistake. I asked her for some water and she just got the glasses mixed up, that's all."

The nurse shook her head. "This could have been serious."

"I know we've been over this a dozen times already, Mr. Andrianos," Albert Brazil said, holding out a cup of coffee, "but I think you have to admit we have reason to be suspicious. I mean, just bear with me one more time. Maybe you'll begin to see it yourself. You're in love with her, am I right? I mean, you've been with her all these years, and you seem very, very protective of her."

Niko remained silent.

"You wanted her to succeed, and maybe at the same time you got access to those names. Maybe she went into trance again later, just the two of you present and you got those names. And then you made sure those predictions came true."

Niko scowled but otherwise did not respond.

"Is it really such a farfetched idea?"

Again, Niko remained stonily silent.

"Nobody was in a better position than you to bring this off. I mean, you have to admit, Mr. Andrianos, and correct me, please, if I'm wrong, but it's very interesting, wouldn't you say, that all of these people, Raymond, Friedkin, Matlock and now Manning, were people with some sort of connection, people close to Bryna Carr? All of those people threatened you, Mr. Andrianos. Isn't that right? They were all trying to take another piece of her, somehow, leaving even less for you."

Christ, the detective thought, *what is this bullshit I'm laying on him? None of it's going to work.* Still, he had to try.

"You worked out at Spectrum on several occasions with Miss Carr. You knew the entrances and the codes, when it would be easiest to get in. You'd seen them do those monkey operations. You left in time last night to get out there and . . ."

Brazil's phone lit up. He lifted the receiver.

"She's here, sir."

"Okay, I'll take her in J-11." Brazil got up and said to Niko: "Stay put."

The girl—*woman*, Brazil corrected himself—was about 22, brunette, beautiful.

"What's your name?"

"Renton. Tracy Renton. And I'd like to know *why* the *hell* I was *dragged* down here at this hour of the morning."

"It's after nine, Miss Renton. Now would you just answer *my* questions? Where were you last night at ten-thirty?"

"Passages."

"That's one of those singles bars, right?"

The girl snorted derisively. "Single *women*, married men."

"I see. And did you meet anyone there?"

"I don't know what business . . . was that jerk *involved* in something? I should have known. What is he, some kind of pervert? He was just *too* good looking. Those pretty boys come down to the straight bars to try to prove how normal they are. Like in *Goodbar*. You know, the film. I've seen that movie six times; I'm not ashamed to admit it. That was *so* true, that movie. It was . . ."

"I saw it, yes. So you're saying this guy was . . . ?"

Miss Renton rolled her eyes. "He was . . . *God* . . . I mean, I've been with a lot of guys, you know, I'm in public relations, but *this* guy, I should have known the minute I saw it . . ."

"*It?*"

"*It.* Yeah, *it,*" Miss Renton said impatiently, staring at Brazil's crotch. "When they're that big . . ."

"I don't under . . ."

"He couldn't get it up," Miss Renton said disgustedly.

"So you . . . ?"

"So I *what?* I mean this guy came on to *me.* I mean, he *advertised* it in those tight pants; I mean, he as much as *promised* me . . . and then, we're in bed, nothing. *Nothing.* He didn't even try . . ."

"What time did he leave?"

"That was the worst of it. I mean we got there around eleven-fifteen, and I couldn't get rid of him until . . . it was after one. He just sat there, staring, brooding, drinking *my* Benedictine. You know what that stuff costs a bottle?"

"What time was it when you first saw him—at the bar?"

"It was ten-thirty or so."

"Is this him?"

Tracy Renton looked at the photo of Niko.

"Yes. God I should have known. What's he . . . ? What did he do? Have you caught him?"

"He's right next door."

"Are you . . . ?"

"We're letting him go, thanks to you, Miss Renton. He didn't do anything."

Miss Renton looked stricken.

Brazil rejoined Niko. "You can go now. Sorry for the inconvenience." Brazil found himself furtively focusing on Niko's crotch as the younger man rose from his chair.

Thirty seconds after Niko left, Harrison Warner stormed in. "I don't give a flying fuck how many alibis he has. I want him watched. All of them. Christ, if *he* isn't the killer he's likely to be the next victim. With friends like her . . ."

"If you'll just bear with me for a few minutes, sir," Brazil said, "I think it's time we considered the possibility that Miss Carr is on the up and up, that she doesn't know anything about any of this, that none of them do."

"None of them *does*, Lieutenant, none of them *does*. Speak English. I think your theory is thin as piss on a slate rock."

"Polls, sir, scientific *polls* show even a majority of scientists think there's something to psychic phenomena. Why should the SFPD homicide division be so hard-nosed on the issue?"

"Oh, Jesus."

"I mean, it makes a lot more sense, sir, if we just assume for the moment that Miss Carr really did see into the future, that she did see who was going to die. Assume that at the time she made the predictions the killer had already made up his mind to kill people connected to Bryna Carr. I mean, it's perfect, sir, just the kind of thing a guy with his sense of humor would do. . . ."

"Sense of humor, Lieutenant?"

"Yeah, well, you know what I mean . . . imagination, whatever. . . ."

"Lieutenant, Lieutenant, hold it. Have you ever heard of Occam's razor?"

"Uh, Occam's razor. I . . . it seems to have slipped my mind, sir."

"Well, if you ever find it, and I suggest you start by looking for it in the dictionary, remember to slit your throat with it. And, in the meantime, keep watching that house. And put the fork to those computer guys. I want that computer code cracked and those last three names puked up before there's nothing left but our resignations—do you get my point?"

"I . . . yes, I do, sir."

"Good, now get out of here and get me the proof I need to put that woman in the gallows."

"There are no gallows here, sir. This is California."

"That's one of the things wrong with this fucking state. Now get out."

"Are you really so blinded by your love for her that you're going to try to stop me?" Mendelsohn said that afternoon, wheeling his chair around to face Ethan squarely. The sudden movement alarmed Tabu, the skinny Siamese, which had been sleeping on his lap. It emitted an ill-tempered yowl, eyeing Ethan accusingly. "It doesn't wash," the psychiatrist said. "It's not like you to be so emotional. You're not your old self. Not the man I knew."

"Thank god," Ethan said, staring fiercely back at the doctor. "I'm not only *not* going to help you, I'm going to fight you. I'm getting an attorney to contest this thing," he said, glancing at the piece of paper on Mendelsohn's desk.

"Well, you can try," the psychiatrist shrugged, "but this will very shortly have the judge's signature on it, tomorrow morning, as a matter of fact. Ethan, listen to reason, in the hospital I can help her, we can *both* help her. It's a fascinating case . . ."

"I don't want to hear it."

"Perhaps you're afraid that if she's locked up you'll no longer have access to her. I imagine by now she's quite an important character in your book."

Ethan cursed under his breath. "If you weren't in that wheelchair . . ."

"What? What would you do, *enfant gaté*?"

Ethan's hands closed into fists. He turned to go.

"You may be next, you know," Mendelsohn said evenly. "The nurse told me about that little mix-up with the pills last night. Do you really think that was an accident?"

Ethan turned to stare at the psychiatrist.

"You needn't look so shocked. We've all suspected it, haven't we? Even poor Manning, I daresay, when it was too late. . . ."

"Are you out of your mind? She doesn't have the strength for one thing, and . . ."

"Oh, no? You should spend an afternoon with me in the back ward of a mental institution. The frailest psychopath might surprise you. . . ."

"She was in the house. . . ."

"We don't know where she was, do we? The day Raymond was murdered, she had adequate opportunity to visit the set of that movie; you were out of town that day, as I recall. And Friedkin, she was alone *that* night, too, wasn't she? Matlock—well, she was closer to him than anyone else. Then our friend Manning, it turns out that though she was with you last night you were out cold. She could have been out for hours without your knowing it. And we both know how she might have left the house unobserved by the police, don't we? At least I *assume* none of you has informed the police of that secret exit."

"And you're *going* to?"

"Only if absolutely necessary."

"I get it. You're building this theory of yours to give you more ammunition to enforce that commitment order."

"Only if I need it," Mendelsohn said, smiling faintly. "Granted, it *is* a theory, and I'd rather keep it all in the family, wouldn't you? All that nasty business about Sabra would come out. It would all be sensationalized, misunderstood. It's all got to be presented properly and at the proper time. . . ."

"Like in a long technical paper, perhaps a book-length case history by Doctor Arthur Mendelsohn? You sicken me!"

"Do I remind you so much of yourself, then? We *could* write it together."

Ethan slammed the door behind him, causing the anxious-looking patient waiting in the outer office to begin laughing uncontrollably.

EIGHT

After Ethan left Mendelsohn's Russian Hill flat, where the psychiatrist both lived and conducted his practice, he drove directly back to Bryna's, observing from his car the plainclothes-man who had been tailing him, none too expertly, for days. Whenever the man got caught in traffic, Ethan would obligingly slow down until his pursuer would charge ahead again, nearly tailgating his quarry. On such occasions Ethan was close enough to see reflected in his rearview mirror the consternation and embarrassment of the other man. Once, Ethan smiled and waved.

At Seacliff, Ethan let himself into the house and met Niko coming down the stairs.

"I suppose you've heard from Mendelsohn, too," Ethan said, stopping Niko, who would otherwise have passed without a word.

"He called me."

"I want you to know I'm going to fight him. I'm getting a lawyer *and* a new doctor."

"As I recall, it was you who recommended Mendelsohn in the first place."

"A mistake, I admit it. Maybe you could help get Hevesey back?"

Niko shrugged.

"Let's talk about it, at least. We're going to have to pull together if we're going to beat Mendelsohn. Since she has no relatives and he's her psychiatrist, the court..."

Niko looked disgusted and started down the stairs.

"Niko, one more thing. Does she know about Manning yet?"

"Yes, she knows."

"Niko, I want you to know, I'm sorry things..."

"Forget it." Niko's tone was truculent, and he turned away.

Ethan continued upstairs and found Bryna watching television, or at least staring at the picture. The sound was off. Ethan touched her face, but still she did not acknowledge him. Her expression was devoid of hope, vacant.

"Bryna," Ethan said softly. "I'm going to get Dr. Hevesey back. You won't have to see Mendelsohn anymore. But I have to tell you, there may be a slight delay, a day or two. It's possible Mendelsohn will make trouble, but I promise you, I *promise* you, it will only be temporary. I *won't* let him take you away."

"I don't want to go away, Ethan," Bryna said flatly, still staring at the TV.

"I'll take care of you."

"Will you, Ethan?" Her voice was still dull, unresponsive.

"Yes, I promise."

His hand was still on her cheek. She touched his fingers with hers.

"Will you make love to me one more time?"

"What are you saying? 'One more time'? Bryna, I'm *here*, I'll always be here."

Bryna looked blank.

"Make love to me, Ethan."

Ethan stared at her.

"I know I've put on weight, that I'm not...that my hair..."

"You're beautiful," Ethan said. "Just shut up. You're beautiful." He began kissing her face, then opened her robe and kissed her breasts, her navel, her thighs. She *had* put on weight, quite a lot of it; she'd been so slender when he first saw her, and her skin—once so smooth and flawless—was now blotched and sickly

253

looking. Ethan silently cursed the nurse for not keeping her cleaner, for letting her stuff herself all day.

Bryna lay beneath him, listlessly, her eyes unfocused.

"What's wrong?" she said, finally.

"Nothing, I just . . ." Ethan was sweating. "It's just . . . wait a minute." Ethan reached down and pulled at himself, trying to get hard. He shut his eyes for a moment and imagined a Vietnamese girl, one he had made love to over and over. He felt himself begin to stiffen, pulled harder, then rolled back onto Bryna, pushed into her and came in a dozen savage strokes. Her mouth sought his, but he kissed her on the neck.

"You should sleep," he said afterward. "You've been thinking too much."

"I want to sleep," she said. "I want to sleep now."

Ethan got a glass of water and dissolved one of the sleeping pills in it.

"Only one?" she complained.

"That's right."

"Not enough. I'll wake up and you'll be gone."

"You're silly," Ethan said. "One is all you get and when you wake up I'll be here."

"The nurse always . . ."

"She gives you too many because she *wants* you to sleep all the time. She doesn't want you bothering her; *I* do."

Bryna smiled faintly and took the water.

Ethan sat on the edge of the bed, holding her hand, as sleep began to come.

"You do love me, don't you?" she said, as her eyes closed.

At five p.m. Ethan rang down to the nurse, who was usually perched in the kitchen, the only part of the house she felt comfortable in, and told her that Bryna was sleeping and was not to be disturbed.

"I'll sit with her," he said.

At seven-thirty p.m., Ethan walked quietly into the kitchen and said, "I'm going out now to get some dinner."

The nurse, absorbed in the thriller she was reading, dropped her book and gasped for air.

"Jesus!" she gasped. "You scared the bilirubin out of me! *Must* you be so quiet?"

"Sorry. I'll be back around midnight. I'm going to try to do a little writing. She took her pills so there won't be any need for you. . . ."

"Food? She didn't want any *food?*"

"No," Ethan said. "She just wanted to sleep."

The nurse shrugged.

"Just relax and enjoy your book," Ethan said. "And if you get too scared, the cops are right outside the door—for *our* protection, or so they tell us."

"Sorry I jumped," the nurse said, holding up the paperback. "Vampires. They do it to me every time."

"Hmmm," Ethan said, "I'm afraid they never did it for me. *Homo sapiens. They* scare me. 'The only real monster is man.' Who said that? Jung? Freud? Count Dracula?"

The nurse shuddered. "I'll stick to vampires."

Ethan smiled and left. He drove to Haight Street and parked in the Cala Food lot near Stanyan. At least, he reflected, nobody would break into his car, not with the cops watching it. The fog was beginning to ooze out of Golden Gate Park; Ethan turned up his collar and hurried down Haight Street. His mind was on sweet-and-sour chicken, the unlisted specialty of Le Bigamist, his favorite Vietnamese restaurant.

At eight-fifteen p.m., Brazil radioed his surveillance men.

"Kendal's still feeding his face," the man outside Cala Foods said.

"Yeah, and only a block up from my wife's place; the guy's got no taste. Hey, you're sure he's in there?"

"Yes, sir. I've been through twice to use the john. He's in there."

Brazil radioed the detectives at Seacliff.

"Nothing new here," one of them responded. "Just the normal quota of gawkers and ghouls. We've got a cruiser out here running them off. Kendal's still the only one out."

"Right."

At eight-twenty p.m. Candice Murray, comanager of the building, knocked on Arthur Mendelsohn's door. The woman standing behind her looked worried.

"I've been coming here for two years now," the woman said. "My appointments are *always* at eight. Something's happened to the doctor. I know it."

Candice knocked on 14-A. There was no answer.

"I hate to do this," she said, looking for the right key, "but with him in a wheelchair and all . . ."

She unlocked the door to Mendelsohn's office.

The outer chamber was black—no light at all. Nor could Candice see any light coming from beneath the inside doors—to Mendelsohn's inner office and apartment.

"Doctor Mendelsohn," she said softly, standing in the doorway.

Something on the carpet just in front of her, illuminated by the corridor light, caught her eye and she reached down. She pulled her finger back quickly and looked at it. It was something red and sticky—she began to feel herself perspire and stepped back into the light. The other woman gasped. Now they could see other dark red stains on the office carpet, making a trail to the inner door of the doctor's living quarters.

Candice felt her legs tingle, as if they were going numb.

"Oh my god," she whispered, pressing the back of her hand to her mouth, still staring into the darkened room. Then she turned around and pounded on the door on the opposite side of the corridor. The other woman froze.

"Please, oh god, please hurry. Somebody, somebody, please." Her voice was higher now, her panic rising. She was certain that if someone burst out of the dark room on the other side of the hall she would not be able to run or resist. A door opened suddenly further down the hall, and an angry-looking man thrust his head out.

"Oh, thank god," Candice gasped. "Father Donahue. Please . . . something has happened to Doctor . . ." She nodded out of breath at the open door opposite her.

"Doctor Mendelsohn?"

Candice shook her head, nearly falling when the door she had been pounding on now also abruptly opened.

"What the hell's going on?" another irate-looking man demanded. A woman peered over his shoulder. "Oh, Father Donahue," the man said, "I didn't see you. . . ."

By now the priest was poking his head into Mendelsohn's office, flicking the light switch in vain.

"There's blood," Candice said weakly, pressing herself against the wall of the corridor. The other woman remained in the corridor.

"The lights won't go on," the priest said.

"I'll get my flashlight," the other man volunteered. "Marge," he instructed the woman behind him, "call the cops." Two more doors opened. By the time the priest was moving cautiously into the gloom of the doctor's office, holding the flashlight in front of him, a small crowd had gathered and was taking up the rear. The priest, who had paused to illuminate each apparent drop of blood, arrived at the closed inner door of Mendelsohn's apartment. The priest knocked softly, then insistently.

"Doctor? Doctor! It's Father Donahue."

There was no answer.

The priest tried the knob.

It stuck, then turned. The priest pushed the door, and it swung silently open. Again the priest groped for a light switch, found it. Again, nothing. The darkness was complete—save for a pale glow coming from beneath a door at the back of the living room.

"That's the fireplace," Candice whispered hoarsely. "In his study."

As the small knot of neighbors approached the study door, some of them falling back, the priest held up his hand, indicating that they were all to wait while he went on ahead alone. He took the last several steps, knocked on the study door, waited a moment, then flung the door open and flashed the light quickly around the room.

Someone, watching from behind, gasped. Mendelsohn was seated in his wheelchair, which was backed up against the rear wall of the study. He was staring directly at the impromptu delegation of neighbors, perfectly still, unblinking, wide-eyed. He looked drugged or crazed. His eyes were fierce. He was in a dark bathrobe. Tabu, his feline companion, was in his lap, licking herself. Then the flashlight shone directly into the animal's eyes. Alarmed, it sprang up with a scream. As it leapt from its accustomed perch, it hit the wheelchair's forward lever. In the shadowy light the wheelchair began to move forward, directly toward the priest and those watching behind him. It wasn't until the automated chair passed the glow of the fireplace that the horror was fully evident.

"Oh my god, my god," Candice Murray wailed.

"No! Oh god, let me out of here!" another woman demanded, holding her hand to her mouth.

"Jesus Christ!"

The priest crossed himself.

Arthur Mendelsohn's decapitated body, borne along by the battery-powered wheelchair, drew nearer the stunned onlookers. The priest hoisted the flashlight up a few inches and illuminated Mendelsohn's head, which still stared implacably back at the assembled—from the point at which it was, by some means, firmly affixed to the wall.

Candice Murray's legs buckled under her and she fell heavily to the floor. Those others who had not already retreated, those for whom the partitioned sight of the late doctor proved transfixing, merely shifted their feet to make room for the unconscious woman.

In what was apparently the doctor's own blood, someone had emblazoned the wall above Mendelsohn's head with a Latin phrase:

ACU REM TETIGISTI

The priest translated the taunting graffito in a whisper:
"You have hit the nail on the head."

At nine-ten p.m., Albert Brazil called Harrison Warner from Arthur Mendelsohn's apartment.

"That's right, sir. That's what I'm telling you. Somebody decapitated him with a very sharp instrument.... I don't know, sir, something like a cleaver maybe. Very clean, sir, And then whoever did this, sir, nailed his head... that's right, *nailed* his head, sir, to the wall.... Oh, no, no, sir, not *through* the skull, sir, that would have taken a railroad spike, sir.... I'm sorry, sir. Nailed through the scalp, sir. The nails were hidden by the hair, and the wheelchair was positioned directly under the head so that the neck, the neck, sir, was wrapped in a scarf, that's what he was wearing, sir, scarf and bathrobe, so that when these people came in it looked like he was just sitting there glowering at them. It wasn't until the cat... I told you about the cat, sir... yes, sir. And the wheelchair just kept going and it didn't stop until it hit that poor woman who had fainted... Mrs. Murray. It just sort of spun its wheels once it hit her and... I'm sorry, sir. I'm *trying* to stick to the story, sir. There's one other thing. His testicles, sir... what? *Doctor Mendelsohn's* testicles, sir. They're missing... what? No, I mean *missing*, sir, as in *cut off. Gone,* sir. When? The same time as the head, I'd say, sir."

Brazil waited. There was silence at the other end of the line. A long silence. Brazil held the phone away from him for a moment and looked at it.

"Are you still there?"

"That woman..."

The Chief sounded as if he were choking. Brazil knew he meant Bryna Carr.

"I sent someone in, sir. It wasn't exactly legal, but I knew you'd want to know. Andrianos wasn't too happy about it, but we saw her, sir, with our own eyes, sound asleep—in bed, sir. No doubt about it."

"The others?"

"As I say, sir, Andrianos was there when our men went in. No one saw him leaving. The only one to leave the house was Ethan Kendal, and we know he had a long dinner at Le Bigamist—that's a restaurant, sir. Then about fifteen minutes ago, he went to his place on the vulcan steps. He's still there."

"Time of death?"

"We're not sure yet, sir. Between six and eight."

"And earlier, where were they, all of them?"

"In the house, sir."

"Christ, *Christ*. Jesus, Lieutenant, whatever happened to ordinary, *decent* murders?"

"I'm afraid I don't know, sir."

"Well, you better know something by midnight, Lieutenant, because when Mendelsohn's name pops out of some fucking computer it's all over unless we've . . . Concentrate on the code, Lieutenant. Break that fucking code!"

Brazil started to speak, but Warner had already hung up.

NINE

Bryna sat up suddenly, bolt upright in the darkness. There was a burning sensation in her eyes and nose, a searing pain in the back of her head. As it subsided she sank back onto the bed. She decided she must have been dreaming, that a bad dream had frightened and awakened her. She felt disoriented, lost in the darkness. That was it, the *total* darkness. Usually at least a little light filtered in through one of the windows, even though the blinds were drawn. The bed felt odd, too, softer than she remembered it. She had begun to drift away again after a few minutes when once more there was that same, sharp sensation slicing through her nose, slamming against the back of her head. And there was a biting odor in the air that quickly evaporated.

She sat up again. The pain was gone now. She groped for the clock-calendar she always kept on the nightstand beside her bed. She read the glowing display. Wednesday: 10:15 p.m. Bryna squinted hard at it. It *still* said Wednesday. She was certain it was Tuesday. It *had* been Tuesday—she was sure of that—when Ethan gave her the pill and she went to sleep. How could it be Wednesday, particularly Wednesday, *ten-fifteen p.m.*?

Bryna felt her heart beating faster. She tried to compose her thoughts. Yes, Ethan had given her only *one* pill; that might account for her awakening at ten-fifteen. One pill was rarely enough to make her sleep for more than four or five hours. But if the clock was right she had slept *too* long, an entire *day* too long. The old fear of "lost time" crept in, the thought of Sabra, of losing the body.

ethan!

He had said he would stay with her, Bryna remembered. Yes, Ethan was there, she could feel him in bed next to her. He could explain it.

—"Ethan, Ethan, wake up, please..."

She shook him gently in the darkness. He did not stir. She leaned over to the nightstand and turned on the small lamp. Ethan was apparently sleeping soundly, facing away from her, the covers pulled up to his ears. All Bryna could see of him was the back of his head, his tousled blonde hair.

"Ethan, please, I'm frightened... the clock..." She shook him again, harder this time, a new fear penetrating the drug-haze that still clung to her, as she remembered the water, the water she had apparently given Ethan, the water with the pills in it.

"Ethan!" she said sharply, her flesh tingling all along the back of her scalp and neck. When he still did not answer, she pulled hard on the blanket that was bunched around him, and he rolled over onto his back, his eyes open wide, unblinking, his mouth and throat sticky with blood.

She could not hear her own scream, so fierce was the pounding in her ears. She pulled back in spasms, retreated in frantic backward lurches until she crashed up against a wall, and all the lights went on. For the first time she was aware that she was not in her own room. The only familiar objects were the small lamp and the clock-calendar on the nightstand. There were mirrors everywhere—the room was paneled with them. No matter where Bryna looked she saw herself—saw *something*.

kali

The image leapt at her, ferocious in its proximity. Bryna looked at her reflection, the horror growing. Her face was swollen and ugly. Her eyes were circled with what appeared to be black paint; her cheeks and forehead were streaked with black and red. Her hair, matted with blood or paint or both, hung in stringy garlands about her shoulders. She was naked, wearing only a crude necklace, a necklace her eyes did not immediately make sense of; instead, she saw her hands on her breasts. Her fingers were red with blood. One of them traced a black stripe that started below her breasts, bisected her navel and plunged into her pubic hair, which was also sticky with red.

kali the black one

Bryna lifted her eyes and saw Ethan's grotesque form reflected in the mirror. She saw blood soaking through the sheet above his genital area. Suddenly Bryna was aware of the necklace that hung around her throat—catgut strung with something, pieces of... Kali's practice of making necklaces of the testicles of her lovers filled Bryna's thoughts with new terror.

goddess of death

Bryna ripped the hideous thing from around her neck and flung it to the floor. She whirled around, staggered forward and bumped into a table spread with glossy nude photos, pictures of a woman both as a blonde and as a brunette. There were men in some of the pictures. Bryna, her movements almost robotical now, started to reach for one of them. Her hand froze as other objects on the table began to register. There was a chrome and plastic instrument that seemed somehow familiar. She picked it up, and then it came to her. It was one of the remote-control devices Ives Matlock had shown her. She dropped it. Her hand darted out again and this time fetched back a piece of paper. She recognized Arthur Mendelsohn's signature at the bottom of it. Then she saw the cartridges, thirty-eight specials.

Bryna, her breath coming in gasps now, her eyes wide and wild, upended the table, scattering the accusatory artifacts in all directions. She lurched forward, losing herself in the mirrors for a moment before pounding on one of them frantically. There was a small clicking noise and the mirror swung out at her, revealing a closet. Bryna saw the clothes—all the beautiful dresses, shoes, wigs. *Blonde* wigs.

her room

Bryna was sure of it now. It had to be.

Some movement in the mirror—perhaps some movement she had made herself—startled her, and she stumbled forward again, hurting her foot. She looked down. She was now near the foot of the bed upon which Ethan lay. At her feet, Bryna saw a bloody flaying knife.

I've got to

Bryna picked it up, awkwardly at first.

got to

Then she gripped it as if it were as familiar to her as her brush or comb.

kill her

She began slashing at the image in the mirror with the

hatchetlike gri-gug, sending slivers of glass flying through the air, intent upon both annihilating the image that assaulted her senses and finding a way out of the room.

Bryna was sobbing now.

No sooner would she "kill" one Kali than another would leap out at her, and there would be yet another mirror to smash. Then one of the mirrored panels, a large one, swung open to reveal a metal lattice guarding what Bryna knew must be an elevator shaft. She peered for a moment into the dark space, spotted a button and pushed it. Pulleys whirred. In a moment the top of the elevator appeared. The door slid open as it filled the space behind the lattice, which now, too, slid back.

There were two figures on the floor of the elevator. Though they were face down Bryna recognized them immediately. Niko and the nurse. They were, she had no doubt, both dead. Scarcely aware any longer of what she was doing, Bryna seized first the nurse, then Niko, and pulled them, in jerks, out of the elevator and into the room. She could see the blood oozing along the back of Niko's head.

must die must die must die

Bryna stepped into the elevator and pushed the button again.

A few moments later, the hum of the descending elevator still audible, Ethan sat up, surveyed the shattered room with apparent satisfaction and quickly began wiping the paint from his face and throat. Except for his shirt, he was already dressed. In the subbasement, Bryna would find her way out quickly enough, he was sure; he had opened all the doors. He would wait another minute, he told himself, before going out the same way, locking up behind him. Once outside she would not likely need any help, but if she did, he would be close at hand, ready to provide it.

Bryna took the path she knew so well, running naked through the chill fog, into the trees. She could already hear the surf pounding below. The path took her near the old highway that dead-ended in the tangle of Land's End. The highway was above her, and she could hear a car and see its lights. Suddenly a light flashed across her face; she froze for a moment then hurried down the slope, off the path and into the thick growth.

"Hey you!" somebody shouted. "Hey, lady! Wait!"

Bryna heard a car door slam, then another. She heard excited voices. Someone—men—were crashing down the hill after her.

If only, she thought, she could get to the cliff before they caught her.

oh god please it's the only way

Barefooted though she was, she felt no pain as she scrambled for the precipice, for the surf and the rocks below, for the free fall of final release. The voices came to her in snatches, borne on the wind that, for a minute, cleared away the fog.

"What in the fuck . . . ?"

"It must be one of those . . . hanging around the Carr place."

Bryna looked back. One of the men's flashlights illuminated a police uniform. She broke out of the trees at last and onto the barren margin of cliff. There were only yards now between her and the death she had chosen. It was not the spot she would have selected had there been more time. There was a higher place, further along, with large rocks at the bottom, a place she knew well. But this would do, it would *have* to do; Bryna felt no fear, only anticipation. She would do now, she told herself, what she should have done long ago.

you're going to die

If victory must cost all, then so be it.

She hesitated on the edge, smelling the sea below. Even as the voices behind her grew louder they became less distinct. She inched nearer, savoring the moment. The fog parted again just long enough to let a ray of light emanating from one of the beacons on the rocks out in the bay reach her. It was golden, beckoning and suddenly ominous. In that instant, the image of Goldie, the doll of her childhood, flashed before her, its face Sabra's face, grinning hungrily, its hands Sabra's hands, grasping at her, tugging, pulling, whispering:

time for you to turn back into a pumpkin.

Bryna screamed as she fell from the edge of the cliff.

"That's right, sir, just below the Legion of Honor. Since it was so close to the Carr place, I thought we'd better let you know."

"Describe the woman again," Brazil said, talking into the radio.

The officer, one of the two who had pursued Bryna to the edge of the cliff, did as he was told.

"Some whacko," the cop concluded.

"The Coast Guard . . ."

"On the way."

"I want choppers out there and a ground rescue crew *right now*," Brazil ordered.

263

"It's hard to see anything down there in the fog."

"*Fuck* the fog. I want that body five minutes ago, understand?" Brazil was only dimly aware that he was borrowing from Harrison Warner. "We can't afford any more surprises. If this is another one of Carr's corpses we've had it. I'll be out there in fifteen."

As Brazil headed for Land's End with two other detectives, he checked in again with his stakeouts.

"Everything calm as a lily pond here, sir," the man outside Carr's house reported.

"You didn't see a crazy-looking naked dame go by?"

"Are you kidding, sir?"

"Stay alert."

He checked with the detective watching Kendal.

"No movement here, sir. His car's right where he left it. I've been up and down those steps a dozen times tonight. The light's on upstairs and I can hear his typewriter going when I go around to the back. There's a window . . ."

"Stay with it."

kill me will you? that's a joke

The woman hit something under water with her foot and realized, with relief, that it was the bottom. The next wave toppled her forward again, and her knees dug into it—hard-packed sand. The wave flattened her, face down, but she laughed through it, sputtering with pleasure and relief as she began clawing her way out of the water, onto the narrow beach at the base of the cliff.

it was yourself you killed you twit. now it's mine all mine.

Through the fog she could see no more than two feet in front of her. Behind her she could hear the waves hitting what surely must be huge rocks. She was nearly out of the water when she felt something seize her roughly about the ankle. There was junk scattered through the sand here, and at first she thought she had become entangled in wire. But then whatever it was began to tighten its grip.

Alarmed, she twisted around to see what it was, as the pain began to rip into her. She saw it, at first dimly, then clearly. It appeared to her to be a gnarled, clawlike hand, reaching up out of the water, digging into her flesh. She stared at it, horrified, then began to feel it pulling her, dragging her back into the water. Through the fog she could now discern attached to the hand a grotesque, misshapen figure, apparently that of a woman. The monstrous thing lifted its head from the water and grinned

264

at her, revealing rotten, pointed little teeth and a black, swollen tongue.

She stared at the thing and felt her pulse pound in her ears, louder than the waves crashing against the nearby rocks.

not real not real not real

Yet, despite her thoughts, it continued to pull at her. She felt herself sliding back into the water and grabbed desperately at rocks, at the bottom, at anything upon which she might gain a purchase. Then she felt her hand close around what was apparently an old iron bar. She gripped it firmly, twisted onto her side and struck the thing on the hand. Its mouth opened, as if in pain, but no sound issued from it. She hit it again, and it released her, then thrashed nearer, obviously meaning to seize her again. Its face, swollen and discolored—corpselike—loomed near.

Sabra—for it was thus that the woman identified herself—hit the thing again, this time across the side of the face.

die die goddamn it

She hit it again and again, each time on the face or head, hammering at it even after it floated, face-down and motionless, in the water. She smashed at it until part of its skull broke away. Then she stood there for a minute, waiting, daring it in her thoughts to move again. When it did not, she stepped back, shuddering with disgust, as much at herself as the thing that now drifted from sight in the fog.

illusion

She dropped the iron bar and turned to face the cliff. She hurried along the edge of it until she came to a narrow drainage ravine. It was steep, but the eroded places around the rocks gave her the footholds she needed to clamber up the side, back to the wooded area above. She reached the top more than a hundred yards from the place where the rescue team was already gathering. She could hear them shouting.

It was simple enough getting back into the house unseen. She went in the same way Bryna had come out. In the service elevator she stepped over the inert bodies of Niko and the nurse. Then, back in her room, ignoring the wreckage, she quickly dressed, applied her makeup and donned a blonde wig and blue contacts. She took a shoulder bag, pressed the panel on the wall that concealed the back of the Void, worked the lock and stepped out into Bryna Carr's house, returning in a moment with a small tape recorder and a large knife, both of which she placed in the shoulder bag. She looked at herself in what remained of one of the mirrors.

my god what she's done to this body

No wonder it had been so difficult to squeeze into the dress. She sighed, realizing that from now on *she* would have to maintain the body. Still, it was a small price . . .

There was a moan. Sabra turned and looked at Niko, beginning to stir on the floor.

"I wish I could stay and comfort you, my darling," she said, knowing he couldn't hear her, "but there'll be time enough for that soon. You're about to get one of the things you always wanted but couldn't have. And so am I. So am I."

Sabra smiled and hurried out, down the elevator and through the secret passage to the waiting Porsche which would speed her to her first appointment of the coming new day.

At eleven fifty-five p.m., just as Sabra was leaving Bryna Carr's house, Lieutenant Brazil was standing at the top of the cliff at Land's End, watching frogmen, far below, attach an apparently lifeless form to a set of hooks suspended from the helicopter overhead. The chopper's powerful rotary blades had cleared away some of the fog, and its powerful lights illuminated the eerie scene below. One of the frogmen gave a thumb's up signal, and the chopper crew began slowly hoisting the body, easing it up to the top of the cliff, then holding it suspended a few feet above the ground—just at Brazil's eye-level, before dropping it at his feet.

"Holy Christ," somebody whispered.

"Have you ever seen . . . ?"

Brazil shook his head at the swollen, purple mass that was only, by the most charitable reach of the imagination, the remains of a woman. Much of the face had been destroyed, apparently, Brazil decided, by the waves pounding it against barnacle-encrusted rocks. There was a large hole in the skull. The tongue, protruding thickly from the mouth, was black.

Brazil turned to the uniformed cop who was standing next to him—the same who had reported a woman had jumped from this spot—and said, "You saw *this* jump?"

The cop, already queasy from the odor of the corpse, stepped back, "I . . . it was a crazy-looking woman. She had black, stringy hair like that but . . ."

"*But*," Brazil finished for him, "this, *this* has been dead for . . ." He curled his lip. "Christ knows how long."

"I don't understand it, sir," the uniformed cop said. "There's got to be another body down there."

"I hope so. I hope so," Brazil said, "for your sake."

266

"Sir! Sir!" Another officer came running over to Brazil.

"What is it, Carlsen? I'm busy."

"You'd better hear this, sir!"

The man's face was flushed.

"What the hell . . . ?"

"Please, sir. Just hear this!"

Brazil followed Carlsen to a police car. The AM radio was playing. It was 12:05 a.m.

"If it's about Mendelsohn's name coming out of a computer," Brazil said impatiently, "we already assumed. . . ."

"Not just Mendelsohn," the other man said.

Brazil looked at the officer sharply. He felt a chill wriggle through his gut; a loose-boweled apprehension grabbed him. He slumped into the police car, sitting at a crazy angle, and listened.

". . . to repeat," the announcer, obviously a deejay rather than a news reporter, was saying, "Mendelsohn's name was number five on Bryna Carr's list. But, and this is that blockbuster we just reported to you, the sixth victim's name has also just come out of a computer, and that victim's name is Bryna Carr, herself! To repeat, the psychic who went into a trance state several weeks ago and, without any memory of any of this later, fed into a secret network of computers the names of seven people she predicted would be the next victims of the celebrity murderer has now herself turned up on that list! Phone calls are flooding in here. It's just total pandemonium. And we've got now on the line Randy Selvridge, our police reporter, who, we understand, has just contacted chief of homicide Harrison Warner. Randy, take it away. . . ."

Brazil snapped the radio off. He dropped his head to the steering wheel of the car, gripping it so tightly his knuckles whitened.

"Sir, I . . ."

"Just . . . shut up a minute," Brazil muttered. He was trying to remember what he was doing here. The report that someone was running through the trees, naked, dissheveled; it had all meant something for a fleeting moment. Something one of the officers who had seen her jump had said. He went over it all again.

"Paint!"

"Sir?"

Brazil looked at the uniformed cop.

"You said it looked like there were stripes on her face. She was painted up. *Kali!*"

"Sir?"

Brazil had seen the pictures, read about her, while researching Bryna Carr and Tantra. The description had reminded him of Kali, only he hadn't realized it until now.

"A decoy," he said. "Maybe it was a fucking decoy." He jumped out of the car and started toward the body. "Maybe somebody just pretended to jump, with that body already down there, to keep us occupied, to. . . ."

He stopped. It didn't make any sense; the stakeouts were still there, outside Carr's house. They hadn't seen a thing. But then there'd been a watch outside Spectrum that night, too, the night Samuel Manning was murdered.

Brazil looked back at his men.

"Let's get over there," he said grimly.

TEN

Sabra parked the Black Porsche on Seventeenth, lit a cigarette and walked up Ord to the bottom of the Vulcan Steps. The steps wound up through thick foliage, with the houses set back, some of them almost hidden in the lush growth on either side. She was careful to keep her distance from the tired man climbing the steps higher up. A police officer, she was certain. A short distance below Ethan's house, she cut into the trees and approached the house from the back. It had, no doubt, been easy enough for Ethan, earlier that evening, to slip in and out unseen by this same route; she was certain he had another car, probably a rental, stashed somewhere down the hill.

She dropped her cigarette, ground it out under her heel, and silently mounted the exterior stairs to a deck on the back of the house. The lower floor was in darkness, but the upstairs—Ethan's study—was lighted. There was a radio or television on; she could faintly make out the excited voice of a newscaster.

Sabra took the knife from her handbag and, using its blade, released the lock on the sliding door. She let herself in, putting the knife back in her bag. Then she stood motionless for a moment, concentrating in the darkness, trying to hear—not the newscaster but Ethan, his thoughts. She smiled. It was so much better now—clearer—without Bryna jamming things up. She felt Ethan's shock. It wasn't the shock of hearing that Bryna Carr was dead but, rather, the shock of hearing that she had predicted her

268

own death—that she was number six on her own list. More than shock, Sabra sensed Ethan's *fear*. It was the fear, building for some time now, that he had lost control, that he had been bested somehow at his own game, used, manipulated by forces he had never acknowledged, let alone understood, by forces he believed were *impossible*.

As she concentrated, Sabra reflected that she had known who and what Ethan was—from the very beginning. It wasn't difficult to understand how Bryna could have fallen in love with him, or *thought* herself in love with him. He was, after all, very much like Bryna's father, very much like Bryan—both were completely self-centered, defining their own realities only in terms of their ability to direct, or misdirect, the lives of other people, real people in Ethan's case, imagined ones in Bryan's. How perfect, she thought, it had been for Ethan, already trained in baiting, betrayal and killing in Vietnam, to commit those murders, each with an existential detachment, and then to exploit his credentials as an investigative and interpretive journalist to write about them for a highbrow publisher, heaping, as he conceived it, the hoax of the century on the crime of the century. To be thus utterly in control, to be pulling all the strings in this macabre comedy was, for him, Sabra thought, ceding him a grudging dash of admiration, the ultimate art and his only salvation.

Sabra silently mounted the steps that would take her to him. With each step she felt more intensely his fear and confusion. She paused halfway up, wanting him to sink further into doubt before she confronted him. He was trying to figure it all out. He was going back over it, over all of it.

Meeting Bryna, he thought, had been a stroke of great good luck, though at first, he was not so sure. Just *before* he met her, the whole situation was beginning to pall. The joke, the punch line to which he alone was privy, had pretty well played itself out for him. He needed to up the ante, increase the risks, do something even more spectacular, something which, at the same time, would give his book the smash ending he longed for, the denouement that would put him at the top of the charts for months.

Then he met Bryna, and it came to him gradually: a psychic, called in to help the police find the murderer, turns out *herself* to be the killer—and even *she* doesn't know it, owing to a dissociated personality. Doesn't know it *until* she begins to come across evidence, little scraps here and there, suggesting that she is, indeed, in her other persona, the murderess. She tries to hide the clues, to deny their reality; she begins to fall apart; finally, convinced she has killed even the man she loves, she kills herself—an act which, along with the other evidence she leaves behind, convicts her beyond public doubt.

Bryna's guilt, her love for Ethan and her dependence upon him, her confusion over the source and nature of her psychic powers, her fascination with and fear of Tantrism—all of these, Sabra acknowledged, had been expertly exploited by Ethan Kendal. It was immaterial to him whether Sabra was real, though of course he thoroughly disbelieved in spirits of any kind; he simply *used* Bryna's beliefs and conflicts to keep her in a state of perpetual imbalance, driving her ever closer to madness and self-destruction, all the while pretending to love her, to protect her, to champion her cause.

Now, as Sabra continued up the stairs, she sensed the dryness that was invading Ethan Kendal's mouth, the same dryness he had briefly experienced that day at Spectrum when Bryna, in trance, had approached him with the dagger of glass, the day Bryna had come closest to letting the truth emerge. Then he had feared for a moment all was lost, that this strange woman really was psychic, that there was such a thing as a genuine psychic, something he had always doubted, that soon she would shout incriminating things, inescapable truths. He had hated her then, to be caught thus in *her* trap, to have so shabby a trick played on him, to have to acknowledge some power greater than himself. But when nothing came of it, when she collapsed, almost submissive at his feet, obviously losing some fundamental struggle within herself, his curiosity had been piqued—and the new, the vast new potential for creative exploitation had presented itself.

Once he had satisfied himself, on the basis of what she told him and of what he discovered himself, that she was in his thrall by virtue of her love for him, he feared nothing. There was, in any event, little evidence that she was any longer, if indeed she ever had been, psychic. And even if she had been, there seemed little likelihood that she would ever be psychic again, so long as she was at war with herself, so long as her love for him convinced her that her psychic channel was closed, denied her by a petulant spirit guide who would divulge nothing without the continued use of her body.

Sabra mounted the last riser. Ethan's back was to her. He had turned on the television, to see if he could get more news there than he had been able to get from the radio.

"*Hé bien voilà, on se revois pour la dernière fois.*"

Ethan whirled around, holding the TV remote-control device in front of him. He held it almost as if it were a weapon. He pushed the OFF button, and the picture—a closeup of Bryna Carr—flickered and faded.

"She's gone," Sabra said, smiling, "but *I'm* still here. You will not find me so easily disposed of."

Ethan, though a master of dissimulation, could not disguise his shock.

"*You*," he said, "but I . . ."

"You saw *Bryna* jump, not me."

Ethan fought to regain his composure.

"Bryna Carr *is* dead. And the prediction was quite accurate, wasn't it? Technically, she's a suicide, but in reality *you* drove her to it; *you* murdered her. Of course, you had a little help you weren't expecting."

Ethan's eyes were full of doubt, questions, fear. And yet, there was still cunning in them, too. He was, Sabra knew, desperately trying to make events bend to *his* will, fit into *his* plans.

"It's ironic, isn't it?" Sabra said. "You thought Bryna was deluded, and you took advantage of that; now you're afraid *you* have been deluded. You're right, you know; you might as well face it. Even before tonight, you had begun to doubt. There were to be only *five* victims; that's all you had in mind, wasn't it? You taught Bryna to hypnotize herself, to become susceptible to your suggestions. All those practice sessions, yes, weren't those wonderful? It was easy for you to plant the five names in her subconscious, along with the posthypnotic signals that would induce her to go into another hypnotic trance and release them. You were convinced her psychic powers were gone, if they had existed at all, but there was still a public ready to believe in her, and that you found irresistible, didn't you? *You* became her spirit guide, the voice that spoke to her in trance, telling her exactly what to do."

Ethan's face was now a mask. He stood motionless, staring at Sabra.

"But then," she continued, "something went wrong, didn't it? *Seven* names went into the computer. There were five in rapid succession, then a pause, then two more. Out of the blue you were faced with a couple of wild cards. You still had the means of putting her into hypnotic trance with a few words and a kiss, so that she didn't even know it was happening. You tried to get the other names out of her, but it didn't work. She couldn't remember, didn't seem to know what you were talking about at all, did she? Still, you *did* get out of her that the first five names were the ones you had given her, and that she had given them in the proper order. So you figured if you could bump off the first five on schedule, the last two wouldn't matter, *provided* Bryna was out of the way herself at that point. The fact that those last two deaths would never take place after Bryna's suicide would only be further evidence of her guilt."

Sabra paused to light a cigarette, offering Ethan one, as well. He looked at her as if she were crazed and remained mute.

She shrugged. "I thought you might want a last one before . . . well, never mind." She put the cigarettes back into her handbag, feeling the sharp edge of the knife. "Of course, you took other steps to insure that she—and everybody else—would eventually think she had done it, killed them. You selected the victims carefully; all five of them, you felt, threatened her somehow. You had already discovered, snooping around in my house, that Friedkin and Raymond were planning to blackmail her. Matlock, Mendelsohn, Manning—they were all challenging her in some way, trying to drive a wedge between Bryna and myself."

Sabra dragged on her cigarette, held the smoke deep in her lungs, tilting her head back, enjoying the little high it gave her, then she exhaled, blowing the smoke toward Ethan.

"How you played into my hands!" she said with relish.

Ethan's mask slipped a little.

"Bryna," he said, "I love you, don't you . . . ?"

Sabra laughed at him. "Save your breath," she said. "You haven't much left."

He let the hand he had extended toward her fall to his side.

"Did you really think you were finding out things I didn't want you to know?" she asked contemptuously. "I knew what you were doing every second. Bryna had her chance. She should have stuck that glass into your heart, but she wouldn't, she blocked it; she blocked out everything about you, except for the lies, the lies that said you loved her. And so then I had to be resourceful. It might have been your idea to do what you did, but *I* made it all possible. . . ."

Hatred flickered in Ethan's eyes. "You're crazy. . . ."

"*I* made sure you got your hands on those pictures. I even posed for some of them, especially for you, for you *and* Bryna, so that she could see me with our dear friend Nestor, with the wig off. I did the same for Friedkin and Raymond; you see, I was helping you each step of the way. You gave Bryna dates, as well as names. That was daring of you, but it made it all so much more spectacular, didn't it. And since *you* knew the dates you figured you could bring it off, get everybody in the right place at the right time. Except it was all a little *too* easy, wasn't it? It unnerved you, didn't it, when Raymond's schedule, set up weeks before, just happened to have him conveniently in San Francisco on the date you randomly gave Bryna, as the date of his death? You had been prepared to go to some creative lengths to get him here or to put Bryna in close proximity to him on that date, but it wasn't necessary. The same with Friedkin. And those phone calls. Everything was going your way, wasn't it? And that worried you, didn't it? It was you who put Matlock onto Bryna, but then you barely had to lift a finger after that. Things just happened. Manning was a piece of pie, just like Mendelsohn. Their due dates fell just as they were closing in on Bryna. The timing couldn't have been better; perfect to convince Bryna that she had done it, to avoid commitment. When you weren't worrying about 'coincidences' you were gloating, convincing yourself that *you* engineered all this."

Sabra sneered, dropped her cigarette on Ethan's hardwood floor and rubbed the ember out with her heel.

"You were had from the beginning," she said. "From the first moment until the last. From that night in the bar when I lured you into following me until now. You did it all for *me*—destroyed those who wanted Bryna to throw me out, disown me, expose me. Raymond, Friedkin, the blackmailers. Manning, Mendelsohn and Matlock, the mad exorcists, each attacking me from a different pulpit. Bryna Carr herself. Yes. She was the most dangerous of my enemies. And *you* killed her for me."

Ethan's face contorted as he struggled to deal with this.

"It *is* funny, isn't it?" Sabra said. "It turns out *you* were the one who was used, manipulated, *fated....*"

"Shut up!"

"The fact that she predicted her own death, you can't find a way around that...."

Sabra reached into her handbag and switched on the tape recorder, pretending to want another cigarette.

"You crazy bitch," he said, his hatred erupting at last, "I killed them all. I started this long before I'd ever heard of you. *You* had nothing to do with it. *I* started this and I'll finish it. The computer says you're dead. Bryna Carr is *never* wrong. We have to protect your reputation, don't we? So we're just going to have to put you back over that cliff, aren't we? And if they find you like that, in your Sabra drag, that's fine. Almost as good as my Kali."

Ethan stepped sideways to the fireplace. His hand closed around a heavy fire iron. He raised it high into the air and started toward Sabra.

"Ethan," she said, her voice changing dramatically, sounding like Bryna. "Ethan, please, no, I *loved* you, I...Oh, god, please!"

Ethan looked at her contemptuously, her evident madness giving him new confidence. "You won't even feel this," he said. "You're falling off that cliff again, but this time you're going to hit your head on a rock." He smiled as he began to bring the iron down.

Sabra hurled herself backward, whipping the knife from her bag and, in one powerful, fluid movement, propelled the weapon through the air and into Ethan's chest. He staggered toward her another step, still holding the iron high over his head, his eyes wide with disbelief. He dropped the fire iron and slumped to his knees, falling toward her.

Sabra heard the click of the recorder and knew that the cassette, which she had intentionally started near the end, had run out. Ethan, who was folded over his knees, one side of his face pressed against the floor, could still hear her, she was certain.

"You poor dear," she said, gently touching his hair. "You *can't* kill somebody twice. I *told* you Bryna Carr is already dead. She was number six. Didn't you ever stop to wonder who was number *seven*?"

Only Ethan's eyes moved, straining to focus on Sabra. She nodded, and Ethan's eyes froze.

The police exploded into the room a moment later, led by Albert Brazil, his gun drawn. Sabra stared at him from across the room. Ethan was on the floor between them, quite dead. Brazil shifted his stance slightly, still keeping his gun trained on Sabra.

"I'm afraid I have to inform you of your rights, Miss Carr."

"You don't understand..."

"Not everything...yet, but enough. We know about the secret passageway. We've been inside your room, Miss Carr. We found the pictures, the remote unit you used to kill Matlock, Mendelsohn's...uh...privates.... Also, we broke the code, Miss Carr, the computer code. We got the identity of number seven." He looked down at Ethan Kendal's body. "Too late, but..."

Sabra shook her head.

"You'll be taken care of, Miss Carr," Brazil said, lowering his gun, signaling one of his men to see to Ethan. He walked slowly toward Sabra. "It's a sickness, Miss Carr, or is it Sabra? What do you call yourself now?"

"I'm...I'm..." She started to cry.

Niko burst into the room and started toward Sabra. An officer tried to stop him.

"It's all right," Brazil said.

Niko stopped and looked at Sabra, who returned his gaze. Slowly, dramatically, she pulled off her wig, blinked the blue contacts from her eyes.

"Bryna?" Nick said, hope rising visibly in him.

She nodded, and he rushed to her.

"She's dead," Sabra cried in his arms. "Sabra's dead. She died when I jumped off that cliff. I had to kill her and that was the only way, even if it meant taking my own life. . . ."

Brazil cleared his throat. "I'm sorry to break this up, but . . ."

"You really *don't* understand," Sabra said, a bit more forcefully than she intended. "Here," she said, in a softer tone of voice. She reached for the shoulder bag, which was on the floor.

Brazil stepped back, alarmed.

"Then you look."

Brazil prodded the bag with his foot.

"It's a tape recorder," Sabra said. "His confession is on it. Ethan Kendal was the celebrity murderer. I didn't know it, not until I regained consciousness after . . . after going over the cliff." She embraced Niko again. "Oh god, I'm so lucky to be alive."

Brazil stared at her dumbfounded as he extracted the tape recorder and played the confession.

"When I came to," Sabra said, breaking the shocked silence that followed Ethan's taped words, "my powers . . . the psychic information, it was all there, everything. I could see it all without any help from . . . from imagined spirits. I realized what a fool I'd been, leaning on that crutch all these years. I saw it all, how Ethan had exploited my weaknesses, how blinded I was by my misplaced love for him, which wasn't love at all but simply guilt over my father. The fall did it! When I came out of the water . . . it was as if a massive block in my consciousness was gone . . . shattered."

Sabra paused for a moment for effect, then looking up into Niko's eyes, certain now that he was hers, she said, "In a way, in a very *real* way, Bryna Carr *did* die in that fall. The *old* Bryna, the one who shared herself, who gave up part of herself to a delusion, the Bryna who couldn't believe in herself, *that* Bryna Carr died tonight."

She looked now at the inert form of Ethan Kendal.

"And oddly enough," she added, nodding at the corpse, "I have *him* to thank for it."

Brazil looked at her, his face a pale green.

"Don't you see," Sabra appealed to him, "he wanted to drive me crazy, to make me think that *she*, that Sabra, was taking over and committing the murders. It was the perfect ending for his book. Finally, tonight, he almost succeeded. When I found him lying in bed next to me with his throat all bloody, I thought I'd killed him, as well as the others, and there was only one thing left to do . . . Then when I, when those officers chased me I . . . I just jumped. I didn't choose my spot, and I hit deep water. I was out, unconscious for a few minutes. I must have been, because I don't remember climbing out of the water. I was on the beach and suddenly it was all very clear to me. I could see it all. I knew what I had to do. I dressed up like Sabra and came here. I had to confront him, take him off guard, make him think I really was crazy. I knew then he would talk freely, that I could get his confession on tape."

Brazil was holding his head in his hands.

"I can see that I'll have to start at the beginning," Sabra said. "You'll see. If his confession isn't enough, you'll find the other evidence you need, some of it here, most of it in an apartment he kept under another name in Los Angeles. Notes, floor plans of his victims' homes, all sorts of things. I saw it all the moment I regained consciousness."

Brazil, groping for a chair, sat down heavily.

"There's one problem," the officer who had been assigned to tail Ethan said, addressing Brazil. "She says he was with her tonight. But I followed him here. I heard him typing. . . ."

Brazil looked up, brightening a little.

"That's no problem," Sabra said, walking over to Ethan's desk. She hit a switch on his word processor and the printer began typing material he had fed into it days earlier.

Brazil looked sourly at the other detective. Sabra managed, with some effort, to transform a smile into a little grimace of commiseration.

ELEVEN

"Look," Harrison Warner said, sounding affable for the first time in weeks, "the heat's off. The murderer has been found. So we didn't save any lives, but who's counting anymore? It's over.

She's the story now. The *whole* story. Nobody gives squat about us, which is just fine."

Brazil sat in the chief's office, staring at the carpet, shaking his head.

"I dunno, I just can't..."

"Jesus," Warner said. "You can't *what*? Let go when a case is over? Kendal was the killer. We've got enough proof to convict *ten* killers. The confession, his notes, all the other stuff we found—right where she said it would be. Christ, they even found microtraces of Mendelsohn's blood on his skin and clothes."

"Yeah, I know. He killed them. No doubt about it. But it all just turned out so... I mean you look at it one way, all those people who died were *her* enemies."

"Oh for Christsake, are you on *that* again? The police don't deal in fantasy, Lieutenant. *Facts*. That's what matters. Kendal was the killer. She didn't know anything about it; he said as much in his confession."

"But we know now that Raymond and Friedkin had found out about her double life and were out to blackmail her; they both end up dead. Mendelsohn and Manning were going to have her committed; *they* end up dead. Matlock, I don't know, maybe..."

"Lieutenant, you're not making any sense. It's all circumstantial. The bottom line is *Kendal killed them*. Can you get that through your skull? *He* picked the people who were going to die. He picked people who were close to her, involved with her, at odds with her, so it would *look like* she had a motive; he wanted her, he wanted *us* to think she did it."

"It just blows me away though, sir, the coincidences. I mean, Kendal couldn't have known, at the time he picked Mendelsohn and Manning, that they were going to try to have her committed. And what if they *had* committed her—earlier, I mean—put her out of circulation, what would that have done to Kendal's plan? It would have blown it all to hell, because—locked up—she couldn't have killed anybody. And how could Kendal have been sure that Friedkin and Raymond would materialize here at just the right times?"

"He couldn't. He took risks. He was prepared to *make* things happen. He was a *manipulator*, and he was lucky, too."

"He's dead. I don't call that lucky. And that's the other thing, sir. I mean, *she* turns up on her own list, and Kendal, too. They're supposed to be victims six and seven. But she's still alive, the only one out of the bunch, and let us not forget, sir, *she* killed Kendal."

Warner shrugged. "It's semantics, Lieutenant."

"Semantics?"

"Yeah. Don't you read the papers? God, they love this story. You know what they're saying. Kendal *drove* her to suicide. I don't dispute it. And that's the same as murder in my book. Granted, she was 'reborn,' but, well... she sure as hell *did* jump. And, as for Kendal, well, they're saying he murdered himself; that's what you do, isn't it, when you *force* somebody to kill you in self-defense? And there isn't any doubt: he did mean to kill her with that fire iron."

"It's just too damned neat, sir," Brazil complained. "I mean she went there, for Christsake, *knowing* she was going to kill him. She took a knife with her for that very purpose. Isn't that premeditated...?"

"Premeditated *what*, Lieutenant? There isn't a jury in this country that wouldn't call it premeditated *self-defense*."

"Yeah, but if she hadn't gone there in the first place, if she'd just called us, say..."

"Look, she saved the state a bundle by offing the creep. The commissioner's happy; *I'm* happy. And Bryna Carr is one fine psychic."

"I thought that was all squat, sir."

"It *was*; it isn't anymore. You see what I mean? Big minds stretch, Lieutenant; little ones don't. Think about it."

"I will sir, I will."

Amidst all the hustle and bustle of organizing the "new" Bryna Carr's life, including negotiations on book and movie deals, in which she would supposedly "tell all" about the double life she had now publicly renounced, Sabra found time for Niko. Especially for Niko. She consulted him on everything—the total redecoration of the Seacliff house, the gleeful junking of several hundred thousands of dollars worth of Tantric artifacts, the equally pleasurable burning of two dozen blonde wigs, the demolition and replacement of the "old" Bryna's wardrobe, everything. *Nearly* everything.

And after a decent interval, she took him to her bed.

"Of course I want you," she said, enjoying his initial awkwardness. "God, I was *so* blind; all those years, it was *you* I loved, and..."

His lips pressed against hers, silencing her, his hunger overwhelming his normal reserve.

"Yes," she kept murmuring, "yes," each time she sensed his questioning, wondering if he dared go further. She stifled a wicked impulse to say no at one point, tempted to see if even Niko had the power of will to stop now. But of course she did not want him to stop. More than anything she wanted him to unleash *all* of his passion, spending all of the animal sexuality that she had always known was in his possession. In time, she told herself, in time she would have all of him. As it was, he was far from deficient in his lovemaking.

Undressed, he was as perfect as she had always imagined. Sabra pulled her eyes from him with difficulty and tilted her head back. She let her long, ebon hair caress her back and shoulders, chastely crossing her arms over her breasts.

Niko looked at her intently, murmuring the name she was already getting used to.

"Bryna, Bryna. God, you're so beautiful, Bryna."

He stepped toward her, and she dropped her arms as he touched her, first her face, outlining her lips with the tip of his finger, stroking her cheek. Then his hands were on her shoulders. His current enveloped her. When his hands cupped her breasts the circuit closed, and she began to tingle all over. His mouth opened hers, and he pressed closer.

He took her into his arms, picked her up, cradled her, kissed her, then put her down on the rug, in front of the fire in her study. He prepared her as if she were a virgin, as if Ethan had never counted, as if none of the others had ever existed. They moved together, breathed together. It was as if they had always been meant to *be* together.

In half an hour, Sabra reflected, she had given Niko more pleasure than Bryna had given him in all the years of her life. It was, Sabra mused, just as Naomi Hevesey—so wise for a mortal—liked to say: "What *seems* to be is often more real than what *is*."

In the vestibule of the morgue, the deskperson, a policewoman, asked Sabra for her autograph. Sabra complied, penning Bryna's signature flawlessly. Brazil came in and beamed at her.

"I'm sorry to drag you down here so soon after . . . Gee, you're really looking great, though, may I say, Miss Carr, you're looking better than ever?"

Sabra smiled.

"What was it you wanted to see me about?" She had already decided it must have something to do with Ethan or Mendelsohn, both of whom, she guessed, were still on ice in the police morgue. She looked at Brazil closely for a moment but somehow could not pick up what it was he had on his mind. That made her uneasy.

He ushered her into an autopsy room. On the table in the center of the room was a corpse covered by a green sheet. Sabra immediately noticed that the body was too short to be that of either Ethan Kendal or Arthur Mendelsohn. She glanced at Brazil and then back at the body, irritated that she could not "see" what was concealed by the sheet or, for that matter, what was hidden behind Brazil's bland countenance.

The detective gestured to her to come closer to the table and then, watching her, he pulled back the sheet, exposing the nude body of a lumpish, malformed female with a broken skull, mangled features and a swollen, black tongue. One of the cadaver's legs was noticeably shorter than the other.

Sabra felt her skin prickle. The body before her was unmistakably that of the thing she had convinced herself, struggling in the water that night, was illusory.

"I was hoping maybe you could tell us something about her," Brazil said quietly.

Sabra pulled her eyes from the corpse with difficulty.

"I'm sorry, I can't," she said, successfully masking the small tremor in her voice.

Brazil waited, saying nothing.

Sabra glanced back at the body again.

"You really can't be dragging me down here everytime you need information on a body, Lieutenant."

"Oh, no, no," Brazil said. "It isn't that we want information on just *any* body, Miss Carr. It's *this* body in particular that interests us. You see, the night you, uh, forgive me, the night you jumped off the cliff, Miss Carr, we looked for your body and . . . we found this." He nodded at the corpse.

"I see," Sabra said drily. "Well, if you're asking me, did I pass her on the way down . . ."

"I . . ." Brazil stopped and looked at Sabra. "You know, Miss Carr, it amazes me, just *amazes* me how cool you are about all this. I mean earlier, too, and now this. I mean, most people in your position, the police find a body at the same place you jump off . . ."

"So you found a body," Sabra said impatiently. "There are probably a lot of them floating around the bay. This one must have been dead a long time."

"Well, you know, that's the thing, Miss Carr, that's the thing that really *kills* me. I *assumed* she'd been dead a long time; I mean to look at her . . . but the boys in pathology—they do such a fine job, Miss Carr—they tell us now that she died the same day, the *very* same day, Miss Carr, that you jumped. In fact, they placed the time of death very close to the time you were seen jumping. Can you imagine! Isn't that wild! I asked them to
280

double check, no, to *triple* check their findings; that's why I haven't called you in earlier . . . you know, they have ways of telling these things, like how long since the last food was digested, the composition of the blood, that sort of thing."

Sabra remained silent, trying to collect her thoughts.

anyway she's dead whoever she is that's all that matters

"She must have been in awful shape," Brazil continued. " 'Walking death' was the way one of the boys put it. Tumors . . . her system full of cancers and poisons, her cells those of an old woman, yet they put her age at *under thirty*. Isn't that incredible! We don't know for sure what killed her, whether she jumped, fell or was thrown into the water. She had a terrible hole in her skull. You can see it there. Of course that could have happened any number of ways. And her face, you can see for yourself, a lot of that was just beat to . . ."

"Please, Lieutenant . . ."

"Listen to me, how I talk," Brazil said, his tone effusively apologetic. "I'm sorry, *excuse* me, Miss Carr. It's just that all of this puzzles me so much."

"Coincidences *do* occur, Lieutenant," Sabra said. "She could have jumped further along the cliff . . ."

"Suicide? Probably, probably you're right, Miss Carr. Although, one curious thing, the lab boys found a trace of barbiturate in her blood, just enough to suggest she'd taken something like a sleeping pill several hours earlier, but not enough to kill her. They think it was only one or two pills, definitely no more. If she had access to sleeping pills and wanted to kill herself why didn't she just take a whole handful of them?"

Sabra shrugged. "Maybe she found one and ate it. Given her condition she probably didn't know what she was doing."

"Probably. Possibly you're right. Oh, it's crazy, I know, but it bothered me somehow, that one sleeping pill, just these crazy coincidences. You'll recall you told us *you* had taken one sleeping pill several hours before you woke up, before Ethan Kendal woke you up with those smelling salts. . . ."

"I told you he gave me one pill, yes, that he *wanted* me to be able to wake up later so that I could find him next to me, so that I'd think . . . Good lord, Lieutenant, thousands of people are taking sleeping pills at any given time. What possible significance . . . ?"

"I know, I know, I'm being crazy. It's just that when you begin to stack coincidence upon coincidence. See, when you told us everything that happened to you that day you mentioned what you had eaten and when. You remember, I pressed you on that?

It turns out this... this lady had eaten the *same* things, Miss Carr. Can you imagine... I mean, the menu, it's all here in these pathology reports. She ate the *same* things you did."

Sabra looked at the twisted flesh on the autopsy table. She felt weak but managed to look exasperated as she replied.

"I told you I wasn't sure, that I couldn't be certain what I had eaten. In any event, I fail to understand the significance of this conversation."

"You're not curious?"

"Curious about what this corpse had to eat? No, I'm sorry, Lieutenant."

"It's just... I can't get it out of mind. It just blows me away that you were both down there at the same time and..."

Sabra looked at her watch.

Brazil shrugged sheepishly. "I'll let it rest, Miss Carr. I just wish..."

"*Yes*, Lieutenant?"

"So many loose ends, Miss Carr. Those people, for example, who were blackmailing you. Friedkin and Raymond. It just seems crazy to me that two so powerful people would want to blackmail you because they found out you were leading this double life."

"*Really*, Lieutenant? Where have you been the last ten years? Watergate, Abscam, the scandals go on and on. Rich and powerful people have never exhibited any immunity to temptation in the past."

"That's well put, Miss Carr; yes, you've got me there, I'm afraid."

"If that's all, Lieutenant..."

"Yes, yes, I know. I've taken up more of your valuable time than... Oh, by the way! Would you... would you mind?" Brazil hunched over and produced a copy of *The Psychic Within* from his ragged briefcase. "I got an extra copy for my wife's sister. Well, she knew I was on the case, and..."

Sabra took the book, opened it and signed Bryna Carr's name. Brazil looked at it closely. Sabra knew he would compare it with Bryna's signature. That didn't worry her. In fact, it cheered her he had nothing left, he was picking at straws.

"That book," she said, as he put it back in his briefcase, "is outdated, as you might have gathered."

"You mean the parts about Sabra?"

"That and other things."

"Sabra then... you really don't... she isn't real to you anymore?"

282

"Just a memory," Sabra said smoothly. "It will all be in my *new* book."

"Yes, yes, I read about that, that you are going to write a new one. That, oh boy, *that* is going to be a dandy, Miss Carr."

"Yes, well..."

"I mean not that the other book wasn't interesting. It *was*. I was just rereading that part to my wife, that part where you talk about Sabra, how you visualized her, this beautiful blonde with blue eyes, and of course none of it had come out then. I mean, you didn't discuss in the book how your personality was split and you actually had two lives, but you talked about her, how you saw her, how she was just what you always dreamed of becoming. And then you mentioned that other dream, the one you had as a little girl, where you saw that old crone, all gnarled and twisted, and how she limped, one leg shorter than the other, how she had this big, swollen tongue, a *black* tongue..."

Sabra followed Brazil's eyes to the corpse. But when he looked back at her she met his gaze firmly.

"Yes, well, Lieutenant, there was a lot of nonsense in that book. At that time I was convinced Sabra was some sort of genuine spirit, a supernatural entity. A fairy godmother rescuing me from a life of drudgery. The Cinderella syndrome. A common enough fantasy, especially among psychics who find it difficult to account for their unusual insights. But that's all it was, Lieutenant, a fantasy; I realized *that* when I... when I came back, out of that water."

Brazil looked at her, fascinated. He shook his head. "I don't know," he said. "This whole case. *Everything* these days, Miss Carr. It's all crazy. Nothing fits anymore. I mean, look at this corpse. Even this corpse is weird. People aren't supposed to be made like this. I mean, this a goddamned monster."

"Oh, I don't know, Lieutenant," Sabra said, smiling faintly, feeling better now. "Somewhere inside there might once have lurked a very beautiful person. Besides, you're a movie fan, am I correct?"

"Yeah, how'd you know that?"

"I'm a psychic, remember? Or maybe you told me. My point is, remember what Bette Davis, one of your favorites if I'm not mistaken, once said?"

"No, no I don't. I mean..."

"She said: 'Until you've been a monster, you can never be a star.'"

EPILOGUE

Sabra closed the door against the distant voices and surveyed the bedroom of her Laurel Canyon home.

"Oh, Nestor," she said, falling into the big man's waiting arms, kissing him hotly. "It's been so long."

"God," he moaned, holding her tightly, "it *is* you, it really *is* . . ."

Sabra pushed away and looked at him, knitting her brow.

"Nestor! Don't tell me you *doubted*." She laughed. "You are *such* a fraud; for all your fascination with the supernatural, after all we've experienced together, you *still* have trouble believing in my kind, don't you? There are times when you *still* think I'm the runaway fiction of Bryna Carr's imagination, don't you? You and Naomi . . ."

Bagehot looked at her quizzically.

"Oh, yes, I told Naomi Hevesey. I told her the truth—that it was Bryna Carr who jumped off that cliff, that it was Bryna Carr who died. *I* survived."

"Was that prudent?"

"Survival is *always* prudent."

Bagehot smiled. "I mean telling Doctor Hevesey."

"Oh, that too. After all, I have to have someone besides *you* to talk to; posing as Bryna Carr, even the reborn Bryna Carr, is no treat. Besides, Naomi is utterly trustworthy. Granted, she was a little worried until I told her I wasn't going to tell anyone else. As far as she's concerned it's no more strange for Bryna Carr to imagine she's Sabrina Jouhaux than it is for Bryna Carr to think she's Bryna Carr. And I think, anyway, that Naomi finds *me* infinitely more interesting than Bryna. She seems to be enjoying our sessions together."

"Hmmm. Wouldn't it have been simpler for you to have said that Sabrina died in that fall, that *she* was the sixth victim?"

"Simpler, perhaps, but you forget, dear man. Bryna Carr was seldom wrong. As a psychic, I mean. And it was so much more fun this way."

"So she *knew* she was going to die? And that Ethan would die too?"

"*Of course*. Well, not consciously, perhaps, but *psychically*, yes. *She* was the psychic, not me. I just borrowed her powers, along with her body. I take what people *give* me. If they forget that it's theirs, fine."

"Just a little opportunist in search of an opportunity?"

"Now you're beginning to understand. Not that I didn't contribute. After all, anything Bryna couldn't cope with, I was there to take the rap for it, to be the source, the responsibility. I was her stand-in, her extra."

"A blank screen upon which she could project her forbidden fantasies?"

"Mmmm, yes, that, too. God knows, there was all that blonde hair and blue eyes. I *hate* blonde hair and blue eyes. And all that Tantric nonsense." Sabra stopped. "Oh, dear, have I spoken out of turn? Well, don't worry, Nestor, I'll still come to your orgies, but really, isn't it time you admitted that whole trip is nothing but a ruse to entice sweet young things into your lecherous and capable clutches?"

Bagehot pulled her to him again, kissing her mouth and neck. She kissed him back, until they were both out of breath. Bagehot looked at the closed door. The voices on the other side were louder now. They pulled apart.

"Is it true what I read in the papers, that you're going to marry him?"

"Niko?" Sabra said, smiling. "Yes, I think I will. But you needn't worry. . . ."

"And *babies*? Did you really mean *that*?"

She laughed. "Why not? That will keep him at home and cement my new respectability. After all, with all the details of my 'other life' profitably pouring out, I have to redeem myself in the public eye. How better than with a husband and babies? And believe me, dear man, Niko takes a lot of the pain out of it. Yes, the new Bryna Carr is going to have tremendous influence. *Everybody* loves a reformed sinner."

"But your figure . . ."

"Don't worry about it. Pregnancy might agree with me, and if it doesn't, I'll have the next one in a test tube and hire one of those surrogate mothers. . . . Anyway, there'll be nannies and that sort of thing. I plan to be on the road a great deal. You'll probably see more of me now than you did before."

"And the business?"

"Not to worry. *That* will be in capable hands—*yours*. It should run ever so much more smoothly now."

"But the police . . . isn't there a chance that's going to leak out, too?"

"Of course not, the reintegrated Bryna Carr is confessing *selectively*. And the only outsiders who knew about Ms. Jouhaux's part in that are dead."

"Yes."

"There's only one thing I regret," Sabra said, looking around. "So many good memories. I hate to lose this place. But, of course, I have to divest myself of all her *hated* belongings."

Bagehot looked as if he might say something when there was a knock on the door. The two stepped further apart.

"Come in," Sabra said.

It was Niko, with the real-estate agent.

"If you'll just sign here, Miss Carr," the agent said, "you can leave the rest of it to us; we'll handle the closing at the bank."

Sabra deferred to Niko. "Is it all right, darling?"

"Yes," he said, putting his hand on her shoulder. "I've checked it all out."

Sabra signed Bryna's name, selling the house.

As they started out, the agent said, "Oh, by the way, Miss Carr, the buyer is still here. If you wouldn't mind, he wanted to meet you, just to say hello."

They stepped into the next room and Sabra, disguising her delight, chastely said hello to Bruno, her former bodyguard and escort. Outside, as they said their goodbyes, Sabra whispered "thank you" as she kissed Nestor Bagehot on the cheek.

In the limousine that took them back to the airport, Sabra and Niko sat silently near one another in the rear compartment, a magical mood enveloping them, one that neither of them wanted to dispel by speaking. Sabra held the flowers that Nestor had given her, and Niko sat very still. They exchanged glances from time to time, each smiling when their eyes met.

At an intersection where they stopped for a traffic light, Sabra felt her attention diverted to the outside. She peered through the window of the car to look at the seedy row of houses that filled the street. The feeling that there was something out there, something she was meant to see, grew. She lifted her eyes to the second story of one of the drab, gray houses. She focused on a window there, the shabby curtains of which parted abruptly, revealing a squat, shadowy figure, apparently a woman. Sabra felt cold.

The late afternoon sun slid briefly from beneath a cloud, brightly illuminating the figure in the window. The woman's eyes glowed, an unnatural blue. She appeared to be wearing a cheap blonde wig. Her makeup was extreme, but it could not conceal the battered and discolored contours of her face. The woman looked directly down at Sabra, her mouth opening in a malignant grin, exposing small, jagged teeth and a swollen, black tongue. As the sun fell behind the clouds again, the curtains on the window slowly closed, and the limo pulled away from the intersection.

Still looking out the window, Sabra held the flowers in one hand and searched for Niko with the other. Her hand found his forearm and clutched it. When she turned to look at him, he was smiling at her.

DON'T MISS
THESE CURRENT
Bantam Bestsellers

The horrifying new novel by the author of
GHOST HOUSE

GHOST LIGHT

CLARE McNALLY

Pretty little five-year-old Bonnie Jackson was the darling of the stage world. Until the night she found herself wandering, terrified, through the darkness of the Winston Theatre—a night that would end with evil consuming the innocent girl in a horrible, fiery death. Now, fifty years later, Bonnie has returned. And she will command the spotlight once again. For pretty little Bonnie Jackson is about to perform her show-stopping act of revenge.